One Wore Blue

One Wore Blue

Heather Graham

A DELL BOOK

Published by
Dell Publishing
a division of
Bantam Doubleday Dell Publishing Group, Inc.
666 Fifth Avenue
New York, New York 10103

Printed in the United States of America

This book is dedicated with many, many thanks to some of the wonderful people we've come to know in Harpers Ferry and Bolivar, West Virginia.

To Mrs. Shirley Dougherty, who has bewitched, intrigued, entertained and taught us so many times with the "Harpers Ferry Myth and Legends" Tour (Ghost Tour!)

To Dixie, for being the gentleman that he is, but especially for his kindness that very first time we came.

To Mr. and Mrs. Stan Hadden for their hospitality and their charm, and for the wonderful Civil War flavor of Stan's "Eagle."

To many of the National Park Service guides for their own love of history, for their enthusiasm, for their patience.

And it is dedicated to Harpers Ferry itself, a town where the mists still hover over the Shenandoah and Potomac rivers, where the mountains rise into the distance, where the past and present seem to collide, and, as Jason says, where a haunting quality seems to settle over the streets by the darkness of the night, and a restless spirit still remains. Perhaps they still walk here, men in blue, and men in gray.

Lastly, but very especially, it is dedicated to my editor, Damaris Rowland, with tremendous gratitude for the enthusiasm and support she has unwaveringly given this project. Damaris, thank you.

One Wore Blue

1

John Brown's Body

Prologue

KIERNAN

Kiernan's world, it seemed, had split in two.

One side was blue, and one side was gray.

Ever since it began to come apart, everything had changed. All that had been beautiful in life had begun to fade. A way of life that had been full of charm and wit and easy grandeur had passed away. They were holding on to it tightly, but it was gone. The world was split apart, and families were split apart—like Camerons.

One wore blue, and one wore gray.

One had been her childhood friend back in Tidewater Virginia. He and Kiernan had tramped through fields together, they had been chastised together. They had told their dreams to each other during long lazy days when they had lain by pleasant, bubbling springs beneath powder-blue skies.

And the other Cameron brother had been her hero. As a child, she had adored him. As a woman, she had loved him. And when the world had changed, she had hated him—fiercely, desperately, as passionately as she had loved him. She had her beliefs, and she had her loyalties.

It was just that she had loved him so long. . . .

Even when she had stood before the altar with another man and promised to love and honor and cherish that man until death did them part, she had loved him.

Almost as much as she had hated him.

She had told him that she hated him the day that she walked away from him.

But he had been destined to ride back into her life that day, Kiernan would later realize.

Jesse. Jesse Cameron.

The one who wore blue.

It began very late in the afternoon of that autumn day in 1861, when the breeze was cool, when the mountains seemed the most gentle.

They came against the beautiful fall colors of the twilight. They were like a great wave, cresting and falling, rising again. Beneath the dying sun they seemed to weave and undulate. A piece of metal—a belt buckle, a sword—would catch a ray of the fading light, and it would flash and shimmer. They came onward still, visible almost like a writhing snake one moment, then disappearing into shadow the next. When they disappeared, the peace, the tranquillity of the coming night in the Blue Ridge Mountains, seemed to deny that they could exist. Here, where fall came so gently and so beautifully, where those last rays of sun and the coming shadow fell upon oaks and rolling fields of green and amber, here at Montemarte, they could not possibly exist.

But they did.

And still they came. Men marching, and more men on horseback. Rows and rows of soldiers.

Kiernan Miller could see them on the distant mount as she stood by the old oaks in the summer garden of Montemarte. In the dim light, it was difficult to see what color they wore. But even as she watched them, she felt panic and dismay rise within her. Her hand flew to her throat, as if she could swallow her despair.

The Confederates had pulled out of the nearby town of Harpers Ferry—she knew that. They had blown up the munitions there and pulled out. They were still near—she knew that too—but they had no large numbers, and so the horde slowly but surely rising toward her had to be Yanks.

As they came closer, she could see the blue uniforms—

standard Federal issue. Union Army. They weren't deserters or guerrilla fighters.

There could be only one reason for them to be riding toward Montemarte.

To burn it to the ground.

She stood very still, only her bright, beautiful green eyes betraying the depths of her tension. The night breeze rippled through the gold and honey-rich fire of her hair. Her slim form was as straight as the old oaks. In better times, she might have been a picture of elegance, for the breeze also touched upon the fullness of her fine gown—white eyelet over a full silver-blue skirt and a low-cut bodice with French puff sleeves. It was a beautiful gown, right out of the pages of Lady Godey's. She didn't know why she bothered to dress for evenings anymore, except that she had found herself plunged into a new world, and she was fighting to hang on to the traditions she knew so well.

The Yankees were coming.

She wanted to scream, and she wanted somewhere to run. She wanted to cast this information upon one of the many gallants she had known in her life. And she wanted one of them to stand up and sweep her up and promise her that everything would be all right, that she would be cherished and protected.

But there was nowhere to run, and no one to run to. Inside the house, the children would have seen the men by now. They would be coming to her. She would have to have something to say to them. It was doubtful that she could save the house—Miller firearms had already been used too successfully against the Union. She had to save her charges, though, and the slaves dependent upon her.

But the Yankees were coming. . . .

A cavalry unit was leading, with infantry in the back, she realized. There must have been a hundred soldiers.

Suddenly, even as they headed nearer and nearer her, the party split. Half now headed toward her, and half toward the Freemont estate down the hill.

"Kiernan! Yankees! For the love of God, Yankees!"

Kiernan swung around. Patricia, her twelve-year-old sister-in-law, stood on the front porch, her fingers clenched into her skirt.

It was curious how very lovely Patricia Miller looked. She, too, had dressed for dinner. Her blond hair hung in a single braid down her back, and her muslin gown filled with soft lilac flowers. She was framed by the house, the gracious and elegant house that looked so very beautiful and welcoming in the twilight.

Montemarte sat upon the hill on the outskirts of Harpers Ferry. Like others in the area, the Millers had found their riches in the production and manufacture of arms, and Montemarte was a monument to those riches. It was not a plantation home but a magnificent manor. There were stables for the horses that had once been the Miller family pride. There were gardens to feed the household, and there were gardens for beauty, but there were no fields for income —just the manor with its classic white Greek columns, and the stables and outbuildings.

"Kiernan—"

"I know, I know!" Kiernan told her softly. "The Yankees are coming." With a sigh she squared her shoulders and fought off a last temptation to burst into tears. She lifted her skirts and hurried for the porch. "Patricia, they're going to want to burn the house."

"No! They can't! What will we do? Where will we go?" Patricia asked, tears in her wide brown eyes.

Despite its beauty, Montemarte was just a house, Kiernan told herself. Their home, yes, but still just a creation of brick and wood and mortar and plaster. They were not destitute; she could bring the Miller children to her father's home, deep in Tidewater Virginia, on the peninsula, where the Yankees would dare not come lest they met up with Stonewall Jackson or General Lee.

She knew why Patricia was so desperate. The war had scarcely begun, but already Patricia had lost everyone. If it hadn't been for Kiernan's reckless marriage to Patricia's brother, not even Kiernan would be here now for the children.

"Don't worry," she told Patricia. "We'll be fine, whatever happens."

"Like hell!" snapped a voice, and Kiernan's eyes quickly rose to meet those of Patricia's twin brother, Jacob Miller. Brown-eyed and tow-headed like Patricia, he was already very tall and very straight, and he carried his father's old rifle. He gazed at Kiernan with hurt and with knowledge that shouldn't have been seen in eyes so very young. "Bad things are happening in a lot of places, Kiernan. Lots of bad things. You'd best get yourself and Patricia hid somewhere." There was a catch in his throat. " 'Tricia's young yet, but when them Yanks see you—"

"Jacob," Kiernan said, and lowered her head to hide a smile. He meant to defend her honor—to the death. She had heard some of the same stories about the invading Union Army that he had, but she couldn't believe that fifty men, riding with such discipline, were coming to dishonor one lone woman. "We're going to be all right. They're coming because of the Miller Firearms Factories. It's revenge, I'm afraid, but nothing more."

"Kiernan—"

She set her hand upon the rifle, lowering it. "Jacob Miller, you can't take on an entire Union cavalry company. In memory of your parents and Anthony, I have to make sure that you grow up and live to a ripe old age. Do you understand?"

"They're going to burn us out."

"Probably, yes."

"And you want to just surrender the place to them?"

"No, Jacob." She offered them both a grave smile. "I want to make the evening as wretched for them as we possibly can. I want you both to go back inside. One of you sit in the library and read a book. One of you go and make sure that Janey has started supper. I'll stay and meet them on the porch, and when they order us to go, we'll go. But on our own sweet time, and with lots of dignity."

Jacob still looked as if he wanted to start shooting. Dear God, the twins had always listened to her in the past! She prayed that Jacob wouldn't pick this moment to defy her.

"Jacob, please, for the love of God. Help me now. I swear I won't bear the sight of any more blood right now. They won't want to hurt you."

"All Yanks ever want to do is hurt southerners!" Jacob claimed, a catch in his throat. He was still just a child. He didn't want to be hurt.

He also didn't want to be a coward. He was the man of the house now, and a man stood up for what was his.

"That's not true," she said. But she herself wasn't certain anymore. War had changed everything. It had ravaged the land, it had torn apart families.

There had once been a time when they in the South had believed that the North would just let them secede, let them go their separate way.

That time was long past.

There had also been a time when they had all thought that the southern soldiers wouldn't need more than a few weeks to whop the North.

That time was also long past, no matter how brilliant the southern generals were, no matter how valiant her men, no matter how gallantly they rode their horses and wielded their swords. It had really started that long-ago day at nearby Harpers Ferry, when John Brown had made his move to seize the arsenal. The old fanatic had been captured and tried. He had committed treason and murder, and he had been condemned to hang.

And he had promised them all, on the day of his hanging, that the land would run red with blood.

"No one is going to hurt you. Put the rifle away."

"I want it close at hand," Jacob said stubbornly.

He turned to put it away. Thankfully, she thought, he wasn't going to throw away his life in a foolhardy quest for valiance.

"Thank you," Kiernan told him, smiling.

But the Yankees were still coming.

"Go in!" she commanded them. "Quickly—now!" She didn't want them to hear her voice quavering.

She clenched her hands before her. She didn't want them to see her fingers trembling.

Suddenly, Janey was on the porch with them. Plump and aging, her anxiety shone in her ink-dark eyes. "Miz Kiernan! The Yankees are coming!"

"Janey, I know that," Kiernan said, surprised at just how calm she managed to sound. "Go back in and start supper."

"Supper's on this minute, Miz Kiernan. But didn't you hear me? The—"

"Yes, yes, the Yankees are coming. Go on in, all of you. This is a house where dignity has always resided. We will go on with our lives. I will wait to greet the—er, visitors. You all go in and go about your business."

They stared at her, all three of them, as if she had gone crazy. But then Patricia—bless her—lifted her little nose, turned about, and walked regally into the house. After a moment, Jacob followed her.

"It don't make sense!" Janey said. Kiernan stood her ground on the porch, and Janey sniffed. "I said that it don't make sense. You want me to go make supper so that they can burn supper to the ground too! You ought to be high-tailing it out of here right now, missy, and that's a fact! They get their hands on you, and they might not just burn the house!"

"Janey, nothing is going to happen to me. Those are obviously not guerrilla troops. Watch them march. I'm not going to be—"

"Maybe they aren't gonna rape you," Janey said bluntly. "But you're the last adult remaining of the Miller family, and after the damage done by Miller firearms, why, they just might want to send you to some northern prison camp, and as I hear it, they aren't mighty nice places to be!"

"Don't be ridiculous, Janey," Kiernan said firmly. "They don't do horrible things to women in the North." A tinge of unease swept through her. They didn't, did they? She wasn't sure, but it didn't matter. She had to stand her ground.

"I wouldn't count on that, Miz Kiernan!"

She and Janey were good friends, even if Janey's status was that of a slave at the moment. Anthony's will had freed her, but all kinds of paper work still had to be done to make her freedom a fact. It didn't matter. Janey would never leave her. Not when they needed each other so very badly.

But for the moment, Kiernan raised her voice just slightly and used the tone she had learned all the long years back home. "Janey, I said to go in."

Janey sniffed one more time and started into the house. "Dear Lord, give me strength! These old bones are too old to be trotting up into a snow-covered northern city to take care of the fool mistress in some jail!"

Janey paused in the doorway, sniffed once more for good measure, and started in. "Can't see why I'm cooking no supper that no human body's gonna get to sink teeth into! Supper's gonna be char-broiled tonight, that it is!"

The door closed with a slam.

Kiernan stood still on the porch and felt the breeze move about her again, lift her hair, and rustle her skirt. The enemy was still coming.

Like the undulating wave of a deep-blue ocean—relentless, unstoppable, they came. And she waited still, silent, her heart pounding, her breath coming too quickly, despite her determination to appear calm.

The Yanks were coming to burn down her home. There would be no help—the deed would be done in retaliation for every rifle ever manufactured by the family into which she had married, the Millers.

She wondered why she was remaining. Why she didn't just run. She couldn't possibly stop them.

Then she knew that she was staying for her belief, for Virginia, for the Confederacy, and for herself, her soul. She couldn't bend to the enemy, now or ever. She couldn't run, and she couldn't bend.

She watched the movement of the enemy troops. The first horses in front broke loose and came galloping up the rise upon which she stood. Her heart thundered. She didn't move.

A moment later, a handsome bay was drawn up before her by a rugged-looking cavalryman with a dark moustache and beard that didn't entirely hide his sneer.

"You must be Mrs. Miller, ma'am."

"I am," Kiernan said.

"Ma'am, I'm Captain Hugh Norris, and I reckon you'd best be out of the place right quick. I've orders to torch the house."

"Whose orders?" she demanded.

"Why, the orders of General—"

"Your general has no jurisdiction here."

"Ma'am, the Union is here. Your Confederates have left you. And I'm going to burn this place to the ground, so you'd best get your kin and help out of here. Lady, you ain't smelt nothing bad until you've smelt burning flesh!"

Kiernan fought very hard to remain still, staring at the man, determined not to give in to his demand.

"Then you'll just have to give me time, sir."

"I'm torching her in ten minutes, Mrs. Miller." He was gleeful. Obviously, his task appealed to him.

"I don't know, sir. I think it would create an awfully bad image if it was found out that Union officers burned down houses with women and children still in them. You will just have to bide your time, sir."

Norris stared at her in a fury. His bay pranced to and fro before the porch steps. Suddenly, he nudged the bay and brought it leaping up to the porch, very close to her. Kiernan raised her chin and didn't take a step back despite the heavy hooves of the bay.

"Lady, let me tell you something. The day of the great southern high-brow belle is over. Real soon, you won't dare be talking to a man like that! So take your time. I won't burn you down. I'll just drag you out. Then it'll look like the darned Yank saved your hide despite your determination for suicide!"

"I think not, sir," she told him. She was insane! What was she going to do? What *could* she do?

She needed to be rescued. She needed the whole southern cavalry under Jeb Stuart to come riding in. She needed a horseman, a hero in butternut and gray.

"Sergeant! Set some tinder!" Norris commanded.

One of his men leaped down from his horse. He called out in turn to several of the men, and they quickly joined him,

collecting dried twigs and sticks and winding them with
dried hay of their own to stuff into the latticed nooks and
crannies at the base of the porch. Kiernan watched them,
powerless to stop them, yet suddenly so furious, she wanted
to tear into the men, to scratch their eyes out, to tear their
hair out by the handfuls.

But she managed to stand still and silently, condemning,
upon the porch.

"Damn you!" Norris thundered. Suddenly, he raced his
horse down the steps and out before his men.

"Prepare to light your torches, men!" he called out.

Kiernan remained still even as they set fire to the torches.

"Prepare to fire the house!"

They couldn't burn it with her standing there—she was
determined! The men in blue looked at her nervously, then
looked at their commander, then looked back to her again.

They started forward.

A cry bellowed out, loud, harsh, and full of authority.

"Halt!"

A rider was coming from behind the others, taking the
path from the town in the valley below that the others had
taken.

He rode with no discipline. He rode like one born and
bred to sit upon a horse, with reckless, absolute ease upon
his steed. He rode as if he knew the hills and mountains and
valleys and more. He rode as if he knew the very muscle and
heart of his mount.

The silver horse raced, churning up dirt and grass, and its
rider was heedless of the speed. Distance was swiftly
breached.

"Norris, halt!"

The order rang out with unmistakable authority, and at
the sound of it, a faint recognition and unease stirred in
Kiernan's blood.

Captain Hugh Norris swore under his breath and rode
down to meet the approaching rider.

A man who also wore blue.

Dark blue, deep dark blue, the blue of the Union Army.
His uniform, too, was cavalry, trimmed in gold braid. His

hat was blue, pulled low over his forehead and topped with a tall plume.

Not a hundred feet from the house, he drew up as Hugh Norris confronted him. And the new arrival produced a piece of paper beneath the captain's nose.

An argument ensued, low-voiced, intense. The men with the burning torches waited uneasily. Countless gazes swept over Kiernan, and she realized that few of these men relished burning down a house.

Even those with eyes that mirrored the death that they had seen. They waited, as she waited.

Someone had come and halted the destruction of her house and of her world.

A Yank. A man in blue.

Not just any Yank, she was beginning to fear.

The two men broke apart.

"Douse your torches!" the new arrival ordered with his indomitable tone of command. He was instantly obeyed. The men thrust their burning torches to the ground.

The new arrival came riding up to the porch on his silver horse. He tilted back his plumed hat, and steel-blue eyes met hers.

The unease that had tinged the base of her spine now swept through her. Her heart skipped a beat, then slammed hard against the wall of her chest.

A Yank had come. . . .

Not just any Yank.

Jesse Cameron. The one Yank she had known most of her life. The Yank she despised the most. The one she had loved once upon a time. The one who now sent her heart and mind into a tumult.

It had been a long time since she had seen him. A long, long time since she had thrown her heart at his feet. Since he had ignored her every plea.

Since he had ridden north, wearing blue.

He hadn't changed.

Or maybe he had. His eyes were every bit as hard as ever, but they seemed to hold an even greater wisdom, a weariness; and a certain ruthlessness. Tiny new lines were etched around them. If anything, his jaw was more firmly set. He was clean shaven, baring the sharp planes and angles of his face. It was a rugged face, but handsome still, for its hard lines were tempered by the dark arches of his brow and the startling color of his eyes. It was given sensuality by the fullness of his mouth—a mouth that was grim and taut now as he stared at her.

"Hello, Kiernan."

She didn't want to admit that she knew him. No, she didn't want to remember that she knew him. She didn't want to remember the last time that she had seen him, and most of all, she despised the fact that she was seeing him now.

With him the victor for the moment, and she the enemy, her life and limb threatened.

She didn't respond. He shrugged, but she was certain that his eyes glittered and that his temper was somewhat frayed. "Mrs. Miller, as of this moment, I'm taking over this property for use as my headquarters, for hospital and surgical space as is necessary, as of this moment. You will kindly inform your household."

Kiernan gritted down hard on her teeth.

He had ridden in to save her home, she realized, to keep the manor from being burned to the ground. She had prayed for a hero in gray.

The house was being saved by a man in blue.

She'd rather eat dirt, she determined, lifting her chin.

"Captain Norris has plans to burn the place, Captain Cameron. I'm afraid you'll have to seek your headquarters elsewhere."

He stared hard at her. He dismounted from his horse and strode up the steps to the porch. He paused, just feet from her. He was tall, over six foot two, and broad-shouldered in his cavalry shirt and skirted cloak. He was dangerous. Jesse had always been dangerous.

As dangerous as the currents that now seemed to riddle the air with him so close—vital, electric. She felt a sudden heat, and it seemed to crackle on the breeze that swept between them.

Jesse could always bring about that kind of tension.

He spoke softly, so softly that his words couldn't possibly carry to the other soldiers, who still formed a ring around the front of the house, watching them.

"I'm trying to save your home and your neck, Mrs. Miller," he told her tensely.

"My neck hasn't been threatened, Captain Cameron," she snapped back.

"Keep talking, Mrs. Miller, and it will be!" he promised her. "Now shut up, and the manor can remain standing."

"Will you really be taking it over?"

"Yes."

"Then I'd rather see it burn."

"I'm sure you would, Kiernan. Common sense was never your strong suit. But what of young Jacob Miller and his sister?"

"Jacob wouldn't want a Yankee turncoat like you living in the house, either, Captain Cameron."

"You'd rather it burned?"

"Yes."

He smiled at last and then started to laugh. He laughed so hard that she wanted to throw herself at him and hit him, despite their audience. He turned away and went down the steps.

Fear swept through her. Montemarte wasn't actually hers —it belonged to Jacob and Patricia. She really had no right to recklessly bring about its destruction. But still, she couldn't seem to swallow her pride.

"Captain Cameron!" she called to him sharply. He paused, his back stiff and straight. "Will you—will you burn it now?"

He turned back to her, setting his left foot on a step and leaning an elbow on his knee. "Well, Mrs. Miller, I probably should do just that. But I am sorry to disappoint you. I'm afraid that I can't burn it now. I had to threaten and cajole and just about turn handstands to get the general to turn the place over to me. You see, Millers aren't real popular among the Union men. Lots and lots of them have had friends and kin killed by Miller firearms. They'd like to see the total destruction of Miller property and Miller people."

"That shouldn't be difficult now, considering that the majority of the Millers are dead—thanks to the Union Army."

"I assure you, several hundred Union men died the same —thanks to the Confederate Army."

"They were on Virginia soil!"

He shrugged, and when he spoke again, he seemed to drop all pretense for the moment. "I didn't start the war, Kiernan."

"But we're on opposite sides."

"So fight me!" he warned her softly. "But I'm moving in, with my staff. Take your little charges and run to your own home. You'll be safe enough there for a while. I probably won't be able to salvage everything in the house, but at least I can keep it standing."

"I don't want any favors from you," she said heatedly. "And I'll be damned if I'll run away from a passel of bad-mannered Yanks."

His brow shot up with surprise. "You're staying?"

She lifted her chin. "Stonewall Jackson will bring his army in here and wipe out the lot of you," she promised. "I might as well wait for him to come. And keep your men from looting the house blind."

"You haven't been asked to stay, Mrs. Miller."

"Are you planning on having your men throw me and the children out—bodily?"

"Heavens no, Mrs. Miller. It's war, and I have managed to send men into battle. But I'm a merciful commander—I wouldn't dream of sending them in after you."

"Then I'm staying."

"Maybe not. I didn't say that I wouldn't come in after you myself."

"What a fine point of valor, Captain Cameron!" she drawled with dripping sarcasm.

"Go home, Kiernan," he told her softly. She hated that tone of voice, hated the way that it washed over her so warmly. The way that it seemed to stroke her, inside and out, and bring back memories.

"This is my home now," she reminded him. "And Jackson will come back. Or Lee will come back. Some southern general will come for this land again, and you will be routed."

"That's highly possible, Kiernan." He stared at her and shrugged. "Fine. Stay. But I'm taking over the house. Be forewarned."

"Forewarned, sir? I'll be looking over your shoulder. I'll be making sure that you treat Reb prisoners with the same care that you would give to your own injured."

Fire flashed in his eyes, an absolute fury. She knew how to set a knife against Jesse's spine because she knew Jesse. She knew his passion for medicine. Casting out the suggestion that he might treat Rebel prisoners with less than his full commitment was like a slap in the face.

But other than the flare of his eyes, he gave no hint of emotion. He arched a brow to her. As always, his control infuriated her.

He took a step closer, and his voice lowered to an even more dangerous tone. He was so near that she could breathe in the scent of him. He didn't touch her, but still she felt his warmth and both the anger and the sensuality of his words. His words were a warning.

"I thought you'd run because of me, Mrs. Miller, like you did before. I won't mind your being around. I'll enjoy it. You're the one who promised never to suffer life with a Yank, remember?"

"I won't be suffering a life with you!" she snapped quickly. "I'll be surviving in spite of you. I'll fight you every step of the way. And the South will win."

"Maybe the battles, but never the war," he told her, and for a moment she wondered if they were speaking about the conflict of nations or the tumult that raged between them.

He stared at her for a several seconds. The wind ruffled her hair, and she was suddenly very cold. It was all she could do to keep from shivering as he stared at her with his steel and smoldering eyes.

"The Confederates will come back!" she vowed to him.

"They very well might," he responded. For a moment, her

will was locked within his gaze, within the heat and tension, riddled with it, shaking with it. There was too much between them—too much hatred, too much passion, too many currents that sizzled and slashed like lightning. "But until your Rebs come back, Mrs. Miller," he warned her, "it's going to be share and share alike."

He swept off his hat and bowed to her with mock gallantry. Then he turned and started back down the steps, calling orders to his men.

Kiernan spun around and tore into the house. Patricia caught her in the hallway.

"Are they going to burn the house down, Kiernan?" she asked anxiously.

"No! No!"

"Then what?" Jacob demanded, arriving in the foyer from the kitchen.

"They're using it as a headquarters."

"As a headquarters! As a place to plan how to kill more of our people?" Jacob asked.

Kiernan shook her head. How she hated Jesse! How she wished that he'd never come!

She'd prayed for a hero in gray. She'd prayed that the house could survive.

And the house had been saved—by an enemy in blue! An enemy she had known long and well.

"Captain Cameron is a—a doctor," she said.

"Cameron!" Jacob said.

"Yes," Kiernan answered. "It's Jesse. Jesse stopped them from burning the place. But he's taking it over."

Jacob stared at her, then swung around in silence. She heard him leave by the rear of the house. Patricia stared at Kiernan a moment longer, then turned and raced after her brother.

Kiernan tore up the stairs.

The twins would have to tend to themselves for the moment. She needed time. She was desperate for time.

Jesse had come.

She threw open the door to her room and threw herself upon her bed, burying her face in her pillow. She wanted to plot, to plan, to reason—but only one thought kept racing in her head. Jesse was here, Jesse was here.

She hated him so very much. And yet she had never stopped loving him. Even when she stood before an altar and swore to love, honor, and cherish another man, she had never stopped loving him.

But not as much as she hated him for wearing blue—when all of his family had donned gray.

When she had fought for the life they had always known, for Virginia, for love, honor, and family.

She rolled over and stared at the ceiling.

If only it were *Daniel* Cameron who had come. The brother who wore gray.

Not so long ago, they had all dressed in blue. The Camerons had both come riding into Harpers Ferry during John Brown's raid.

Jesse had come to her rescue then.

Back when the world had still seemed sane.

How very much had happened since then!

One

October 16, 1859
Harpers Ferry, Virginia
Near Midnight

"A shot's been fired!"

Kiernan bolted upright in her bed. Lacey Donahue, her gray hair covered in a nightcap, was carrying a candle to the foot of Kiernan's bed, and hovering over her in distress.

Half awake, Kiernan struggled to understand what was happening. "A shot? Fired by whom?"

"I don't know!" Lacey murmured.

"When? Where?"

"I don't know, but I know that I heard it!" Lacey swore.

"Lacey, I didn't hear a thing," Kiernan assured her.

What Lacey wanted was companionship, Kiernan realized as her plump hostess curled up on the foot of her bed. "There's something going on in the streets. I woke up and there were people out there!" Lacey said.

"Lacey, out where? These are public streets—" Kiernan began, but Lacey nervously interrupted her.

"No, no, dear! There are strangers running around with guns. No, wait, they're not running around—they're sneaking around. Oh, Kiernan, you must know what I mean. They are people with no right to be out there!"

Kiernan leaped out of bed and hurried to the window,

drawing back the frilled curtains. To the far left she could see the Potomac and the railroad crossing over to Maryland. A little closer, she could see the buildings of the armory. The moon was out, and the street was gently lit.

"I don't see anything," she said.

"Step back!" Lacey warned her. "Don't let anyone see you there!"

Kiernan hid a smile and moved back. She looked out, thinking that she loved the night and the beauty of the mountains and valleys here where the Shenandoah and the Potomac rivers came together. There was a beautiful story about the Indian maiden Shenandoah, who had loved her brave, Potomac, too deeply and too well. And when they were parted, it was her tears that had formed the rivers.

Kiernan's home was in the Tidewater region of Virginia, far down on the peninsula, right on the James River, and not at all far the from the original Jamestown settlement. Virginia was a big state, and she'd come a long way to reach Harpers Ferry, several days ride. But the country was beautiful. She loved all of it. From the low-lying land along the James to Williamsburg, to Richmond, Fredericksburg, and all the way over here, where they were in the point of the state that joined Maryland, and where one actually had to look to the south to face Washington, D.C. She loved the peninsula where she lived. But at night, when the moon beat gently down upon the town, with the Blue Ridge Mountains rising all around and the waters rushing between, she didn't think that any place could be more beautiful.

Or more peaceful, like tonight.

Lacey was just nervous, Kiernan thought. Her husband, Thomas, was away with Kiernan's father and Andrew Miller and his son, Anthony Miller. They were looking for a site farther south on which to build a second factory. Since the federal armory was at Harpers Ferry, Andrew Miller wanted to stay in production there, but he also wanted to expand and explore new possibilities. And he wanted to be away from the ever-watchful eye of the federal government to do that.

The political situation was not an easy one at the moment.

Southerners were swearing that if Abraham Lincoln was elected president, there would be war. Discontent was sweeping the country. If it did come to war, the federal government would have to take an immediate interest in Harpers Ferry because of the armory.

Kiernan was fascinated by politics. She knew she wasn't supposed to be—her aunt Fiona had told her it was a most unladylike trait, and that she would pay for it somewhere down the line. Her father had chastised her, too, mainly because Aunt Fiona had done so.

But Kiernan was an only child, and she had been her father's companion and his best friend as she grew up, except for the time she had gone away to Lady Ellen's Finishing School for Girls. She knew her father's mind very well, and she thought that he had been right when he warned his friend Andrew Miller that no one really knew what Virginia would do in the end.

"South Carolina is the one screaming states' rights the loudest, Andrew," he had stated at the dinner table. "Why, the majority of the Founding Fathers were Virginians! Washington, Jefferson, Madison, Monroe—all Virginians. Patrick Henry—a Virginian. Why, Virginia is the very heart and soul of this country. It has never been proved that a state can secede!"

"If Lincoln is elected," Andrew had argued back, "then South Carolina will secede. And once she leaves the Union, I promise you, her sister cotton and tobacco and slave states will follow suit. You mark my words."

Kiernan wondered if it would happen, or if the uproar was just the political climate of the day. The real trouble was out in the wilds of the West. Abolitionists were racing out westward to Missouri and Nebraska and Kansas—"bleeding Kansas" as they called it, for all the bloodshed. There was a war going on in the West already. Proslavery men and abolitionists were at one another so viciously, it had become a string of raids and murders rather than battles. Slaveholders were racing out, too. Everybody was trying to claim the new states for their own side.

Horrible things were happening, really horrible things,

things that made some of the stories about Indians seem
tame. A war was already going on between the slaveholding
factions and those determined that Nebraska would be a free
state. Cities had been attacked. Unarmed men, women, and
children had died. Among the abolitionists, one name stood
out: John Brown. Even in Virginia, they had heard stories
about him, about the way he had taken his followers into
Missouri, ripped unarmed men from their houses, and
butchered them then and there in front of their loved ones.
Retaliation, he had claimed it was.

But it was murder, Kiernan thought, horrible, heinous
murder. She was grateful that such things didn't happen in
Virginia, even this far west in the mountains. She was convinced that anyone who was running around killing people
in either Kansas or Missouri ought to be prosecuted.

The problems weren't just in the West, she knew. A
woman named Harriet Beecher Stowe had written a book
called *Uncle Tom's Cabin,* and in it she had created the
cruelest human being who could be imagined to own and
persecute slaves.

But it wasn't always like that! Kiernan wanted to shout to
the newspapers. Most of the slaveowners she knew were
good people, determined to enforce good conditions for their
slaves, seeing to it that they received proper religious train-
ing. There were *some* cruel men, she had to admit, but none
she knew were as bad as Simon Legree!

Most southerners didn't even own slaves. The problem
really had to do with the economy. The South was a cotton
kingdom, and slaves were necessary to work the plantations.
That didn't mean that everyone was happy about it. Why,
Jefferson, when he wrote the Declaration of Independence,
wanted all men to be free—including the slaves—when he
had been a slaveholder himself. Other statesmen had convinced him that the Declaration would never get past the
Continental Congress if it contained such a clause, for
the very reason that the South still needed slaves today—the
economy.

But whether a master or mistress was a good person or a
bad person wasn't the point in the long run, the way

Kiernan saw it. The point was freedom. She couldn't begin
to imagine being owned by anyone. Her father was a wonderful man. No master could be kinder, or more gentle. But
he was an old-time Virginian—the son, grandson, and great-
grandson of planters. Her view on the slavery question was
not the same as his, or that of any of their neighbors or
business associates.

Kiernan didn't know Lacey Donahue's thoughts on the
subject, but Lacey and her husband, Thomas, owned no
slaves. They had no servants living in the house at all, for
that matter. Her maid was an Irish girl who came in every
morning, and Thomas, a lawyer, had a clerk and an assistant
who came in every day to his office below the living floors of
this three-storied house right on the main street of town.

The women were very much alone in the house tonight.
That was surely why little bumps in the night and the idea of
people walking about in the street bothered Lacey. She was
a sweetheart. Childless, she clung to her husband. To the
best of Kiernan's knowledge, Lacey and Thomas had never
been separated before, but Thomas and Andrew Miller and
Kiernan's father were all planning on investing in the new
armory together.

Kiernan was aware, too, that her father and Andrew Miller were interested in another alliance—a marriage between
her and Anthony. She cared for Anthony, cared for him
deeply. He was tall and almost gaunt, with golden hair and
mahogany eyes and the most charming and elegant manner
imaginable. He was dedicated to his father, and to Virginia.
He was bright and fun, a wonderful dancer, a man quick to
plan a picnic with her or a daring horse race with a friend.

Maybe she did love Anthony. They had everything in
common, and she enjoyed him tremendously. Yet for reasons she didn't understand herself, she waited and stalled
about marrying him. She didn't mind flirting with him in the
least, and she loved dancing with him and being with him, it
was just . . .

She had dreamed of love being something different, something that would make her whole body tremble. She would
feel a vast excitement knowing that she would see the man

she loved, of feeling a rush of heat and fever every time that he was near.

Feelings she tried to push to deep corners of her heart and mind plunged forward despite her best efforts.

She wanted love to feel the way she had once felt about Jesse Cameron.

Oh, but that was so long ago! she thought. When she had been a very little girl, she had thought that the sun rose and set on him. No man had ever sat a horse better. No man had ever managed to shoot quite so well, or tease a little girl so gallantly.

Jesse was ten years her senior. She had just been leaving her dolls behind when he had first returned from West Point in his uniform. No one had been as fascinating as Jesse in that uniform. No one had ever had quite such an effect upon her. He was always cordial when he saw her, his flashing blue eyes filled with humor and affection when he greeted her in his husky Virginia drawl. "Mornin', Miss Mackay. I swear, but you do grow more lovely by the day." Naturally, he teased her. He was always surrounded by girls, the belles of the South—and the North.

Or at least he had teased her until recently, she thought. Not that she saw him very often. He had come out of West Point to move on to medicine, and he had been spending an awful lot of time in Washington. And then she had spent time with her father, and with Anthony Miller.

Now she had to remind herself that her feelings for Jesse had been a childhood infatuation and nothing more. Their families had been friends for decades. Jesse's brother Daniel had been one of her best friends, and he had admitted to her that Jesse had often laughed at her mischief-making and said that she was a "wayward little dickens," and that any man had best watch out when she was in the vicinity.

Of course, she'd never *really* been a "wayward dickens." Jesse had overreacted. She had simply been careful to stand up against some of the pranks that others played around her. In school one day Tristan Tombey had tried to get her attention by dipping her hair in an inkwell. Well, she'd just gotten back at Tristan. Admittedly, she'd flirted with him, teased him, smiled, tugged upon his heartstrings. But that had been the only way to attach the inkwell to his suspenders so that every single thing he was wearing and his body could be coated in ink. As it happened, Jesse had just been on his way home, passing by the schoolyard, when Tristan had first put up his fuss.

Jesse had laughed, but he'd also pulled her up on his horse and insisted on taking her home. "Miss Mackay, you are an outrageous little flirt, and I pity the poor young lad who falls for you next!" Jesse had told her firmly.

Then he'd taken her home, and despite her outraged protests, he'd laughingly told the entire story to her father. She'd gotten into horrible trouble, of course, but Jesse had still been amused. On his way out he had taken hold of her chin, and those striking eyes of his had lit like blue fire into her own. "Take heed, Miss Mackay, you're too young to be practicing such a talent for flirtation. Someday, some poor soul may fight back."

"A gallant southern gentleman?" she had taunted sweetly in turn. "Such as yourself? To cause a lady—oh, no! a child! —distress?"

"Ah, but men will not always be gallant southern gentlemen," he had warned her. And with a tousle of her hair, he had left.

And she had been furious.

But even then, she had dreamed about him, about those blue eyes of his, and about the deep, husky taunt of his voice.

Because Jesse didn't always tease. Once before, she had determined to go swimming down in one of the creeks and on her way she'd come across little Cissy Wade, one of Old Man Evan Turner's slave children, and on an impulse, she'd talked the skinny, frightened-looking little girl into coming with her. When they'd come back, Kiernan had been astounded by Evan Turner's fury with Cissy. Kiernan had confidently explained that it had been all her fault, but Turner had taken a cane to Cissy and warned Kiernan—rich little lady that she might be—that she'd get the same if she didn't run along. Poor farmers needed what slave help they had.

Well, Kiernan hadn't run. She'd stayed to see Turner strike Cissy. And she understood why her papa had always called Turner white trash, but that hadn't helped any. She'd heard Cissy scream, and she'd come running for help, though she knew she'd never reach Papa in time to do Cissy any good.

As soon as she had hit the roadway home, she had nearly plowed right into Jesse on one of the Camerons' beautiful black racing horses. He dismounted and caught her before she could race on.

"Kiernan! What now? Who did you tempt into doing what?"

She didn't care if Jesse teased her or not. There were tears in her eyes. Jesse held her shoulders and tried to shake free. "I took Cissy swimming. Just down to the creek, just for an hour. And he's beating her! Old Man Turner is beating her with a cane. Jesse, he's going to kill her!"

Jesse stepped back with a weary look in his eyes.

"Kiernan, Turner *owns* Cissy. By law, he can beat her."

"He'll kill her!"

"Kiernan, you should have thought about Cissy's position before you invited her along."

"I just wanted her to have some fun. He works her so hard. She always looks so very tired. I didn't mean to hurt her. I'd never hurt her! Oh, I'd like to tear his hair out!"

"A few more years on you, Miss Mackay, and you'd probably try," he said lightly. Then he added, "All right, all right. Go on home, Kiernan. I'll do what I can."

She hadn't gone home. She'd followed Jesse back to Turner's farm, and she'd hid back in the bushes. Jesse had ridden in on the action, dismounted from his horse, and stripped the cane right out of Turner's hands. Old Man Turner swung around, but even though Jesse hadn't quite reached twenty, he was very tall and broad-shouldered and Turner wasn't about to wrestle with him. Still, he had his say.

"You ain't got no right, boy, you ain't got no right. Even if you do come from Cameron money!"

"You're going to beat this child to death, Turner!" Jesse had exclaimed.

"She's mine, and she was a runaway."

"She wasn't any runaway, and you know it!" Jesse said angrily.

Turner's voice lowered, and the two of them argued onward.

At the end of it all, Jesse produced a large wad of money, and suddenly Cissy, dazed and silent now except for her sniffles, was on the back of Jesse's horse.

Jesse had bought her from Turner. A week later, the Camerons bought the rest of her family—her mother, her father—a rickety old field hand—and her baby brother.

Maybe it was then that her infatuation really began.

Ah, but Jesse could still infuriate her! He treated her like a child!

When her father had staged her coming-out ball, she'd thought that Jesse was off with the military, either in Washington or out in the West fighting Indians. It had been a wonderful night for her. She was tied into an incredible corset, wearing what seemed like a million petticoats. For the first time her father allowed her a fashionable adult gown with a daring, daring bosom. Her hair was curled and elegantly piled on top of her head. She felt beautiful and very grown-up—and more. She felt very confident with herself as a woman, and she had the time of her life flirting, smiling, and dancing. The young men flocked to her, and it was wonderful. She knew that she must never really torment a young swain, but it was certainly proper enough to be a very charming flirt, and she couldn't help but enjoy her power.

That is, she had enjoyed it until she saw Jesse. He had been leaning in a doorway watching her, and she realized that he had been watching her for quite some time. There was a very irritating amusement in his eyes and in his lopsided smile.

And then he came to her to claim a dance and swept her

into his arms, even though she had promised the dance to someone else.

"Ah, but you are growing up to fulfill your every promise of beauty, Miss Mackay!" he had assured her. But his blue gaze had still been alight with laughter, even when he had bent over her hand and brushed it with a kiss. The kiss brought a flush to her cheeks, and she wanted to kick him even as she felt palpitations pulsing beneath her breast, right in the area of her heart. "So who are you out to dazzle tonight?" he asked.

"The world, Jesse Cameron," she told him sweetly. But when he laughed again and released her, she had been careful to accidentally tread upon his toes with her new leather pumps.

Jesse could go hang! She had outgrown Jesse Cameron, outgrown that kind of infatuation, she told herself firmly that night in 1859 at Harpers Ferry. She wasn't in awe of Jesse anymore. She had grown up—and she had grown up with definite opinions, so she was probably—to Jesse—more than ever a "wayward little dickens."

Jesse could be amusing and polite. He could even be charming—when he chose to be so, she thought. He never minced his words or opinions, and he had never given a fig for popular thought. He was incapable of bending or compromising, she reminded herself. If she married him, he would surely never accept her advice the way Anthony did.

Nor would he tolerate indecisiveness on the question. Jesse would demand all or nothing if he demanded anything.

Anthony was by far the more civil man.

Jesse was really nothing compared to Anthony.

It was the feeling she had had for Jesse that she remembered. The excitement when he was near, the wild, challenging excitement, the shivers, the tremors. It was that feeling she missed with Anthony. It wasn't Anthony's fault. She simply wasn't a child anymore, so naturally she did not feel those things.

"Look! Oh, Kiernan! Someone's moving down there again!" Lacey called.

Kiernan hadn't been paying attention. By the time she looked, whoever had moved—if he had moved—had disappeared.

"Lacey, I'm sorry. I just don't see anything."

"You're not trying!" Lacey told her.

"All right, all right, I'll keep my eyes open this time, I promise," Kiernan assured her.

A moment later, they heard the whistle from the night train. It was about one thirty.

"Everything is all right. The midnight train has come through," Kiernan said.

Lacey shivered emphatically. "I tell you, something is going on tonight."

A fierce chill swept through Kiernan. She still hadn't seen a thing, but she suddenly sensed that maybe Lacey's fears were based on something real.

Kiernan looked from Lacey back to the window. She blinked, certain that she had seen a movement by the shadowy buildings. Little pricks of unease danced up and down her spine. Lacey was right—there was something going on.

But it didn't affect them, she thought. Surely they were safe in Lacey's home.

She turned back to her hostess once again. "Lacey, have we got a gun in the house?"

Lacey slowly shook her head, and Kiernan almost laughed. They were alone because the men were off to find a spot for a new weapons-productions plant, and they hadn't a single firearm in the house.

"Oh, Kiernan! Do you think we're in trouble?"

"Of course not," Kiernan told her. "Maybe it's just a late meeting down there or an inspection going on or something of that sort."

"Then why would they sneak around? And why would I have heard a shot?"

Kiernan shrugged. She wanted to assure Lacey, but she herself was now convinced that something wasn't right. The people below did seem to be slinking, or making movements that just weren't right.

"I'm sure we're in no danger," she told Lacey. After all,

why would they be? It was a big town. And as two women alone, they certainly offered no one any kind of a threat. Lacey and Thomas lived comfortably, but they weren't particularly wealthy, so there were no great treasures in the house.

But whoever had come into Harpers Ferry hadn't come for wealth or riches. Kiernan knew that, just as she knew that something was happening.

"Why don't we go down and have a glass of sherry?" she suggested.

"We can't see the town from downstairs," Lacey told her.

Kiernan smiled. "Then we'll bring the sherry up here. How's that?"

That suggestion appealed to Lacey. The two women lit the candle by Kiernan's bedside and hurried downstairs to the parlor by Thomas's office for the sherry.

They must look like a pair of wraiths, Kiernan thought. She had on a lace-trimmed white cotton gown that seemed to float as she moved, and Lacey wore a pale blue gown, an eerie color in the night. Harpers Ferry already had ghost stories. It was said that down by the old Harper house, a ghost could often be seen in the windows. It was supposed to be Mrs. Harper, watching over the gold her husband had supposedly buried somewhere in the yard. Some said that George Washington, who had been determined that this would be the site for the armory, still walked the streets upon occasion, checking out his interests.

And there were the Indians, of course. Potomac and Shenandoah were still shedding their tears.

Back in the guest room, Kiernan poured them each a glass of sherry. They took up sentinel in rockers on either side of the window, sipping the drink. Lacey seemed happy enough, either content that they were safe, or enjoying their impromptu party.

Kiernan was growing increasingly more uncomfortable. There *was* movement out there, by the firehouse, and by the armory buildings. And the night was passing swiftly. Looking out at the sky and toward the mountains and the rivers,

Kiernan thought that the first pink streaks of day would soon reach delicately over the water.

Lacey was telling her about a party she had attended in Washington recently, marveling at how quickly the railroad had taken her into the capital city. Kiernan swallowed more sherry. She had just begun to relax when she heard a fierce pounding on the door below.

She and Lacey leaped out of their chairs at the same time, staring at each other.

"What do we do?" Lacey cried.

"Ignore it!" Kiernan suggested.

"What if someone is trying to help us?"

"What if someone is trying to hurt us?"

Wide-eyed, they continued to stare at each other.

And then they heard the glass of the office door below shatter as it crashed open. Lacey yelped, and Kiernan managed to swallow back a scream. It wouldn't help to let anyone know where they were.

"Lacey, we need something, anything! Why is there not a single weapon in this house!"

"I don't know, I don't know—we never needed a weapon in the house!" Lacey countered, wringing her hands.

Barking at poor Lacey wouldn't help a thing, Kiernan realized. She was just as terrified herself.

Then they heard footsteps coming up the stairs.

Kiernan saw a parasol in the corner of the room. She dived for it, wondering what earthly good it would do her. But she couldn't just stand there and accept whatever happened. She couldn't allow anyone to come in and harm poor dear Lacey. She would have to fight.

With a parasol!

They heard the door to Lacey's bedroom across the hall being thrown open and footsteps moving about.

"Hide!" Kiernan whispered to Lacey.

"Where?" Lacey demanded.

There was nowhere to hide. It was a pleasant, comfortable room, warmed by Lacey's special touches, but it was small and sparsely furnished. There was the bed, a wardrobe, the two padded rockers, and a nightstand.

"Slip under the bed!" Kiernan suggested, then realized that Lacey could not slip her round form into any such space.

"*You* hide, Kiernan Mackay," Lacey told her. Her command was heroic, for Kiernan could see the frantic race of Lacey's pulse above the ruffles at her throat.

"I'd never leave you alone—" Kiernan began, but the question suddenly became moot as the door to the room burst open.

Two men stood before them, and both were armed. One aimed a Colt at Lacey's heart, and the taller of the two, a bearded black man, held a rifle pointed straight at Kiernan.

Her own heart leaped with fear, and she forced herself to stand tall and indignant.

"Who in God's name are you, and how dare you burst into a private residence to threaten vulnerable women!" she cried out with vehemence that surprised her. Her hands were clammy. She'd never been more frightened in her life.

"We're soldiers for freedom, miss," the shorter, white man told her. "And you're Kiernan Mackay, the daughter of John Mackay, slaveholder."

"I am Kiernan Mackay," she acknowledged coldly. "And you—"

"We're the revolution. It's starting here, tonight. The country will rise here, this very night."

She swallowed hard, realizing that he was talking about a slave revolution.

Such things had happened in the Caribbean and South America, she knew. Slaves had risen against their masters and mistresses, and the carnage had been horrible. People had been butchered in their beds—little children, anyone.

But she couldn't believe that that could happen here. Certainly not in Lacey's home—when Thomas had always made it clear that he would never own another human being.

"You have no right to come here!" she said. "Revolution, indeed! You'd hurt anyone in your reckless endeavors."

"We don't mean no harm to Mrs. Donahue," the man said, frightening Kiernan further. He knew them both! He knew that it was Lacey's house, and he had known that Kiernan would be in it. Whatever was going on had been well organized. "But Miss Mackay, you're to come with us."

"No," she said flatly.

Lacey wedged her plump body between Kiernan and the men in the doorway. "You'll not touch this girl, you ruffians! I don't know what you think you're going to do with a young woman—"

"Nothing evil, ma'am," the tall black man assured her. "We've come under the guidance of John Brown, and John Brown comes under the guidance of the Lord. But the war has begun, and Miss Mackay is to come with us—a hostage for John Brown."

John Brown. Her blood simmered hotly, then chilled to ice. John Brown had ruthlessly butchered men. He was a fanatic, and he did believe that he killed men in the name of God. She badly wanted to disdain these men, but she was very frightened. Surely John Brown didn't wage war upon women and children!

"We don't want to hurt you," the short white man told Kiernan. "If you'll come along quietly . . ."

She didn't want them to hurt her either. But if she went with them, what then?

She shook her head slowly. "No, I can't come with you. I'm not dressed."

"That's right!" Lacey said. "You can't take a young woman out on the streets like this!" Lacey played for time because Kiernan was playing for time. But what good was time going to do them? If they meant to harm her, Kiernan wasn't going to allow them to do so without a fight. She still held the parasol. She wrapped her hands tightly around it. But what good was a parasol against guns?

"Miss Mackay, you're to come now. If you resist us any longer, I'll truss you up like a Christmas turkey, and Cain here"—the short man indicated his tall black companion— "will carry you over his shoulder."

She must not be tied up, Kiernan thought. If she had any chance at all of escape, she couldn't be tied up. "All right. I'll walk down the stairs," she said.

"Wait!" Lacey cried. "If Kiernan goes, you'll have to take me too."

"No, Mrs. Donahue, we don't want you!" Cain, the black man, spoke emphatically.

"Lacey, please stay here," Kiernan said, staring at Lacey and praying that the woman would understand that she would be better off without her.

"But Kiernan—"

"Lacey, please."

Lacey stepped back, her small mouth pursed indignantly. She was holding up rather well, Kiernan decided.

Better than I am at this moment, she thought.

"Miss Mackay." Cain stepped back politely for her to pass by. Kiernan did so, walking by him. She still held the parasol. She was wonderfully dressed, she thought to herself, with her laced and smocked white cotton nightgown and small blue parasol. She wasn't even wearing shoes.

"Fine," she said curtly. She stepped past them and started down the stairs. If she could leave the house ahead of them, perhaps she could run. These men seemed to know a lot, but they couldn't possibly know this town as she did—the alleys, and where the trails led almost straight up to the heights.

She moved quickly, but they were right behind her.

She came into the parlor. In the growing light of dawn, she could see the poker by the fire. A much better weapon than a parasol! she thought.

Not that it could stop a bullet either.

She hurried through the parlor to the office. The shattered glass lay before the door. She stopped in her tracks.

"Gentlemen, since you won't allow me shoes, I'd appreciate it very much if you could sweep up the glass before we proceed."

"What!" the white man demanded belligerently.

"My feet," Kiernan said flatly. "If you want to impress the rest of the world, you shouldn't have your hostages bleeding and in pain."

"There's no need to hurt the girl now," Cain said.

The other shrugged. "Oh, hell!"

The two of them stepped around her to collect the broken glass. Kiernan waited until they were bent over at their task, then turned and fled back through the parlor for the back-porch door.

She could hear swearing behind her. When she reached the back door, she found it bolted. Swearing to herself, she slid the bolt and rushed through.

She stood on the back step for a moment, surveying her options. She was almost dead center in the town, and the cliffs rose high above her. The Roman Catholic church jutted out almost straight above her, and the climbing pathway to Jefferson's Rock and the cemetery were straight above that. She knew the area well—knew that a treacherous path hewn out of the foliage led precariously up the path.

She could leap from the steps and run quickly around the house for the street.

Or she could run for the footpath up the hill and try to disappear into the jutting cliff and dirt and the foliage that clung tenaciously to it.

The footsteps were close.

She threw the parasol behind her and raced across the yard, painfully aware that she was barefoot. She found the overgrown path up the steep cliff and began to climb, hoping that the foliage would fall back around her and hide her. She grabbed for bushes, for handholds as well as footholds, moving as quickly as she could.

"She's started up!" one of them shouted.

"Stop, or I'll shoot!" his companion warned her.

Was it an idle threat? She had a feeling that the two of them had been ordered to bring her back alive. She kept climbing.

An expletive rang out in the cool dawn.

And then someone was following her, climbing up behind her.

"Kiernan!"

Her name was called from the street. She could hear the sound of horse's hooves. Someone was out there, calling to her in a husky rich voice.

But she was still being followed.

"I'll kill the bitch!" she heard.

She kept climbing, nearly mindless as her desperation grew.

"Climb, Kiernan, climb!"

She didn't need the husky warning. She could only pray that the rider in the street had dismounted and was following her own pursuer.

Her breath came quickly, and her heart hammered. She was gaining ground, though—of that she was certain. If she could reach the crest, she could race to the church. Perhaps she could wake Father Costello—perhaps he was already awake and at prayer. Maybe the church would provide a refuge.

As she reached the crest, her nightgown caught on a branch. Gasping for breath, she paused to tug it free.

Then hands fell upon her shoulders. She screamed as she was dragged to the ground. She struggled fiercely, seeing the hard-lipped white man atop her. She screamed again. His hand fell flat over her mouth, and she tried to bite. His fist went up in the air, and she knew that it would connect shortly with her jaw.

But it didn't.

Instead, the man's eyes went very wide. Kiernan was dimly aware that a leather-gloved hand had clamped onto the man's wrist. Someone was behind him. The rider, tall and fierce, dragged her attacker from her.

She heard a wicked-sounding blow connect with the man's body.

But she screamed anew, for the earth beneath her had broken under the conflict. She couldn't catch herself, and she started to fall over the side of the cliff, above sheer rock.

"Kiernan!"

For a moment she saw him, tall and in uniform, dark in the shadows, holding on to her attacker.

He thrust the man away and pitched forward to come rolling after her.

His body covered her, and his weight threw them both far to the left and back to the trail. They tumbled endlessly together back to the yard.

They landed with her on top. Coughing, dizzy, she tried
to rise. And stared down into endlessly blue eyes.

"Jesse!" she gasped. "Jesse Cameron!"

He smiled his lazy, taunting smile. "Hello, Miss Mackay.
It's been a while, hasn't it? But then, a man never knows
quite when he'll run into you, eh, Kiernan?"

Two

"When you'll run into me?" Kiernan repeated. It was too incredible that he was there. She was straddled over him in her white nightgown with its lace and smocking, now torn and disheveled. Her hands rested upon his chest, and her hair trailed over the navy blue of the uniform cavalry shirt he was wearing. His hair, like her own, was in reckless disarray, dark strands trailing over his forehead. "Oh, my God, it's Jesse!"

"In the flesh," he agreed.

She suddenly cuffed him upon the broad chest. "And rude and abrasive at that!"

He slipped his hands around her waist, lifting her to his side. She should have risen instantly, Kiernan thought, mortified, but he had only moved her in order to rise to his feet. Once he was up, he reached for her hands, pulling her up before him. "Kiernan—"

"What are you doing here?" she demanded. "How can you be here?"

"The night train spread the word," Jesse said. "I was sharing a late whiskey with a general friend, and he ordered me here to tend to any wounded. Troops will be here soon."

"What's going on?"

"Kiernan, that will have to wait. I have to find that man."

"Jesse, he knew *who* I was and *where* I was!"

"I know."

"But what—"

"Get back into the house." He strode away, picking up his hat where it lay in the dirt.

"What if he comes again? There were two of them."

He strode back to her, pulling a Colt six-shooter from the holster that hung on his hip. "You know how to use this?" She nodded. He grinned at her and touched her cheek. "He's probably long gone by now. Get back into the house, Kiernan, and stay there until I get back. All right?"

She nodded slowly. A quivery warmth spread through her limbs. She stretched out her fingers and clenched them tightly again.

Jesse Cameron was back in her life. He'd ridden in just when she needed him most. He could have captured the man, except that he had thrown himself upon her to save her from a deadly fall.

In his dark clothing, he blended into the foliage, even as the sun unerringly began to rise. She heard rustling and knew that he had found his way back up the cliff. But she was certain, as he had been, that the man was long gone. The cliff rose all the way to Jefferson's Rock, where Thomas Jefferson had surveyed the area, and on to the cemetery; it was hard, rugged ground. But there were numerous other ways down, and even a stranger to the area would have found them by now.

She felt her cheeks grow warm, and she pressed her hands to them tightly. Jesse. He shouldn't have been there, but he was. He lacked Anthony's manners, perhaps, but manners weren't necessary to save her life.

She turned and quickly hurried back toward the house. Lacey was waiting for her by the back door. "Kiernan! Oh, thank heaven! What happened? Who was that man in the yard? Why, I almost came out with the rolling pin, except that you were on top of him and you seemed to know him. Really, Kiernan, that wasn't at all proper behavior if you did know him—or if you didn't," Lacey mused worriedly. "But then, what difference does it make? You're back here, and you're safe—and you do know him, don't you, dear?"

"Yes. Oh, Lacey, something very big is going on. You

know him too. It was Jesse—Jesse Cameron, one of our neighbors back home."

"What's he doing here?"

"An alarm went on via the night train. He didn't explain everything. Some general sent him here. There will be troops soon."

"But why?" Lacey began. "Oh dear, yes! He's a doctor, isn't he? Still serving in the military. Oh, my goodness!" She stared at the Colt in Kiernan's hand. "Can't we put that thing away somewhere?"

"I think I'd like to have it close."

"Those men aren't coming back," Lacey said with confidence.

"How can you be sure?"

"Come with me." Lacey led Kiernan through the house to the front, where the shattered glass still lay before the door. "Look," Lacey said, pointing through the door.

Kiernan looked down the street. A crowd had gathered outside the arsenal buildings now. Armed men were milling in the streets. Someone was in charge, and shouting was going on.

"It's all out in the open now," Lacey murmured.

Kiernan heard footsteps on the wooden sidewalk to their right and swung around quickly. One of Lacey's neighbors, Mr. Tomlin, was hurrying along. He carried a rifle and was speaking to his sixteen-year-old, Eban, who followed behind him. "Give me some more o' them nails, boy." He stopped in front of Lacey and Kiernan. "Don't that beat all, ladies? We produce guns here, and just when you want it, there ain't no ammunition to be bought. But heck, that's all right. We'll nail 'em just the same, eh?" He winked at Kiernan, and she saw that he was loading his rifle with nails.

"Mr. Tomlin," she murmured, "what are you doing?"

"There's a rebellion in the streets, Miss Mackay, ain't you seen?" He stared at her for the first time and saw her torn and ragged gown and the tufts of grass that stuck to her hair. "Bejesu, Miss Mackay, are you all right?"

Kiernan nodded as Lacey answered for her.

"She's fine now! But she wasn't so terribly fine an hour ago!"

"They tried to take you! They tried to take you too!" Eban Tomlin said, staring at Kiernan with awe.

"Who else did they try to take?" Kiernan demanded tensely.

"Try? Why, they got all kinds of people. They got the mayor! And the master armorer. And they even rode five miles out and got Colonel Lewis Washington, George Washington's kin! They say as how Colonel Lewis had things belonging to George, and John Brown wanted those things," Eban said excitedly. " 'Course, Brown come in here calling himself 'Isaac Smith,' but it didn't take no time for someone to guess who it really was!"

"Oh, my Lord!" Lacey breathed.

"And they got more. Reckon they got at least twenty people hostage, maybe more."

"Lacey heard shots," Kiernan said.

"Hell, yes!" Eban said. His father's look of warning brought a flush to his face. "Sorry, ladies. Yes, there's been shooting. And it just beats all, it sure does. Old John Brown, he wants to free the world. Well, ladies, he comes into Harpers Ferry and shoots down poor Hayward Shepherd, the free black man at the railroad station. Guess they didn't want no alarm going out. But then the train came through, and he let that train go on by, and it seems they know what's going on down here as far as Washington and beyond. You'd best get back inside now, ladies. There's all manner o' ruckus going on in the streets now. Some o' those people out there get a little scared and get a gun and shoot up everything in sight."

Kiernan glanced at his nail-filled rifle. "Yes, I know," she murmured.

He tipped his hat to them. "Come on, boy," he told Eban.

Kiernan headed back into the house, and Lacey followed after her. "We'll sit tight, Kiernan. News will come to us. I'm so glad you want to stay in the house!"

"Lacey, I'm not staying in the house. I'm going to get dressed as quickly as possible!"

She tore into the kitchen and pumped up water to bring to her room. She started up the stairs, smiling as she passed Lacey.

"Oh dear, oh dear!" Lacey wailed.

"I'll be all right. I've got a Colt with real bullets, and I know how to use a gun."

Lacey stood at the foot of the stairs calling up to her. "Kiernan, dear, please! Heaven only knows what's really going on!"

Kiernan dumped the water into her wash bowl. She whisked off her torn nightgown and slipped quickly into a chemise and pantalets and a petticoat. She hesitated, then decided that in the midst of a revolution, she could dispense with a corset. Clad in her undergarments, she turned back to the water and scrubbed herself quickly.

"Kiernan—are you listening to me? Oh!" Lacey murmured suddenly.

Rinsing her mouth out, Kiernan wondered what had brought that quick exclamation to Lacey's lips. She looked up, then froze.

Jesse was back. He stood in the doorway, leaning casually against the frame, a lazy smile curving his lip as he watched her.

Color flooded through her, rising from her toes to her hairline. What did he think he was doing? No gentleman in the world would come upon a lady in a state of undress and stare at her so.

But Jesse would. Despite her rising fury, she also felt a sweet, exciting sensation ripple through her. Damn him! He was still one of the most handsome men she had ever seen, with his coal-black hair and wicked blue eyes and lazy, sensual smile.

"Jesse—"

"Well now, darlin'," he drawled softly, and those eyes of his raked over her thoroughly with laughter, humor, and something else. Then his eyes landed upon her own. "You've grown up while I've been away."

She should have blushed to kingdom come. She probably had a right to throw a screeching fit or hysterics. But the sense of danger and excitement rippling through her demanded that she stare him down. If he wanted an innocent feminine reaction from her, she decided, he wasn't going to get it.

"Captain Cameron, if you don't mind"—she faced him, her hands set disapprovingly upon her hips—"I'd appreciate it if you'd wait below until I'm decent to recieve company."

He laughed. "Kiernan, you must be the most decent thing I've seen in a month of Sundays. Isn't it just like a woman? The town is in the grip of history, and you're worried about being seen in your knickers."

"I don't wear knickers, Captain Cameron."

"All right, then, petticoats."

"Jesse—"

"Come on down as soon as you consider yourself decent. I can't stay long. In fact, I may not be able to stay long enough to—"

"Don't move!" Kiernan commanded him. She strode across the room to the wardrobe and quickly found a white cotton day dress with flounces and a sophisticated black pattern. She pulled it over her head just as Lacey reached the doorway to chastise Jesse.

"Captain Cameron, what do you think you're doing?"

"Ah, Mrs. Donahue, I've known Kiernan since she was squalling around in diapers."

"But Captain Cameron, I'm responsible for her welfare, and she isn't in diapers any longer."

The dress fell over her head. Kiernan's eyes met Jesse's, and she felt the sizzle in them just as he replied softly to Lacey, "No, ma'am. She isn't in diapers any longer at all."

She couldn't speak for a moment, and his eyes remained on hers. He, too, was silent. Kiernan felt electricity sweep through the air between them like invisible lightning. Not even Lacey spoke to break the tension between them.

Then Kiernan discovered that she could move. She walked toward Jesse, facing him as she turned her back to Lacey. "Would you be a dear and get the buttons, please?"

Lacey quickly began to button up the long row of tiny

pearls that served as buttons for the dress while Kiernan continued to stare at Jesse.

"I take it, Jesse, that you did not find the man."

"No, I'm afraid he's joined his companions."

"Companions?"

"The people in the street say John Brown has a force of about twenty men with him."

"What about the other man?"

"I didn't see him, Kiernan. I wish I could have kept my hands on the one. But . . ." his voice trailed away. He was worried, she thought. "I could have kept my hands on him, or you. I chose you," he said lightly.

"Oh!" Lacey breathed. Of course it had been true. If he hadn't thrown himself upon her, she would have pitched down the rock instead of rolling down the trail. But the way he made it sound . . .

"Lacey, he had to break my fall," Kiernan said with what dignity she could muster.

"Oh," Lacey repeated, this time understanding.

But Jesse wasn't going to let her understand anything. His eyes raked over Kiernan like blue flames, taunting her, and his smile was overtly sensual. "You've definitely grown up," he told her. "You're sophisticated and elegant." Then he ruined the handsome compliment by reaching over to remove a twig from her hair. "And almost domesticated."

She snatched the twig out of his hand, then smiled, fighting for control. The excitement stirring in her was exhilarating. She wanted it to take her somewhere, even if she wasn't sure where.

Even if the world was in revolt all around her.

"I'll never be domesticated, Captain. Barnyard animals are domesticated."

"So they are. Let me see, Kiernan. What is a lady such as yourself—untamable?"

"I'm not a wild horse, Jesse."

"Horses need to be broken to the saddle, Kiernan. Women upon occasion also need to be tamed."

"And have you tamed many women?" she demanded.

"A few," he admitted, lazily slouching against the doorframe.

"Well, Captain Cameron, *I* cannot be broken or tamed!"

"Kiernan, Captain—!" Lacey began, distressed.

Jesse didn't seem to realize that Lacey, still buttoning Kiernan's dress, was even there—or else he didn't mind. He laughed lightly. "I don't remember making such an offer," he drawled.

Lacey inhaled sharply. "Captain, this isn't at all proper."

"Jesse, you never do make offers or say anything concrete," Kiernan said, inadvertently as mindless of Lacey as Jesse was. He had that effect upon her. No, he had it on everyone. He could make people laugh, he could make them furious, he could make them relax.

And he could create an excitement, a tension that demanded awareness of itself.

"It's all insinuation," she told him, keeping her brittle smile intact. She wanted to hit him!

"Captain, Kiernan, please!" Lacey implored. "I must protest! This just isn't proper."

"That's because nothing at all is proper about Jesse," Kiernan said sweetly.

"Now I protest!" Jesse said. "I can be extremely proper, Mrs. Donahue, when the occasion warrants. But Kiernan and I are very old friends. Actually, Mrs. Donahue," he whispered conspiratorially, moving very close to her and offering her his most charming smile, "I even saw Kiernan buck naked when she was a little thing."

"Oh dear, oh dear!" Lacey breathed as she buttoned Kiernan furiously.

"Never!" Kiernan snapped.

"Oh, yes," Jesse assured Lacey charmingly. "As a child, she used to love to strip off every blessed bit of clothing and jump into the lake."

"You're absolutely despicable to remember such things, Jesse," Kiernan told him sweetly, "and to bring them up!"

"Ah, but you speak of my fond memories!" he protested, as if he were wounded.

The last of her tiny buttons was done up. "Really?" She

challenged him with a superior air. "Lacey, I'm quite certain he hasn't thought a thing about me for the last year or so until the moment he came after me."

"Came to your rescue," he reminded her.

"Humility is his greatest asset," she murmured with dripping sarcasm.

Jesse grinned. "Her kind and gentle ways are surely Kiernan's greatest attributes!" he countered.

"Oh dear, what is going on here, Captain?" Lacey interjected. "This just is not proper, not with Kiernan practically engaged."

"Engaged?" His brows lifted with surprise. A flurry swept Kiernan's heart at his obvious interest. "Who's the lucky man? Ah, never mind, I know. It's young Anthony Miller, the arms heir, I do imagine. Well, there's a nice mannered pup for you, Kiernan."

"Anthony is the very soul of propriety," she assured him angrily.

"Indeed. I imagine you maneuver him about with the twitch of your little finger," Jesse agreed. He was laughing at her, she thought, and once again she wanted to hit him. But there also seemed to be a bit of an edge in his voice. Could he possibly be jealous?

"He is completely charming," she said sweetly.

"Then you *are* engaged? My congratulations."

"No," Kiernan admitted. "We're not engaged yet."

"He's madly in love with her!" Lacey said.

"And well the lad should be!" Jesse stated, still laughing. "Beauty, grace—and a mind like a whip!"

Kiernan kept her smile intact. "If you'll excuse me, I'm going to size up the situation in town myself."

She swirled around, but he caught her arm. "Kiernan, stay in. Come downstairs, and I'll tell you both what I know."

He didn't wait for an answer but went downstairs ahead of her. Kiernan shrugged to Lacey, who was concerned that she had completely failed to chaperone a young and innocent woman.

Kiernan wished she could have told Lacey that anyone

would have failed with Jesse around. And she was furious with herself because he always had the ability to lead her along, then step back. The older, wiser, very masculine—male!

Times have changed, she wanted to shout at him. I'm very much grown up now, and I can hold my own in any battle!

But she wondered if she really could hold out in a battle with him.

She gritted her teeth. She could—and she would!

Jesse found his way into the parlor with Lacey and Kiernan following behind. The teasing was gone from his eyes and his manner as he politely waited for both women to perch upon the loveseat. He pulled up a chair before them and straddled it backward to face them very seriously.

"What I've managed to get so far is that John Brown has been planning this raid for months. He was over in Sandy Hook, Maryland, laying out his strategy. He must have hoped that many more people would rise to fight against slaveholders with him. I imagine that he wanted a revolution to start here, with slaves rising against their masters and slaying them in the streets. He really believes that only a bloodbath can cleanse the land."

"My God!" Lacey gasped.

Kiernan watched Jesse, shaking, imagining the scene that Jesse had so bluntly painted. "Are you sure it won't come to that?" she demanded.

"No," he said flatly, "it's not going to come to that. John Brown is already holed up."

"There's been bloodshed," Kiernan whispered.

He arched a brow. "You heard?"

"A neighbor came by. Loading up his shotgun with nails," Kiernan said. "Oh!" she exclaimed passionately. "What right has this man to come to Virginia? How dare he think to command our lives!"

"He dares," Jesse murmured. He quit looking at her for a moment. He seemed to look beyond her, to the future that stretched before them all.

He seemed worried by what he saw there.

"It seems that the townfolk had their own way of dealing

with the events that happened," he said. "A man was killed right away."

"Hayward Shepherd, at the station," Lacey said, her eyes round. "He was a good soul, a gentle man."

"Gentle men get caught up in the deeds of others," Jesse mused.

"There's more?" Kiernan asked.

He returned her gaze steadily. "Yes. One of the hostages has been shot."

"No!" Lacey murmured.

"I'm afraid so. A local farmer named Turner has been killed."

They were all still for a moment. Then Lacey burst out, "Oh, my dear God, Kiernan! What if—"

"Lacey, I'm fine," Kiernan reminded her gently. She stared steadily at Jesse. "They—er, they don't usually shoot women anyway, do they?"

"Of course not," Jesse told her. But watching him, Kiernan shivered inside. She might have been one of the hostages.

"They still have—people?"

"Yes. Mayor Beckham, among them. Colonel Lewis. Mr. Allstadt, the armorer."

"What will happen now?" Lacey asked worriedly.

Jesse smiled. "The cavalry will ride in, Mrs. Donahue," he said, rising. "Actually, Jefferson Davis, the secretary of war, has ordered Lieutenant Colonel Robert E. Lee to bring in troops. They'll handle things, ma'am. I've got to go now. There are some people I have to see, and things I have to do before I meet up with those troops."

"Wait, don't go yet, Captain Cameron!" Lacey implored, jumping to her feet. Kiernan cast her a quick glance. She could have sworn that Jesse had very much unsettled Lacey. Then Lacey smiled, looking down at her hands. Lacey might be unsettled, but she was also charmed.

And she didn't want to be left alone in the midst of all that was happening.

"Mrs. Donahue, honestly, you're going to be all right," he told her. "John Brown and his men are holed up in the firehouse down by the armory. You'll be safe from him. I'm not sure about some of your gun-toting neighbors. Just stay off the streets."

"But what if those people come back for Kiernan?"

"They've tangled with Kiernan once. I don't think they'll be willing to do so again." He winked at Kiernan over Lacey's head, and she had to smile again.

"Coffee!" Lacey said. "Just stay for a cup of coffee. Breakfast. I make a very good plate of ham and eggs and sausage. And very good corn muffins. You must have a little time," Lacey argued.

To Kiernan's surprise, Jesse agreed, pulling out his pocket watch. "All right. I've got an hour, Mrs. Donahue. No more."

Kiernan stood to join Lacey in the kitchen. "I'll help you," she said.

"No!" Lacey gasped. She had been worried about Jesse's sense of propriety upstairs, but now she was determined to keep him just as long as she could—even if that meant leaving Kiernan to flirt with him.

But he was no longer in his taunting mood, Kiernan realized as Lacey left. He wandered to one of the front-facing windows, pulled back the drape, and stared out broodingly.

Kiernan felt a quickening in her heart. "Jesse, what's wrong? Are you lying to make Lacey feel better? Are we in serious trouble here? Do you think that a full-scale revolt will break out?"

He turned back to her and shook his head slowly. "No, Kiernan, I'm not lying. John Brown can't expect any more help. If he could, it would already have come his way. No, I'm afraid that Mr. Brown is doomed."

Kiernan snapped, irritated, "The man is a murderer. He *should* be doomed. Are you in sympathy with him?"

Again, Jesse shook his head. "No, I can't condone what he's done. If I were judge or juryman, I'd have to condemn him to death. And if he isn't killed when the troops ride in, I'm sure he will hang."

"Then what's wrong?" she asked him.

He looked at her again, really looked at her. "You were

always an intuitive little thing," he told her softly. He felt warmth—startling, deep—ripple through him. So often she had read his mind and his thoughts. He remembered coming home from West Point determined to go on to medical school. He had stopped to pay his respects to her father, and she had been sitting at the piano. And she had looked up and smiled when he had come into the room. "Are you going to tell your pa that you want to be a doctor more than a planter?" His interest in medicine was no real surprise to anyone—he had always been fascinated by the field. But he was the eldest son of a very prosperous cotton and tobacco planter. He'd made the decision to go on to medical school himself, without leaving the military. He wanted to combine his interest in medicine with the military, and he thought that he could do very well. He hadn't explained it all to his father, his sister, or even to Daniel yet. But when Kiernan had looked at him that day, he knew that she understood.

"Intuitive," Jesse murmured again now, his smile curving ruefully. "Either that, or you've always known me."

Kiernan wanted to know him—very much, at that moment. She wanted to know him better than anyone else in the world knew him. In fact, she wanted to rise and rush over to the window to him and feel him put his arms around her and hold her close. But she was afraid—she didn't know why—of the emotions she was reading in his eyes, in his manner.

"So what *is* wrong?" she repeated, curling her fingers into the sofa.

"I'm not sure, Kiernan. It won't end here—that's what I'm afraid of, I think. That these events will go on and on. The bloodshed between the abolitionists and the proslavery men will not end out in Kansas. The cry for states' rights will go on, and the split between people will drive more and more deeply into the land itself. I won't like the way our world begins to move. I love my life the way that it is. I love Cameron Hall, and my brother and my sister, and the sloping grass and the James River and—" He broke off, then shrugged, and she realized that he had let her glimpse far more of himself than he had intended.

"Nothing is going to change," Kiernan said quickly. "Cameron Hall has stood for centuries now! And Daniel will always be near." She smiled. "We're all Tidewater people. We'll all remain that."

"Ah—not if you marry this mountain man, this Anthony of yours," he said. He was teasing her again—and he was doing it because he didn't want her to pursue the conversation in the direction it had been going.

Still, she flushed just slightly. "I haven't made up my mind to marry Anthony," she said.

"Why not?" he demanded.

Kiernan rose and strode across the room to the other window. She wanted to offer him a charming smile and tell him that it was none of his business.

But the truth suddenly flooded through her, and she didn't want to tell him the truth either.

That she had been waiting for him. Always.

She lifted her chin, smiled at him, and decided to offer a half-truth. "I'm not sure that I love him."

"Ah. Is there someone that you do love?" he asked softly. But he suddenly seemed angry, both with her and with himself. "Never mind, don't answer that," he told her.

"I didn't intend to. My feelings are none of your business," she snapped quickly.

"Kiernan, I—" He took a step toward her, then paused. When he stepped toward her again, she was stunned when he suddenly pulled her into his arms, pulled her hard against him. His fingers threaded through her hair at her nape, and she almost protested the pain, except that she could feel his passion. He gazed down at her with intensity. "Kiernan, you don't understand. The world is going to change, and I'm afraid that I'm going to disappoint you. I wish that I could make you understand." He stared at her searchingly. "Kiernan!" He shook her slightly. Her head fell back farther, and her eyes met his—not with alarm, but with surprise and curiosity, and with a flame to challenge his words. "Oh, hell!" he whispered. He cupped her chin, and she felt the rough texture of his palm and fingers, his stroke gentle and provocative as he deftly moved his thumb against the softness of her flesh. He lowered his head and kissed her.

It was like no other kiss she had ever known.

Anthony had kissed her, brushed his lips against hers. It had been pleasant enough. She had considered the experience with a certain amusement.

But now she knew that his pleasant touch had been oh, so tepid.

This was fire—sweet, savage fire. He asked no permission, gave her no chance for the least hesitance. His lips molded over hers, claiming them completely, giving fire and heat and passion and demanding it in return. He kissed her the way no gentleman should ever kiss a lady.

But Jesse had never pretended to be a gentleman. Not with her.

And with the moist searing heat of his lips against hers, she wanted to be no lady.

He pulled her ever closer against him. Her hooped petticoats rose to her rear as her body pressed decadently close to his. His tongue wedged through the barrier of her lips and teeth and delved wickedly into the dark and secret recesses of her mouth. It seemed to enter deeper into the secret chambers of her soul and body. The excitement she had always felt when he was near took soaring flight. Her heart hammered, her limbs felt weak—and the heat was part of her now, urging her to slip her arms around his neck, to taste the kiss, to give way to the sweet, evocative passion.

Still he kissed her, his tongue playing with hers, his lips commanding, his body so close, so tight. She could feel so many raw, exhilarating sensations, the shape and form of him, the feel of his clothing, the heat and desire that lay beneath it. She could feel herself molding the length of his form. Longings that were reckless and wild crept into her mind and heart, winding throughout her like a serpent—the serpent that had brought Adam and Eve to the brink of damnation in Eden.

Jesse . . .

His lips were coercive, moving against hers, molding them so hotly. His tongue flicked here and there.

Ah, if this was damnation, let the fires begin! She would gladly have abandoned all for him. She would have walked naked with him into a field of green grass and flowers and lain down beside him. . . .

He broke the kiss at last, just lifting his lips from hers. The warmth of his breath stirred an even deeper quivering within her as his whisper touched her. "If he can't kiss you like this, Kiernan, don't marry him."

"What?" she demanded sharply. Furious, she tried to pull away. She raised a hand to strike him, but he caught it, and his laughter, husky and rich, rang out.

"If he can't kiss you like that, sweetheart, don't marry him."

"Bastard!" she charged him, struggling to be free.

But he pulled her tight once again. "Hold out for the best there is, Kiernan. You should have it. Make sure that there's fire. Maybe there'll be ice, too, but hold out for the extremes, for the best, the brightest. Don't accept anything lukewarm. Because you're fire and ice, and you're the brightest and the best, Kiernan."

"Kiernan! Captain!" Lacey called to them, hurrying to the parlor doorway. "Breakfast."

His eyes remained locked on hers. Then at last he released her.

Kiernan took a quick swing, slapping him hard against the cheek.

"Oh dear!" Lacey wailed.

"You don't play fair," Jesse told Kiernan, smiling slowly as he raised a hand to his reddening cheek.

"Fair! Jesse Cameron, you—"

"Ah, ah, careful, Kiernan. Watch out for Mrs. Donahue's tender ears," he warned her quickly, laughing at her again. Both his hands touched her shoulders as he set her aside to move past her. "She can swear like a mule driver when she wants to, Mrs. Donahue."

"I can kick just like a mule too," she snapped, seething.

"Now, both of you—" Lacey began.

"*Can* you?" Jesse interrupted, his hands suddenly on

Kiernan's shoulders again. "Miss Mackay, I don't suggest
you try it with me."

"Oh, and what *will* do, Jesse?"

"You don't want to know, Kiernan."

"Fine gentleman you are, Jesse."

He grinned. "Ladies aren't supposed to kick like mules,
Kiernan."

"And gentlemen don't—" She broke off. She wanted to
tell him that an honorable gentleman would never ever have
stolen a kiss like the one he had just stolen.

"Gentlemen don't what, Kiernan?"

"I'd move to safety, Jesse," she warned him sweetly.

He laughed again. "Take care, Kiernan, with me. Test
your powers on that charming almost-fiancé of yours, but
not on me. Anything you start, Kiernan, I'll finish."

"Really!" Lacey implored. "If we could all just sit down
and have breakfast—"

"Don't dare *me,* Jesse."

"I made griddle cakes!" Lacey wailed.

Jesse released Kiernan and turned to Lacey. He bent
down to kiss her cheek. "I have a feeling I'm persona non
grata at the moment, Mrs. Donahue. Thanks for the invitation. You be a good dear and keep yourself safe in the house,
eh? I've got to go."

"But Captain Cameron—"

"Behave, Kiernan," he warned, suddenly very stern as he
stared at her over Lacey's head. "Please be careful. I'll be
outside town to meet the troops tonight. And I promise you,
the streets are wild."

"These people are my neighbors!" Lacey murmured.

"Yes, and I'm sure you'll both be fine," Jesse agreed. "But
for my peace of mind, stay in, all right?"

He started out. Kiernan glanced at Lacey briefly, then
went racing after him.

She still wanted to kick him, hard.

She called to him. "Captain!"

Startled by her use of his title, he swung and waited, a
coal-dark brow inquisitively arched.

"Are you coming back, Jesse?"

He nodded. "I'll come in with the troops, Kiernan."

"Be careful, Jesse," she warned him

He grinned and took a step back toward her. She shrank away quickly. "Oh, no, Captain! Keep your distance. You don't play fair."

He shook his head suddenly. "No, Kiernan, you're the one who doesn't play fair." He smiled, but she sensed that he was serious too.

"What do you mean?" she asked. She felt warm again, flushed, with subtle rivers of excitement running through her veins.

"Kiernan, you always wanted to make all the rules. That's not fair."

"Don't they say that all's fair in love and war?" she murmured. She didn't want to make all the rules. She just wanted to keep her heart safe.

"That's what I'm afraid of," he told her huskily. He touched her again, just her hands, meeting her eyes. "Love —and war."

"I don't understand."

"And I can't explain. But you take care, Kiernan. I'll be back soon."

He kissed her again, just brushing her lips with his own. And still she felt his touch like a sweep of staggering warmth.

She met the blaze of his cobalt-blue eyes just briefly, and then he was gone.

Three

During the long morning, Kiernan waited in the house. It was obvious that Jesse had appalled Lacey—but Lacey seemed equally upset that Kiernan had somehow driven him away when he had promised to stay for breakfast. "I felt so much safer with the captain in the house!" she said nervously, sitting at the breakfast table. There was still a great commotion in the streets. But the events now taking place were happening far down by the armory and firehouse, so they couldn't see terribly much. They heard shots being fired, and still there were many shouts. The drama unfolding seemed to put an almost tangible tension in the air— Kiernan could feel it, even in the house.

"He wouldn't have left us if he felt that we'd be in any danger, Lacey," Kiernan assured her.

Lacey clapped her hands together. "How delightfully romantic! You mean, he would have defied duty to stay with two ladies?"

"No, not Jesse," Kiernan said wryly. "He would have packed up the two ladies and dragged them along with him." She wished he had dragged her along with him. She couldn't bear sitting still when so very much was going on. The town was at war! She didn't know what she could do, but she felt she should be doing something.

"Oh, dear," Lacey said with a sigh. "Just how well do you know this young man?"

"I've known him all my life," Kiernan admitted. "We grew up together over in the Tidewater." She was eating her third stack of griddle cakes. She wasn't the least bit hungry, but she had eaten and eaten, exclaiming over the deliciousness of the food, to assuage Lacey. After all, Lacey blamed Kiernan for the fact that the captain was not wolfing down a good portion of the meal.

"What will happen when Anthony returns?" Lacey asked worriedly.

"What do you mean, what will happen?" Kiernan asked her.

"Well, he's—he's very much in love with you, dear! When he sees Jesse Cameron—"

"He knows Jesse Cameron, Lacey. You know Jesse, Lacey!" She counted on her fingers. "You met him at my coming-out ball, the barbecue at the Stacys' in Richmond, and oh, yes! I believe you both were at Anthony's sister's birthday party two years ago up at Montemarte."

"Yes, I met him. But you know him so well."

"Anthony knows him very well," Kiernan asserted with an amused smile. "They're all good friends—Jesse, his brother Daniel, Anthony, and a number of others who were at West Point during the same years. And they've met socially time and time again, both at Cameron Hall and out here at Montemarte."

Lacey was disgruntled. "How amazing that the captain stumbled upon you in the nick of time."

"I don't think he stumbled on me," Kiernan assured her. "He must have known that I was up here. I wrote to Daniel Cameron recently, so Jesse knew that I'd be in Harpers Ferry with you while Papa and your husband and Anthony and his father were on their business trip. He heard about the attack in Washington after John Brown's men let that night train come through. He was ordered down to tend to the wounded. Despite appearances, he does have his own peculiar sense of honor. He would have felt he owed it to my father to see to my welfare."

"Hmph!" Lacey stated.

"And what does that mean?"

"It means that there's no fool like an old fool, but I'm not an old fool, Kiernan Mackay. That man came here for a great deal more than a sense of obligation to your father."

Kiernan's heart was beating too hard, and a flush was warming her cheek. She chewed her griddle cake and sipped her coffee quickly. "We fight like cats and dogs, Lacey. Surely you noticed."

"I noticed a great deal," Lacey said sagely.

Kiernan shrugged. She didn't know how to explain to Lacey that maybe, just maybe, she was in love with Jesse. Or that if she was, it didn't mean anything. It wasn't because Jesse didn't care about her—she was sure that he did. She had felt it in his kiss. Jesse knew women—his was a practiced, arrogant, masterful kiss. He could elicit emotion from a woman even if he himself felt no more than longing, of that she was certain. Jesse knew how to seduce.

She could still feel the warmth of his mouth where he had kissed her. She could taste and breathe the sensation, and hunger for more, hunger to explore everything that had always been forbidden.

But he hadn't offered her anything. All he had said was that she shouldn't marry Anthony if he couldn't kiss her like that. What did Jesse himself want?

And why had it seemed that he was in pain? Talking about love and war, then telling her what scared him.

Why should all of it scare him? Nothing had ever seemed to frighten Jesse before. He had stayed with the cavalry, and he had fought Indians out in the new territories in the West. If war came, and if Virginia seceded, she'd stand behind him. She'd agonize when he rode away, but they were both Tidewater Virginians—fierce, independent, and loyal, passionate lovers of their land and the Tidewater region.

Maybe he wanted to know if she was in love with Anthony. Maybe he himself wasn't ready to settle down.

But maybe he didn't really care a whit for her. After all, she was a young woman to taunt and tease and practice seduction upon. Maybe she had only dreamed that he was waiting for her to grow up.

She knew through rumor that he'd had his share of affairs. Jesse had a way about him. There was something in his eyes. Even if he was as silent about his personal life as a man could be, one could sense things.

"What will poor Anthony say?"

For Lacey, it was almost as if his name were Poor Anthony.

"Say about what, Lacey?" Kiernan asked with a weary sigh.

"Everything that has happened. He'll be so upset that you were threatened by those horrible men. And he'll be very upset that he wasn't here to rescue you. And he'd be very upset if he knew—"

"But Lacey, poor Anthony won't know anything," Kiernan said. "Jesse will ride away with the troops tomorrow, and by the time Anthony and the other men return, this will all be history. We won't tell them that I was threatened."

"But Kiernan, Anthony has a right to know. And everyone in town will know what happened here!" She waved a handkerchief before her. "And your father—"

"Lacey, please. There's no reason to worry Papa needlessly. They'll know what happened here, but they will also know that we're fine. And I'm not engaged to Anthony. I haven't figured out what I want to do yet." She smiled at Lacey.

"But your father *has* to know! You were nearly taken a hostage because—"

"Because my father is a wealthy man."

"A slaveowner," Lacey corrected.

"Like many Virginians!" Kiernan protested.

"Like most wealthy Virginians. Why, you know as well as I do that very few of the poorer farmers own even one slave, young lady. And not all wealthy Virginians are slaveowners, at least not in the western counties," Lacey stated. Lacey opposed slavery, Kiernan knew. Not violently, not the way that John Brown did. But in her own quiet way, she was very much against the institution.

"Lacey, please, there's no reason for Papa to know anything. I'm fine. Nothing happened to me in the end."

"Because of Jesse Cameron's timely arrival."

"Yes, because of his timely arrival," Kiernan admitted. She smiled, and began to clear their dishes. Lacey decided to let it be—for the moment. But several hours later, as they sat in the parlor together, she began anew.

"Kiernan, I just worry so."

"And you really shouldn't. In fact, you absolutely mustn't. I think I'll take a little walk," Kiernan said suddenly. She would go out and find out what was going on. She couldn't bear to sit and wait any longer.

"But you can't go out there! You promised Captain Cameron you wouldn't go!"

"I didn't promise anybody anything, and I don't owe Captain Cameron any allegiance!" she said firmly.

"But Kiernan—"

"I have Jesse's Colt, Lacey, and I know how to use it. I can't stand it anymore, not knowing what's going on out there." She leaped up and squeezed Lacey's cheeks together with her thumb and forefinger. Lacey's mouth made a big round O and a sound escaped her, but she couldn't protest further as Kiernan planted a kiss upon her forehead. "Don't worry! I'll be fine. I'll be careful, and I know how to shoot. And I have real live ammunition in the gun—which is apparently much more than anyone else has."

She hurried from the kitchen to the parlor. Lacey called after her, but she moved quickly, finding the Colt on the mantel. She felt a twinge of guilt about defying Lacey, but that couldn't be helped. Momentous things were happening, and she had to understand what they were.

"I'll be back soon!" she called, then she hurried out to the street. She looked up and saw that the sun was already beginning its descent. In another few hours, darkness would fall over them again.

There was no one before the house, but down the street to her left, a crowd had gathered before the firehouse—out of range of shot, it seemed. Militiamen were surrounding the firehouse, she realized, and the citizens of Harpers Ferry were surrounding the militia.

Things seemed fairly quiet and subdued, but still, an air of electric tension seemed to have settled upon the town.

People were talking about how the townfolk had battled John Brown until he'd had no choice but to take refuge in the firehouse.

Kiernan hurried down the street. When a hand fell upon her shoulder, she nearly jumped sky-high and swung around. Dr. Bruce Whelan, white-haired with a drooping moustache, stared at her sternly with a pair of clear, dove-gray eyes.

"Doc Whelan—"

"I was told to look out for you, young lady," he said gruffly.

"What?"

"Captain Cameron came through to help with the wounded." He waved a hand in the air. "People were all kind of cut up, what with firing shotguns filled with whatever debris they came across. There's been a heap of death today, young lady. A heap of death."

"Jesse doesn't have the right—" she began.

"Yes, Jesse does. He said that he come upon you in a bit of trouble, Kiernan Mackay."

Her heart sank. If Doc Whelan knew about last night, her father would know. He'd be loath to leave her alone ever again. Anthony and his father would be loath to leave her, but she really did love her independence.

"Nothing catastrophic happened—"

"You might be in grave danger at this very moment!" he corrected her. "Jesse said you managed a good fight on your own, but hell, girl! Not even a man can stand up against a bullet. And now John Brown has his hostages holed up with him in the firehouse. Colonel Lewis Washington is in there, girl! They're saying that Brown wanted to have the sword Frederick the Great gave to George Washington and the pistol Lafayette gave him, and so they've taken that fine brave gentleman. And Mr. Allstadt, his neighbor, and his young son. You could have been among them!"

She gritted her teeth. Jesse must have described her flight from her pursuer with full dramatic license, she thought.

"But I am all right."

"And you should be off the streets."

"Doc Whelan, the whole town is on the streets!"

"The whole town is out here, right. But the things happening to the whole town haven't been good! Kiernan, Mr. Beckham has been killed."

She gasped, thinking of the kindly mayor. He had been such a gentle man!

"And young lady, when Mayor Beckham was killed, a lynch mob broke into the Wager Hotel and seized one of the raiders who had been taken prisoner. They dragged him on out to the bridge and shot him up on either side of the head. Half the maniacs in this town are still pumping bullets into the body."

"My Lord," Kiernan breathed.

"Go home, Kiernan."

"I will, soon. I promise."

"There's more, young lady. There was shooting all around, what with the various militias coming in. Seems like there were about twenty raiders to begin with. Some of them were wounded and killed. Some were shot trying to escape across the river. It just isn't a good day to be out, and I do mean it."

"I know, Doc Whelan. Really, I do."

He tried to look stern, but then he shrugged. "Don't imagine I could get you to go home if I talked myself blue in the face. So be careful, and head back in by nightfall. Hell, some assistance could still come this way before we get federal troops in here to deal with this." He stared at her for a moment. "Too bad Captain Cameron isn't around. I reckon he'd get you back inside." He grinned, then laughed out loud. "He'd pick you right up over his shoulder and see you back to the house." He grinned again and started on his way. He paused to laugh again—no, to cackle—then he started down the street once more.

The shooting was over for the moment, Kiernan realized. She hurried onward.

Jesse wasn't about, but she wasn't going to be told what she could and couldn't do.

* * *

Jesse Cameron was a lot closer than Kiernan thought.

Colonel Baylor of one of the militia companies had taken matters under control as best he could. Negotiations hadn't gone very well between the townsfolk and the raiders holed up in the firehouse. Two of Brown's men had been shot under a white flag of surrender. One had crawled back into the firehouse, and one had been killed, his body mutilated by the people.

But someone had asked for a doctor, and Jesse was regular army. He was sent in with one of Baylor's militiamen, a man called Sinn.

The firehouse was a brick structure, about thirty-five by thirty feet. The doors were heavy wood, and they were soundly battened down. Under a white flag of truce, Jesse and Sinn approached the firehouse. The doors opened briefly, and they were let in.

Jesse had been with the cavalry in Kansas, and he'd heard about the doings of old "Ossawatomie" Brown for years, but he'd never met the man.

When he did now, he was startled, physically moved, by the fires burning in the old man's eyes. He'd never seen anything like it. Brown's face was haggard, aged, and lined. It was full of character, with a long beard and thick bushy brows. But that blaze in his eyes was arresting. He was a murderer, a cold-blooded one, Jesse was convinced.

But he was also convinced that he had never before seen a man who so truly believed that he committed murder for God's own cause.

"The cavalry is here," Brown commented.

Jesse shook his head. "I'm a doctor. I've come to see to your wounded."

"Then take a look at the boy."

The boy was on the ground, to the far left of the entrance and the old fire engines. Jesse nodded and strode over to his side.

He was a handsome young man, no more than twenty. As soon as Jesse stooped down beside him, he knew that that the boy was going to die. He was gut-shot, and badly. There wasn't a thing that any man could do to save him.

Sinn was getting ready to address Brown with terms from Colonel Baylor, but Brown, with his fire-edged eyes, was watching Jesse. "He's my son, Oliver."

Jesse nodded again. The young man's pain-filled eyes touched his father's. "It hurts, Pa. Can't you shoot me?"

"You'll get over it," Brown said.

Jesse stiffened. He could swear that despite this abrupt answer, the old man cared deeply for the boy.

He opened his surgical bag and found bandaging to bind up what he could of the fatal wound. The lad's eyes were on him now. He pulled out a syringe and a bottle of morphine. At least he could ease the lad's pain. He set the needle just beneath the boy's skin and administered the drug.

"Thanks, mister," he breathed. There were tears in his eyes.

His eyes closed, and he moaned again. "If you must die," Brown suddenly thundered, "die like a man!"

Jesse's gaze snapped to the old man's. For a long moment they stared at each other. Brown saw the condemnation in Jesse's gaze.

He seemed sorry for his harsh words, but that blaze was still about his eyes. He didn't mind offering up his own life for his cause, nor his own flesh and blood.

Sinn told John Brown that he'd murdered Mayor Beckham when the man had been unarmed.

Brown gave his attention to Sinn. "That, sir, was regrettable."

Jesse had done all that he could. He saw that the hostages and the other wounded were gathered in the rear of the firehouse.

He recognized Colonel Washington immediately. Washington nodded his way, tall and straight. Jesse saluted him, and Washington returned the salute.

"We'll see you soon, sir," Jesse said to him.

Washington offered him a half grin. "Either that, or in hell, Captain!"

Brown and Sinn broke off in their negotiations. "Captain!" Sinn said to him. "Are you ready, sir?"

"A moment."

Jesse saw to the others, though he could do little for them under the circumstances. He bandaged what he could and set a few limbs on splints, removed a nail from an arm muscle, and gave some advice for staying still until real medical help could be given.

"A man doesn't need to be in good health to hang," one of the raiders said dryly.

"Hang?" the lean young farmer Jesse had been helping said.

"Sure, for treason," he was told.

His eyes went wide, and he searched out old John Brown. "Was this treason, sir?"

"Sure was," John Brown answered.

"Heck, I didn't want to be guilty of treason," the young farmer said. "I just wanted to free the slaves." He gripped Jesse's arm. "I just wanted to free the slaves. We didn't mean nothing else."

Jesse nodded, thinking the man might not live to hang anyway. "I understand exactly what you meant." He could have told him that innocent people had been killed, but he decided not to. He was a doctor, not a judge, and if John Brown thought he knew what God intended, Jesse sure as hell didn't.

"Captain?" Sinn called to him.

He closed his bag with a snap, straightened, and joined Sinn at the door. The two men exited the firehouse.

Jesse felt the searing eyes of old John Brown boring into him. He turned back.

Indeed, the man was watching him with his blazing gaze.

A coldness crept along Jesse's spine. He wasn't afraid of John Brown, he knew that. He was afraid that John Brown foretold some kind of doom.

The heavy doors closed behind them, and he and Sinn went back to report to Baylor.

Then he was free once again to ride through a town gone mad.

* * *

Kiernan saw Eban at the edge of the crowd and circled around until she could reach him.

"Eban, what's happening?" she demanded.

"Some of the hostages have escaped," he told her.

"Oh, how wonderful!" she exclaimed. Then she asked softly, "Has anyone else been—"

"No more of the hostages have been killed," Eban told her. "But you should have seen what they did to Daingerfield Newby."

"Who?"

"He was a free black man. I hear tell he joined up with John Brown because no matter how he tried to earn the money to buy his wife and family, her master kept raising her price. The poor man was shot down with anything you could imagine and left there in the alley." He pointed up the hill a little way. "I hear they let the hogs get ahold of him then."

"Oh!" Kiernan gasped. She felt ill. Yet something drew her to the spot—maybe she couldn't quite believe that people she knew so well had been driven to such violence. But she walked uphill toward the alley, then paused with horror.

Blood still stained the alley. It was on the ground, and splashed against the wall.

Hogs were still rooting around the alley. She backed away, feeling ill.

Daingerfield Newby would never buy his wife and children.

"Miss Mackay!" Eban stood behind her. "Are you all right?"

She nodded. Pieces of burned nails lay at her feet, and she bent down and picked one up. The citizens had fired these at the poor man. She stared at Eban, and he was instantly on the defensive. "For pity's sake, Miss Mackay. John Brown's men killed Mr. Turner, just 'cause he owned slaves. They meant to rouse all the slaves in the area against us. They meant to have us murdered in our beds! But we stopped them. We fought back with nothing, and we holed them up in that firehouse. We're going to get them. But it's too late

for Turner. They put a gun right up to his head and pulled
the trigger and killed him. And they killed Hayward!
They're supposed to be so good and kind and all-loving to
the black men, but they come in here and shoot down a free
black man themselves. It's frightening, Miss Mackay,
darned frightening. We fought back, that's all we done. We
fought back."

Kiernan nodded again. Who was to be condemned in this
madness? John Brown? But John Brown seemed to believe
that God whispered in his ear and gave him his orders.

"Is Brown still in the firehouse?" Kiernan asked.

"He is, Miss Mackay." Eban tilted his hat to her. "And
he's still got hostages. No one knows what he intends to do.
The militia have been talking with him. If they rush him, he
might kill the captives. We're at a standstill now, waiting on
Washington, D.C., and the federal military."

A chill rushed through her, and she was suddenly very
afraid. Many militia units had been called in, it seemed.
People were grouped in the streets. She could still hear shots
and wild cries.

And in that awful alley the blood still lingered.

She was afraid, with the kind of fear that Jesse had been
talking about himself feeling.

We didn't start this tragedy, she thought, trying not to
imagine the mutilated body of the black freeman. John
Brown had ridden into town and awakened the terror of a
peaceful people. But John Brown hadn't started the debate
on slavery. She couldn't blame him for that.

She could blame him for bringing it and all this horror
and bloodshed to Virginia.

" 'Scuse me, Miss Mackay," Eban told her. "I'm going to
find out what's going on."

Kiernan stayed at the edge of the crowd as the day waned.
The sun began to set in earnest. She learned that Colonel
Robert E. Lee had a detachment of marines stationed just
outside of town, and that he'd be taking over from the militia soon enough.

She wondered if Jesse was with Lee.

She heard shots again, by the firehouse. The crowd was

shoving. Before she knew it, she was being pushed nearer
and nearer the firehouse.

Suddenly she nearly tripped over the body of a man, a
man so filled with shot that he must have been heavy with
the lead. His face and body were ruined beyond recognition.
She was pushed again as the crowd gathered nearer. She
was almost shoved upon the man. She looked down at sightless holes where eyes had been, and she started to scream,
panic growing within. Another shot was fired into the body.
The young farmer who had aimed the rifle seemed heedless
of the crowd around the dead man.

"No!" Kiernan screamed again. She had to get away from
those horrible sightless eyes.

Suddenly, she was swept up high into strong arms. She
looked up, her horror mirrored in her gaze.

Deep blue eyes stared sternly down upon her. Jesse. Jesse
wasn't with Lee at all. He was here.

With her.

Come to her rescue once again.

Her arms locked around his neck, despite the fury in his
eyes.

"Jesse," she whispered.

"Make way!" he demanded, and the crowd parted. His
long strides brought them quickly through the crowd and to
his waiting roan horse.

He set her atop it, then leaped up behind her. Within
seconds they were cantering down the street, and the clean
wind was blowing against her cheeks and washing away the
scent of tragedy and blood.

And the chill that had seeped into her was warmed away
by the heat of the arms around her.

Four

He didn't take her back to Lacey's house.

The well-trained roan quickly traveled through the town of Harpers Ferry, climbing the hill to Bolivar Heights with what should have been frightening speed.

She wasn't frightened—not with Jesse.

She felt the muscled heat of his chest hard against her back as she rode, and the events of the past two days seemed to fade away. Nothing could happen to her now that Jesse's arms were around her.

He didn't stop in the town of Bolivar, but climbed up to the woods atop one of the hills. He spurred his horse all the way to the top, where the tall trees looked down at a great distance on the little cleft of land where the Shenandoah met the Potomac and old Harper had started his ferry service across the river. The townspeople seemed tiny now, and the buildings looked tiny, too, like toys.

Jesse leaped down from his horse and reached up for her. She set her hands on his shoulders and slid down into his arms. She was trembling, and he kept his arms tight around her.

"Oh, Jesse, the things they're doing down there are so horrible!"

His hands moved gently, soothingly, over her hair. "It's all right. It will all be over soon enough. A tempest in a teapot." He stroked her cheek, meeting her eyes, then spun her around so she could see down the far distance of the cliff. Again, the people and buildings were like toys. The white rushing waters of the rivers could be seen, meeting. "Today will end. Shenandoah and Potomac will continue to shed their haunting tears, and the mountains will be beautiful again." His arms were about her, his fingers entwined at her waist and over her belly. He must have felt that she had ceased to tremble.

His tone suddenly changed, and he swung her around so that she faced him again.

"And I told you not to leave the house!"

"Damn you, Jesse, you're not my father!"

He uttered an oath beneath his breath, and she placed her hands upon his arms. She broke free of his touch, backing away from his tall, muscular form, a form that suddenly seemed threatening.

"If you'd stayed inside, you'd never have been exposed to all this!"

"But Jesse, so many people are down there! So many people I know are pumping lead and debris into a man's body!"

"And with any luck, they won't pump it into one another," Jesse said. He came toward her again. She couldn't back away any farther on top of the mountain cliff.

"Jesse—"

"You little fool!" he said heatedly. "You could have gotten hurt!"

"The whole town could have been hurt."

"Some people *were* hurt! The mayor was killed, gunned down unarmed."

"Jesse—"

He was really angry. But when he stopped before her again, his fingers gripping her upper arms and pulling her close, she couldn't think of another argument. He stared down into her eyes, and his were alive with cobalt fire. Her heart suddenly seemed to flutter like butterfly wings against her ribs, and a weakness seized hold of her knees. She was just as angry as he, she told herself, and that anger made her weak.

"Jesse—" she started, but his mouth touched hers,

smothering her whisper. His touch was both fierce and coercive, a sweep of dazzling fire, stealing away both breath and reason. Her fingers curled on his chest, her lips parted, fascinated, to the pressure of his. The hot sultry fever of his kiss pervaded her, touched her mouth, and stole and curled through her body like slow-moving nectar—or lava. Her senses seemed so very much alive. Her flesh burned to the slightest brush of his hand. His body against hers was hard but like the fever inside her, so very hot, and pulsing, and alive. The closer she drew herself against him, the more she knew about the fever that threatened to consume them both. For even as she tasted the texture of his tongue, she felt the pressure of hips hard against hers, and the fever of that touch that should have been so forbidden to her did nothing but entice and seduce her into a longing for further discovery.

His lips parted from hers, touched them again, parted, and touched—sweet, open-mouthed, hotter, and hotter. Her mind began to reel. She shouldn't be here with him. She should be scandalized, horrified.

There was someone else in her life. . . .

Someone with whom things had never been like this.

Still, she had to draw away, she had to stop.

"Jesse . . ." His name was barely a whisper on the breeze, yet he heard it. He suddenly emitted a soft oath and drew away from her. To Kiernan's surprise, he nearly thrust her from him. He walked away, placing a booted foot high on a rock as he leaned upon an elbow to stare out at the valley below them.

Her mouth was still damp from his touch. She could still feel the touch. He seemed to be a knot of fury again.

"Damn you, Kiernan!" he swore, spinning around to stare at her. "If you would just do what you're told now and then!"

"Jesse, you've no right—"

"Your father isn't here, and your precious beloved Anthony isn't here either. Where the hell is he?"

She flushed, feeling her temper rise, and dizziness assailed her again. She should never, never allow Jesse to touch her.

He was as volatile as a forest blaze, erupting in passion, erupting in anger.

"You know where Anthony is," she began as primly as possible.

"Never mind, never mind," he said suddenly. He strode back to her. "Just listen to me and stay the hell inside, away from the melee out there, will you? Look what you've done to us!"

"Me!"

"Kiernan—"

Her eyes narrowed, and she took a wild swing at him. He caught her wrist and their eyes met in a flame, and then he smiled slowly, ruefully.

"I'll take you back to Lacey's."

"I'd prefer to walk!"

"It's a very long walk."

"I'd prefer a very long walk."

He shook his head. "Sorry." Before she knew it, she was up in his arms and upon the big roan, Pegasus. And he was up behind her, his arms wrapping around her.

He nudged Pegasus, and the roan took them down the face of the mount.

Kiernan's temper waned with the warmth of his arms around her. By the time he had delivered her to the front of Lacey's house, she was aware only of a sense of desolation and loss. He dismounted from Pegasus to help her down, and she knew that he was leaving her. She should have been scandalized and horrified that he had kissed her so, touched her so, but she wasn't. It was simply what came between the two of them. There had been something just and sweet and right about it, and she refused to be ashamed of it.

"Stay in," he commanded her curtly.

She smiled, allowing her lashes to fall over her eyes. "Captain Cameron, I am my own keeper."

"Kiernan—"

"But I choose to stay in," she told him hastily. "Oh, Jesse, people are behaving so horribly!"

"Yes," he told her simply, "they are." He mounted Pegasus once again and looked down at her. "Things might get worse, and it's getting dark. So please . . ."

She curtsied to him regally, then turned and fled into the house.

The shattered glass had been swept up, but where the office door pane had been, there was a big hole. She decided to patch up the door with some canvas and spend the evening reassuring Lacey. She needed to stem her own feelings of guilt for having deserted her.

"Who's there?"

She heard the sharp call as she opened the door. "It's me, Lacey. I'm back."

"Oh, and just in time!" Lacey appeared in the doorway, holding a candle high against the darkening shadows of the night. "Thank heaven! I was getting so worried!"

"Everything's fine, Lacey. Well, not really fine. Let's go into the parlor, and I'll tell you about it."

Lacey nodded, her eyes wide, and preceded Kiernan into the parlor. Kiernan told her about the events in town, but she did so very carefully, softening the violence. Still, Lacey was horrified, and very nervous.

She insisted on serving Kiernan a cup of tea, then on making supper, so Kiernan went into the storage closet and found some canvas and a hammer and nails and set about doing a makeshift job of repairing the door.

The two women ate a quiet supper, all the while aware of the drama down the street.

"Didn't the captain say that he'd be back?" Lacey asked Kiernan anxiously.

"Well, he may make it. Then again, he may not."

"He should be looking after you," Lacey insisted.

Kiernan smiled ruefully. "No, Lacey, remember? Poor Anthony is supposed to be looking after me."

Lacey had the good grace to blush. "Never mind. Oh, I wish that this night would pass!"

"I don't think needlework will do it tonight," Kiernan murmured. In fact, nothing was going to ease the evening for her. She was torn between the horror of the sights she had seen, and the pulsing magic that returned to her lips when she thought of Jesse.

It had been a forbidden kiss, because of Anthony.

"How about some cards?"

"Hearts?" Kiernan said.

"Good heavens, no! Poker!" Lacey shocked her, and Kiernan burst into laughter. "Lacey! How very decadent. Wouldn't your husband be shocked?"

Lacey sniffed. "And what about your father, young lady? You know how to play."

"I grew up in my father's company," Kiernan reminded her, grinning broadly. "Get the cards and shuffle, Mrs. Donahue. You're on. We'll play for pennies."

"Done!" Lacey agreed.

Playing did help to pass the time. Something about the taboo aspect of the game for ladies made it exciting. It would always be a secret between them that they had passed the night so.

The hour grew late. Jesse didn't return.

Finally, Lacey yawned and admitted that she was exhausted. "But how will I sleep?" she demanded.

"Nothing is going to happen," Kiernan assured her.

But Lacey was still nervous, so Kiernan suggested that they put on their nightgowns and bunk in together. Lacey enjoyed that idea. "We'll sleep with Jesse's Mr. Colt right by our bedside," Kiernan said cheerfully.

"The bed in your room is nice and big. We should both be comfortable in it!" Lacey agreed. But when they were settled, she moaned again.

"I shall never be able to sleep!"

But to Kiernan's amusement, Lacey closed her eyes as peacefully as a babe soon after they crawled into bed. It was early still, Kiernan thought, and that was why she couldn't seem to close her own eyes. Or maybe she was frightened. She had come close to being kidnapped that morning, and she very well could have been one of those hostages still being held by John Brown.

John Brown must be desperate by now, she thought, with his few followers holed up in the firehouse. He must realize that his grand revolution wasn't coming. The countryside had not been stirred to great revolt.

The United States Army was coming for him, and in the morning, he would have to face the fire. Would he kill the hostages because of his despair?

Or could the bloodshed be kept down? Kiernan fervently hoped that it could.

She wondered what John Brown looked like, and she wondered if he could really rationalize murder into a crusade. But then she remembered *Uncle Tom's Cabin* and how furious she had been when she read the book.

Then again, she had to admit that some people were cruel and took much better care of their horses and their dogs than their slaves. She tossed about in bed. Then suddenly Lacey inhaled deeply with a shake, and exhaled with a long, low snore.

It was the end of trying to sleep.

She stood up and wandered over to the window. To her amazement, two men were standing below the window. They were both tall and dark in the shadows of the night. For a moment she held her breath.

One of them stepped forward and stooped low, plucking a pebble from the ground. He looked up and tossed it high toward the window. Just before she stepped back, Kiernan released her bent-up breath, smiling. The face that had turned upward toward hers was familiar.

Jesse was back.

The pebble landed with a little crack on the window. Kiernan stared down below.

Now both faces were upturned to hers. Jesse was with his brother Daniel, and both were dressed in the uniforms of the United States cavalry. Both were wearing their handsome plumed hats, and both were grinning broadly at her. They were very much alike. Like Jesse, Daniel had the ebony-dark hair and near cobalt-blue eyes that ran in the Cameron family. His features, too, were similar—handsome, well defined. His mouth was full and sensual. He was several years younger than Jesse, though, and his shoulders were not quite as broad. His manner was lighter—dramatically gallant. He was Kiernan's good friend, and she loved him, while Jesse . . . ah, Jesse!

"Sh!" She brought her finger to her lip and shook her head when she realized that Daniel had a pebble, too, and was about to throw it up to her.

She threw open the window and called down softly, "Stop the rocks!"

"Then come down and let us in!" Daniel called. "There's a nip in the air."

"It's downright cold," Jesse corrected, casting his brother a wry glance.

Kiernan looked quickly over to Lacey, who was still sleeping soundly.

Kiernan waved to the Cameron brothers—a wave that promised she'd be right down. Daniel grinned and gave her a thumbs-up sign. Jesse's easy smile curved into his lip.

Kiernan left the room behind, raced down the stairs to the back, and threw open the door.

Daniel was just on the other side of it. He swept her up high into his arms and swung her around as he came into the narrow hallway. "My Lord, Kiernan!" he teased, setting her down at last. "Every time I see you, you get prettier, more grown up, more sophisticated, more elegant. More—"

"Voluptuous?" Jesse suggested.

Kiernan quickly cast him a glance. As he leaned in the doorway, there was definite amusement in his suggestion. His eyes flickered over her, and his glance instantly warmed her.

His eyes could do things to her that actually seemed indecent.

Yes, he had always liked to tease her. This afternoon, though, he hadn't teased. He had gotten caught in his own fire, she realized, and that was why he had grown so very angry with her.

They both realized it, she knew, as their eyes met and held.

"Yes, voluptuous," Daniel said. He laughed. "Forgive us, Miss Mackay," he said, stepping back and sweeping off his hat to hold it to his heart. "We army men do have our failings. Days on the trail, and all that."

Kiernan tore her eyes from Jesse's at last. "Days on the trail, indeed! Jesse came straight from a bar in Washington. What about you?"

"I was at a party at a friend's house when a messenger came from Jeb Stuart." Stuart was a dashing young cavalry commander and a good friend of both Camerons. "He knew that Jesse had already been sent in, and that Jesse was concerned about you when he heard about the ruckus here."

"That's what I imagined," Kiernan said, looking from one to the other. "You're both going to be with the troops challenging John Brown in the morning? Christa will be worried sick." Christa was their sister, a year younger than Kiernan, the last of the immediate Cameron clan. Like Kiernan, she had trailed after Daniel as a child, and the three of them had always been very close.

And a bit in awe of Jesse, although Daniel denied it. Now the brothers were thick as thieves, and no brothers could offer each other greater loyalty or friendship.

"You wouldn't have some apple pie here somewhere, would you? And some hot coffee for a frozen soul?"

"We do happen to have apple pie," Kiernan admitted to Daniel. "And I'll make coffee. But don't try to side-step the situation, Daniel Cameron." She swirled around and headed for the kitchen, the brothers following behind her. They both took seats at the kitchen table and spread their long legs beneath it, as she started the coffee and placed the pie and plates and Lacey's embroidered napkins before them.

"What's going to happen in the morning?" she asked stubbornly.

"They'll ask John Brown to surrender," Jesse answered flatly.

"And if he doesn't?"

Jesse shrugged, cutting pieces of pie as she stood over him. "We'll storm the firehouse, I imagine."

"And there's no danger in that? The both of you? You've really no right to risk both your lives that way. I'm telling you—"

"And I told you not to leave the house today," Jesse interrupted suddenly, waving the pie spade before her nose.

"The whole town was out on the streets, Jesse," she told him.

"The whole town," Daniel laughed, "including Doc Whalen. He told me that you were out on the street, and he'd heard tell Jesse had already gotten his hands on you."

Kiernan quickly lowered her eyes. "Indeed, he had," she said sweetly.

"Whalen's suggestion, so I heard," Jesse murmured, "was that you should be trussed like a turkey over a shoulder and taken to a woodshed. I wasn't nearly as crude."

"You were barely short of it!" Kiernan responded quickly.

Jesse raised a brow to her, and she felt a hot flush rise over her body.

"Do I detect a note of tension here?" Daniel asked.

"No!" Jesse and Kiernan snapped simultaneously.

"Oh, excuse me!" Daniel said, and grinned.

"I wasn't at all crude," Jesse said.

Kiernan leaped up to see how the coffee was doing, but she suddenly felt a clamp of steel upon her arm.

"This time," he told her softly.

"This time?" She arched a brow. Storms were brewing between them, she could feel it. She felt tension hot and sweet on the air. She wanted to do battle with him. She wanted to argue and fight—

And touch him.

"Hey! The coffee is boiling over!" Daniel cried out. Jesse's eyes still burned into hers. He released her wrist slowly, and she tore her gaze from his at last and hurried to salvage the coffee.

Daniel started talking and he kept talking, eating his pie with relish.

Kiernan and Jesse drank their coffee, listened, and watched each other warily. Thankfully, Daniel didn't seem to need much help with the conversation.

Jesse stood up suddenly. "We've got to get back," he said.

Daniel nodded regretfully. "Yes." He stood up and pulled Kiernan to her feet and kissed her cheek then hugged her tightly again. "Tomorrow, Kiernan, please stay in until it's all over!" he begged her.

"She'll stay in," Jesse said with an edge. "I can guarantee it."

"Oh?" Kiernan said sweetly.

"Yes. Because I'll be around tomorrow. And I will see to it, even if I have to carry you around like a sack of potatoes."

"Sir, your gallantry is overwhelming!" Kiernan drawled.

"I call it as I see it," Jesse told her.

"I can't imagine your being so cavalier if my father were here!"

He arched a dark brow and grinned. "Kiernan, I would be the same no matter who was here, and you know it." He paused a second, his grin spreading. "Including the saintly Anthony!" He turned around, heading out. Daniel grinned and followed him. Kiernan hurried along the hall behind them to the rear door.

"Please take care!" she urged Daniel on the back porch. Their horses were tethered in back beneath a tree by the uphill trail, sheltered by the cliffs.

He paused. "I promise."

Jesse reached his horse and mounted smoothly. The roan trotted over to the steps, and he smiled down to her. "Am I to take care, too, Miss Mackay?"

"Of course, Jesse," she said coolly. "I'd be deeply grieved to see anything happen to you. For Christa's sake."

"Only for Christa's sake?"

"You *are* a good neighbor," she said sweetly.

He laughed and dipped low from the horse's back to find her hand.

He kissed it lightly. "How very sweet and honorable, Miss Mackay!" He freed her hand. "Now, please make sure that you keep your very sweet and honorable derriere indoors tomorrow!" he charged her firmly.

"Jesse, darlin', you do have the manners of an orangutan. Someone should take a horsewhip to you—sir!" she told him sweetly.

"I mean it, Kiernan."

"So do I."

"I'll find you if you're out, I swear."

"A promise, Jesse, or a warning?"

"A threat—and take it that way," he advised. Then he smiled and lifted his hand to his hat in salute.

The big roan swirled, and he was off into the night.

"Jesse, take care!" she whispered softly. It was far too late. He was gone, and he never heard her words.

Standing next to her in the moonlight, Daniel was still watching her. He shrugged, laughter in his eyes. "He has his way," he told her, offering no explanation and certainly no apology.

"Yes, he does. Oh, Daniel, do take care. Both of you."

"We will," Daniel promised her. He hugged her again, then leaped up onto his mount, as comfortable on horseback as his brother was. He lifted his hat and waved to her. "Scrape up a good dinner for us tomorrow night, eh?"

"I promise!" she called. "Daniel!"

"Yes?"

"See that you—that you and Jesse come to me as soon as you can!"

"I will."

He waved, and rode into the night after his brother.

Kiernan shivered fiercely, then hurried back inside. There was certainly no comfort in this night. She was suddenly very much alone. All the warmth had gone from the evening, and it was very chilly indeed.

And like Jesse, she was afraid.

Of love—and war.

Five

Jesse hadn't ridden more than a minute or two before Daniel was beside him, watching him and about to say something.

Because of the way that they had left Kiernan, he thought.

No, because of the way that *he* had left Kiernan.

It was probably a good thing that Daniel hadn't been around during the day, Jesse reflected. He'd be fielding questions right and left if he had.

But now he was in for some brotherly concern no matter what, Jesse realized.

"You're awfully quiet, Jess," Daniel told him.

"Reckon so," Jesse murmured. He knew darned well that Daniel wasn't going to leave an answer like that alone.

"Because of tomorrow and John Brown? Or because of Kiernan?"

Jesse cast him a quick glance and discovered that his brother's eyes were dancing. Maybe Daniel had seen a lot more over the years than Jesse had imagined. Maybe there was more to see than he had even seen himself.

Who was he kidding? There had always been something about Kiernan. Even as a child, she'd had the most extraordinary eyes, green eyes that defied and challenged and laughed and dared.

By ten, she'd had a certain way of walking. Jesse remembered feeling darned sorry for her father because she had become such a brazen little piece of Tidewater baggage so quickly. Kiernan was beautiful, and Kiernan could steal the heart and soul and taunt the body. But she was also proud and stubborn, and no one was ever going to sway her mind.

She could play and she could tease, but she did so only within the bounds of propriety. Naturally, she liked attention. She could flirt with the best of them, but she was certainly no sweet and naive creature—she had her opinions about life and about her place within it, and she never minded voicing them.

He knew her so well, Jesse thought, because he'd watched her for years from Cameron Hall. He'd watched with definite amusement when she was little. She'd always had her way. She was sometimes gentle, sometimes kind, but always proud, and always inquisitive about the world around her. She had been quick to test her powers, and she had been very quick to realize that she was a woman in a society where women were born to be revered. She was just as quick to understand her father's business, but she still loved to dance and to ride, casting aside her cloak of innocent femininity when necessary, donning it again when it was convenient. She was a little witch in her own way, Jesse thought. But she was all woman, with a mind like a whip and a heart like steel.

Jesse had retained some of his amusement as he watched her grow older. But at her coming-out party, she had been stunning, so stunning that she had taken his breath away. And maybe that night he realized that he had always been waiting for her.

Anthony Miller had seemed to be just perfect for her. He was the son of the perfect family—southern, aristocratic, rich. And he was more—he was the perfect gentleman. Anthony Miller was handsome and could be charming. He was quick to compliment her and quick to be at her side to fulfill her slightest whim.

Actually, Jesse had to admit, he liked Anthony Miller. There wasn't a thing wrong with Anthony Miller. At Montemarte he had mastered all the things a young man was supposed to master. He was cordial, proper, a loyal son to his father, a fine young man with a code of ethics and all the right ingredients of southern chivalry.

It was just that he wasn't right for Kiernan. Kiernan would run him ragged in a matter of months.

Jesse grinned, realizing that he considered himself to be the only man right for Kiernan. When he had watched her play with others, he had always thought that he was the right one for her. The one to love and understand her, the one to let her win upon occasion, yet the one who knew her ways enough to stand firm when she wanted or need a steadying hand.

A certain tension gripped him. Until today, he had never known just how much he felt that way. Until he had touched her with the breeze stirring by them on the top of the cliff and he had felt the lightning and the longing that swept through them both, he had not known.

He had not known how hungrily he would crave her, how the desire would grow to be something unimaginable. Yes, he was the man to tame her, to seize the fire and the flame, and to watch it burn in beauty.

The right man for her . . .

Except that suddenly he wasn't right for her anymore. She believed passionately in causes, in her sense of loyalty, of right and wrong.

Maybe he was wrong himself about the things that the future might bring. Congress had been fighting and squabbling about many issues for years. South Carolina had wanted to secede once before, and old Andy Jackson had had to go down and assert that a union was a union.

But maybe Jesse wasn't wrong. Maybe the nightmare he felt brewing before them was destiny, and it really would be a storm that no man would be able to stop. Jesse couldn't condone the actions of a fanatic like John Brown, but it was hard not to listen to some of the things that the man had to say.

John Brown was going to die one way or the other. But things wouldn't end here in Harpers Ferry.

He couldn't say certain things to Kiernan. He could try to tell her that Anthony wasn't right for her—he wasn't hard enough, he wasn't strong enough, dammit, he just wasn't passionate enough. But Jesse himself had nothing to offer her, nothing that she would want.

Anthony, too, was caught up in her spell, Jesse thought. Few men could be immune to her. Her sweet backside should be met with a hickory stick for what she was doing to Anthony Miller. She didn't love Anthony, Jesse was convinced of it. But Anthony was everything that she *should* want—the perfect southern gentleman again—and she was definitely entertaining herself with him.

Waiting, Jesse thought wryly with humor. There were times back home when he was convinced that she watched him just as he watched her. There were times when he was convinced that they had been made to be together, bred to be together. And maybe it was something even deeper than that. He felt it when he touched her, he tasted it when he kissed her. Something sweet and electric and so volatile that it had to be older than time itself.

He caught himself in his thinking and unconsciously he squared his shoulders and straightened on his horse. He was wrong, dead wrong, to be thinking about Kiernan so. The world was revolving differently these days. His world was moving on an uneven axis, a very precarious axis. He was very much afraid that the world he knew and loved was coming to an end. He wasn't sure where he stood, but he was becoming more and more aware that he was going to have to choose sides soon. He would have to choose by his conscience. A number of the people he loved dearly would hate him for making that choice. He would have to learn to live with their hatred.

But a man couldn't betray himself, then learn to live with his own betrayed heart and mind and soul. It couldn't be done.

Kiernan might be the one to hate him the most fiercely when he made up his mind. There would be no areas of gray for Kiernan.

Then again, it could all unfold differently from what he was imagining, he told himself. Maybe South Carolina would not vote to secede. Maybe none of the other southern

states would want to go with her. Hell, Virginia had provided four of the first five presidents of the United States.
Maybe Virginia would not pull out of the Union. A number
of the state's western counties had no wish whatsoever to
pull out.

"Well?" Daniel said.

"Well, what?"

"What's bothering you? The situation or the girl?"

"Both," Jesse said briefly.

Daniel was silent for a moment, then said lightly, "Seems
to me like there's been something brewing between the two
of you for a long, long time. Seems to me like—"

"Seems to me like it isn't your business, brother," Jesse
cautioned him lightly.

But Daniel laughed. "I've known you both all my life.
You're my blood and she's a whole lot of my spirit, so I
reckon I've a right to my say."

"You reckon so," Jesse said dryly.

Daniel grinned. "Do something!" he told Jesse. "Marry
her, before she does decide to marry Anthony Miller."

Jesse sighed with exasperation. "I can't marry her."

"Why the hell not?"

"She wouldn't be happy."

"Oh? And she's going to be happy with Anthony Miller?
Well, hell, all right, if you say so."

"She shouldn't marry Miller. She doesn't love him," Jesse
said flatly.

"Lots of people marry people they don't love," Daniel
commented. "And some of them do damned well. Just like
Kiernan might. She and Miller have everything in common
to make it right. They've the same background, the same
loyalties. But then, so do the two of you."

"Yeah," Jesse murmured, "so do the two of us." But conviction was missing from his voice. He didn't know how to
explain what he was feeling to Daniel, because they, too,
came from the same background. They should have shared
loyalties. He turned to his brother, determined to say as
much as he could. "Daniel, there's going to be a war."

"It's not going to be a war, Jesse. It will be a skirmish at

best. After today, old John Brown can't be in very good
shape. He's had men killed, and he's had men wounded. It
won't be much of a battle. If he doesn't surrender, it'll be
over in a matter of minutes."

Yes, old John Brown did have men sick and wounded.
He'd seen young Oliver Brown, and he couldn't forget his
father's words to him. *Die like a man.* He saw the light, all
right. Old John Brown saw the light.

"Brown's frightening," Jesse said out loud. "He's just
about the most frightening man I've ever met in my life."

"Damn, Jesse, that man did get to you!" Daniel was silent
for a moment, watching him. "Hell, Jesse, you can't think
that the old fanatic should get away with this."

Jesse shook his head vehemently. "No, I don't. As far as
I'm concerned, he committed murder in Kansas, and he
committed murder here. Hell, I'm no judge or jury, but it
sure does look like what he did here was treason as well."
He thought of the young followers of Brown who had suddenly seemed to realize that what they were doing could be
construed as treason. "Daniel, I just don't know how to
describe it. There's a light in his eyes. He knows he's going
to die, and he knew his son was going to die. But it's like
he's on a holy mission."

"He's a fanatic, and he should hang."

"I'd be the first to say that he should," Jesse agreed, and
exhaled slowly. "But you should meet that old man, Daniel.
He's frightening, I swear it."

"I've never seen you afraid of anything, Jess," Daniel
commented.

Jesse grinned. "Then you didn't always see real good,
brother. Every living man has been afraid at some time in
his life. I'm not afraid of going up against a man in battle,
and I don't even think I'm afraid of dying. But I've been
afraid."

"Of what?"

"Of things that I can't touch, things out of my reach,
things I can't even understand. Things that I can't get my
hands on, and things that I can't stop from happening."

Daniel stared at him. For a long moment, Jesse thought

his brother was going to make a joke. But then, as Daniel's eyes met his, he realized that his brother knew exactly what he was talking about.

"Only time will tell, Jesse. Only time will tell."

"Yeah, I guess so." They were alike in so many ways. Back at Cameron Hall, they'd grown up with the same rights and wrongs drilled into them. They both had a sound sense of ethics and loyalty and honor. And both of them would follow it.

But the paths that they followed might be completely different.

"We're blood, Jesse, no matter what."

Daniel had reined in and now extended his hand across the chasm between them. Jesse took his brother's hand. "Blood, Daniel. No matter what."

"It's a pact."

"It's a pact."

They held hands in the road, their eyes meeting, their grips firm. Then Daniel grinned. They hadn't come to an impasse yet. "Jesse, you're awfully damned grim tonight."

"It was a grim day." He thought about Kiernan, and his voice softened. "Most of it."

"Do you know what you need? A drink!" Daniel announced, convinced.

Jesse grinned slowly. "Well, what the hell. You must be right. What I need is a drink."

"And since we're still both officially on leave, it seems like a right good thing to do with the rest of the evening," Daniel told him. He kicked his horse to quicken his pace.

It was a peculiar set of circumstances that had brought them both to Harpers Ferry, just as it was a peculiar set of circumstances that had brought their West Point commander, Brevet Lieutenant Colonel Robert E. Lee, and their old West Point and army friend, Lieutenant Jeb Stuart, in on a situation that was being manned by U.S. marines. When word of the raid had reached Washington, all that President Buchanan had on hand had been this navy unit under Israel Green. Green had immediately headed out from Washington with his troops.

Jeb had been visiting relatives in north Virginia when he
was summoned to the war department. Jeb had invented a
new way to attach a saber to a belt. He was interested in
selling his patent, and the government was interested in buying it. He'd been waiting when all of a sudden things had
started to happen. was sent out to Arlington House to bring
back Lee.

Jesse had already been sent the night before. The old general, Winfield Scott, had heard something about the goings-
on, and while things had still been rumor at that time—and
Brown had only identified himself with the alias of "Smith"
—the old war horse had known that real trouble was afoot.
Daniel, on the other hand, had been with Jeb. Stuart had
volunteered to come with Lee as an aide, and Daniel had
volunteered to come with Stuart as an aide.

Now, the two brothers rode to the Wager Hotel for their
drink. Since neither of them was officially attached to the
troops, they were at their liberty to choose their own accommodations, and they chose the hotel. They were due to meet
up with Lee and Jeb by six the next morning.

When they reached the Wager, the situation was being
boisterously discussed in the hotel's barroom. "Let's have
that drink upstairs, shall we?" Jesse demanded of his
brother.

"Sounds like a good place to me."

They left their horses to be stabled, and Jesse retired
straight to their room. Daniel bought a bottle of good Ken-
tucky bourbon and brought it up. They shared a drink while
Daniel brought Jesse up to date on what was happening at
Cameron Hall.

The Tidewater plantation home itself was actually Jesse's,
since he was the oldest son. But the family's land holdings
were vast, and there were a number of other fine structures
built on the Cameron land, so they shared the responsibility
for it. It was unspoken but understood to their family of
three—Jesse, Daniel, and Christa—that whenever one of
them married, he or she was welcome to make their home
on the family estate.

In fact, Jesse thought, Daniel knew the land a lot better

than he himself did. Daniel was closer to it. Jesse loved Cameron Hall, and he loved his family history. But he wondered if he loved it as much as Daniel did.

And then again, he wondered if he could ever give it up. No one had asked him to, not yet.

After a while, he and Daniel fell silent. It was a comfortable silence. Then Daniel yawned.

"I still don't get it, Jess."

"What don't you get?"

"You and Kiernan. Why don't you just sweep her up on that steed of yours and carry her away?"

He'd done that, Jesse mused, he'd done that very thing just that afternoon. He could have ridden on forever with her. He could have kissed her, and he could have let the kiss become more. If he ever kissed her again, he thought, it *would* become more. He wasn't Anthony Miller, he wasn't the gentleman he should be, and he was suddenly certain that none of the standard rules could come into play between Kiernan and himself.

"I want her to make a choice," Jesse said.

Daniel snorted. "Between you and Anthony Miller?"

"There's nothing wrong with Anthony Miller," Jesse heard himself saying. He almost grinned in the pale moonlight that settled over the room.

"I like Anthony just fine," Daniel said. "But I repeat— what's the choice?"

Jesse grinned broadly. He took a long swig on the bourbon and handed the bottle back to Daniel. "Thanks, brother." He inhaled deeply. "Hell, there may be lots of choices soon. Let's get some sleep. Morning's going to come soon enough."

Morning did come soon enough.

By seven thirty, the storming troops lined up in position in front of the firehouse. Lee, following both diplomacy and procedure, offered the militia units first crack at storming John Brown's position. The militia commanders declined. Too many of the militia were family men. Federal troops were paid to risk their lives.

The marine commander, Israel Green, told Lee with ceremony and honor that his marines would be proud to enter the fray. John Brown was to be offered one last chance to surrender. Jeb Stuart brought Lee's terms to Brown.

Jesse accompanied Jeb Stuart when he brought the terms to Brown. Jeb read Lee's order, which first identified Lee and his command under President Buchanan of the United States. Then it demanded the release of the hostages and went on to advise Brown that he couldn't possibly escape. If he would surrender himself and restore the armory property, Colonel Lee would keep them safe until he was given further orders from the president. If Brown did not surrender, Lee could not vouch for his safety.

Old John Brown opened the firehouse door a four-inch crack. He told Jeb that he wanted his freedom to take his followers back across the river to Maryland.

There was an uproar from the hostages inside. "Have Lee amend his terms!" someone cried out.

Then there was another call from the prisoners. "Never mind us! Fire!"

Jesse grinned. He recognized the voice—it was Colonel Lewis Washington. The spirit of revolution did live on, Jesse thought.

Jesse couldn't hear what happened next, but Stuart and Brown spoke for some time. Then Brown shouted out, "Lieutenant, I see we can't agree. You have the numbers on me, but you know we soldiers aren't afraid of death. I would as lief die by a bullet as on the gallows."

"Is that your final answer, Captain?" Jeb demanded.

There was a silence for just a moment. The sun was rising, beautiful in the morning sky. Jesse could hear the chirps and cries of birds.

He glanced around. His old West Point teacher, the gentlemanly and indomitable Robert Lee, stood at some distance by a pillar of one of the buildings.

He wasn't armed. He looked upon the situation as one of little consequence, one that the marines would handle quickly and efficiently.

That was all it was, Jesse told himself. Lee was right. Why did Jesse himself insist on making more of it?

"Yes," Brown announced flatly.

Stuart stood back and waved his hat. It was the signal to Israel Green to bring in his troops, with bayonets only to reduce the risk of injuring the hostages.

The marines began to pound on the heavy doors with sledgehammers. The wood shuddered and groaned and splintered, but did not give. A halt was called, and a battering ram was formed. A ragged hole was dug into the doors, and the men burst through. Jesse followed.

It was over quickly. The marines stepped in with their silver bayonets flashing. After Colonel Washington greeted them all and identified Brown, Green struck Brown, who fell.

The raiders swept the firehouse with gunfire. A marine clutched his stomach near the doorway and fell. Smoke began to fill the firehouse. A few more marines rushed the place, and one of the raiders was instantly killed. Another, wounded, was dragged outside.

Colonel Washington pulled on his gloves before leaving the firehouse. Jesse was behind him, helping one of the hostages out, when Washington was greeted by a friend. "Lewis, old fellow, how do you feel?"

"Hungry as a hound and dry as a powder horn!" Jesse heard the disheveled Washington say, and he grinned again, touched by the man's spirit and pride.

That's it, he thought to himself, that is the grandeur we've created here in Virginia. We have bred such men!

It was, he realized, part of what he was afraid of losing.

More went on, but Jesse could no longer heed any man who was walking and well. His duty was first to the civilians and then to the marines—and then to the raiders.

Jesse learned later from Jeb Stuart that John Brown had been taken to a room at the Wager. Assembled to question him were Lee, Stuart, Senator Mason, Virginia's governor Henry Wise, an Ohio congressman, Colonel Washington, and Congressman Faulkner of Virginia.

They quizzed him for hours, Jeb said. John Brown wouldn't incriminate others, but he was damned forthright about himself and his determination. He said that he had only meant to free the slaves, that he'd meant no harm to others. When he was reminded that innocents had died, he had assured them that no man or woman of any innocent nature had been harmed to his knowledge. Jeb admitted that Brown was an extraordinary man. A fanatic, a doomed man, but also much more.

While Brown was being quizzed, Jesse did what he could for the wounded. Another of John Brown's sons, a boy named Watson, lay dying during the long afternoon. There was nothing that any man could do, but Watson, too, was grilled endlessly for his part in the affair.

A boy named Anderson lay on the grass, waiting to die. As the boy continued to breathe, a man walked by him and callously remarked that it was taking him a long time to die. But eventually, his death silenced the voices of his tormenters.

At last a pit was dug, and the dead were buried, except for Anderson's body. He was claimed by doctors from Winchester. Jesse gritted his teeth when he learned that the boy had been stuffed headfirst into a barrel, then rammed and packed down so hard that blood and bone and sinew all seemed to crack alike.

It wasn't so bad that the body of a boy who hadn't understood that he was involved in treason was going to medical science. It just seemed horrible that any human being could be so abused, so stripped of his dignity in death.

For Jesse, it was the final straw. He'd done what he could do. He'd seen to the wounded, he'd stormed in with the troopers, and he'd tended the wounded again.

He didn't want to see any more at Harpers Ferry. A place that had always been beautiful and peaceful to him would never be the same again. Something about the misuse of Anderson's body had been the final straw. When they had rolled that barrel away and he had come too late to do a damned thing about it, something inside of him had seemed to snap. A tempest raged in him like something he hadn't begun to imagine.

He mounted his horse. He probably should have looked for Daniel, but he didn't know where his brother was. He was angry, but had no outlet to vent the anger.

And he felt curiously as if he had been hurt, and he didn't know why he felt that way.

All in all, he was like a tempest brewing.

It was the best time in the world for him to stay away, far away, from Kiernan.

But he didn't. He discovered himself riding for Lacey's house.

Kiernan hadn't expected to see Jesse that early in the day. She had ventured out that afternoon when she had heard that it was all over, that the firehouse had been stormed, that John Brown was now a captive. But she hadn't gone far. She'd seen what people had done to the wounded and slain raiders the day before. Although she was appalled and horrified by the innocent lives that had been lost at Harpers Ferry because of the raiders, she couldn't help being disturbed by some of the things done to them in retaliation.

She was a Virginia lady, she had told herself, gazing at her reflection in the glass that morning. She was delicate and protected and tender, and she wasn't supposed to be exposed to anything evil.

But she knew that she was anything but delicate, and she had never allowed herself to be overprotected. What had happened was simply horrible, and she didn't want to see more.

She was sitting in the parlor, reading a newspaper from a nearby Maryland press, when she heard a tumultuous pounding on the rear door. She started, alert and wary for a moment. The attempt to kidnap her and take her hostage remained with her, and she wasn't immune to a sense of unease if anything resembling danger threatened.

But kidnappers did not knock at a door, certainly not so violently. Lacey had ventured out, when all was well, to hear the latest on what was happening at the hotel.

Kiernan rose and hurried to the door, throwing it open quickly since the pounding threatened to tear it from its hinges.

Jesse stood before her. His plumed hat was pulled at a rakish angle over his forehead. He was in uniform, a shoulder-skirted regulation cape around his shoulders.

"Jesse!" she murmured, and stepped back. She could barely see his eyes, shadowed as they were by the brim of his hat. She sensed a deep tension about him, an energy even greater than that which he usually exuded. "I wasn't expecting you or Daniel yet. I've nothing ready. Oh, but come in— I'm so sorry! I didn't mean to be rude. I'm sure there's something to drink, and—"

He moved through the doorway, his presence powerful. He swept his plumed hat from his head, and she saw his eyes at last. They were dark and seemed filled with a whirlwind emotion.

"I don't need anything to drink," he told her.

"Then—"

"Ride with me," he said briefly.

Kiernan stared at him. He was in a dangerous mood, she sensed. She shook her head uncertainly. "Jesse, Lacey isn't here. She's gone down—"

"Leave her a note," he commanded.

She should have told him right where to go for so commanding her. No lady would ever do such a thing, but she had never pretended to be the perfect lady around Jesse.

"Jesse, I should tell you to go straight to hell!" she whispered softly to him.

He set a hand against the doorframe and moved closer against her. His face was just inches away. "But you're not going to, are you?"

Despite his arrogance, there was something almost desperate about his words.

For the first time, she realized, Jesse needed her, really needed her, as an adult.

As a woman.

She lifted her chin. "I'll come with you, Jesse," she said. "This time."

He didn't smile, didn't even seem to note her taunt. He took it fully for granted that she would come with him. But she realized that, equally, she needed to be with him.

"I'll be right with you," she murmured. In the kitchen she wrote Lacey a note, saying only that she was with Jesse. She ran up to her room for a cape and hurried back down.

Jesse was still by the rear door, pacing the small area of the rear entry like a caged lion. Kiernan felt a fierce shiver seize hold of her. He ceased moving at last, not realizing that she had returned, and stared out into the small rear yard at the golds and grays of the autumn afternoon. A lowering sun cast its gentle rays upon the rock and shale of the mountain cliffs. He stared, she thought, but he didn't see.

"Jesse," she said softly.

His dark blue gaze shot quickly to her. He opened the door for her, and his eyes followed her as she left the house. He didn't speak.

His sleek roan stood waiting in the yard. Jesse lifted her up onto the horse, then mounted behind her with smooth agility. She thought that in his present mood they would race again, but he walked the horse from the yard, then reined in.

"What is it, Jesse?" she asked him.

"I don't know where to go," he admitted, an edge of raw frustration to his voice.

Kiernan should remain silent, she knew, absolutely silent. Jesse's present state of mind couldn't be good for either of them.

But something of his wild, reckless, and even tormented mood was entering into her heart and, like the dark winds of a storm, into her soul and body. "Head west along the river," she told him.

They passed quietly out of town and headed down the pike that lined the water. They passed the old mill and kept riding until they were several miles out of town. They could hear the rush of the white water passing over the rapids, but they couldn't see it through the abundance of foliage and

trees growing on the strip of land between the road and the
river.

"Turn here," Kiernan advised him.

Jesse might have missed the narrow, overgrown trail
heading toward the water if Kiernan hadn't pointed it out.
But he didn't question her wisdom in taking it. He knew
they were near Montemarte, the Millers' estate.

A small wooden fishing shack sat almost on the water
with a dock that stretched out over the rocks. In the dim
twilight, the shack was almost invisible.

Kiernan felt Jesse hesitate, felt a greater heat building
inside him. "Anthony's?" he inquired dryly.

"His father's," she replied flatly. He'd come to her for a
place to go, and she had been generous enough to offer this
quiet haven.

He nudged the horse forward. At the shack he dismounted and reached up to her. She slipped down into his
arms, but he released her quickly and walked down to the
water by the shack. The water was low. He set one shiny
black boot upon a rock and stared out at the ever-moving
water.

Kiernan ignored him and hurried into the shack. There
wasn't much there. It was rebuilt every summer after the
waters of the river rose and receded. There was a fireplace
and a pot for making coffee and a skillet for frying whatever
fish might be caught. There was a rough-hewn table and
four chairs, and one sleigh bed shoved into the far corner of
the room. There was a ledge with a handy supply of whiskey
and tobacco and a few glasses.

She and Anthony had last been there, Kiernan thought, at
the end of summer, not long ago. In a pleasant twilight, the
other men had debated politics, but Anthony had dropped
out to teach her the proper way to fish.

It had been nice. Not exciting, just a pleasant twilight to
while away . . .

She dragged a chair over to stand upon to reach up for the
whiskey. Jesse might well want a drink once he came into
the shack.

But as she stood upon the chair, the door burst open.

Jesse stood in the doorway. The dying orange glow of the afternoon framed him with his low-brimmed plumed hat and his shoulder-skirted navy cape.

In the coming twilight, with the hectic rush of the water tearing over the rapids behind him, she felt his recklessness, his energy, his tempest, more certainly than she had ever felt it before.

She stopped reaching for the glasses and rubbed her palms over her skirt, watching him, sensing the passion and heat and need within him. Her mouth was dry. Her heart pounded. Her blood seemed to race through her system as swiftly and wildly as the water rushed over and around the ancient rocks.

Jesse didn't want a drink, she realized.

Jesse wanted her.

Six

Suddenly, he slammed the door shut behind him and advanced upon her, his long strides bringing him to stand before the chair. She was silent, staring down into the cobalt depths of his eyes.

She'd thought that he'd have so much to say, that he would speak and she would listen, that she would soothe the anguish that swept his soul. She'd thought there would be many words to share.

But there were no words. He reached out to her, wrapping his arms around her. The tempest and the passion and the heat in his arms were so great that she instinctively wound her own arms around him, and for a long moment, his head lay against her breast. Indeed, she thought, she soothed him.

But his was a wildness that did not seek to be soothed.

His hands wound around her waist, and he lifted her from the chair. She slid slowly, evocatively, against the length of his body. She felt again all the things that she had felt in that previous touch.

Felt his body, the hot corded tension. Felt the deep power of his chest, the hardness of his thighs. Felt the taut demand of his hips and the unyielding strength of that which lay within his loins.

His lips touched hers hungrily. He did not seek to slowly seduce—there was nothing leisurely about his kiss. His lips

took and consumed hers, ravaged them. He did not seek a
subtle entry to her mouth. Instead, his tongue plunged between her lips and teeth and demanded the sweetness of her
mouth.

His arms held her with magic, with fire and fervor and
tempest, with something that entered deep into her body
and demanded a response.

He broke away and stared down at her in the shadows
cast by the dying sun. For a long, long moment she didn't
move. They stared at each other, caught up in the heedless,
swirling excitement that hurtled and slammed between
them. Feelings raced through Kiernan, hungers and yearnings, and dark forbidden things.

She had imagined them before. She'd tasted hints of aching and wonder in his arms before.

He began to kiss her again.

She closed her eyes and swept her arms around his neck.
She met his kiss as a new-found thirst and desire brought a
trembling to her lips.

She was learning swiftly what to do with those lips.

An innate sensuality blossomed and grew within her,
there in the wooden shack, in the late afternoon of a day
that had been beset by blood as dark as the crimson of the
dying sun.

Their lips met again and again, open-mouthed, in hungry,
wet kisses, kisses that melded their lips and their bodies, that
brought the searing heat from that sweet touch to burn deep
into the heart of unleashed desire.

Kiernan knew what she was doing all the while. She knew
before his lips trailed from hers to touch her earlobes and
her cheeks, to slide provocatively along the narrow column
of her throat, to rest against her pulse and travel onward
along the length of her collarbone.

The touch of his fingers upon her shoulder sent her cape
falling to the floor. And his lips fell against the naked flesh
of her throat once again.

The things he did with his tongue . . .

She felt that she was falling, that his touch had already
entered into her body. She trembled as her senses reeled.

The warmth was so sweet, entering, like nectar that caressed her inside and out. She concentrated so on the wonder of the sensation that she barely realized that Jesse had found the tiny hooks and buttons at the back of her gingham day gown, and that she was slowly losing it as he slipped it downward to her waist.

His fingers lifted the delicate strap of her chemise, and his mouth pressed against the spot where it had been. That same wet warmth was placed over the fine silk where it molded the very tip of her breast. He caressed and nurtured the flesh beneath the fabric, wet against the hardening bud of her nipple.

Like lightning it moved, the searing ecstasy of the sensation. It touched her breast, and like his kiss, it touched so much more. It spread like the summer rays of the sun, spiraling down to her stomach and beyond, entering low into intimate places between her thighs—shocking places.

"Oh, Jesse!"

She whispered his name at last—not with protest but with wonder. She discovered herself swept up into his arms, held tight against the rough fabric of his cavalry cape. As he carried her to the bed, she didn't care.

She didn't care about the dust that had settled upon the woolen blanket and down mattress. The room was surely cold, but she felt no chill. None of it mattered. She had mused and pondered and imagined, as any young woman might, this first time with flowery, chivalrous phrases, with soft candlelight and the scent of roses on the air.

But none of that mattered, none of it at all.

It didn't even matter that no words of God's blessing had made them man and wife.

She was with Jesse, and she trusted him as much as she desired him. Perhaps therein lay the beauty of this tryst in the cold and rugged cabin in the woods.

When he saw the dust, he set her upon her feet, swept his cape from his shoulders, and laid the garment with the soft lining upward upon the sleigh bed. Then he turned back to her, and again he paused, and she realized that he was trembling too.

He lifted a ringlet of her hair from her shoulders, and she saw the slight movement in his fingers. He buried his face against it, then she was in his arms once more, tasting his kiss, tasting all the sweet and mysterious and haunting things that it promised.

He found more hooks, and she felt her gown whisper down to her feet, leaving her in the bone of her corset, her delicate chemise, her petticoat, and her pantalets.

He was an experienced lover, she thought. Despite his haste and fire, he was at ease with the complexity of her clothing. He could kiss and tease and tantalize, his lips never leaving her flesh. Her petticoat crumpled to her feet. The softness of her chemise was stripped away, the material rustling over her naked flesh, as sensual as his touch. Still his mouth and the moist searing heat of it kept her in wonder as he cast aside the restriction of her stays, tossing the bone far from them.

Her shoulders and breasts were naked to his gaze.

He paused briefly to just stare at her. In the twilight, his eyes reflected flames, flames that smoldered and elicited both desire and shyness, a need to be known, and a need to hide. But before she could react fully to the fires that blazed in his eyes, she was within his arms again.

There were words at last, words that touched her flesh in hot whispers. They told her that she was beautiful. Words of poetry—

And words of raw hunger.

She found herself swept up again and laid both fiercely and tenderly upon the satin lining of his cape. He lay quickly down beside her. The brush of his fingers and the warmth of his tongue raged over the mounds of her breasts, explored contours and creamy skin, and set fire to the pebblelike peaks of rouge and crimson that tautened instantly at his touch.

She had thought before that his kiss could enter deeply into her. Now it seared a trail so hot that it denied her all thought. All she knew was longing. She arched against the palm of his hand as he pulled the tie to her pantalets. A flush —soft pink in the twilight of the shack—flooded her cheeks.

But she felt the husky tenor of his delighted laughter, and when his lips found hers again, his whispers eased her from embarrassment.

He had wanted her so very long. He had waited, and he had known, he had always known, just as he had known the summer gales that swept the Tidewater, that one day they would come to this.

Her pantalets were shed, her shoes were tossed aside.

And her stockings were removed more erotically than she had ever imagined clothing could leave the human body. The stroke of his fingers, feather-light against her thighs, moved upwards toward that center of flame.

His shoulders were broad and bronzed in the light, his chest dusted with a heavy spattering of dark hair. He was well muscled but whipcord lean, so taut in the belly, lean in the hips . . .

And passionate within the dark nest of his loins.

She saw him completely for only seconds because he crawled over her and straddled her hips. She gasped as his sex touched her, as hard as steel but as hot as fire against her flesh. With almost the curl of a smile to his lips, his face was still very tense. He stared at her again. She felt shuddering within him and knew that no matter how badly he wanted her, he would pull back now if she wished it.

The sun suddenly fell farther. Red light flooded into the shack, washing away the shadows. His flesh was toned red, and when she lifted her own hand, she saw that it too was caught in that glowing reflection.

Like a reflection of blood.

She started to shiver, suddenly very afraid. But she wasn't afraid of Jesse. She wanted to hold him tighter than ever.

"Jesse," she whispered.

"It isn't right," he told her. "I shouldn't have you here. I shouldn't have swept you away, I should never have touched you. Your father would have a right to take a rifle to my heart this very moment."

She blinked away the illusion of the red light. The shivering stopped. Her soul was on fire, her body was on fire. She wanted to touch his flesh, to run her fingers over the muscled breadth of his shoulders, to test the tight ripples in his belly, to press her lips against his chest. Most of all, she wanted to appease the longing inside her. She wanted the emptiness to be filled.

She reached out and touched his cheek. She spoke a truth that she never thought she would utter.

"I love you, Jesse."

A soft oath escaped him, and she was swept back into his arms. She felt the fervor of his kiss, and the heat and fire began to build and spread anew within her. Hungrily he feasted upon her breasts.

And hungrily she tasted him in turn, twisting, turning, to press her lips to his shoulders, his throat, and softly, wetly, drew patterns down the rippling muscles of his chest.

He shifted upon her suddenly. The thrust of his knee parted her thighs, and the weight of his body spread her further. She felt the erotic touch of his hands again. His fingers caressing, exploring, ever more boldly. She felt him touch her intimately in the very place where she seemed to feel the spiraling heat most deeply.

A cry tore from her lips and she surged against him. And still he touched her, more deeply, more intimately.

Tantalizing . . .

He had created a tempest within her, and she rocked and undulated against his touch. A spark glowed deeply inside her, and each sweet stroke of his sent the fire burning more and more brightly.

Again he shifted, and it seemed that all of his body parted her. Incredibly, impossibly, he demanded more from her, and he gave more to her. His kisses lingered upon the softness of her upper thighs.

She must protest, she knew that she must—just as she knew that her cheeks were flooded with color. She tried to whisper his name, but the word wouldn't come.

She couldn't protest. The feelings were too exquisite, the longings too intense.

Then he took his boldness a step further, and she felt the searing moist heat of his kiss, of his tongue, against the most intimate of virgin flesh. Nothing, not the wind, not the fire,

not the ice of winter, could ever cause such sensation. She
gasped and sought to rise, but his fingers curled around hers.
The ecstasy was so sweet that it was anguish. She could
bear no more of it. She was faint, she was dizzy, she was
trembling, and she knew that she must reach some promised
explosion or perish soon for the longing and the soaring.

It was then that he took her, when she needed him so
desperately. The pain came swift and staggering. She cried
out with it, stunned, her fingers tightening upon his flesh.

But so quickly it was gone!

She had been empty, and now she was filled. His kisses
held her while the thrust of his body entered within her,
deep, deeper. A velvet blade cut her in two, brought agony,
a certainty that she could never bear the intrusion.

But his kiss, his touch, his slow, shattering movement—
all these brought her feelings and senses reeling into play
again. The agony receded, and the sweetly soaring ecstasy
came to the fore once again.

He moved so slowly, thrusting against her until she cried
out, then rose again. Then once more he moved, slowly,
achingly slowly . . .

Until she discovered that she was rising against him. Until
the need within her was so rich and so great that she could
not bear his absence. Oh, how it grew, this need! And still he
took care, planting kisses upon her breasts as he moved. She
arched against him, thrust and writhed against him.

Suddenly his arms wrapped tightly around her, and she
knew that Jesse would wait no more. She arched against
him, and he willingly availed her of her longing, bearing
down upon her deep and hard and fast, creating a rhythm
that flew with a pulsing beat. She lost all sense of what was
around her. She heard the water beating over the rock, and
the sound swept into her. She hungered, she wanted, she
ached. She needed all that she received, but she reached, and
she did not know why she reached. The sweetness, the ecstasy filled her until she thought that she must die with it,
that she must explode, and still he moved. . . .

Then it seemed that she *did* die, and that her senses *did*
explode. Shattering light burst all around her, the rays fell

from the sun, a thousand stars seemed to burst and shimmer down upon her all in one. She could not move, for the stars disappeared and the world went briefly black, and when she could see again, the stars were still cascading down upon her. Warmth radiated through her body and to her limbs, sweet nectar filled with warmth. Her body was racked with shudders.

And then she felt Jesse. He went deadly taut above her, muscles bunching and constricting, and he moved against her once again, thrusting so very deeply.

A sweet warmth burst from within him, showering into her. To her amazement, it brought a new flow of ripples within her own body, tantalizing, wonderful little after-shocks of splendor.

His weight rested briefly upon her until he rolled to his side. His arms curled around her, and he brought her with him. She leaned her cheek against the sweat-sleek flesh of his chest, and her lashes closed over her eyes. She had never felt such exhaustion.

She had never known such wonder.

Jesse was silent, stroking her hair. She herself couldn't speak because she couldn't think what to say. It had been one thing to share such absolute intimacy in the heat of the moment, but now, in memory, much of it made her blush. And now, as the cold night air settled over her and darkness began to replace the multitude of colors of the sunset, she realized that she should not have done this. Her father would be horrified; indeed, any man or woman within her world would be horrified.

She'd never really even kissed Anthony.

And Anthony would have never even thought of making love to her like this. It would not be proper. If she married Anthony, they would probably go through years together with neither of them ever knowing the other as intimately as she now knew Jesse.

And yet doing this couldn't be wrong. She loved Jesse. She had told him so. He had given her every opportunity to stop what had happened between them.

She shivered from the briskness of the air. "Cold?" Jesse asked her.

"Very," she whispered.

He pulled her close and kissed her forehead, then balanced his weight to roll over her and leap lightly to the floor. Naked and comfortable in his nakedness, he walked over to the fire and knelt low. "There's kindling," he murmured. He strode back to his pants for his striker, and within a few minutes he had a warm fire going. Kiernan had not waited for that warmth to draw his navy cavalry cape around herself. She wasn't sure if she was ashamed of her own behavior or not, but she simply couldn't be as comfortable in front of Jesse as he was in front of her. When he returned, she was sitting up and watching him somewhat nervously.

He smiled. His dark hair was totally disheveled and fell in an ebony lock over his forehead. He seemed younger than the man who had carried her here in such a tempest. His smile was crooked and wicked, yet broad and filled with both humor and tenderness.

"I saw you reaching for the liquor when we came in. Need a drink now?"

"Yes," she said. "No—I mean, I don't need a drink. I really shouldn't be drinking whiskey. Ladies don't . . ." She paused and her voice trailed away, and then she looked up at Jesse. "Oh, Jesse, ladies don't ever do what I did here today, do they? Ever."

He found a glass and wiped the rim carefully, then splashed whiskey into it. He took a long sip himself, then came to sit beside her. He drew her close to him, and the roughness of his cheek rubbed against her forehead when he spoke. "Only the very greatest ladies could love so deeply and so well," he told her. He offered her the whiskey. She sipped it and coughed and choked, and he patted her upon the back, smiling.

"Don't! Oh, please don't laugh at me!" she implored him.

"Kiernan, I would never laugh at you. Lord, sweetheart, today has been the most tender day in all of my life, and I will thank you for it always."

He seemed sincere, and she discovered that she could no

longer meet his eyes. She stared at her hands. His were so large and so bronzed—the palms roughened from constant riding, but the fingers so long and precise and dedicated to his medical calling—very dark against the whiteness of her own.

Those fingers curled around hers. "I think that this has been coming all our lives."

"I am practically engaged to another man," she murmured.

"Ah, yes. Poor Anthony," Jesse said dryly. She didn't like the tone of his voice. He rose and reached for his long johns and then his trousers with their yellow piping. He pulled them on and headed to the fire, poking it to stoke up the flame. The firelight played upon his chest. For a few moments she dared to survey him. She relished the play of gold and orange and fire that danced over his flesh. In his very masculine way, he was beautiful, toned and hard and beautiful. He had held her in his arms, he had held her against his flesh, and he had given her so very much. She had no experience, yet she was shrewdly convinced that she had been seduced by a rare man, that what she had touched was indeed a form of magic. And without Jesse, she might never touch that magic again.

She could never have shared this experience with any man but Jesse, she thought. Never. Maybe she had always known it.

"There's no reason to be rude about Anthony," she murmured, drawing the cape more tightly about her as if it were a shield of respectability.

"No," he said, sounding bitter. "There's no reason to be rude about Anthony."

"Jesse, I hadn't seen you in months, and suddenly—"

"And suddenly I was back in your life," he interrupted. His voice was quiet, thoughtful.

"You came to me this afternoon," she began, but she didn't finish. This time he strode back to the bed and came down on one knee before her, taking her hand.

"Yes, I came in a tempest to steal you away like the wind.

And you came with me," he murmured, and brushed aside her hair.

She smiled. "Yes, I came with you," she told him. She let the cape fall to reach for that straying lock of black hair upon his forehead, and she smoothed it back. She didn't want to talk about Anthony again. She didn't want to hear or say words that might dispel the closeness between them. She didn't want the magic broken.

She didn't want there to be anything else in the world except for the night, and the two of them.

Anthony was surely in her past now. Jesse, despite his recklessness and stubborn streak and even the wildness that sometimes brewed in his heart, was a man of extreme honor. There was no question that he would marry her. But that was the future. Anthony would have to be dealt with first, gently. And there was her father. He might be difficult to handle. He'd be appalled that she'd come so close to one man while nearly engaged to another. But it would all work out. It was just a matter of diplomacy.

She didn't want diplomacy now. She didn't want anything to spoil the memory of this night.

"Jesse, what was it? Why were you so upset?"

"I had no right to come for you. Really, I didn't."

"But what was wrong?"

He shrugged and sat up beside her, folding his legs beneath himself and pulling her close. "What was right?" he murmured.

"John Brown is in custody. It's over."

"It's not over. Don't you see? It will never really be over, and nothing will be the same again."

"I don't know what you're talking about."

"You saw only some of what people were doing. You didn't see it all." He stood again and paced to the fire. He stared into the flames. "Kiernan, in the West, I saw terrible things. The Indians did terrible things to the white men—a number of which they learned from the white men, I might add. Because the white men were doing terrible things to the Indians. I saw things just as horrible here. People weren't just shot, Kiernan. They were abused. Atrocities were committed here."

She understood him, yet she didn't understand him. She had felt a vague sense of horror herself, but Jesse's seemed deeper, seemed to touch something within him that she didn't comprehend, or seemed to relate to something that he knew and that she did not.

"Jesse, John Brown attacked these people. He shot the mayor, one of the nicest, most gentle men I have ever met. People reacted."

"Yes, but people reacted badly to people all the way around," he murmured.

"Jesse, you're scaring me. I don't understand you."

"That's what I'm afraid of. You'll never understand me."

"Then tell me what you mean!" Kiernan flared.

He shook his head. "I don't know what I'm saying myself, Kiernan."

But suddenly, she did. She leaped up, pulling his cape along with her, and stared at him hard. "John Brown is a fanatic," she said flatly, staring at him. "And so is that Lincoln. If he wins the election, the country is going to split. It's going to split right in two."

"You don't know that, Kiernan."

"Yes—yes, I do. Because of sectionalism, Jesse, and because of the economy. And because there is a way of life for us, and a way of life for them."

"You can't pull a country apart, Kiernan."

Kiernan was suddenly more frightened than she had ever imagined she could be. She'd had everything in her hands. She'd had Jesse. She'd made love with him. She should never have done it, but she'd never been conventional, and neither had Jesse. It had been the most beautiful thing in the world, and her future had been bright, as beautiful as the blazing stars that had touched her in the aftermath of his touch.

And now it was slipping away from her. It was as if she had held water in the cup of her palm, then suddenly opened up her fingers. It was all trickling away.

"Jesse, you're a Virginian!"

He stiffened. "You can't tear it apart, Kiernan. You just can't tear it apart."

She spun away from him. Half blinded by the tears that stung behind her lashes, she hurried about the shack, looking for her strewn clothing.

She couldn't handle the corset alone. She needed his help, but she couldn't bear accepting it.

Suddenly he was behind her. "Don't touch me!" she snapped.

"It's too late for that," he murmured, a hint of amusement touching the tension in his voice.

"Let go!" She tried to wrench free, but he had her ribbons. As she pulled to free herself, he pulled harder and she jerked back against him.

"Stand still!"

She had little choice but to let him finish tying the garment. But once he was finished, she pulled free again, hurriedly finding the rest of her clothing. She felt his eyes upon her, but she didn't want to look his way. At last she had to. "I'm going, Jesse."

"When I'm ready."

"I'll walk back."

"No, you'll ride back with me."

"Jesse—"

"You came with me. I'll take you back."

He started moving at last, his eyes on hers while he grabbed his shirt off the floor. Her gaze nearly fell from his, but she forced herself to meet him with her growing fury.

How could he argue against the rights of the southern states? How could he argue against her father, against his own brother, against his own way of life?

It didn't matter, she tried to tell herself. It *couldn't* matter.

But it did. She felt as if she were being buffeted in a tumult, dragged down the rocks of the river. People were already talking about war.

If it came to war, would Jesse be on the wrong side of it?

He tucked his shirt into his pants, sat, and pulled on his boots.

Then with a mocking curl to his lip, he swept up his hat and set it low upon his head, then reached for his cape.

The cape on which they had lain together.

She swirled around, heading for the door. He caught her arm, jerking her back. "I thought you said you loved me."

"I can't love a traitor."

"I'm not a traitor."

"You're on the wrong side."

"There are no damned sides!"

"Then swear!" she told him suddenly. "Swear that you would be on the right side—"

"What would the right side be, Kiernan? Tell me that, please, will you?"

She paused, staring at him. She wanted to burst into tears and throw herself into his arms. She wanted to forget it all and to lie down now before the fire beside him. She wanted to see the flames upon their naked flesh as they made love again.

She wanted him to love her and for him to be the man she had always wanted. The man who lived the life she knew so well—the Virginian.

She wanted him to be with her, no matter what.

"My side is the right side, Jesse," she told him rigidly. She waited for him to agree, to promise that he would always be with her.

But he was silent as his cobalt eyes bored into hers. She spun around again, tears about to fall. And once again he caught her, spinning her around to face him. "Kiernan, marry me. You're going to be my wife. You *have* to."

"I don't have to do anything, Jesse Cameron."

"Do you think you can run back to Anthony Miller after this?"

"I don't need to run anywhere, Jesse. But Anthony's loyalties lie with mine."

He swore savagely. One last time he wrenched her against him. She tried to twist from his hold, but he caught her chin and held her face to his, and he kissed her again. He kissed her ruthlessly and passionately until he forced a response.

He lifted his head from hers. "Don't play foolish games with our lives, Kiernan!" he warned her.

She broke free from his hold and hurried outside. He was quickly behind her, his arms sweeping around her waist when she would have gone on. Before she could voice more than an oath, she was sitting upon his roan once again, and he was mounting behind her.

"Where are you taking me now?" she demanded.

"Home!" he snapped.

He did not walk the roan. He gave the animal free rein, and the hungry horse galloped into Harpers Ferry.

He urged the horse to the front of Lacey's house. Still furious, Kiernan slid down from the horse on her own.

"Kiernan!"

She stopped and swung around. Jesse would have to come around to siding with Virginia. She would have to make him understand that he must.

He jumped off his mount and headed toward her. But a rakish grin suddenly slashed across his handsome features.

"What?" She backed away, afraid that he would touch her again.

He did, pulling her against him although she struggled against his hold. She went rigidly still and repeated, "*What,* damn you?"

His voice was low, husky, soft. "I warned you before not to marry him if he couldn't kiss you as I did. Now I can warn you that you'll never have anything like you had tonight with him. Not in a thousand years, Kiernan."

She broke free, lifting her hand to slap him. He caught it and chuckled softly.

"Kiernan—"

"Go to hell, Jesse," she told him. She pulled her hand free and spun around, heading for the house.

"Kiernan, I cannot change my conscience!"

She kept walking, calling back to him, "And I cannot change mine!"

She felt his silence, felt the tension of it.

Then she heard the sound of his horse's hoofbeats as he rode away, and she swirled around again.

"Jesse!" she whispered in anguish.

But it was too late—he was gone.

She stood in misery. The night wind suddenly picked up, and it was cold.

So very cold.

As cold as a world without Jesse.

Seven

Kiernan didn't see Jesse again that night, nor did Daniel make it back. She heard a report of a slave rebellion in Pleasant Valley and that Jesse and Daniel had ridden out there with Lee and Stuart.

There was still nervousness in town that the nearby slaves would rise and rebel—even if it was too late for them to join John Brown's cause.

Kiernan knew that she should be worried, too, but she was far too involved in her own inner conflict to dwell on fears that might be unfounded.

She spent the evening trying with all of her heart to be calm. She tried to enjoy the dinner that Lacey made in case the Camerons managed to come back.

But the truth of it was Kiernan could hardly stand sitting there with Lacey. Just being polite was the most difficult thing she had ever done. Her mind didn't stop racing for an instant, and at the first opportunity, she begged exhaustion and hurried up to her bedroom.

And there she went into a frenzy of washing her face, which alternately seemed to burn with shame and grow cold with chills of wonder. She went over every minute detail of what had happened, and she began to wonder how on earth she had been so brazen. Then she reminded herself that it had been Jesse, that she loved Jesse.

Ultimately, no matter how she chastised herself, a sweet

quivering started up deep inside her, and she knew she could be certain of one thing.

She wanted to be with him again.

But she was angry, too, furious that he seemed to be living on a different plane of reality. It occurred to her she had told Jesse she loved him—but he never said those words to her.

Jesse had said that he would marry her. No, he had said that she *must* marry him! His duty called, she thought wryly. Perhaps there was more of his upbringing in him than he cared to admit. But she would never marry him if he thought it was necessary because of what had happened between them. She would only marry him if he loved her.

And if he loved Virginia.

She wondered if she was wrong to feel so passionately about her state. It was not proper for her to care as much as she did about the politics of the day. It was not an admirable feminine trait, her father warned her often enough. But she and Anthony shared the same passions. He did not mind what she had to say, for he agreed wholeheartedly.

She couldn't marry Anthony, she knew, had probably always known. Not while Jesse existed in her life.

A warmth swept over her that brought her to a renewed and different trembling. What if there were . . . complications from today? She had been innocent until that afternoon, but she wasn't naive. She could be carrying Jesse's child at this very moment.

To her amazement, the idea did not bring horror or shame to her. Instead, excitement seized hold of her, and she knew that she would love to have Jesse's child.

Because she loved Jesse.

And perhaps, if she were in the family way, she would be able to forget their differences, no matter how devastating they seemed now.

She hugged her pillow close to her body. She walked to the window, wondering if he would appear beneath it again. But he did not, and the cold of the evening swept around her. She closed the window and stepped back. She lay back on her bed, again hugging her pillow to herself.

At last, she slept.

If the day ended in a tumult, her night was haunted by the sweetest of dreams.

Kiernan had barely opened her eyes when she heard Lacey calling to her excitedly, "Kiernan! Come down. We've company!"

She leaped up, her hands shaking. It was Jesse, she was certain, and Daniel. They'd come back for breakfast.

She washed hastily and searched through the gowns she had brought. She decided on a soft green gown with a sweeping wide skirt and a green velvet jacket. The sleeves were elegantly large beneath the elbows, while the jacket was snugly fitted. She struggled a bit with her corset since Lacey was not available to help her, and a sudden nervousness caused her to fumble. How would she greet him today? Would it be different to see him?

Yes, it would never be the same again.

At last she was dressed. She picked up her brush to do something dignified and elegant with her hair, but she hadn't time and besides, her fingers were trembling. She brushed it out over her shoulder, then swept it into a simple coil at her nape. Its honey color was caught by rays of light and glistened with gold highlights. She stared at her reflection and bit her lips for color. Her cheeks were already flaming. Her eyes, brilliant with her reckless excitement, were flashing like emeralds.

She couldn't blush so!

She was furious at him, she reminded herself, and she had to remain furious at him.

She gave her hair one last pat, then spun around with her skirt swirling and headed for the stairs. She forced herself to walk slowly and came down the staircase with commendable decorum.

Her heart was thundering. Jesse was back.

But Jesse was not back. Her heart swung heavily against the wall of her chest as she reached the landing in the parlor.

"Kiernan!"

It was Anthony who called her name, and it was Anthony

and his father and her father and Lacey's husband who had all come back this morning.

Her father, whom she loved dearly. His misty gray eyes were upon her, damp with emotion, and his wrinkled and weathered cheeks split into a glad smile of appreciation. She knew instantly that he had heard of the trouble at Harpers Ferry and that he had worried himself sick over her.

"Papa!" she whispered.

Although she had really been longing for Jesse, she ran to her father.

She didn't reach him. Anthony said her name again and stepped forward. She found herself plummeting into Anthony's arms as he rushed toward her.

"Kiernan, oh, sweet Kiernan! You're here, you're well, you're unhurt!"

She looked up at him. Anthony Miller was a handsome man with golden hair that had a tendency to curl. His eyes were a soft brown like the hue of mahogany. His features were lean and finely honed.

And his concern for her was real and deep. She read it in the anguish that tightened his face and burned in his eyes. She would have pulled away from him except that guilt suddenly and swiftly tore through her. She couldn't marry him, she knew that, but she couldn't hurt him either.

She set her hands upon his arms and smiled, then reached for his cheek to reassure him. "I'm fine, Anthony. Absolutely fine." She had never realized how deeply he cared for her until now, when she was going to hurt him so deeply.

"Oh dear, there's the door again!" Lacey murmured, and hurried to see to the rapping.

Anthony didn't release Kiernan.

He pulled her closer, crushing her to his chest. His chin rested upon the top of her head, and she felt his trembling as his fingers smoothed over her hair, cradling her head. There couldn't have been a more tender picture of concern.

It was then that she heard Jesse's voice.

"Excuse us. It seems that we're interrupting."

She pulled back quickly, meeting Anthony's eyes first, then turning to see Jesse and Daniel. Jesse was greeting

Kiernan's father, but his eyes were on her, blazing blue orbs of condemnation.

Damn him! He must realize that she couldn't possibly be cruel to Anthony!

"Jesse, my son, you're not interrupting us in any way!" Kiernan's father told him, taking his hand and clapping him on the back. "I've not had a chance to greet my own daughter yet, what with young love and all, but you lads are always welcome."

"Indeed," Jesse said pleasantly, smiling at her expectantly. "Young love. How touching."

She wanted to throttle him. He stood shaking her father's hand, staring at her.

Lacey was suddenly back in the room, bearing a silver tray with small wineglasses upon it. "My very best blackberry wine, gentlemen. And lady!" She acknowledged Kiernan with a wide, brimming smile. "We must celebrate, everyone being here and well and beneath my roof!"

"Hear, hear!" Daniel said, laughing and availing himself quickly of a glass.

Kiernan wasn't sure how or when, but at last she was disengaged from Anthony. She hugged her father fiercely, realizing that she was heartily glad to see him again.

But then she found herself uncomfortably close to Jesse. His head bent low, he whispered to her.

"Haven't quite told him that you're not marrying him?"

She lifted her chin, smiling, trying to appear every bit as casual as Jesse did.

"Why, Captain Cameron, I haven't even begun to make up my mind about such things as yet!"

"Perhaps you should. Soon."

"Perhaps you should see to your own affairs, Captain. To my mind, they are in grave disarray."

"Perhaps *I* should ask your father for your hand. Perhaps we should bare our souls before him—and about the other things that have recently been bared."

She swung around, seeing amusement in his eyes.

And a warning.

"You wouldn't dare."

"Kiernan, I'd dare anything, you know that."

"But you won't, please. For my sake."

He inhaled sharply, watching her, and she knew that she had hit the proper note with him. Jesse *would* dare anything. But pleading with him had a different effect.

For the moment, she was safe.

Safe? But she loved him!

And she hated him for the stand he was taking.

Lacey soon had everyone seated. John Mackay and Thomas Donahue and Andrew and Anthony Miller all demanded to hear the details of everything that had happened in their absence.

"It was right distressing to be in the mountains hearing about the things going on down here," John Mackay said. "Right distressing. Word was so vague. One minute, the whole town was up in arms. The next minute, it was nothing but a little bitty skirmish. Daughter," he told Kiernan, shaking his head, "I'll not be so quick to leave you alone again, ever."

"Pa, I'm just fine," Kiernan said.

"Thanks to Captain Cameron," Lacey murmured vaguely. Kiernan froze. Lacey looked up and realized that everyone was staring at her. "Oh, I am sorry!" she said with distress.

"Lacey Donahue, what are you talking about?" John Mackay demanded. He was on his feet facing Lacey, who looked as if she were about to cry. John swung around on Kiernan. "Young lady, what is she talking about?" He didn't wait for Kiernan to answer, but swung on Jesse. "By the soul of my dear friend, your departed father, young man, I demand an answer."

Jesse shrugged and looked at Kiernan, giving her the option to answer.

"Oh, Pa, it was nothing, really. A few of those scoundrels surprised Lacey and me, and they decided that I would make a good hostage."

"Lord!" Anthony exclaimed in horror.

"But nothing happened!" Kiernan insisted. "Jesse came along, and they took off. It was nothing, really."

"Nothing, really! Why young woman, I do hope you displayed a proper gratitude to Jesse."

"John," Jesse murmured. His eyes were on Kiernan again, and she didn't much like either the amusement or the hint of danger within them. "I assure you, Kiernan displayed a gratitude unequal to any I have ever known."

Damn him! Her cheeks were flaming, but she determined to fight fire with fire. She smiled sweetly for her father. "Indeed, Father, I thanked him fully. After all, Jesse was such an incredible . . . gentleman."

"One cannot say enough for your daughter's strength and courage and . . . passion, sir!"

Oh, if only she could throw something!

But suddenly Anthony stood up and faced Jesse. "Captain, I am in your debt. I am ever so beholden to you!" Emotion trembled in his voice.

Jesse looked at Anthony, and for a long moment Kiernan thought that he would explode with some damning words.

But he did not.

Beholden indeed, Jesse thought. Anthony, you poor fool, you owe me nothing. I took what was dear to you on your very own property, and now we are both here playing to her whimsy.

He leaned back, sipped his drink, and replied casually, "Kiernan and I are old friends, Anthony. I happened along at the right time." He sat forward, and his eyes met Kiernan's again. "Heaven might have found some pity for Mr. Brown after all, had he managed to seize Kiernan." He smiled to take the sting—and the truth!—from his words. "Perhaps we'd never have needed to storm the place had he snared Kiernan. She'd have given him a political tongue-lashing and sent him running instantly to surrender!"

John Mackay roared with laughter, while Anthony looked uncertain. Kiernan cast daggers upon Jesse with her eyes, and Lacey hastily refilled the glasses.

Kiernan's father sobered. "Still, Jesse Cameron, in truth, we are in your debt. All ended well here, but you young people do not remember the Nat Turner rebellion in the Tidewater region back in '31. Fifty were killed then, dragged from their beds and murdered. Women and children. Bless the good Lord that a like thing did not happen here."

They were all silent. Kiernan glanced at Jesse, and he watched her very soberly.

Jesse, I *am* grateful for everything! she thought. And I do love you.

But there was no way to let him know her thoughts. Nor did she want to—he was holding himself away from her and from everything that he should profess to love.

His somber eyes did not leave hers as talk continued.

Though he was invited, Jesse declined dinner. He swept his hat off to wish them all a good day.

There was nothing that Kiernan could do then but watch him leave the house. She felt a touch on her shoulder. It was Anthony. He put his arm around her. "My God, Kiernan, you're safe!" he whispered. "It is all that I prayed for, night and day, since we heard the news. I vowed my life for yours, but there was no way to give it."

I can't marry you, Anthony, she thought. The words were in her heart and on her lips.

But she couldn't say them, not now. She forced a smile, and feeling ill, she returned inside with Anthony.

Daniel Cameron had remained. He told them that their trip to Pleasant Valley the night before had yielded no sign of rebellion. "Just sleepy farmers and slaves who were afraid of John Brown more than they were intrigued by him."

"So it's really over with then," John Mackay said with satisfaction.

"All but the trial and the hanging," Daniel said.

The men continued talking, and Kiernan realized that Daniel was watching her closely.

She pleaded exhaustion and fled from them all, upstairs to the haven of her room.

In the morning she learned that Jesse had been called back to Washington.

Kiernan didn't see Jesse again until John Brown's trial, which began on October 27.

Brown had been brought to Charles Town, which lay a

few miles from Harpers Ferry, the day after his capture. He and four other captured raiders were arraigned on the twenty-fifth, and the next day they were indicted for treason against the Commonwealth of Virginia, for conspiring with slaves to rebel, and for murder. Each defendant pleaded not guilty, and each asked for a separate trial.

The trials began with Brown's.

John Mackay was determined to attend, as were Anthony and Andrew Miller and Thomas Donahue.

They all frowned upon Kiernan's attending, and she wasn't sure if she wanted to be there herself.

But she knew that Jesse would be there. She was certain that the prosecution would demand that he be on hand if they needed him as a witness.

Anthony had remained very kind. She did love him, she realized, as a very dear and important friend, one whom she would never injure, if it was in her power to avoid it. There would one day be a way to talk him. But for now she managed to evade his determination to propose an engagement. When he pressed her, she came up with the excuse that she hadn't received all the education that she desired.

"Kiernan," he had told her politely one evening, "we are not getting any younger."

He didn't mean *we*—he meant *her*. For some reason, men were allowed to marry at any age they chose. He was, as always, unerringly tactful in reminding her that she was already eighteen, several years older than most women in her social class were when they married.

"Then Anthony, perhaps you should look elsewhere."

"We'll speak of it later," he assured her quickly. "Kiernan, take your time, study where you will. All the more will you grace my house."

"Anthony, I am not sure—"

"There is no other woman I could want."

"Anthony," she said in a rush, "I'm not sure that I love you."

"But I love you. Enough for both of us. Kiernan, nothing that you can say will dissuade me."

Not even the fact that I have slept with another man? she wondered in silence.

Or that I love that other man? Have always loved him?

She knew that she had to speak the truth. But she didn't know how to do it without wounding him.

When they arrived at the Charles Town courtroom, she knew that she should have been more decisive. Anthony was escorting her when she looked across the room and saw that Jesse had already arrived—and that he was watching her upon Anthony's arm.

It was amazing that he had spotted her so quickly, she thought. The courtroom was packed.

There was a tremendous commotion, but then Judge Parker brought the court to order.

John Brown, still suffering from his wounds, was brought in on a cot. Kiernan stared at him, searching for something in the man to confirm what she had heard. She was not disappointed. His eyes did burn. As they moved about the courtroom, she felt a distinct unease.

The prisoner had barely come in and order had just been called when one of his defense attorneys began to make a plea for him. He read a telegram from A. H. Lewis of Ohio who stated that there were many instances of insanity within Brown's family. Clemency was the suggestion.

It was an intriguing defense stratagem, Kiernan thought, one that might well save the man's life.

Except that John Brown wasn't about to allow it. He stood, rising from his cot with considerable dignity, and denied that he was insane.

He would not be sent to an institution; he would not have his life salvaged. He had known what he was doing, and he believed in the right of it.

Watching him, Kiernan was startled by the pity she felt for the man. He frightened her, and yet she was sorry for him. She could not admire him, yet she could admire his conviction.

As the day dragged on, proof of his treason was read out time and time again, and she believed more and more that he truly thought himself a servant of God, and that although he had shed blood, he regretted that blood must darken the land.

She left the courtroom that first day with a great deal of confusion. And in that confusion, she wanted to see Jesse.

She saw him sooner than she had expected. As she was leaving the courtroom on Anthony's arm, she ran right into him. He stepped back, and lifted his hat to her and to Anthony. "Kiernan, Anthony. What a pleasure."

His voice was edged with sarcasm, and his eyes held a distinctively mocking light when they fell upon her.

Anthony shook Jesse's hand and greeted him enthusiastically, and then her father was there and Andrew Miller and Thomas Donahue, and the men became quickly involved in conversation. Before she knew it, they had invited Jesse to dinner with them.

Well, she had wanted to see him. But not with half of the world present, and the only conversation that of the trial.

She held her breath, waiting to see if Jesse would decline the invitation.

He did not. "I'd enjoy the companionship," he said, and turned to Kiernan. "And of course, the presence of such a fine lady."

They met in two hours in the restaurant of the hotel where they were staying. Eager as she was to see Jesse alone, Kiernan was hard pressed to remain graciously with the others for long as they spoke outside the courtroom. She tried to respond appropriately to their conversation, she tried to remain calm and demure lest her father grew suspicious. But the first second that she could, she excused herself and bolted for her room. In the short time she had before dinner, she ordered a bath and scrubbed her hair with perfumed shampoo. With furious energy, she towel-dried her honey-colored tresses. Then she dressed in an elegant peach and yellow gown with draping white linen sleeves and tore down to the dining room, hoping to meet Jesse before the others arrived.

The place was a madhouse with all the people in town attending the trial. Kiernan looked anxiously about but did not see Jesse. The tuxedoed maître d' of the restaurant found her, and bowing low, he informed her that Captain Cameron had reserved a room for their party.

She reached the doorway and saw Jesse standing by one of the chairs, sipping a full drink. He was in full dress uniform, dark, handsome, exciting. Her heart was suddenly still as she watched him.

He sensed that she was there and turned to her. Their eyes met, and for a moment, her need to rush into his arms seemed to be overwhelming. In only a second, her heart and limbs would have taken flight.

"Ah, here you are, Cameron, Kiernan. Jesse, I do say, what a fine thing you've done for us all, thinking to reserve this privacy!"

She didn't move. Her heart sank, and her limbs did not take flight. Anthony was behind her, setting his hands tenderly upon her shoulders. Though Jesse's eyes continued to meet hers, he spoke casually to Anthony.

"I was expected that there might be a crowd and thought of reserving space."

Then her father came in, and Andrew and Thomas. Kiernan found herself seated in between Anthony and her father, and across from Jesse.

"Well, Jesse," John Mackay demanded, making a broad motion as he unfolded his napkin and set it upon his lap. "What did you think of the proceedings today? Brown could easily have grabbed hold of that insanity plea, by Jove! There's a madman if I've ever seen one."

"Sir, he's a fanatic, certainly. If that makes him a madman, I'm not certain."

"Bah!" Andrew Miller said irritably. "He's mad. And dangerous. And a fool. He thinks that he has the word of the Lord in his ears! Well, let me tell you, the Lord says otherwise. In the Bible the good Lord said, 'Slaves, obey your masters.' Isn't that right, Captain Cameron?"

Kiernan stared at Jesse, praying that he wouldn't be difficult at the dinner table.

Jesse shrugged. "Mr. Miller, I'm afraid that I wasn't a very good Bible student."

"What are you saying, sir?" Andrew Miller, his face

flushed, demanded. "You don't think that Brown will hang
—or that he deserves to?"

"Oh yes, he'll hang," Jesse said. "And by any law, he
deserves to do so."

Andrew settled back. Lacey's husband, Thomas, looked
acutely uncomfortable. He was Andrew's friend and a
strong advocate of states' rights, but he didn't believe in
slavery himself.

Jesse leaned forward. "Gentlemen, we've a lady present at
the table. I suggest we cease to discuss politics for the duration of the meal."

Kiernan was deeply annoyed when her father literally
snorted, "Kiernan? Why, Jesse, you know my girl as well as
anyone!"

Jesse smiled at her. "Probably better," he offered pleasantly.

"Then you know she's not in the least offended by talk of
politics."

"My, my," Kiernan murmured sweetly, "it must be the
company I keep!" She side-kicked her father. He yelped and
stared at her and frowned warningly, but she continued to
smile sweetly. "Humor me, Father," she said. "Let's do
cease with all of this for a while."

There were plays to discuss, their land, the military itself,
the trip that the men in partnership had taken into the
mountains. The food offered by the hotel was very good, but
Kiernan barely tasted hers. She grew restless as coffee was
served to them in elegant silver pitchers. The meal would
end soon. Maybe then she'd have a chance to talk to Jesse.

But it wasn't to be. Jesse barely touched his coffee. He
stood and told them that he had an appointment for a drink
with an old army friend and bade them good night, bowing
handsomely to Kiernan.

The trial lasted two and half more days. Kiernan sat
through the entirety of it. She listened to John Brown, and
she listened to the witnesses. She was torn. What had happened had been horrible—John Brown had committed murder. He had come with hundreds of pikes with which to arm

slaves. If he had created an insurrection, hundreds of people might have been brutally murdered in cold blood.

Yet there was something about the man. He would not be quickly forgotten.

On October 31, closing arguments were given. The case was handed over to the jury at one thirty in the afternoon.

The jury deliberated for forty-five minutes. The verdict came in. John Brown was guilty on all three counts. Old Ossawatomie Brown was going to be hanged by the neck until dead.

Kiernan had expected shouts and cries from the crowd that so often upon the steps of the courthouse had shouted threats and insults upon the man.

But there was silence, dead silence.

Brown himself merely adjusted the pallet on his cot and stretched out upon it.

Kiernan looked across the courtroom. Jesse took his eyes from Brown and stared at her. He seemed sad—no, stricken, almost anguished. She felt his stare like a touch. But people stood all around them. In seconds, they were lost to each other in the crowd. "Daughter, it's done. Let's go," her father told her. She was led from the courtroom on his arm.

With the trial over, Kiernan knew that Jesse would be riding back to Washington. But she had to see him alone one last time.

She didn't know when she would see him again.

He would be joining them for dinner again, as he had every night, but sitting through those meals with the others in attendance had been pure misery. She would have escaped those occasions if she could have. No matter how polite Jesse was, how careful with his words, he still refused to lie about his convictions about the political situation. Sometimes his comments were nearly traitorous to the life that they led, traitorous for a Tidewater Virginian.

When he wasn't creating tension at the table, he was watching her and Anthony with that rueful twist of his lip and pained and bitter mockery in his eyes.

This last night, Kiernan dressed carefully for dinner. She chose a gown with a soft underskirt and an overskirt and bodice of deep blue velvet. The sleeves and low-cut bodice were trimmed lightly with fur against the chill of the night. She swept her hair back cleanly but allowed tendrils of golden-red curls to escape the coil and frame her face. She stepped back from her hotel room mirror and surveyed her image.

Anthony was right—she *was* growing older. Her eyes seemed very old. But she wasn't displeased with her image. The gown was beautiful, and it displayed an ample amount of bosom and shoulder without being too daring. The color was perfect for her, and the gown was perfect for a proper evening out with her father and friends.

And it was perfect for reminding Jesse that she was a grown-up woman, one with whom he had made love.

She wasn't going to mind dinner that night, she determined. She was going to find a chance to tell him that she needed to see him alone.

She hurried down to the dining room they had shared every evening. To her dismay, her father and Andrew were already seated. Thomas Donahue came in immediately behind her. A smile crinkled his pleasant, weathered old face, and he paused to tell her that she was a beautiful sight for old and weary eyes. She smiled in turn. Thomas was very dear.

When Anthony arrived, he brushed her cheek with a kiss and pulled back her chair.

"I wonder where Jesse has gotten himself to," John Mackay said to no one in particular.

"There's a lot of military brass around," Anthony said, unknowingly defending his rival. "Perhaps he has been waylaid."

Their waiter arrived with a message on a small silver tray. John took the message and crumpled it in his hand. "The boy's running late. He says that we should go ahead and order, and he'll be along as soon as he can."

Kiernan jumped out of her chair, so restless that she could no longer bear it. She had to see Jesse.

All eyes turned to her.

"There's a chill in the air," she told her father regally. "If you gentlemen will just excuse me—"

But Anthony was up too. "If you need a wrap, Kiernan, I would be delighted to fetch it for you."

"Oh, thank you, Anthony, but I'm not sure that I left the stole I want in my room. I might have left it in the sofa by the registrar. Stay, please." She gave him one of her most charming smiles, then added, "Really, you gentlemen go on and talk without me. I'll be just a few minutes."

Her father's blue eyes were downright suspicious, but Kiernan ignored them. She left the room and moved quickly through the dining room beyond.

She knew that she'd have to have a wrap when she returned, so she raced upstairs to her room and grabbed the stole, which was on the foot of her bed—exactly where she knew it would be. She raced back down the main stairway and outside to the huge veranda that surrounded the hotel.

It was quiet out there. All the conversation was going on inside. The night was cool and beautiful.

She looked down the street, into the darkness of the night. Jesse was staying at a different hotel and would arrive from the north.

But when would he come?

She gazed across the road to the livery stable, and with a sudden spurt of energy she flew down the few steps from the porch to the road and hurried across the street.

To her amazement, she discovered him coming around the side of the stable. There was foliage all about, and she might not have recognized him in the darkness, except that she knew him so well—his walk, the tilt of his hat.

"Jesse!"

She breathed out his name, and he saw her. Before she knew what she was doing, she raced along the trail toward him.

She threw herself into his arms, pressed her lips to his with a starved hunger, and nearly burst with the sweet fervor of the kiss he gave her in return, his tongue filling her mouth, his passion robbing her of breath and reason. As he held her against him, she felt their hearts beating like the wings of eagles. She felt the coolness of the night and the soaring heat between them. Slowly, he eased her down to her feet and stared into her eyes. She flushed and lowered her face.

"Where's poor Anthony?" he asked her.

"In—in the restaurant."

"Did you tell him that you're not going to marry him?"

"I tried to."

"Tried?"

"He can be very stubborn."

"Just tell him that you're going to marry me."

She looked up at him, searching his eyes. Her fingers wound around the button of his cape. "But I'm not going to marry you, Jesse. Not until you see things the right way."

"Your way?" he quizzed. He arched a brow and spoke very softly. He bent down and pressed a kiss to the corner of her mouth. He rubbed his tongue lightly, slowly, across her lower lip, caught it between his teeth, then kissed it very tenderly. She pressed against him, savoring the warmth of him and the sheer luxury of touching him. "The right way is your way?" he repeated.

"Yes, my way," she murmured. "Oh, Jesse—"

Suddenly, swiftly, he set her aside. "So now what, Kiernan? You flirt and tease and torment poor Anthony until I come around to your way of thinking?"

Her eyes narrowed sharply, furiously. "Who is to say that I am tormenting him, Jesse? Dear Lord, he's a better man than you, so it seems!"

She was suddenly seized so tightly that she could scarcely breathe. "In what way, Kiernan? Is he a better man when he kisses you, touches you? Have you decided to test your greatest powers upon Anthony too?"

"Let go of me, you arrogant Yank!" she spat out. "How dare you suggest such things! Anthony is far too noble—"

"Anthony is far too besotted a fool, Kiernan," Jesse said bluntly. "He hasn't been making love to you in dark corners. He allows you to dangle him along at your whim and asks for nothing in return but one of those devastating smiles. Well, I'm not Anthony, Kiernan. I love you, but my mind is my own, and I cannot change what I see as right or wrong for you or for anyone else. Do you understand that?"

She understood that he was rejecting her—and his own life-style—because of something that might or might not happen in the future.

She tried to wrench free of him, torn by the pain. "Don't you ever touch me again, Jesse Cameron!"

"Touch you? Why, Miss Mackay! Do correct me if I'm wrong, but I could have sworn that you came soaring across the earth to land in my arms."

"How very, very rude of you to put it so."

"That, too, is because I am not the driveling Anthony."

Once again, he pulled her closer, so close that she could feel the hot whisper of his breath, so very close that she could feel the excitement of his body. Enter her . . . warm her, stir her.

"Kiernan, I love you. I am the man for you, the only one to know you and to love you. But you won't rule me. Do you understand? I'd give you everything that I can give you, but there are certain things that I cannot give. When you're ready to accept me for what I am, for what I believe, come to me." He smiled at her then, a smile that was bittersweet, anguished, and crooked with a wry humor that mocked himself as well as her. "If you're lucky, I'll be waiting."

"Oh!" she cried, but he was holding her too tightly against him for her to injure him. "You bastard!"

"I know," he agreed. He kissed her again, her hard, with passion and insinuation. He kissed her so long and so completely that she felt that she had been ravished there on the streets. He kissed her until she had no breath, until her limbs were powerless, until the hot fires of desire raced ruthlessly through her.

Then he set her down. "Until then, little girl," he demanded harshly, "torment me no longer!"

He tipped his hat and walked on by her. Kiernan was left to look after him in amazement.

For a moment she felt as if he had given her a physical blow, a strike to the cheek—no, to her heart.

Then her pride raced to her salvation, and she swept past

him. With her back to him she said icily, "Please inform my father that I've retired for the evening because I'm feeling ill."

He caught her arm and pulled her back. His eyes were light, and his smile was tender.

"No. He'd never believe that you were suddenly ill. You're simply not the type for vapors, Kiernan."

"Fine!" she snapped. "We'll dine!" She strode on before him, pausing only once to swirl back around. "Don't wait for me, Jesse. My loyalties are fierce."

She preceded him across the street, and they dined. The conversation was easy-flowing and polite, and anyone in the room would have said that it was a comfortable dinner among good friends.

And then it ended. Jesse rose and bade the men good night, telling them that he was riding back to Washington that evening.

He paused by Kiernan. He lifted her hand to his lips, and his eyes met hers. "Good evening, Kiernan," he told her softly. "It's been a pleasure."

"Indeed, it has, Captain," she said with regal dignity. She withdrew her hand and kept her eyes steady upon his. "Good-bye, Captain," she said flatly.

He nodded, pulled the brim of his plumed hat low, and exited the room in long strides.

Moments later, she heard the thunder of his horse's hooves as he rode out of town.

And out of her life.

Eight

Kiernan would not attend the hanging—Jesse knew that. She wouldn't even be allowed, and if she were, she would not come. He had no chance of seeing her there.

And he shouldn't see her. They had both laid their positions on the line. He couldn't compromise on this. If he saw her, he would want her, want to insist that she forget Anthony, that she marry him and cling to him as a wife should.

And accept whatever he chose to do in the future.

He'd already asked her to marry him. He couldn't force her to do so. Even if he wished a thousand times over that he could kidnap her and force his will upon her, he knew it would never work. Anthony would feel honor-bound to challenge him in some way, and he had no desire to hurt Anthony.

But she didn't love Anthony. Jesse knew that she was in love with him—she had told him so.

He'd never meant to touch her. But when he had seen her standing upon the chair and looking down upon him in the shack along the river, he felt as if he had always meant to touch her.

Maybe he'd been in love before that day. But seeing her in the sunfire light of that shack, seeing the gold of her hair and the sparkling emerald of her eyes, the softness of her flesh, and breathed the scent of her he knew he'd never be free of her again. He could deny that he was like Anthony, but it wasn't true. She haunted his days, as she haunted Anthony's, and she was a tempest in his nights.

He'd had no right to her, knowing that his conscience came between them. But in his arrogance he had thought that she wouldn't be able to stay away, that she would love him more than any belief or ideal once they had been together.

He had been wrong.

Still, he came back to Charles Town. He was stationed in Washington, and he had plenty of leave time as the day set for John Brown's hanging drew near. So he determined that he would ride out and attend. He had been there at the beginning of the drama involving old John Brown. He might as well be there at the end.

It was December 2, 1859. The day was cold, but clear.

Since the trial, a number of restrictions had been placed on Charles Town. Many feared that an escape plot was being hatched outside the city, and a proclamation had been handed out that visitors would be arrested for trying to enter Charles Town. Only the military were allowed to the immediate execution site.

But that didn't keep civilians from the Charles Town streets, or from following the events as closely as they could. People came out in masses to see old John Brown head out for his hanging.

Jesse rode into the town alone with his military pass and remained upon Pegasus, keeping his distance from the general fanfare. A curious mood of a celebration was stirring much of the crowd, along with a somber element too. John Brown had committed murder, and he had committed treason, but he had comported himself well in court. Jesse sensed that he would become a martyr in the North. Even Governor Wise, after questioning him about the raid, said that he was "the gamest man I ever saw."

"Cameron!"

Jesse was startled to hear his name called, and he turned to see Anthony Miller. Miller was with his local militia unit, but he broke away from them to ride to Jesse's side. A broad grin was spread across his face as he offered Jesse his hand. "Come for the hanging, eh?"

Jesse shook his hand, then shrugged. "I've come to see the end, I guess."

"And a damned good thing it is," Anthony announced flatly. Jesse didn't have a response to that, but Anthony didn't seem to need one. "There are a number of interesting folks here for this. One of our esteemed senators, over there. And that man with the Richmond Grays is an actor. I've seen him perform—he's excellent. His name is Boots or something like that. Booth, that's it. John Booth. If you ever get a chance, you should see him perform. Yes, there are lots of interesting people gathered here."

"Any of my neighbors?" Jesse asked. He wanted to know about Kiernan. She wouldn't be at the hanging, but she could be in town. He couldn't bring himself to ask.

"You mean John Mackay?"

He meant Kiernan Mackay.

"Yes."

Anthony shrugged. "No, I'm not expecting John." Anthony tilted his hat back. "Kiernan's gone and gotten this idea she needs more education. What a girl like that needs with more education, I'll never know. I just want to get married and end all this back-and-forth business. I guess I could never make you understand just how badly. But she's got it in her head to go to Europe for a while. Says there's a fine finishing school in London." He shook his head, confused and hurt. "John's on the coast, seeing her off."

Jesse nodded. His heart leaped to his throat, then slammed down hard against his chest.

So she wasn't with Anthony. She wasn't a complete fool. She was heading across the ocean to watch things from a distance.

"When is she coming back?"

"I imagine in about a year."

A year. So much could happen in a year.

"Excuse me," Anthony went on, "I've got my troops over there. You're welcome to join us. There'll be a dinner at my father's house later."

"Thanks, but I've got to ride back to Washington tonight," Jesse told him.

He couldn't get into a party mood after a hanging. Whether a man deserved to die or not, it was an ugly way to meet one's maker.

And still, he understood the way a lot of the folks felt. John Brown had attacked them. He had come into Harpers Ferry to create an insurrection. When he had gone after the slaveholders in the West, he had murdered them in cold blood, dragging the men from their beds, slaying them with swords before their loved ones. The battle in Kansas and Missouri had been an ugly one. John Brown had shown no mercy. It was fitting that he should die.

But still, he really believed in the freedom for all men that he preached.

"You're not one of those—" Anthony began. "You're not one of those people who think that Brown should be set free?"

Jesse looked at him steadily. "He broke the law," Jesse said. "He committed murder and treason. No, Anthony, I'm not one of those—people—who think that."

Anthony grinned, abashed. "Sorry. I didn't mean to imply that you were one of those bleeding-heart abolitionists. Hell, you've got slaves yourself back at Cameron Hall."

Yes, he did, Jesse thought. A number of them. Cameron Hall was still a working plantation, and he understood the economic position of the South as well as anyone.

They had freed a number of their slaves, though, he and Daniel and Christa. He'd discussed the issue with his father several years ago, before his death. They'd agreed they wouldn't buy any new slaves at auctions. If a slave married a slave from another plantation, they'd purchase the wife or child. They'd also establish a way for the men and women to earn their freedom and hope that they'd want to stay on as paid workers.

But it was compromise, Jesse realized. All compromise, and he was guilty of it. Washington and Jefferson had made the same compromise. They'd believed in freeing slaves. Jefferson had wanted the slaves freed when he'd written the Declaration of Independence.

But he'd been convinced that he'd never get the states together if he tried to do such a thing.

All these years later the situation hadn't improved.

"It's been good to see you, Jesse," Anthony told him. "Don't forget, you're welcome anytime."

"Thanks, Anthony."

Anthony lifted his hat again and rode off. Jesse watched him go.

He felt the sun on his face and looked up, hearing the movement of restless cavalry horses. The troops were well disciplined, even if there was a tremendous amount of fanfare.

His mind wandered to Kiernan.

She was gone, Jesse thought. Kiernan was gone, to where he couldn't reach her. It was just as well.

Jesse waited, feeling the sun on him. He felt a little bit numb.

At the appointed time, John Brown appeared. He was brought along in a horse-drawn cart, his hands bound behind him. He rode in silence, sitting straight with quiet dignity.

He sat upon his own coffin.

He stepped from the cart with dignity and walked to the gallows the same way.

A hush fell over the military crowd. Sheriff John W. Campbell pulled a white linen hood over the prisoner's head, then set the noose around his neck. The jailor asked Brown to step forward onto the trap.

"You must lead me," Brown said, his voice steady, "for I cannot see."

The jailor availed him and adjusted the noose.

"Be quick," Brown said.

A hatchet stroke sprang the trap, and with an awful sound, the body dropped through.

John Brown was dead.

There was complete silence. Suddenly, the voice of a militiaman broke the silence.

"So perish all such enemies of Virginia! All such enemies
of the Union! All such enemies of the human race!"

Jesse felt no such sense of elation. By due process of law,
John Brown had been hanged on a beautiful winter morning.

Brown had said little enough at the moment of his execution, but Jesse couldn't forget some of the things that the
man had said and written earlier—especially the words he
had written to one of his guards not long before his date
with the hangman.

"The crimes of this guilty land: will never be purged
away; but with blood."

John Brown was dead. It was over.

It was just beginning.

Jesse turned his horse.

And in his heart, he rode north.

2

A House
Divided

Nine

Near Cameron Hall, Tidewater Virginia
December 20, 1860

Kiernan sat on her dapple-gray mare high atop the forested ridge overlooking Cameron Hall.

The morning sun had just risen. Dewdrops played upon the sweeping lawn like a carpet of diamonds. The main house, regal with its soaring white columns, stood in the center of the manicured portion of the property. Behind the house were handsome gardens that in the summer were filled with the scent of roses. The house was one of the oldest in Tidewater Virginia, the original structure having been built soon after the Indian massacre of 1622. Jesse's great-great-great—she really wasn't sure how many greats—grandparents had lovingly laid the first brick and set their names upon it. They had built with beauty and a deep affinity for their new land.

The house had weathered the ravages of time to remain one of the most gracious plantation homes on the James River.

There was a wide breezeway, and on pleasant days, the doors on both ends of the house were cast open so that the soft cool air from the river whispered throughout the wide-open hallway and into the house. The porches became an extension of the hallway, open, inviting, touched by the breeze.

Two large wings had been added to the house just after the Revolution, and they extended gracefully to either side. The kitchen, smokehouse, laundry, bakehouse, stables, and slave quarters entended from the right of the house toward the cliff, from which Kiernan now looked upon the activity of the busy plantation. Close to where she sat upon her mare, near a copse of trees and foliage and the river's edge, was the family cemetery. Camerons had been buried there ever since Lord Cameron, who had built the place, and his beloved Jassy had been tenderly laid to rest by their heirs. Now handsome monuments stood in the plot, enclosed by an ornate wrought-iron fence, with beautifully sculpted angels and madonnas and renditions of Christ. The cemetery itself was beautiful and graceful and spoke of a rich heritage.

From where she sat her horse, Kiernan could see past the sloping lawns that fell from the left side of the house and to the numerous fields beyond, fields of the stuff that had built the South: cotton and tobacco.

No one could ask for a finer home or a more prestigious heritage. The sons of Cameron Hall had always been held up to gentlemen of the state and beyond as fine prospects for their daughters. It was a home that any woman would envy. From her sentinel upon the mount, Kiernan thought it embodied everything stately and gracious and beautiful in the world. How she had missed it during her year abroad! With a tinge of shame she realized that she loved Cameron Hall more than she loved her own home nearby. It too, was beautiful, built of brick and mortar and stone, and it was gracious and pleasant. But it was barely fifty years old. It hadn't weathered the centuries as Cameron Hall had. It didn't have the personality of its James River neighbor. It didn't seem to live and breathe and be so much a part of this world.

She breathed in deeply. The air was sweet with the scents of early morning bread-baking and ham-smoking. The air that came in from the river was decidedly cold today, but she didn't care. She knew the dampness and the cold of winter, just as she knew the humidity and heat of summer.

This was home. She had been away a long time, and this
morning she wasn't at all sure why she had tormented herself for so long.

At first, leaving had seemed to be the only way to escape
marriage to Anthony without being downright cruel.

It had also been a way to escape Jesse. His assignment had
been Washington when she left, and that had been far too
close. She knew that Jesse had wanted his assignment to be
close to home when he was just out of West Point. His father
had still been living then, and his father had been military
all of his life.

Then Jesse had traveled with the cavalry out west and had
spent time fighting Indians at the tail end of the action in
Mexico.

And he had spent time in "bleeding Kansas" as the government tried to put some kind of restraint on the horror
there. Kiernan had known a great deal of what was going on
in his life then. She and Daniel had always been good correspondents. He had felt the need to put things on paper to
her, and she had been more than willing to keep him advised
about things back home. She had always scanned his missives for information about Jesse. She had always known
what he was doing.

And she knew now.

The year she had spent in Europe had been a tense one on
this side of the Atlantic—electric, frightening. In London
she had avidly sought every piece of information about the
states that she could find. She had read political commentar-
ies by the dozens.

Old John Brown had become a martyr. The northern abolitionists had rallied to make sure that his death would never
be forgotten. They sang, "John Brown's body lies
a-moulderin' in his grave." And Harriet Beecher Stowe's
Old Tom's Cabin continued to fan the flames of fury.

But the worse thing that had happened had been the election of Abraham Lincoln. The South just couldn't stomach
it.

Before the election, Kiernan had hoped that the political
climate would quiet down, that various sections of the coun-

try would manage to live with their differences—as they had been doing since the Revolution.

But as soon as she had heard the results, she had come home. She had arrived in time to discover that South Carolina was planning a convention and that it would vote on the matter of secession. Other states were following that example—Florida, Mississippi, and Tennessee, just to name a few. The feeling was that South Carolina would secede. So would the other states.

So far, though, Virginia seemed to be watching the action. Careful, cautious, dignified, the homeland of so many of the founding fathers, Virginia would watch.

Many Virginia sons, however, were not so cautious. Young men and old men everywhere were forming up into new militia units. Rich men were buying up horses and designing uniforms and purchasing arms. Poor men were seeking to serve beneath them.

If it came to war, they would be prepared.

Many of the South's finest were either enlisted men or commissioned officers in the United States Army—Robert E. Lee and Jeb Stuart, among others.

And the Cameron brothers.

Daniel had written that he had been considering resigning his position, but neither he nor Jesse had done so as yet. Few men had resigned their positions. It remained to be seen just how many would. And of course, it remained to be seen what South Carolina and the other states would do.

The sun rose further into the sky as Kiernan sat upon her mare, surveying the scene below her. She had headed for home the moment that she had heard about the presidential election. From the time her ship had left the London docks, she had felt a growing excitement. Every step of the way, she had wondered why she had ever left home at such a crucial time. London was fascinating, her school for young ladies was entertaining, but she realized the moment she arrived that she had outgrown school. It had been a time of waiting for her, a time for reflecting.

And a time for dreams, for she had not managed to leave Jesse behind. She had been disappointed the previous November to discover that she was not in the family way. Such a situation might have swayed her hand. *Would* have, she thought, a small smile tugging at her lips. Her father would have had Jesse walking down the aisle at gunpoint had it been necessary. But it was not necessary.

How had she slept through so very many nights, when all she could do was remember him? She thought endlessly of him, reliving all that had happened between them. She had met many young men in London, some of them titled, some of them very rich. She had played the games by all the right rules that a young woman should play, and she had tried to fall out of love with Jesse and into love with someone else. She watched as many of her friends were married off according to the dictates of their parents, and she had been extremely grateful for her father's leniency. But none of it mattered. She didn't need a wealthy man, for her father was a wealthy man. She was unimpressed by titles, and she was, in truth, far more fond of Anthony and Daniel than she was of any of the young men she met in London drawing rooms or chose as escorts for a night of London theater.

Perhaps Jesse was right about her, she mused. She had enjoyed the flirting. She had enjoyed having young men flock about her and marvel at her soft Virginia accent, lose their voices when they spoke with her, and turn beet-red in their attempts to be charming in turn. It had been fun to test her power, she reflected.

Except that she had returned to her small school bedroom every evening to feel a painful ache where she should have felt triumphant. Games could never again be as innocent as they once had been. If she tormented others, it was because she was tormented herself.

She was very afraid that she would be tormented until the day that she died. Jesse had done that to her.

She sighed softly and heard the whisper of her breath join with that of the breeze.

What now? What could she do? Stay in love with Jesse, hold Anthony off indefinitely, pray that he would find someone else himself?

Or give up her own beliefs?

No. She could never give up her passion for this place, for this land. Surely, surely, Jesse would never really be able to do that either.

Now that events were growing critical, Jesse would have to change his heart and his mind. This very place, Cameron Hall, could be in jeopardy. Everything that he loved.

"My, my. To what do we owe this fine pleasure?"

Kiernan nearly leaped from her side-saddle when she heard the husky drawl. Her heart thudded against her rib cage as she turned quickly with surprise. It was Jesse. She knew it long before she saw his face. She would know his voice anywhere, she had heard it in her dreams a thousand times, she had felt the sensual whisper along her spine in long cold nights when she had fought hard against the memories of that she had sworn she would forget.

She looked at his face. She wondered how he had come upon her so silently, or if she had simply been so lost in her reflections that her senses had betrayed her.

He stood some distance from her, having dismounted from his horse, the fine huge roan, Pegasus. He had bred Pegasus at Cameron Hall, and he had brought him into the cavalry with him. Pegasus was impeccably trained, but no horse standing nearly seventeen hands high could tiptoe through brush.

And neither could Jesse—but there he was, indisputably, almost upon her. Tall, striking, standing still in the tall grass, the breeze lifting his hair and pulling upon the cotton of his white open-necked shirt. He was dressed as a civilian in buff-colored breeches and high black boots, dressed as the master of Cameron Hall. His hair seemed exceptionally dark, and his eyes, even at this distance, seemed exceptionally blue. He held Pegasus's reins and stood with his feet planted firm, his legs apart upon the incline of the mound, as a slow smile curved his lip.

"So you've come home," he said softly.

"And so have you."

His lashes fell over his eyes and his smile was broad when

he raised his gaze to her once again. "I'm not supposed to be here?"

"I—I did think that you were in Washington."

"Please, don't let the rudeness of my presence destroy your visit. Is my sister expecting you?"

She shook her head. "No one is expecting me."

She had changed—and then again, she hadn't, Jesse thought. She appeared more sophisticated than ever. Surely her riding habit was the latest in French fashion. The cut of the green velvet creation was a very tailored one, but the sharp-angled brim of her green-feathered bonnet lent both femininity and elegance to the outfit. Beneath the closely fitted jacket of the ensemble she wore a laced shirt that added to the very feminine grace of the habit, despite its almost masculine cut.

She wore it well. Seated atop the dapple-gray mare, she was the very height of sophistication and beauty. In fact, she was stunning. Her eyes defied the emerald splendor of the dew-kissed grasses. Her hair, entwined in rich braids and pinned at her nape, took up the colors of the sun and shone with a fiery splendor. And she seemed older, and perhaps wiser, for there was a curious sadness about her gaze.

Watching her, Jesse felt the pain that he thought he had buried come to life again. He clenched and unclenched his fingers, and a heat like the radiating play of the sun upon naked flesh in summer came upon him. It was bittersweet to see her, to have her here before him, to remember what it had been to touch her.

Surely there was no difference among women, he told himself. One was surely the same as the other in the darkness.

But it wasn't true at all. No woman felt the same as Kiernan did, even in the dark. No woman carried the same sweet scent, no one whispered or sighed the same.

With dark fury, he suddenly wished with all his heart that she had married Anthony. He might have purged her from his dreams and his life if only she had done so.

"What are you doing here, Kiernan?" he said suddenly, fiercely.

She stiffened upon her mount. "It's wonderful to see you too, Jesse," she said coolly.

"You're trespassing."

"My Lord, your manners haven't improved—" she began, but he dropped the roan's reins and strode toward her with long steps. She started to back her mare away, but his hands were already upon the mare's bridle, holding her steady. Before she knew it, he was reaching up to her.

"Jesse, what do you think you're—"

She fell silent, for she knew what he was doing. He was lifting her down and into his arms. All the winter's cold was instantly dispelled as he wrapped her tightly into his embrace. He kissed her hard and savagely, suffusing her body with all the warmth of his own, and with the memory of all the splendor.

His hand gently moved over her chin, exploring bone structure and texture. But his eyes were savage as his thumb caressed the softness of her cheek, and his body was rock hard as it pressed against hers. She was caught between the man and the horse, and she was vulnerable to the ferocity of his power.

"My God, I have missed you!" he whispered. "You can't imagine what it's been like. In every drawing room where I have been a guest I've listened to the sound of rustling silk, and I've prayed that I could turn and see you there. And every damned night I've lain awake and thought of you, and even when I've slept, my dreams have been plagued by you. Every time I touched a woman's hair, it seemed coarse in my hands because it was not yours, it wasn't the color of fire, and it did not have the sheen of satin and the feel of velvet and silk. Words whispered have never been the same, you witch! Damn you. Damn you a thousand times over!"

She stared into his eyes, and she felt the heat and the hatred within them.

And she felt so much more. She felt the need in his touch. She felt the hunger and tension in the body pressed so closely to hers. And when he ruthlessly lowered his mouth to hers once again, she parted her lips by instinct and responded with a sweet memory that swept away the time that lay between them.

She was back in his arms again. Nothing else mattered.

She broke away from him, aware of the fires that had been ignited between them. Desire that lay dormant when he was not near rose to the surface of her being. It felt as if her heart beat for him, as if her every breath was for him, as if her limbs flamed for him, as if she were split apart by the fires that burned and radiated from deep within her. She needed desperately to be with him.

She moistened her lips and met his hot gaze. She struggled for breath, then for the sound to make a whisper. "Where can we go?"

He grinned broadly, and she realized that he had voiced that question a year before.

And that she had taken him to the haven.

"I'll show you," he replied softly.

They left the horses in the field atop the mount as he caught her hand and brought her running swiftly down the slope. It seemed in only seconds that they were racing by the cemetery and plunging into the dense foliage that lined the river to the left of the docks. They scurried through a trail of brush and trees until they came to a copse wherein stood an elegant white gazebo, a summer cottage. Like the manor, it was built with a breezeway. Octagonal in shape, its etched-glass doors would welcome the breezes from the river if opened, and yet warm the place against the damp chills of winter. She should have known the place. She had come there often enough as a child.

Now Jesse opened the double doors, which had been closed against the December cold. He led her inside, closed the door again, and leaned against it. For a long time he stood staring at her, and she was suddenly afraid of why she had come, and at the same time she felt a growing pleasure and longing sweep through her. He looked so damned good. The white of his shirt emphasized the bronze of his face and throat. The simple cotton enhanced the structure of his shoulders and torso and arms. His face seemed more lined, she thought, etched more deeply around his eyes. But he seemed more handsome to her than ever, grave, taunting, demanding. They were both growing older, and Jesse was growing even more sensual.

And more determined, she thought briefly.

She would soon be in his arms. And they would stand together, now that he had come home.

"Jesse—"

He swore something unintelligible that held a note of anguish, then strode toward her once again. "No, dammit, I do not want to talk!" He swept the elegant little hat from her head, and before she could stop him, his fingers were in her hair, freeing it from the pins. He spread it out to frame her face, and his lips and mouth touched hers again with such fervor that decency seemed lost, and the fierce flames of desire were awakened. Was it right to love so deeply and so desperately? Kiernan didn't know—she only knew that she lost her soul within his arms, that she sought to touch his tongue with her own, that she was surrendering to the simple ecstasy of his lips upon hers, caressing, seeking, touching again and again.

There was no chaise, no bed, no lounge within the gazebo. But a cloth lay over a wrought-iron table. Jesse swept it up and laid it out upon the floor, then returned for her.

Not even the wildest fires of raw desire could strip away the cold within the summer house. And so he did not seek to divest her of her clothing.

He swept her up and carried her to the cloth, and he bore her down upon it as her eyes met his with the emerald blaze of her longing, and her fingers curled into the ebony hair at his nape. When she was upon the floor, she felt the wetness of his kiss again, warmly raging, touching her lips, drawing away, his tongue seeking, his teeth catching her lower lip lightly, and then again, his tongue meeting hers just outside their parted mouths, and their lips closing finally around the exotic hunger of the kiss.

Velvet still encased and enclosed her, bringing her warmth, a warmth that melted into the growing heat of her body as she thirsted for his touch. His touch came so sweetly. Her velvet jacket was loosened, her breasts spilled free in a froth of lace and silk undergarments. Her skirt was loosed, the ribbon tie of her pantalets was freed. Beneath the textures of the fabrics, his hands roamed freely. His palm began a sultry movement beneath the velvet of her skirt to caress the naked flesh of her hip, of her buttock, of her thigh. Warm velvet brushed against her as his touch traveled on. A heightening expectation, sweet and sensual, then raw and erotic, snaked through her, for with his touch, his kiss never ceased. Always it was there against a part of her. When his lips left hers, it was only for his mouth to form and cover seductively the rouge pinnacle of her breast. His tongue teased the tautening peak, then his lips formed again to suckle upon it deeply, sending startling waves of moist sweet heat rippling through her body to soak her with shattering desire that centered bluntly at the point between her thighs.

With his touch he found that point. With bold, excruciating precision, he stroked her where she most longed to be stroked, centered in upon all the shocking heat and sweet nectar and stroked. Stroked until gasps escaped her throat and she undulated to the rhythm of his hand. The velvet of her skirt bunched high atop of her hip, then she felt the rock-hard point of his erection burn erotically against her naked belly. She reached down to touch him. Her finger closed around his surging hardness and heat and vital life, and she almost pulled away, startled by the searing power and that very masculine life and power and pulse. His fingers closed around hers, holding her there. His kiss caught her lips again, and as his lips played wickedly with hers, she became fascinated with him and explored that living steel, trembling as she stroked and caressed, discovered the dark nest of hair at his groin, the soft sacs within it, and again, the driving rod of his sex. His hoarse cries and whispers drove her on until he was suddenly atop her, and the cry within her own body was answered by the hard and thundering thrust of his shaft deep, deep inside her, seeming to touch to her womb and to her heart.

Bringing with it splendor.

And so if winter winds blew around the summer cottage,

the cold inside was dispelled. Her every dream from far-away England was answered, her nights of loneliness, her time of waiting, the endless days when desire had lain dormant because the man to fuel the fires of that desire had been denied her—by her own choice, perhaps.

But time was swept away now, and the world was eclipsed. She had barely seen his face again, she had heard so very few of his words. But here she was again, swept into the rhythms of his passions, caught up in the desperate and heady desire of the excitement that sparked between them. Oh, where was discipline, where was conscience, where was honor, and dear Lord, what had happened to restraint?

In his arms, she did not know, nor could she care. The sweet winter's scent of the river came in along with the breeze, mingled with the subtle scent that belonged only to her lover. Movement went on constantly, exquisitely, the twist and spiral of his body, the taunt when he was away, the gratification when he came again, growing wet and sleek and surging harder and faster with each thrust. She realized suddenly that whimpering sounds, soft eager cries, were coming from her, and that she surged in a likewise frenzy to have more of him, to join with him, to meld their bodies completely. And then suddenly, with one stroke, the wonder burst upon her. The delicious crest was met, and she went stiff, feeling heady, searing pleasure burst forth over all of her body. She shuddered as it swamped her again and again. She drifted as Jesse moved again, and then once more, then fell atop her as the sweetness from him pervaded all of her.

He fell to her side and pulled her against him. For a moment he was still, but then he held a tendril of her hair and brought it against his face, breathing deeply.

"Oh, Jesse," she whispered.

"I wonder," he murmured, "how I lived without you."

She twisted into his arms, delighted just to be held against him, to luxuriate in the warmth and the tenderness that he offered. "Oh, Jesse, is it always like this?" she asked.

He pressed a kiss against her forehead. "No. It is never like this."

"What are we going to do?" she demanded.

To her dismay, he gently eased himself free from her and stood. He absently buttoned his shirt, stuffed the ends into his breeches, and buttoned up his pants. Kiernan sat up, and with far greater difficulty, she rearranged her own clothing.

He strode to where the windows looked toward the house. Through the foliage the back porch with its regal and gracious columns could barely be seen. But as he looked more closely, his eyes grazed over the tops of some of the beautiful monuments within the family graveyard.

"I love this place," he said suddenly, passionately. "My God, I love this place."

I love you, Jesse. She almost said the words, except that she had said them before. She knew that he loved her too. And so she spoke as he did, and her words, too, were true.

"I love it, too, Jesse," she said softly.

He turned to her suddenly, his hands planted firmly on his hips. His hair was rakishly disarrayed, and he appeared very much the man he was, older and wiser than many she knew, perhaps even world-weary. He was strikingly appealing, sensual, bold, sexual, hard—very much the master of his world.

"Then marry me," he said.

To her own dismay, her eyes fell and she started to shiver. She loved Jesse, she wanted to marry him. She wanted to live with him here as lady of Cameron Hall, and she wanted to grow old sipping cool drinks with him upon the porch in the summer, watching their children grow.

She couldn't speak at first. Then she murmured, "What if there is war?"

"There is no war right now."

"Lincoln will soon be president," she said.

"Why the damned hell did you ever have to know anything about politics!" he demanded savagely. "It's a despicable trait in a woman."

She cried out in protest, rising upon her knees. "Oh, Jesse! You don't mean that, you've never meant it before—"

"Well, maybe I mean it now," he muttered. He stared at her again. "Marry me."

She rose, straightening her skirt. She walked to him and

leaned against his chest and felt the beat of her heart. Yes! Yes, I'll marry you, there is nothing that I want more in all the world! The words were on the tip of her tongue, aching to be spoken.

"Oh, Jesse!" she murmured miserably. She turned entreating green eyes up to his. "Promise me that you'll be with me, that you'll always be with me!"

His lip curved. "Right or wrong. On your side."

"Oh, Jesse! This *is* your side!"

He smiled a bittersweet smile and lowered his lips to kiss her tenderly, his fingers curving with a tender touch around her skull.

Suddenly, he pulled back, frowning. For a moment she didn't understand, then she too heard the sound of hoofbeats.

"Jesse, Jesse! Confound it, where the hell are you?"

It was Daniel's voice, sounding both excited and anxious. Kiernan stepped back quickly, smoothing her hair, her eyes downcast.

Jesse instinctively stepped before her, shielding her, then strode to the breezeway doors of the summer house.

"Daniel, I'm here. What is it?"

Convinced that she was as put-together as it was possible for her to be, Kiernan stepped up to Jesse's side. Daniel was riding through the trees, as excellent a horseman as his brother. His blue eyes were alive with fire. He opened his mouth to speak, but then he saw Kiernan.

"Kiernan! You're home and you're here!" He leaped down from his horse, and before she knew it, she was in his arms and he was swinging her around, then giving her a sound kiss upon her lips. Jesse watched from the doorway, bemused as he always seemed to be when they met, a dignified figure watching the meeting of children.

"Yes, I'm home!" She laughed and hugged him in return. "I told you I was coming home."

"Yes, but I didn't know that you were here already."

He suddenly stared from her to Jesse, and then back to her again. He must have noticed that her hair was somewhat disarrayed.

But whatever he thought or whatever he knew, he kept it to himself. Before he could speak again, Jesse was striding toward them both, saying, "Daniel, what is it? What brought you racing down here?"

"Oh, oh my Lord. It's happened!"

"What's happened?"

"Secession, Jesse. Secession! South Carolina has just voted herself out of the Union."

$\mathcal{T}en$

Word of the vote for secession in South Carolina spread through Virginia like wildfire. The decision had been made on December 20, and by that evening, the bells throughout Charleston were ringing to herald a brand-new era for the state. It was not much of a surprise. Ever since the election of the Republican president—and Lincoln was adamantly against the institution of slavery—it had seemed that little else could be expected to happen.

Other conventions were planned throughout the South. As Christmas Day 1860 arrived, tensions were high, and excitement was rampant.

Jesse and Kiernan were both quiet.

On Christmas Eve, Kiernan came to Cameron Hall's Christmas party. Guests came from miles and miles around, including Anthony and his family. It was the first time that Kiernan had seen Anthony since her return to Virginia, and when she greeted him, she tried very hard to be warm. Anthony had not changed during the past year. He seemed to believe that she had now sown whatever feminine wild oats she may have had to sow. His eagerness, his tenderness, were apparent in his eyes.

She saw him first in the open breezeway. Christmas Eve was cold that year, but the doors had been thrown open because the many people present at the affair created an astonishing warmth within the house. Flames burned brightly in every fireplace throughout the stately manor. Cameron Hall had been decked for the occasion with holly boughs and bayberry candles and beribboned wreaths. Mulled wine simmered upon the hearths, and the sweet smell of cinnamon filled the air.

Kiernan had arrived early with her father, and was hugged enthusiastically by Christa and Daniel. Jesse had taken her shoulders and placed a perfunctory kiss upon her cheek, and their eyes had met. There had been little that they could say before others.

They had been able to say little to each other since Daniel had first brought the news of the secession. Daniel had been with them when they returned to Cameron Hall to tell Christa, and Daniel had insisted upon accompanying her home to tell her father the news.

Excitement over the news ran very, very high. The only one subdued about events was Jesse.

"They insist in South Carolina that it will be a peaceful split," Daniel had informed them.

"There will be no peace," Jesse said quietly.

"Well, now it is up to the other states to choose sides," Daniel mused. They all knew it didn't matter much what the others did—all that mattered was the choice Virginia made.

Kiernan had had no further opportunity to speak with Jesse alone. Others arrived at the Christmas Eve party just after she did.

It was a joyous occasion. Even though speculation and excitement rose with an ever-increasing fervor, it was still Christmas Eve, a warm and poignant occasion. The guests arrived in beautiful apparel, the men in distinguished frock coats and elegant tuxedos, the ladies in every manner of velvet and silk and fur. And despite the cold, bosoms were bared as daringly as fashion would allow. Fiddles and flutes joined the music of the pianoforte, which had been brought into the huge hallway, and reel after reel was played for dancers who knew no exhaustion.

When Anthony and his family arrived, Kiernan was in the breezeway with Christa. Christa, the last of the Camerons, was a beauty with the family blue eyes and raven hair set against a cream complexion and fine delicate features. She had a will to match that of both her brothers. Christa whispered against Kiernan's cheek to let her know that Anthony had arrived, then swept by her in her velvet and taffeta skirts to greet the Millers herself. Anthony and his father were there, as well as Patricia and Jacob, his younger sister and brother. Kiernan stayed back, watching the four Camerons converge on the breezeway, welcoming the new arrivals. The Millers had come a long way. They would be guests of the estate and probably stay until the new year.

Anthony was, as ever, perfectly polite. But after he had shaken hands with Jesse and Daniel and kissed Christa on the cheek, his gaze swiftly roamed over the crowd and came to rest upon her.

She felt pinned down by the cast of his eyes, captured in some mockery of circumstance. The tenderness in his gaze was almost unbearable. He moved swiftly through the crowd of dancers and diners and merrymakers to reach her side.

Even as he walked, Kiernan knew that Jesse was watching him, watching her.

Anthony reached her side and touched her shoulders with trembling fingers.

He pulled her close and offered the most proper and still emotional kiss upon her cheek. He was loath to set her free. "Kiernan, I've missed you so very much. Are you home now for good? I hope so. Things are happening quickly now. There may be war. You can't go running around the world anymore. You have to stay home—and marry me. Let me make an announcement this Christmas, Kiernan. Please, let that be your gift to me!"

She stared into the warm brown of his eyes and felt the tension in his arms upon her. "Oh, Anthony!" she told him miserably. "I can't. I just can't!"

Disappointment darkened his eyes and he swallowed hard, but he spoke softly and quickly again. "I've rushed you again. Forgive me."

She wanted to scream at him. *He* didn't need to be forgiven—*she* did. But she couldn't tell him that she was in love with another man. Perhaps she should—perhaps that would end it. But she couldn't put still more pain into that dark gaze of his.

Not even with Jesse watching.

Or maybe *because* Jesse was watching. Maybe Jesse needed to remember that there were other men who could love her—men who did not betray their own kind.

"I'd love to dance, Anthony," she told him. She looked over his shoulder and gave Jesse a brilliant smile, then moved into Anthony's arms.

It was Christmas, and it was a party. She danced with Anthony, and Andrew, and Anthony's young brother, Jacob. She danced with her father, and she danced with Daniel, and she danced with any number of the other guests. Handsome men, young Virginians, planters, military friends of the Camerons, neighbors —dashing, exciting young men. She flirted outrageously.

Jesse danced, too, with his own sister and with Andrew's pretty sister, Patricia.

Then he danced with Elizabeth Nash, the steel heiress from Richmond. Then he danced with Charity McCarthy, the widow of a senator, still residing in Washington.

She lived very near where Jesse was stationed, Kiernan found herself thinking bitterly.

Jesse danced with Charity again. In the arms of a Virginia militia lieutenant, Kiernan watched Jesse again with the sable-haired, very elegant Charity.

The woman's head was cast back as she laughed, revealing an ample expanse of her shoulders and breast and the diamond locket she wore to emphasize her natural assets. Jesse's hand was upon her waist, and his eyes seemed caught within hers. It seemed, too, that nothing in the world mattered to him except for the elegant woman in his arms.

"I am in love."

"What?"

Startled, Kiernan looked back at the young lieutenant with whom she was dancing. He was a very good-looking boy, with ash-blond curls, warm hazel eyes—and cheeks that barely needed shaving. He smiled sweetly at her. "I'm in love. Truly, Miss Mackay, you are the most beautiful woman I have ever seen. Dare I hope that we might become better acquainted?"

She was probably a year older than he, Kiernan thought. She stared at him blankly, then realized that Jesse was sweeping by again with the widow from Washington. She flashed the boy a smile. "I do cherish my friends, sir. And I'd be delighted to count you among them."

A few minutes later she was startled by a firm hand upon her arm, and she was swept into Jesse's arms. His eyes flashed a dangerous, wicked blue, as hot as they had ever been. They stared arrogantly into her own.

"What now, Miss Mackay? Another conquest? Is it not enough that young Mr. Miller must trip over his tongue every time you are near? Would you have another young man panting on the whisper of a promise? Or have you taken love up as sport?"

Her hand went rigid, and she would have slapped him. But his hold upon her was tight, and his words were quick and harsh. "No, no, careful, love! Imagine, what would they all think if you suddenly slapped your host upon the dance floor? Your father would be aghast—I would be forced to tell him the truth about our relationship. Anthony would be horrified and honor-bound to come to your rescue to salvage your honor. He would be forced to challenge me. And in the duel I'd have to try damned hard to stay alive and at the same time manage not to kill the poor young fool. Is that what you want, Kiernan? The two of us—or three or more of us—fighting over you?"

She still wanted to strike him. But more than anything, she wanted to cry. She lowered her eyes and shook her head. "No. No, that's not what I want." She looked up at him again, her eyes damp. "What I want is you, Jesse."

He smiled, a slow, somewhat painful grin that curled his lip in self-mockery. "But you have had me, Kiernan. And you have me still."

They whirled around the dance floor once again. Kiernan knew where he was taking her. They whirled to the open doorways and then beyond. He slipped off his handsome frock coat to set it about her shoulders as they moved down the porch. They could hear the sounds of laughter and singing from the slave quarters. Delicious aromas wafted on the air from the smokehouse and the kitchen and the bakehouse. That sweet smell that was Christmas was on the air, a smell of cinnamon, cloves, bayberry, holly, mulling wine, rum, and fruitcake, and so many other special scents.

Kiernan felt as if she were going to cry again. She lifted her arms and encompassed the scene, the porch, the winter garden, the lawn sweeping down to the river, the stables and other appendixes to the beautiful estate, the graveyard with its long history. "This!" she whispered. "This is what I want."

He smiled, sitting up atop a latticed railing at the far end of the porch and drawing her close. "This? The hall? You could have married Daniel long ago for this."

She blushed. "No, I don't mean the hall, although I do love it." She turned to him very seriously. "Jesse, I want you. And I want the life that we have always led. I want the river, and I want the land, and I want years of Christmases just like this one. I want the elegance—"

"You know how much work a plantation is!" he reminded her sharply.

Yes, she did know. It was dawn-to-dusk work, no matter how many slaves a man or woman owned. It was constant supervision of a massive household. The laundry, candles, beeswax, baking, sewing, cleaning, buying, harvesting, and always listening to problems, solving them, and starting all over again. But Kiernan had never minded. She had been her father's hostess since she was a child, and she had learned so very much that way.

And all the work was for moments like these, moments when she could look out upon the river.

"I want this," she murmured. "I want you and me and this. I want to grow old throwing such parties, and sitting upon this porch. And watching my grandchildren tumble down the lawn. I want to be buried in that little graveyard, with a headstone that says Cameron."

"Then marry me," Jesse interrupted. "If I can promise

you nothing else, I think I could see to it that you are interred in that plot with a Cameron headstone."

She pulled away from him and glanced at him sharply. "You're laughing at me, Jesse."

"No," he told her softly, "I am not."

His eyes were dark, a dusky blue. He watched her with a combination of tenderness and warmth. For a moment, she thought that they shared everything. He understood exactly how she felt. He loved the things that she loved and he loved her.

Maybe it was just the moment itself that they shared. But she felt compelled to move closer to him and to watch him with growing wonder as he bent down and just touched her lips with his own, lightly, gently, oh, so tenderly, so sweetly.

They broke away, watching each other.

It was then that she heard the sharp sound of a man clearing his throat. Jesse looked up over her head, and Kiernan spun around with dread.

It was her father. A blush suffused her cheeks, and she wondered what he had seen.

He had seen enough. He was staring hard at Jesse.

"Kiernan, get in the house," John Mackay advised her firmly.

"Papa—" she began to protest.

"Kiernan, your father asked you to go inside," Jesse reminded her firmly, his eyes upon John.

She had never been in terror of her father. She loved him, loved him dearly. He had always been a good, giving, and even tender parent. They were, after all, all the family that each other had. But his eyes, which were usually such a soft and gentle blue, were now as hard as steel. She wanted to protest, but she looked from him to Jesse and back to him, then to Jesse once again. Neither seemed to be paying her any heed.

"Papa, Jesse—"

They both turned on her. Their words were unanimous. "Go inside, Kiernan."

Trembling and furious that both would order her about

so, she gritted her teeth, inched her chin up, and headed for
the doors, decrying her sex.

But she paused just inside the doors and tried to listen to
their words, her heart seeming to spin within her chest.

She heard Jesse's voice first, assuring John that his inten-
tions were entirely honorable. He had, in fact, asked
Kiernan to marry him. As yet, she had not agreed, and that
was why Jesse had not yet come to John.

Her father was curiously silent.

"Mr. Mackay," Jesse began again. "I assure you—"

"I know, Jesse, I know. You have grown up honorable,
and five years ago I would have welcomed your suit. I would
have deplored my daughter's handling of young Miller. I
cannot fault her behavior now, for she has refused an engagement with him. But I have to tell you, Jesse, that if you
came to me now, I could not give you my blessing."

Kiernan could not see Jesse, but she knew that he was
stiffening, that he was standing very tall, that his backbone
was rigid, that his temper was held in check out of respect
for her father.

"You won't be here much longer, will you?" her father
asked softly.

Jesse was very quiet. "I don't know, Mr. Mackay."

"It will depend which way the wind blows, won't it?"
John asked him.

Again, Jesse was quiet.

"Perhaps you should stay away from her until we know,"
John suggested.

"That will be difficult, sir," Jesse said.

"And why is that?"

"Because I love her, you see."

"Indeed," John said quietly. "Then, sir, I must ask you
for prudence. Let things go on as they have been. We'll
watch the wind."

"All right, Mr. Mackay," Jesse agreed. "We'll watch the
wind."

Kiernan was still at the doorway when her father came
bursting back through it. He stared at her, and his shaggy

brow went flying up. "Hmpf!" he exclaimed. "I should have suspected you were there!"

She looked anxiously to the porch, but her father caught her arm and pulled her back into the hallway and into the dance in progress. "I should have kept you in Europe a bit longer, eh, daughter? I've been warned that a beautiful woman is trouble, and trouble you're proving to be!"

"Papa!" she wailed.

He winked at her, softening his words. But when the music died, he said, "Bid Christa and Daniel and Jesse goodbye. And be especially polite to young Anthony—his father and I are business partners. Then we'll be going."

"But it's early!"

"I have a feeling that it's already too late," John Mackay said with a weary sigh. "You'll do as you're told this once, daughter. Now I mean it—run along."

Much as she was unaccustomed to his giving her orders, she knew that he meant his words. The party had barely begun, but it did not matter—they would leave.

She hugged and kissed Daniel, fought for regal control as she said good-bye and thank you to Jesse, and was as demure and charming as her father could have wanted when she bade good night to Anthony. She would see them all again, soon, she knew. Her father would hold a twelfthnight dinner at their home.

But she was suddenly very much afraid. It was one thing to hold Jesse off by her own desire and determination. But now that her father was involved . . .

Her father had seen the same torment in Jesse that she knew he had about the political situation that faced them all.

She loved Jesse. But was her love stronger than whatever might happen in the country? Could she ever really be Jesse's enemy?

Yes, she could, she thought, and was more bitter because of that love.

Yet she could not believe that when the time was really upon them, that Jesse could leave his home—that he could leave her—because of a misguided disagreement with Virginia's political stance.

She did not want him to be torn away from her. She wanted to hold him, to hold him as tightly as she could.

And so before she left, she found Christa. She dared to take her friend, Jesse's sister, into her confidence.

"Christa, please ask Jesse to meet me at the summer cottage tomorrow, at dusk."

Christa's eyes grew large and wide. "All right, Kiernan."

"And please—"

"I won't say anything to anyone else, Kiernan. I promise."

Kiernan smiled. The two girls hugged one another, then Kiernan hurried out, not wanting to risk her father's temper.

In the carriage, John Mackay stared at her. "So it's been Jesse Cameron all along, has it?"

"Yes, Papa," she said primly.

"You love him, huh?"

"Yes!"

"Do you love him enough?"

"Enough?" She flushed, and suddenly she found herself defending Jesse's position. "Virginia has not seceded, sir. We are not at war."

Her father wagged a finger at her. "You listen to me, missy. Virginia will secede, and there will be a war. Jesse knows that. That's the only reason he hasn't pressed you. If he weren't the man that he is, if he didn't love you enough to know your own heart better than you do yourself, he would have been at my door long ago. You mark my words, young lady, guard your heart."

She'd guard her heart, all right.

But she would still meet him at the summer cottage tomorrow. She had a Christmas gift for him.

He arrived at the cottage at exactly noon and saw that Kiernan had come before him, for a fire had been lit. He could see the smoke drifting softly from the chimney. He smiled. She wouldn't worry about the smoke attracting attention. She knew he came here often, and that his family respected his privacy.

He entered, and for a moment he blinked, trying to adjust to the dim light in the room. All that gave it luminescence was the fire that played in the grate. The room was bathed in a very pale glow of gold, otherwise touched in shadow.

And then he saw her.

She was only a few feet away from the fire, upon the floor. But the floor was not bare—it was covered in fur.

And like the floor, she was covered in fur. A beautiful white fox was draped over the length of her. Her hair, loose and free and set to shine like fire from the glow of the blaze, rippled and waved over the fur.

Then, as he stood, she let the fur fall. She was naked, naked in the achingly soft and sensual pool of the fur.

"Merry Christmas," she whispered. Her emerald eyes were green in the glow, the eyes of a cat, mysterious, haunting, compelling.

He paused—God in heaven, he didn't know how he did so, but he did—and allowed his eyes to rake over her, to relish and savor, to savage and adore the woman that he thought he knew so well. He knew the sweet scent of that glorious golden hair, knew its feel between his fingers. He knew those eyes, the elegant shape of her face. He knew the taste of her flesh, the curve of her hip, the fullness of her breast. He knew the length and shape of her thighs, knew the musky sweet secret femininity between her legs. He knew so very much about her . . . but not as much as he thought he knew.

She rose. She seemed to glide from the elegant cocoon of fur, like Venus sweeping from Poseidon's shell. She stood before him, sensual, exciting, sweeping his breath away. The boldness to her movement was belied by the sudden shyness in her eyes, by their uncertainty as her gaze met his.

A soft, tender question curved her lips, lips that were full, shapely, moist, waiting to be kissed.

She stretched her arms out to him, wanting him, arms soft and creamy, heightened the beauty of her breasts as they rose. Alabaster, touched by the tiny blue lines of veins, crested by nipples as rouge as a rose in winter. His eyes swept lower still, taking in the golden nest at her thighs, the curve of her hip.

A cry, ragged, hoarse, tore from his lips, and she was within his arms. He tore his clothes from his body, and soon he was next to her before the fire.

Upon their knees, they met one another. The fire glowed over their bodies, making his shoulders sleek, making the curves of her body, her breasts, her hips gleam. Their fingers met and meshed, and then their lips caressed and parted and caressed again.

Soon their bodies were dampened and slickened by the torrents of kisses and caresses that they shared and exchanged. The fire glowed upon them still.

It glowed until he pressed her back upon the fur and sank hard within her.

The winter's cold became summer with its heat.

After the blaze had swept through, the fire still played within the grate, and the glow remained to warm them.

Mississippi seceded from the Union on January 9, Florida seceded on the tenth, and Alabama on the eleventh.

The four states needed only Georgia for the seceded territory to stretch from North Carolina's southern border to the Mississippi.

Joseph E. Brown, Georgia's strongly secessionist governor, asked his legislature to call for a convention. Speeches were made by visitors from the already-seceded states.

On January 19, Georgia became the fifth state to secede from the Union. Louisiana seceded on the twenty-sixth, and Texas on February 1.

By the end of the month, Jesse and Daniel had both ridden back to join their units. Virginia had made no move to leave the Union.

Her legislature had suggested that a convention be held in Washington, at the Willard Hotel, in the hope of preventing war. It convened on February 4 and was known as the Washington Peace Convention.

But delegates from the lower South were conspicuously absent. On the same day, they were holding their own convention in Montgomery, Alabama, to form a new government, a Confederacy of seceded states.

So while peace was discussed in the North, the Confederacy was becoming a reality. The Confederate delegates rushed to perform important tasks to solidify their own union before Abraham Lincoln could take office. In Montgomery, Jefferson Davis—once President Buchanan's secretary of war, the man in charge of that department when John Brown had raided Harpers Ferry—was elected to the highest office of the new Confederacy.

The Confederate Constitution was ratified. The "stars and bars" was adopted as the flag. An army was authorized. The laws of the United States were also adopted, with exceptions regarding states' rights and the instituion of slavery. The Mississippi River was declared open for navigation, Texas was admitted to the Confederacy. The provisional government authorized loans, contracts, and treasury notes—and prepared for war.

Much of this went on while the Washington Peace Convention was still playing with hope at the Willard Hotel.

At home, Kiernan waited, wishing desperately that she could be where all the action was taking place. She read every newspaper she could get her hands on, and she waited.

Virginia remained steady for the moment, and both Cameron brothers remained with their regiments. Kiernan heard frequently from Daniel, who was eager to explain his position. "My heart lies with this new Confederacy," he wrote, "with the states and the people with whom we have so very much in common. I think that I am a southerner, a Confederate—a Rebel, if you will! But first and foremost, I am a Virginian, and I will abide by the will of the state I love so dearly. Actually," he went on to admit, "I believe that I have stolen that sentiment from Colonel Lee, but then, you know how we both admire him, and he expresses what we feel." The letter rambled on. It ended with a postscript. "Jesse sends his love."

His love—and his silence, Kiernan thought.

Throughout the South, major events were taking place.

In Florida, warlike actions had begun even before the

state had seceded. Militia had been trained. In Pensacola, Federal troops had been forced off the mainland forts of McRee and Barrancas to Fort Pickens in the harbor. Fort Marion at St. Augustine had been seized, and Alabama and Florida troops had taken over the navy yard at Pensacola. Southern military leaders wanted to attack Fort Pickens, but they also wanted to avert war, and so they waited.

Similar events were taking place throughout the Confederacy. In South Carolina, Brigadier General Pierre Beauregard watched the Union troops at Fort Sumter and feared that Washington would send reinforcements.

Everywhere, the tension increased.

And still Kiernan waited. Anthony no longer plagued her with his constant, patient proposals, for he had hurried home. He had left his position with his local militia, for many of its members were pro-Union, as were many of the western counties of the state. Politically, Anthony was everything that Kiernan longed for Jesse to be—passionately, loyally, unshakably sympathetic to their cotton and tobacco neighbors.

Anthony scarcely even wrote, though his words were passionate when he did. He and his father were recruiting and arming a unit of cavalry. They were busy buying horses and designing uniforms.

Then, in early April 1861, Kiernan's time of waiting came to an end.

Christa came riding by to tell her with a great deal of jubilation that both her brothers were soon coming home. "I'm so delighted! They've both gotten leave to come for my birthday. I wanted to tell you as soon as I heard from the both of them. Thank goodness Daniel is such a wonderful correspondent!"

"Yes, thank goodness," Kiernan agreed.

"Oh, I can't wait to see them!"

"Neither can I," Kiernan told her fervently. "Oh, neither can I!"

Two days later, Christa was back. She met Kiernan on her porch and did not dismount from her horse. She smiled mischievously. "A soldier just stopped by, a friend of Jesse's who resigned his commission."

"Oh?" Kiernan said, her heart thundering.

Christa laughed. "Well, it seems that Jesse is capable of writing after all. He sent me a note, and in it is a request for you."

"Yes?"

Christa handed her an envelope. Kiernan raised a brow to her, then reached for the letter inside.

Her eyes scanned the brief but affectionate passages to Christa, asking about the house, servants, the weather, and Christa's state of mind and health.

The last paragraph referred to her.

Christa, please see Kiernan for me. And ask her to meet me at the summer cottage. Dusk, the night of the sixteenth.

"What do I tell him?" Christa asked her.

Kiernan lowered her lashes swiftly, not wanting Christa to see the wild elation within her eyes. She fought for control, then raised her eyes to Christa's once again and smiled demurely. "Tell him I'll be there."

Christa smiled and started to turn her horse away. Then she paused, turning back. "Oh, I forgot. There's a postscript on the back. He says that it might be cold. He suggests you wear fur."

Kiernan smiled and lowered her head quickly. She folded her hands before her, but despite her best efforts, her voice was filled with a soft tremor.

"Tell him . . . tell him I'll wear fur."

She turned and ran back into the house, unable to look into Christa's eyes any longer.

She'd wear fur. It was what Jesse wanted.

Jesse was coming home.

Eleven

Looking out from the breezeway doors of the gazebo, Jesse could see the monuments of the cemetery and beyond in the evening light. The lawn sloped up to the house, and the garden was just coming out from its winter's cloak of green to flower again.

It had been a beautiful day.

April in Virginia was often a whimsical month. Sometimes a dead heat lay over the coastal land. The heavy humidity of summer came creeping in early, and the nights were sultry and warm. Sometimes, it was just the opposite. The day could be bitterly cold, and it was even possible for a light spattering of wet snow to fall, the kind that could chill you to the bone.

Then sometimes, it was just beautiful, everything that came with the promise of spring. The sun would shine throughout the day, hot and radiant, throwing a bold new yellow light over the soft new grass that was just bursting through the old. The first of the spring flowers would be bathed in that light, their colors the brighter for it. But the heat of the sun was softened and tempered by the coolness of the air coming in from the river, and it was easy to walk, easy to breathe, easy to love to be alive. Newborn foals frolicked and played in the fields, and the horses bred from Arabian stock whipped their tails up incredibly high and seemed to dance within their paddocks.

It had been one of those days today. A cool day, tempered by a warm sun. The night coming on was a gentle and balmy one. The whisper of the breeze was itself sensual, seeming to wrap around him as he waited in the summer house.

He wondered if she would come.

The wire services were alive with the latest developments between the Union and the new-formed Confederacy.

In the early hours of April 12, the southern troops under General Beauregard in Charleston had fired upon the Union position at Fort Sumter in Charleston harbor.

Major Robert Anderson had been in command at Sumter, with Captain Abner Doubleday his second in command. Beauregard had set up batteries in Charleston because South Carolina was offended by the Federal troops sitting on its sovereign territory. The Federals had been asked to surrender, but Anderson, expecting supplies from Washington, had refused. He'd had only sixty-six cannon, many of them unmounted, and he was short of powder-bag cartridges.

At 3:20 A.M., hostilities came to a head. One last demand for a surrender was made and refused, and the Federals were warned that they would soon be fired upon.

And so they were. Two hours later, a Confederate shell broke over Fort Sumter, and the shelling continued. Anderson gave Doubleday the honor of firing the first Union shot at seven, and the uneven contest began.

It went on all through the day. By nightfall, the shelling slackened, but by dawn of the thirteenth, it came again. Anderson and Doubleday kept their men low to the ground against the smoke inhalation. The supply ship Anderson had awaited came—but it was held in the harbor by the Confederate artillery.

Soon after noon, a Confederate shell blew away the fort's flagstaff. Secessionist Colonel Wigfall rowed out to Sumter, having seen the flag go down, and demanded a surrender of the fort.

Anderson, having no way to fight, conceded. To that point, he had not lost a man.

Surrender ceremonies were planned for the next day, and Anderson asked and received permission from Beauregard to salute the American flag before hauling it down. The hundred-gun salute brought about the death of a Union soldier when the fiftieth gun exploded.

Throughout South Carolina, there was tremendous jubilation. Union forces had been thrust away.

In Virginia, the situation was at a crucial peak. A legislature would now decide the fate of the state. Lincoln had made a call to arms. War seemed imminent.

It seemed impossible for Virginia to take up arms against her sister states.

Would Kiernan come? Jesse wondered again in the summer cottage.

Even as the question plagued his mind, he saw movement in the foliage beyond, and then she burst into the clearing and raced into the gazebo.

She closed the doors behind her, leaning against them. Her eyes touched his, filled with life and a blazing green excitement. Her breast rose and fell swiftly with the force of her breathing. Her hair was free and wild, tumbling around her shoulders and down her back in a sweep of sunlit waves.

The fur she wore rimmed an elegant gold cape that swept evocatively around her body.

"Jesse!"

She whispered his name, and then she was in his arms. He quickly discovered that beneath the cape she wore a simple cotton day dress and nothing more. As he slipped the tie on the cape and it fell softly to the floor, he felt her hands upon him, tugging his shirt free from his breeches. He felt her fingers upon his naked flesh and marveled at the touch, shuddering as the hot fires of desire snaked through him.

In the days to come, he would remember this night, remember it with aching poignancy, and he would tremble anew, thinking of all that he had held in his arms.

For in all the long years when they had watched each other and waited, when he had wondered at the beauty she would be when she grew up, he had never imagined this.

He knew that she was his. He had been her first lover, the first to touch her, to teach her. And she had learned to give so very much to him. She had never questioned propriety, she had simply loved him. And in that, he had never known a feeling more exquisite, never known a power so great. She was sensual, elegant, beautiful, and in his life, he had never imagined a love so great.

She stroked his back, her fingers playing upon muscle and sinew. She rose against him, the soft curves of her body haunting and evocative beneath the simple cotton of her dress as she pressed against his naked chest. She nibbled against his lower lip, then rose to meet him in a wild and sweet open-mouthed kiss that drove every demon known to man to tear into his groin and his blood. He had stripped her of the gown and borne her down upon the fur that had offered them so sweet and heady a haven before.

In the days to come, he would indeed remember this evening! Remember the feel of her lips, moist and searing warm, moving over his body, the feeling of soft, exhilarating fire, wet upon his chest, trailing patterns, circling his nipples where her teeth teased and played. He felt the flow of her hair following the taunt of her lips, soft velvet to bring him to an ever-greater need. And still she loved and teased and taunted him with tender kisses upon his flesh, exotic, erotic, decadent kisses upon his flesh, moving lower and lower against him until, incredibly, she touched the pulsing fullness of his sex with her mouth.

Lightly at first, with kisses that were so soft and sweet that they tormented him nearly to hell. He grabbed hold of her, unable to bear the bursting desire, when suddenly she closed her sweet caress hard around him, and in all his life he had never felt so searing an explosion of desire.

He drew her to him. The hot blood surged and raced throughout his body, and he pressed her down hard into the velvet-soft fur upon the floor. His fingers became entangled in her hair, and he ravished her with burning kisses as her long legs wound erotically around his hips, and he swept inside her, thrusting deeply into the welcoming, sheathing warmth.

When the sweetness of the tempestuous climax claimed them both, he scarce let the cool breeze of the night whisper over them before he turned upon her again, fiercely, needing the night. In the coming darkness, he smiled down into the misty beauty of her eyes and began to make love to her again.

Kissing, caressing, finding sweetly erotic places, the pulse at her throat, the lobe of her ear. He shimmied his body down the length of her hers, and his kisses grew slow and sultry upon her naked flesh, teasing her breasts, loving them tenderly, demanding their fullness. Still his body caressed hers as he moved again, kissing the point at the back of her knee, the softness of her thighs, and the beckoning warmth of the sweet petals between them. She cried out, and he caressed her still, stroked her, whispered to her. But she was up on her knees to meet him, her lips searing his, her fingers entwined about his nape, curling into his hair. Windswept yearnings became a tempest in the tranquil quiet of the night. The end burst upon Jesse with shattering volatility, drawing everything from him. The world spun as he stared down at her, her lashes fallen over her eyes, her hair a tangle about them both, her delicate, beautiful features flushed and damp. Her eyes opened to his, and he kissed her again and fell to her side, pulling her close.

"Oh, Jesse," she murmured.

"I was afraid that you wouldn't come," he told her.

"Why?"

He kissed her forehead. "Never mind. Let's not get into it. I don't want to argue with you."

Even as he tried to pull her close, she stiffened.

"Why, Jesse?"

He leaned up on an elbow. "Because war is imminent. I'm sure you've heard about Fort Sumter."

She blinked, staring at him. "Yes, I've heard about Fort Sumter. The wire services carried little else. Jesse, the Virginia legislature is meeting on the matter of secession."

"I know," he said quietly.

He wondered what it was in his tone that she heard. She pushed away from him, shaken, hugging her arms about herself in the sudden coolness that came once they had parted.

"Jesse, what is the matter with you?" she cried. "How can you turn against everything that—"

"I've not turned against anything!" he said irritably. He pushed up and stood, staring down at her. "Kiernan, it's never been anything but one way with you. You've never even looked at the big picture. Not once."

"What big picture?" she demanded. Her eyes were open wide now, and very dangerous in their luster.

He sighed.

He wanted life to go on, too, exactly the way it had been. He loved Virginia, he loved his home. He could never explain to her just how much. He and Daniel and Christa used to walk down and set flowers on the graves of their parents, and when his sister and brother were gone, Jesse had stayed, closing his eyes, thinking of the past that had been theirs, the times and trials that the house had weathered, the triumphs, the agonies.

He loved the James River. He loved to watch the steamers come in, and he loved to hear the singing and the chanting as the slaves loaded the bales of cotton onto the decks of the ships.

Why in God's name did she think that he was turning against everything he loved? Couldn't she understand? There was something greater at stake than slavery and states' rights. They were all Americans.

" 'A house divided against itself cannot stand,' " he quoted softly.

"What?"

"It's something that Lincoln said a few years ago," he told her, "in Illinois, after he was nominated for senator."

He could tell from her reaction that she didn't have much interest in Abraham Lincoln.

"It's true, Kiernan. My God, we aren't even a century old as a nation. Americans bested the English, some of the finest soldiers in the world, because they joined together. Because Virginia stood up for Massachusetts."

"Because we had help from the French," Kiernan murmured dryly.

"Because we stood together," Jesse said flatly. "We're

one country. And we can be great because of the farmlands of the South and the industry in the north."

"You want to fight against Virginia."

"I want to fight *for* Virginia."

She leaped up, facing him, very beautiful and dignified in her nakedness. Her fingers wound into fists at her side as she faced him. "Jesse, you talk about a house divided against itself! Cameron Hall is your house. Virginia is your house. I am part of your house! Don't you see? You're against slavery? So are a lot of people! Maybe, eventually, we'll manage to free our own slaves! Without being told to do so by fanatics. Damn you, Jesse, *you* still own slaves. You haven't figured out how to change the world yourself!"

"My slaves will be freed!" he told her passionately. But then he curbed his anger, swallowing down a taste of pain and bitterness. "Kiernan, I love Virginia."

"Then what will you do if Virginia secedes?"

"I don't know," he told her flatly. He took a step toward her. Even after the hours they had shared together, she stepped away from him. Anger spilled from him again, and he pulled her back into his arms. "I love you, Kiernan!"

Tears filled her eyes as they met his. "Do you love me enough, Jesse?"

"Damn you!" He exploded. "Do *you* love *me* enough?"

She jerked free from him and spun around for her clothing. She snatched up her dress and started away from him again, but he caught her arm and pulled her hard against his chest. He kissed her, sweetly, savagely. He refused to let her go when she fought his hold. He kissed her until her lips parted to his, until she offered up a surrender to at least that demand. The hair on his chest chafed against the softness of her breasts, and he felt the hardening of her nipples against his flesh. She twisted her lips free from his at last.

"Let me go, Jesse."

"No, not tonight."

"Please."

"I can't," he told her. "Dammit, Kiernan, don't ask me to let you go tonight!"

Suddenly, the force she had exerted against him was gone.

She rested her cheek against his chest, and he felt the dampness of her tears.

He swept her up into his arms and carried her back to the furs.

He kissed away her tears, and she curled into his arms again. They made love, slowly, tenderly. The night around them was achingly sweet.

When they rose at last, Jesse was the one to move first. He rose and dressed and helped her into her things.

"I'll take you home," he told her.

"I know my way."

"I'll take you home," he insisted.

He set her in front of him on Pegasus, and when they reached her mare tethered under trees, he kept Kiernan with him and led the mare along.

When they neared her house, she stirred. "Jesse, you should leave me here. My father—"

"I'm taking you home, Kiernan."

As it was, John Mackay was waiting on his front porch. It, too, was broad and handsome, with its brick facade, its pillars tall and regal. John Mackay sat with his pleasant, lined face in repose, his pipe in his mouth, a tumbler of whiskey in his hand.

"Though you might be bringing her home, Jesse," John said. "Else I might have worried about the time."

"I'd not have let her come alone, sir."

"I'm sorry, Papa," Kiernan began.

"It's all right. I knew you were safe with Jesse."

Someone else might not have considered her safe in Jesse's company. But Mackay was a different man. Even if he suspected that his daughter and Jesse were lovers, her life and her happiness mattered more to him. He was indeed a rare man, created within a rare breed.

"I'll just go in so you two can say good night," John offered.

Jesse dismounted from Pegasus and reached up to lift her down. She leaned against him and accepted the tender kiss he placed upon her lips.

She lowered her head against him.

"I love you, Kiernan."

"I love you, too, Jesse," she said. But then her emerald eyes, brimming with dampness and fire, rose to meet his. "But if Virginia secedes and you don't resign your commission in the Federal army, I won't see you again. Ever."

She pulled away from his arms and raced for the door.

There was nothing he could do but watch her go.

Jesse awoke the next morning with an incredible headache.

A great deal of the pain was his own fault. After he left Kiernan, he'd come home and spent the better part of the night with a bourbon bottle and Daniel, discussing times recently past, and times long past. Christa had found them down in the den in the first faint hours of daylight. Being a good Cameron, she had shared a sound swig of bourbon with them—and then ordered them both up to bed.

His headache was his own fault. And it was a damned mean and nasty one. It wasn't helped a bit by the screeching and shouting and carrying-on that was coming from outside the house.

Staggering from the bed with a sheet wrapped about his waist, he stumbled across the room to the wide double doors. They led to a balcony that looked out over the rear porch and the gardens and all the way down to the river. He saw that Daniel was outside, greeting two riders. One of them was Anthony Miller, a fact that seemed to make the pounding in his head all the fiercer. The other was a closer neighbor from the Williamsburg area, Aaron Peters.

The two had ridden in, whooping and hollering. Having listened to them, Daniel suddenly swept his hat from atop his head and threw it high into the air. A thunderous war whoop escaped him, as if he were out west joining in with the Cheyenne or Sioux.

"What the hell?" Jesse muttered. The sound of his own voice hurt him.

He pulled on his breeches and his boots and drew a shirt from the heavy armoire in the corner of his room. Suddenly, he stopped. He ran his hands over the armoire, then stood back to look at the room.

It was the master's room of Cameron Hall. He hadn't taken it over until several years after his father's death. As the oldest son, he had inherited the hall. Not that it had meant anything in the years gone past. He had been involved in his medical career and the service, and Daniel had been just as avid a horse soldier. They came from a long line of fighters. The first Cameron on the Virginian shore had battled the Indians, survived the massacre, and lived on to create a dynasty. Camerons had battled pirates, and his grandfather had fought for the fledgling colonies in the American Revolution.

Jesse moved his hand over the armoire. It had stood where it did now as long as Jesse could remember, just like the big master bed and the elegant glass-paned doors that led out to the porch. The desk had held the Cameron ledgers for years and years.

He moistened his lips, feeling a cold sweat break out on his skin. A feeling of dread was already falling over him.

He slipped on his shirt and hurried from the room. Again he paused, for though he rarely gave the portrait gallery at the top of the stairway much attention, he now felt as if each and every Cameron were staring down at him. He paused and studied the pictures. Lord Jamie Cameron, and his beautiful barmaid bride, the indomitable Jassy. His grandmother, Amanda, cool and elegant, accused of being a Tory spy, but standing by her husband in the end. And Eric Cameron, a slight twitch of amusement to his lips, his eyes painted a startling deep blue. He seemed to question Jesse— to dare him to hold to his own faith.

And then there was his father. The portrait had been painted late, when he was older, his hair was snow white, his eyes still a startling blue. There was something wise in the gaze that seemed to follow him. Something, too, that seemed to warn him that there could be no course for him except the one he believed in most deeply.

"But I would betray you all!" he whispered. He realized that the whisper hurt his head, and that he was in worse shape than he had imagined if he was talking to his long-dead ancestors.

He came down the stairs and strode through the breeze-way. A larger grouping of men had gathered on the porch by then.

Anthony Miller cried out, shooting a gun off into the air.

"For the love of God!" Jesse exclaimed. "Will someone tell me what is going on here?"

"Hell, yes! It's secession, Jesse! Old Abe Lincoln up there in the North is begging the states for troops. Well, Virginia will not take arms against her southern brethren. The legislature has voted her out! Hell, Jesse, we're seceded! We're out of the Union!"

Jesse felt a churning in the pit of his stomach. No one seemed to notice his discomfort. They were all shooting off their guns like a pack of fools, talking about whopping the Yanks in a matter of weeks if the Yanks thought to fight about anything at all.

He sank down into a whitewashed wrought-iron chair. Christa, sitting there too, looked at him and reached out to pour hot coffee into his cup.

"Jesse?"

"Thanks," he muttered to her. He looked out onto the yard. Even Daniel was behaving like a fool, throwing his plumed hat up into the air and letting out a cry like a banshee.

"Jesse, Daniel's going to resign his commission today."

Jesse nodded blankly, sipping his coffee black.

"Jesse, there's more news," she said in a rush, her beautiful eyes dark on his. "Lincoln sent an emissary from Washington across the river to Arlington House."

Arlington House was Colonel Robert E. Lee's home. The message had come to him through his wife, who was George Washington's step-great-grandchild. Her father had built Arlington House, and she possessed many fine household items and furniture that had belonged to the first president. It was a beautiful and graceful home, where Colonel Lee had raised his children. It was on a mount and looked right across the river over to Washington, D.C. It was a very strategic location.

Jesse leaned back. "And?" he asked Christa.

She spoke in a rush. "Lincoln was ready to offer Colonel Lee command of the federal field forces, Jesse. Why, everybody knows that he's one of the finest soldiers in the field, even Lincoln. But, Jesse"—she paused, leaning forward— "Jesse, Lee refused him. He was against secession—at least, that's what Daniel told me. But now that Virginia has seceded, Lee has tendered his resignation. Jesse, everyone is doing so."

He nodded blankly and looked at her with a lopsided smile. "Christa, why did you let the two of us drink so much last night? By God, but I am in pain this morning!"

He rose and stretched and stared at the men still caterwauling on his property. Someone had just trampled over a rose bush.

"Excuse me," Jesse muttered. He strode back inside, and entered the parlor. The April morning was chilly, and Christa had seen to it that a fire was set against the cold.

He leaned against the mantel, feeling curiously numb now that secession had come.

Someone suddenly burst in on him. He swirled around to see the young, anxious, and highly flushed face of Anthony Miller.

"Oh! Sorry, Jesse. I didn't mean to interrupt you. You look like a man seeking solitude. But, hell—you should be out there celebrating with us!"

Jesse stared at Anthony, at the wild exhilaration in his eyes. Suddenly, raw anger ripped through him. "Anthony, there has been firing. There's going to be a war. What the hell is there to celebrate in that?"

Anthony stared at him blankly, then flushed. "Hell, Jesse. I never took you for a coward."

"Don't make the mistake of taking me for one now," Jesse warned him sharply.

Anthony lifted his hand to his hair. "Captain Cameron, I apologize. I'll leave you, sir, to your own deliberations." He swung around, but then paused, looking back. "You know her mighty well, Jess. Think she'll marry me now? What with war being on the brink? I'm banking on her finding a little romance in it all. I'll be her soldier-boy, marching away to war—well, riding. It's a cavalry unit we've recruited." He grinned with a boyish appeal. It should have been difficult to be angry.

But Jesse still felt slow burning fury.

"Do I think that *who* will marry you now, Miller?"

"Why, sir, I refer to your good neighbor here in the Tidewater region, Miss Mackay. Kiernan."

There was something so painstakingly eager on Anthony's face that Jesse looked back to the fire. "You don't want to marry her, Anthony."

A silence followed his words. Then the sharp sound of Anthony's voice queried him again. "Cameron, I demand you explain yourself, sir!"

Jesse gazed at Anthony, who was as straight as a poker. What was he to tell the misguided sap? That the girl he adored was in love with Jesse himself? But was she so much in love with him anymore?

"There's nothing to explain, Anthony. Forget it."

But Anthony wasn't about to forget it. He came striding across the room, pulling off his riding gloves in his agitation. He faced Jesse at the fireplace. "I demand, Captain Cameron, that you explain yourself!"

"And I'm telling you, there is nothing to explain."

"You have cast aspersions upon the woman I love!"

"I cast no aspersions upon her! I merely suggested that she might not be—that she might not be the woman that you want to marry!"

"Because she has meant something to you, sir? How dare you suggest any impropriety on her part!"

"I did no such thing!" Jesse snapped irritably. "If anyone suggested such a thing, Anthony, I'm afraid it was you."

Anthony took a wild swing at him. Instinctively, Jesse ducked, but Anthony swung again. This time Jesse dropped low and swung beneath him, turning back to come up with his right fist flying in self-defense. He caught Anthony square in the jaw, and the younger man landed hard by the mantel.

Anthony rubbed his jaw, staring at Jesse. Jesse gritted his teeth and walked over to him, offering him a hand. "Ask her to marry you. Maybe war *will* change her mind."

But Anthony's anger had risen too high. He eschewed the hand offered to him and rose. "I reckon we're not even going to be on the same side in that war, are we, Cameron?"

"I won't celebrate bloodshed. That's the only decision I've made so far."

"She won't go with you because she doesn't want you," Anthony stated aggressively.

Jesse lifted his hands, clearly stating he wanted no part of a fight.

But Anthony's glove came flashing across his face in a stinging blow. Startled, he touched his cheek and stared at the younger man as if he had gone insane.

"What the hell—?"

"I'll meet you, sir, with pistols. By the old chapel in the glen, this evening, at dusk."

"What?"

"I said—"

"I know what you said! Damnation, Anthony, no one meets with pistols anymore!"

"Then let it be swords!"

Jesse swore softly. "Jesus, Anthony, I don't want to kill you."

Anthony bit down on his lip as if he regretted his hasty challenge.

Again, Jesse tried to dissuade him. "Anthony, there is no one in this room except you and me. No one saw what happened here. Let's not meet with pistols or swords."

Anthony worked his mouth as if he were about to agree, but then he stiffened. "I have my honor, sir!"

"God in heaven!" Jesse began.

"What's going on in here?" a soft voice suddenly demanded. Jesse looked past Anthony to see that Christa had come into the room, and Daniel and the others were behind her.

"Why, Mr. Cameron and I have just agreed upon a meeting with pistols over a personal and private matter."

"What?" Daniel demanded increduously.

"Aaron, I'd look kindly upon it if you'd agree to be my second. Daniel, I'll naturally assume that you'll stand for your brother," Anthony said.

Jesse threw up his hands in exasperation. "What the hell is this desire for bloodshed?" he demanded.

"Sir, I will meet you at dusk!" Anthony insisted. "The challenge was mine, therefore the choice of weapons is yours."

"Well, why not bring everything that you have?" Jesse drawled sarcastically. "Let's do this up well!"

"This is not a matter to be taken lightly!"

"Very well, then, Anthony. Meet me at dusk!" Jesse said with disgust. He bowed low to Anthony with an elegant, cavalier mockery, then looked upward. "God help me, for I do not seek to kill this poor fool!" he muttered.

Anthony turned crimson, but Jesse ignored him. With everyone staring at him, he swore a sudden, savage oath and strode swiftly from the room.

Twelve

Few people were as thrilled by the vote for secession as Kiernan's father. John Mackay was totally convinced that the southern cause was right. When the colonies had felt unjustly treated by England, they had broken away. They had fought a revolution and gained their independence. He saw the present southern situation as very much the same.

Oddly enough after a sleepless night, Kiernan rose early. She spent time in the laundry advising Julie on how to remove a custard stain from one of her father's favorite shirts. There were several deer and a wild hog to be properly preserved, so she had then spent time in the smokehouse. There was plenty to keep her busy. But no matter how preoccupied Kiernan became, she couldn't keep her mind off Jesse.

By the time her celebrating father remembered that she was down at the smokehouse, it was late in the afternoon.

She heard a gunshot and looked up at old Nate, who was hanging a slab of the venison. She hurried around the structure, wiping her hands on her apron and smoothing back some tendrils of hair that were escaping the bun at her nape. She looked up to see her father on horseback, racing up and down the path through the manor house appendixes. At one end he stopped, turned, and saw Kiernan. A broad grin split his weathered face, and his misted blue eyes came alight.

"They've done it, girl! They've voted us out! Virginia is out of the Union!"

His pistol exploded in the air again. A nearby chicken
squawked in panic. Nate looked at Kiernan.

She wiped her hands nervously on her apron again.
"We're out?" she repeated to her father.

"Indeed, we are, missy! Let them hothead Yanks breathe
hard and threaten and ramble on about sedition now! The
heart of the country, the heart of the revolution, is southern!"

He turned his horse away and raced back toward the
house. From her distance, Kiernan could see that riders
awaited him by the front porch. His old cronies had come by
with the news, she thought. They'd retire now to his den and
drink themselves into being heroes.

She sighed softly and reminded herself that her father had
been a military man, West Point like so many of the others,
and that he had served in Mexico. She smiled softly. He had
been very handsome and dignified in his uniform.

A uniform he would never wear again.

But Jesse!

It had reached the crisis stage for Jesse, she realized, and
the blood drained from her face. She had told him not to see
her again, but she suddenly realized that it was imperative
that she see him. She had to convince him to resign his
commission with the Union Army.

She smoothed back her fallen hair again and pressed her
palms over her apron. She was a mess, she thought. Beneath
her apron she wore a simple gingham dress and a single
petticoat, and her hair was sodden and limp from the
smokehouse, and she probably smelled like a good old country ham. Her heart beating furiously, she had to hurry back
to the house and bathe before going to Cameron Hall. It
would be one of the most important occasions of her life.

"Nate, just finish here, please," she advised him. He was
one of her father's few free black men, a talented worker
who had earned the money to buy himself from John Mackay by tinkering on the side. But Nate had liked his home,
he had liked John Mackay, and so he had stayed on. Now,
looking at Kiernan, he rolled his eyes as if wondering at the
strange ways of the gentry, then nodded solemnly. He made

Kiernan smile, and she waved as she left him, but her smile faded as she ran quickly for the house. An instinct was warning her that she hadn't much time.

A half-dozen horses were standing in her yard, their reins hanging, and she surmised that the men had gone in for a drink to celebrate the occasion. She had heard church bells ringing earlier, and she now realized that they must have heralded the final vote in the legislature.

As Kiernan started to run up the brick steps, she heard her name cried out.

"Kiernan!"

She turned to see Christa was riding up, bareback and wild. Christa leaped from her horse with little concern for her skirts or for ladylike dignity and raced to her. "You've got to come! Now!"

Kiernan felt the blood drain from her face. A trembling swept raggedly through her body. Something had happened, something horrible.

"Jesse—" she voiced his name. There had been an accident. He was hurt, he was dead. "Oh, my God! He's dead?"

"He's not dead!" Christa told her quickly. "Not yet, anyway. Kiernan, you've got to stop them."

"Stop who, from doing what?"

"Jesse and Anthony—"

"Anthony?"

"He and Andrew were in Williamsburg on business when the news came in from Richmond. He rode straight out to tell Daniel. And then he and Jesse got into a confrontation."

"What? What was it? Over what?"

Christa shook her head, her blue eyes bright. "I don't know!" she wailed. "Neither one of them will say anything at all! They're just planning to have a duel."

"A duel!" Kiernan exclaimed.

"Yes! Oh, I thought that I could shame the two of them out of it at first. I thought they could not be serious! Jesse tried to refuse to fight, but Anthony insisted that his honor would be tarnished if Jesse refused to satisfy his demand. I don't even know what it's over. One moment everyone was throwing their hats in the air, and the next moment I came inside to find Jesse and Anthony at each other's throats. I can't explain any more, Kiernan. We have to go. I haven't been able to stop them, and Daniel hasn't been able to stop them. You have to come and do what you can!"

"Oh, Lord!" Kiernan breathed in misery. Was this over her? What had Jesse said to Anthony? Had he told him about their affair? But Jesse would not have done that. What was it then? Jesse's determination that secession was a mistake? No, the lines were clearly drawn now. If Jesse believed in something different, Anthony would have felt honorbound to allow him that belief.

He wouldn't kill Jesse unless they came face to face on a battle line.

"Kiernan, come!"

Kiernan tugged off her apron and looked at the assortment of horses in front of her. Her father's big stallion, Riley, was eating grass just down the walk. After Christa took a leap and remounted her horse, she offered Kiernan a hand. "You haven't time to get your mare. Ride with me!"

"I'll take Riley."

Christa arched a brow. Riley could be deadly. John Mackay's pride and joy was big and powerful and had a will of his own.

"You'll break your neck!" Christa warned her.

"I need to be there!" Kiernan told her. She leaped up onto Riley, her skirt swinging. She was a good enough rider to handle him, and for all his temperament, she'd never seen a faster horse. John Mackay had won money on him time and time again.

She looked to Christa. "Where?"

"In the glen past our property, down by the old burned-out church."

Kiernan nodded and nudged Riley. He set off like lightning. Christa cried out something from behind her, but Kiernan didn't hear.

Her heart was thundering as loudly as Riley's hooves against the ground. The reckless pace and the seething energy within the massive stallion seemed to join with the shivering that had set up inside of her. She ducked down low against the horse, riding tightly against him, heedless of the wind and brush that sped past her as she reached the road. She careened by a wagon and tore past a group of revelers. Christa was far behind her.

She had to reach them. She couldn't let either of them die, not for her! There had to be a way to reason with them.

She could remind them that they could shoot one another in battle soon enough.

Jesse couldn't die—but she couldn't bear life herself if he were to kill Anthony. Anthony loved her, and Anthony was willing to die for her. This was her fault because she'd never told him the truth. She'd put him off, and she'd put him off, but she had never explained that she didn't love him.

She saw the trail off to the glen and plunged down it, unaware of the branches that reached out to snare tendrils of her hair. She raced on—and heard a shot.

Riley heard it too. Startled, the stallion came to a stop, then reared up on his hind legs, standing almost straight up. Kiernan struggled to remain seated. "You overgrown fraidy-cat!" she yelled at the horse desperately, clinging to its neck. "Get down!"

He did, but when Riley reared once again, she went flying off.

She landed softly, with tears stinging her eyes. She had to get to the copse where the shot had come from! But if Riley went off without a rider, there would be all hell to pay. Her father would have her blood.

Blood! Dear God, a shot had been fired!

Riley suddenly went trotting into the bushes.

She leaped to her feet and raced after him. As she did so, she heard hoofbeats charge by on the trail. "Wait!" she cried out, but the rider did not hear her, or give her heed. Growing more and more desperate, she charged after Riley.

The horse had paused to munch a long clump of grass. She lunged for Riley's reins. He pulled back, snorting, his dark brown eyes wild. But her strength was great in her growing panic. She managed to subdue the horse and mount him again.

Returning to the trail, she raced again until she reached the copse by the old church. She pulled in hard on the reins.

Someone was lying on the ground with two men beside him. Daniel was one, she realized, and the other man she barely knew, but she thought his name was Aaron.

And the one on the ground . . .

She screamed and leaped down from her father's wayward stallion and ran over the cool, shaded earth.

Her heart slammed hard against her chest. It was Jesse! If he was dead, her world was over, and she wanted to die herself.

Daniel looked up at her and saw the raw terror in her eyes. His smile reassured her. "Just a wound," he said quickly. "A flesh wound."

She fell down to the earth upon her knees. It wasn't Jesse. Jesse was nowhere to be seen. The man stretched out on the ground was Anthony Miller, and his shirt and sleeve were soaked in blood.

"Oh, my God!" she breathed.

His dark, deer-brown eyes opened to hers, and he tried to smile. "Kiernan." Then his eyes shut again.

"Anthony!" she cried.

"It's all right," Daniel told her softly. "Jesse gave him a shot of morphine."

"What?" she whispered.

Daniel rose, drew her to her feet, and placed his hands on her shoulders. He pressed her away from the fallen man. "It's all right, Kiernan."

"Jesse—"

"Jesse is fine. He allowed Anthony to take the first shot, and then he just clipped him in the arm. His shooting arm. Anthony wanted to take another shot, but Jesse told him there would be plenty of fighting soon enough. Anthony said that he still wasn't satisfied."

"So what happened then?" Kiernan cried.

Daniel grinned. "I gave Anthony a good pop to the jaw. He fell, and Jesse came over and looked at his arm and gave him a shot against the pain and advised that we just wrap it up real good. Anthony is going to be fine."

"Oh!" she whispered, then she hurried back to Anthony, falling down by his side, determined to see to the truth of it for herself. She ripped up the fabric of his white shirt and found that the wound that had soaked his clothing had already been carefully and neatly bandaged.

She looked up at Daniel. "Jesse tended to him here?"

"Yes," Daniel said, and added wryly, "my brother has to be one of the very few men who would bring his own medical bag to a duel."

He was trying to make her smile, but she couldn't. "Jesse saw to his arm and gave him morphine?"

"Yes, after I slugged him. I didn't want to slug him—I had to, or he would never have let Jesse tend to the wound. Jesse had to dig a bit for the bullet—that's why the morphine."

"Buy why did Jesse leave him like this? Why didn't he—"

"Because someone else has to take care of Anthony now. Aaron's brother has gone for a wagon. He'll take Anthony into Williamsburg, where he can be seen again by a doctor." He paused for a minute. "And because Jesse is leaving."

She felt as if she had been physically struck, slammed across the face and the chest. She stood dead still, staring at Daniel. "Leaving? What do you mean, leaving?"

"Leaving, Kiernan. I don't know when he'll be back."

"But I don't understand!"

"I've resigned my commission, Kiernan. I've written and posted my letter. But Jesse isn't resigning. He has decided that in all good conscience, he can't."

"No!"

Tears were forming behind her eyes, tears she wouldn't allow herself to shed. "Where is he?"

"Probably at the house."

She twirled around, clutching her stomach, and leaped up atop Riley. She slammed her heels hard against his side. The horse seemed to leap into the air, and then they were running again, tearing through the foliage.

She took the shortcut through the fields, through the rows and rows of spring planting. She passed the workers in the fields, felt the sun upon her face, and felt the harsh wind against her as she rode.

The stallion was hot and lathered by the time she reached the back steps.

"Jesse!" she screamed and raced up the steps.

Jigger, the Camerons' very proper black butler, met her at the breezeway door.

"Where's Captain Cameron, Jigger?" she demanded.

"Which one, Miss Mackay?" he asked politely.

"Doctor Cameron! Jesse!"

"Why, he done packed up, Miss Mackay. He won't be coming back to the house." Her face must have crumpled along with her heart, because Jigger spoke quickly. "You might still catch him down by the graveyard, Miss Mackay. He said there were still a few folks he wanted to say good-bye to."

She twirled upon the top step and looked down the sloping lawn, over the garden, and to the cemetery.

Pegasus was standing beneath one of the heavy oak trees just outside the wrought-iron gates.

Jesse stood within, she saw. His plumed hat was in his hands, and his head was bowed.

"Jesse!" she shrieked, and tore down the steps, across the expanse of lawn, her heart beating furiously, creating a thunder in her ears. She ran and ran, sobs tearing from her lips.

He looked up as she neared him and smiled slowly—slowly, tenderly, wistfully, and with an aching bitterness.

"Kiernan." Her name on the breeze seemed a caress.

"Jesse!" She suddenly stopped dead still. He was on one side of the wrought-iron fence, she on the other. Her heart slammed against her chest. Her anguish must have been naked in her eyes.

"I did my best, Kiernan. God knows, I didn't want to hurt him." He shrugged. "I didn't tell him anything about us. I guess he sensed something, I don't know. But he'll be all right."

She nodded jerkily. She didn't want to hear about Anthony now. She knew that he was all right.

"Jesse, you can't ride away," she told him.

"I have to ride away." His smile took on a wry twist. "I don't want to fight a duel with every friend and acquaintance I ever had."

"Jesse!" she cried it out with pain, with anguish, with all her love.

He said softly, "Are you going to kiss me good-bye?"

He was really leaving. The crucial moment had come. He loved his home, but not enough.

And he loved her, but not enough.

"Jesse, if you leave this place now, I will hate you forever!"

He stiffened. "Kiernan, if I stayed here now, you could never really love me, for I would not be able to abide myself."

"I hate you, Jesse Cameron! I swear, I hate you with all my heart! And I will despise you forever. No rebel enemy will ever loathe you as completely as I do now!"

He was silent for a long while. The river breeze rustled by the trees. He raised his head to look toward the river, and then the foliage, and then the house.

He glanced down to the graves of his mother and father one last time.

Then he turned and strode from the cemetery. He walked to the oak and picked up Pegasus' reins.

Then he strode back to her and pulled her into his arms with a force to deny her any thought of protest. His lips burned her lips—no, burned into her being, like a brand of memory that would last a lifetime and beyond. It was a brief reminder of all the sweet passion that had been between them.

He was leaving. She broke free and slammed her hands against his chest, shaking, her voice trembling. "I hate you Jesse Cameron! I'll take arms against you myself if I ever see you in the South again!" She raised a hand high again to strike him, to scratch out at him, to hurt him the way he was hurting her.

He caught her arm. "I'm sorry," he whispered. His blue

eyes were intent upon hers. "For I will love you the rest of my life."

He released her and walked past her, leading Pegasus.

Suddenly weak, she sank down to the ground, her back her to him. She heard a soft, feminine cry and a rustle of silk and realized that Christa and Daniel had come up behind them.

"Good-bye, Jesse. Take care."

"I'm a doctor, Christa. I'll try to save what lives I can," Jesse told her.

Kiernan, listening, closed her eyes tight, and the tears squeezed out. She heard Christa sob softly.

Jesse walked to his brother. Kiernan turned at last. Jesse waved a hand out to encompass the place, the house, the James River, the grand docks, the fields, the cemetery—and her.

"Take care of things, Daniel."

"I will."

They embraced tightly, two brothers. It was Daniel's face that she saw, clenched tight, his jaw hard against the tears, twisted in pain.

Damn Jesse. Damn him!

Jesse released Daniel and looked back to her one more time.

"Kiernan—"

She turned away, bowing her head.

She heard his footsteps as he walked again. Heard his easy movement as he leaped atop Pegasus. Heard the hoofbeats as the horse rode away.

She looked up, her tears blinding her. "I hate you, Jesse. . . . I love you, Jesse," she whispered almost in silence.

Moments later, Christa came and tried to force her to rise. She shook her head vehemently. Then Daniel was by her side, but she didn't hear his words.

"Leave me, please!" she pleaded with both of them.

Though she knew that Daniel would not leave her, that he would be near, she felt alone as the darkness fell over the trees.

She felt numb.

But she wasn't going to remain so, she swore to herself. She would get over Jesse. She would hate him the way she should hate an enemy.

If he ever did come back, she would take arms against him.

Her heart seemed to cry out as she sat in the growing dampness and dark of night, her head bowed before the old cemetery.

The pain washed over her, and she allowed it to.

Then she felt numb again.

At last she rose and furiously told herself that her strength was greater than his.

"Come on," Daniel said. "I'll take you home."

She looked at him and wiped the last tears from her cheeks, shaking. "How can you be so calm, Daniel? He's a traitor! He's a Yankee, a damned Yankee."

He smiled awkwardly. "But he's my brother."

"And what if you meet on a battle line?"

"Then he's still my brother!" Daniel snapped heatedly. He sighed. "And my enemy. Hell, Kiernan, I don't like what he's done one bit. But I understand it. When the lines are drawn and there is no more neutral territory, a man has to fight for what he believes is right. And if he doesn't, he ain't no use to anybody. I understand him, and I forgive him."

"Well, I don't understand him," Kiernan said icily, "and I will never forgive him!" She added softly, "Never."

She turned from Daniel and started for the house.

He followed after her.

"Kiernan, I'll take you—"

She swung around. "Thank you, Daniel, but no. I will stand on my own from now on."

She smoothed her fingers over her gingham skirt, squared her shoulders, and walked toward the house.

Someone had tethered Riley to a ring by the columns. She slipped the tie and mounted the stallion.

She looked out to the river, then to the house.

And then she rode away, very proud, very straight, and very much alone.

* * *

When she reached her house, her father was waiting for her once again. He was waiting upon the porch in the white-wood swing, watching the path for her.

She stiffened. He would be furious with her. She had caused a duel between two men. Thank God Anthony hadn't been killed or seriously injured.

He stood up when he saw her. He walked down the steps and looked up at her while she was still mounted. He scanned her weary, tear-stained face reached up to help her dismount.

"A bad day, eh, girl?"

"Oh, Papa!" she whispered.

He looked into her eyes, smoothing back her hair. "I've heard, Kiernan, I've heard all about it."

He led her up the steps, calling for someone to come and take Riley. He sat her down and slipped an arm around her, and in a moment he was pressing a glass to her lips.

"Brandy," he said.

She looked at him through damp eyes. "You hate it when I drink."

"Take a sip now. I've a dozen things to be mad with you for, girl, a dozen more this day. But I'm not mad, and I wouldn't think of punishing you, for it seems to me that you've punished yourself enough already."

She took a sip, then more than a sip. Shuddering, she swallowed it all down.

"You were right about Jesse."

He rocked quietly for a minute. "I like Jesse Cameron. Always have, always will."

"I hate him."

"Yes. Well, maybe that's for the best."

"I don't ever, ever want to see him again."

John Mackay didn't say a word to her. He just sat with his arm around her, rocking on the swing.

The night passed on as they sat there. John spoke at last.

"Ah, Kiernan, time will tell, eh? Many a young man we'll not see again. For honor is a splendid thing. But blood and death are forever. And if there's anything in this world I'm certain of, Kiernan, it's that we're headed for war."

The swing creaked upon its hinges, and her father drew her close.

"War."

Thirteen

Events suddenly moved very quickly in the Old Dominion. Virginia had officially passed her ordinance of secession on April 17, and within a week, the Confederate vice president, Alexander Stephens, arrived in Richmond to negotiate a military alliance between the Confederacy and Virginia. Stephens alluded to the possibility of Richmond becoming the Confederate capital, and the Virginia delegates quickly reached an agreement with him.

In May, the Confederate government dismantled its offices in its first capital, Montgomery, and moved to Richmond. They had chosen Richmond as a capital because of its close proximity to the approaching conflict. Only a hundred miles lay between Washington, D.C., and the new heart of the Confederacy.

John Mackay, staunch Confederate that he was, watched the happenings in his home state and shook his head. "It's a mistake," he told Kiernan. "Mark my words. It's too close to the conflict. Northern armies will cross that hundred miles. There will be a bloodbath. Why, they're already screaming, 'On to Richmond!' in the North. They are determined that the Confederate Congress will not convene this month."

Kiernan, listening to him at the dinner table, smiled bitterly. "But Pa, I hear the Southern boys are going to tear up those Yanks in a matter of weeks. I'm quite sure that Richmond will be safe."

He narrowed his eyes on her. "You're one of the most ardent little rebels around."

"I am," she assured him. She moved her fingers up and down her water glass idly. "I've listened to some of Daniel's friends. They're spoiling for a fight, like little boys. They think that they're bigger and stronger and that they can just beat the Yanks up and then everything will be fine."

John reached across the table and patted her hand. "We've the very best horsemen, and the very best marksmen. And the very best military leaders. How can we lose?"

But one of their very best men was in the North.

She had vowed that she was no longer going to think of Jesse. It was July, and he'd been gone a long time now. They had been quiet months for Kiernan, easy months in the Tidewater region. A hot, lazy summer was coming on.

As Kiernan had watched the events taking shape around her, she had avoided Cameron Hall. It was too painful to go there. As it was, her nights had been torture. Due to the pain that Jesse caused her, she really began to hate him. She prayed that the pain would ease. She had even avoided Daniel and Christa.

But they were her friends and her closest neighbors, and she couldn't stay away forever. Daniel, a cavalry captain, had recently left for the Confederate Army. Troops were gathering at an important railway station, Manassas Junction, and Daniel was with them.

Anthony was with those troops, too, or would be soon. The army was still being organized, and Anthony's company had yet to move in from the western side of the state.

She didn't know where Jesse was.

She tried very hard to convince herself that she didn't care. At some moments she actually felt numb, and she relished those moments.

The conflict moved ever closer.

Alexandria, just across the Potomac from Washington, was occupied. It was the Union's backyard, and it had surprised no one when forces marched in. The first Union casualty had occurred there. The very popular young colonel Ephraim Elmer Ellsworth had spotted a Confederate flag atop the Marshall House hotel. He climbed to the roof to tear it down. Coming down the stairs, he was shot to death by the hotel's proprietor. The proprietor, in turn, was shot to death by one of Ellsworth's men.

Kiernan felt sorrow that a Union man had been killed. From what she read, he had been a handsome, gallant, and giving man—and a very close personal friend to Abe Lincoln. His body had lain in state at the White House before it was sent home to upstate New York for burial.

Ellsworth, like John Brown, became a martyr in the North, stirring men to cry out and clamor for more bloodshed.

It seemed very sad.

But it also seemed very sad that Robert E. Lee, after refusing an offer from the North and accepting a commission in the Confederacy, had been forced to leave his home. She could imagine Lee and his wife talking through the night of the decision that he'd been forced to leave. He would have known that the Federals couldn't possibly let him be there at Arlington House. And so his wife and his children had been uprooted along with him. The enemy now tramped through the halls where his children had played.

So much seemed so very sad.

Perhaps the duel between Jesse and Anthony had been fought over her, but it never would have happened without the prospect of war. And if not for the prospect of war, she would have married Jesse. No questions of honor would have been raised. Jesse would never have had to tell his brother good-bye, and he would never have had to walk away from his home.

But she wouldn't waste her time thinking about Jesse. If anything, she would worry about Anthony.

She had gone into Williamsburg to see him the day after the duel. She cared very much about him, but she had to admit to herself that it was guilt that forced her to visit him rather than deep affection.

In Williamsburg, she had felt more guilty than ever, because Anthony had assured her that he was fine, that his pride was wounded more than anything else.

He had told her again that he loved her, that he'd fight a thousand duels for her, that he'd die over and over again for her.

But Jesse, who claimed to love her too, would not even remain to fight in his own state for her. He claimed that as a doctor, he wanted to save lives, but lives could be saved on this side of the conflict just as well.

She had been thinking about Jesse when Anthony had demanded, "Well, Kiernan?"

"Well?"

"Will you marry me now? Or will you at least think about it? I'll march soon enough, now that Virginia has seceded, I know that. We'll be going off to whip those boys in blue. Let me carry the memory of your love into battle with me!"

"Anthony, I don't—"

He pressed his finger against her lip. "Don't say no to me, please. Tell me that you'll think about it. Let me live on that hope."

She hadn't had the heart to tell him no.

It would not be only Anthony against Jesse. It would be Daniel against Jesse too. Brother against brother.

But that was war. And as Kiernan's father had told her, war was coming. Everyone spoke of it. Everyone seemed to long for it. "On to Richmond!" As her father had said, the North was very determined to swiftly end the rebellion. Patriotism ran high on both sides.

One morning in July, John Mackay lifted his head and quickly folded up the paper he had been reading at the table. He frowned. "Listen!" he told her.

She didn't hear anything at first, but then she heard horses, a large group of them, coming down the long drive.

John stood quickly, and Kiernan followed him to the door. Suddenly, she heard a loud Rebel cry, and the sounds of pounding hooves came closer and closer.

"What is it?" Kiernan asked.

"Seems to be a Rebel company," John replied, grinning. "But what it is doing on my front lawn, I surely don't know."

He strode out onto the porch, Kiernan following him.

There was, indeed, a Rebel company on their lawn. They were a handsome lot, even if they moved with a wild confusion, their horses prancing everywhere. They were dressed in butternut and gray, the handsome new uniforms of the South. The uniforms didn't seem to be government issue, but ones specifically designed and lovingly hand-sewn for this particular company. The Rebs wore cavalry hats, just like those in the Union cavalry, except that these were gray. Gray, pulled low, and finely plumed.

There were about twenty-five in the company, tramping across the lawn, reckless, loud, and constantly cheering.

"What in the Lord's good name—" John Mackay began. But a rider broke away from the melee and trotted toward them. He pushed back his hat.

"Anthony!" Kiernan gasped.

He grinned broadly at her. He was wonderfully, engagingly handsome with his warm, dancing brown eyes, his golden curls beneath the fine plumed hat, and his perfectly curved moustache and finely clipped beard. He sat his horse so well, and his smile, so endearing, touched her that night as it had never touched her before. She did not love Anthony. And she could never love anybody with the wild and desperate passion with which she had loved Jesse.

As he stood before her that night, so gallant and so comical, she laughed in delight as she had not laughed in some time.

Not since Jesse had left.

"Mr. Mackay!" Anthony called, and he grinned at Kiernan again. "Despite your daughter's very inappropriate laughter at such a fine pack of soldiers for the Confederacy, I have come to ask you for her hand in marriage. No, sir! Your pardon, I take that back! I have come to beg you for her hand in marriage!"

John Mackay's brow shot up.

"Well, son, if you're going to be begging and pleading, I'm the wrong one to be doing it to!"

Anthony grinned, and he leaped down from his horse. The men of his company quit their wild prancing and brought their horses to a standstill behind his, as disciplined now as they had been unruly just seconds before.

Anthony walked toward the steps to Kiernan, pausing with a booted foot atop the first step. He reached for her hand. "We're riding even now for Manassas Junction. We will barely arrive when we were ordered to. But all these fine fellows know how deeply I pine for you. I have told them, of course, that you have moments of heartlessness. I have told them that you have refused me for years. But the last time I spoke with you, you didn't actually refuse me. So you see, we decided to waylay our journey just a bit—"

"Just a bit!" Kiernan exclaimed. "You've ridden well over a hundred miles out of your way! You came all the way over here to the peninsula!"

He grinned again. "Yes. So it would be churlish for you to refuse me still again!"

He walked up the last step and pulled her close against him. "Kiernan, I've no time, no time at all. Not even a night to spend with you, not a day to take you anywhere, not even home. But I've got a preacher with me—Captain Dowling is also Father Dowling of Charles Town—and if you would consent to be my wife this night, I promise that I'll come back for you. And I'll take you anywhere in the world that you want to go once this skirmish is over. I'll take your kiss into battle, and with the sweet promise of you in my future, I swear I shall lead these fine gents to sure victory."

Kiernan stared at him blankly for several moments. She felt numbness steal over her.

Yes. Yes, marry him, marry Anthony. She had known him so long, and she did care for him very deeply. And she owed him, because she had led him on in a way, when she had known in her heart she loved Jesse.

She didn't love Anthony, but he loved her enough for both of them he had told her once.

Marry him, marry him, marry him, she told herself. Erase forever the hope that Jesse will come back.

"Anthony," her father answered for her, "this has been a cavalier and highly romantic deed on your part, but perhaps it might be best to wait until—"

"Yes!" Kiernan exclaimed.

"What?" Anthony and her father voiced the word simultaneously.

Anthony, she realized, had not really dared to hope. Her father, she thought, knew her too well.

"I said yes!" Kiernan exclaimed.

"Kiernan," John said, frowning, "this is so fast."

"Nonsense, Papa, we've known each other for years. Anthony has been asking me for years! And he's about to ride away into battle—" She broke off, for his troops were shouting and whooping, cheering her on.

"It seems that I'm outvoted here," John murmured. He stared at Anthony. "Young man, give me a moment alone with my daughter."

He drew her into the house, closing the door so they could have privacy in the hallway. He set his hands upon her shoulders.

"Daughter, do you know what you're doing?"

"Yes, Papa, I do."

"You were in love with Jesse Cameron."

She didn't blink. She stared steadily into his eyes. "I hate Jesse Cameron," she said flatly.

"That's what scares me," John told her. "There's a very thin line between love and hate. All these years, young lady, I never forced your hand, never arranged a marriage, so that you could fall in love and marry the man of your choice."

"But if you had arranged a marriage for me, you would have arranged it with Anthony," she reminded him.

He sighed softly. "Kiernan, don't do this."

"Papa, I must!"

"You're always too passionate, Kiernan, too reckless."

"Papa, don't stop me, please. He's riding into battle. He came miles and miles out of his way."

"And he's riding out again as soon as you say the word. I

won't stop you, Kiernan, but listen to me first. If you marry him tonight, he will ride back into your life. You will be his wife, and when he returns for you, you will go to his home. You will share his bed at night, and you will take care of his family. Do you understand that?"

She shivered deep inside. Images of Cameron Hall flashed through her mind. She had always dreamed that she would be the lady of the hall.

"Yes," she told her father.

"You really want to do this?"

"Yes, with all my heart."

John sighed softly again, then opened the door. Anthony was waiting on the porch, handsome and dignified in his new uniform, straight and tall. Only his eyes betrayed his anxiety.

"Seems my daughter is now all-fired determined, Anthony. All these years, and we have to have a wedding here tonight with the supper dishes barely off the table. Well, then, it's what you both want. Come in, men, come in."

A cry went up like nothing Kiernan had ever heard before. Anthony let out a whoop and threw off his hat and plucked her up high into his arms. She stared down into his eyes, and she was glad.

It was just that she felt cold and numb.

"Lieutenant Miller, let's get to it!" one of his men advised. Suddenly the gray-clad soldiers were filing into her house, and her feet were back on the ground.

Anthony's adoring eyes were still staring into her own. "Thank you!" he told her.

She tried to smile, but her lips would not move. She stared at him gravely until her father caught her arm, pulling her back into the house. "Anthony, come on."

She remembered very little of the ceremony. Her father stood by her side and slipped her hand into Anthony's. Captain Dowling—Father Dowling of Charles Town—said all the proper words while Anthony's men stood witness behind them.

Her father had pulled a handful of daffodils from a vase, and she curled her fingers around them as she listened to the words. Anthony had to nudge her to repeat her vows, but she did so. She repeated them firmly, even if she was so cold that she didn't know what she said.

Then the same cries went up in the air, and Jubilee, her father's housekeeper, who had been very much a mother to Kiernan, started to cry. Father Dowling said that the groom could kiss his bride, and she was in Anthony's arms.

He kissed her.

And then she knew that she had made a big mistake. His kiss was filled with love and warmth. It was tender and restrained.

And it was little else. It wasn't demanding, passionate, or filled with fever. It wasn't a kiss to cause the world to cease spinning, a caress to warm her inside and out. It did not touch her blood or reach into her limbs, or into the very center of her being. It wasn't hot and wet and reckless and . . .

It wasn't Jesse's kiss.

Tears stung her eyes, but she swore that she would not shed them. She forced herself to curl her arms around Anthony's neck, to return his kiss, to try to give him a hint of the love that he was so determined to give to her.

The war whoops and hollering continued. The men stamped the floor. She heard the pop of a champagne cork.

She allowed herself to break away from the kiss, and she forced herself to keep her eyes upon Anthony's. She hadn't really thought this out at all. She didn't love him.

But she would be a good wife to him, she swore. She'd be a wonderful mother to his little brother and sister, she'd keep the house while he went to war, and she'd learn what she could about his business. She'd be good for him, she really would. She'd make up for the fact that she'd love another man until the day that she died.

But Anthony would never know that, she vowed.

"Kiernan, I love you. If I died tonight, I'd die happy, knowing that you love me."

She forced a smile to her lips. Her father brought them both champagne and shook Anthony's hand, and he welcomed him as his son-in-law.

It felt as if her cheek were kissed a hundred times as each of Anthony's men filed by her. Her father's supply of champagne, cool from the wine cellar, was drunk, and Jubilee managed to get out enough pies and cakes and breads and smoked meat to create something of a wedding feast.

It all went by so fast. Then a nervous private urged the company on. The troops filed out until only Anthony was left, holding her hands in the hallway.

"You've made me the happiest man on earth," he told her. He pulled her against him again and kissed her. She tried very hard to return his emotion, to fight the tears that stung her eyes.

"Take the greatest care, Anthony."

"I will. I'll come for you as soon as I can. Oh, Kiernan, thank you! I love you so very much."

He kissed her one last time, then released her, looking over her head to her father and thanking him.

"Care for her for me, sir."

She sensed her father's smile. "I've been doing so all these years, young man. I reckon I can manage awhile longer."

Anthony grinned, and he was gone.

Her father came up behind her, setting his arm upon her shoulder as they watched Anthony and his company ride away. They were beautiful—all of them, Kiernan thought, all young, and elegant in their new plumage, excellent horsemen.

God protect them all, she thought.

"Well, Mrs. Miller?" her father said. He spun her around to face him. She lifted her chin. She was close to tears, but she knew she had to smile.

"I'm happy, Papa. Honest to God, I'm happy. I'll be good to him, honest I will."

He lifted a brow. "Most men don't want a wife to be good to them, Kiernan. They want a wife to love them."

She lowered her head quickly. "Papa, I care very much for him." She raised her eyes to his. "He was so handsome tonight, wasn't he? Handsome and gallant and wonderful!"

"Handsome and gallant and wonderful."

And that, John Mackay agreed, young Anthony Miller

had been. Everything was right about the boy. He liked his new son-in-law just fine.

But handsome and gallant and wonderful didn't mean everything. The real measure of a man was inside him. While one man might not be any worse or any better than another, it was largely the qualities inside of him that made him what he was.

She was still in love with Jesse Cameron. John Mackay understood that better than she did herself at that moment. He still liked Jesse himself. There was something special about Jesse Cameron, and something special about the way he and Kiernan connected.

But Jesse was gone with an enemy army, and it was best that Kiernan learn to forget him.

She was on the right track, John determined wryly. She was married now, legally wed, forever bound.

He hoped she understood that.

"I'm tired, Papa. I'm going up to bed," she told him.

He studied her eyes, nodded, and kissed her cheek. She smiled brilliantly and hurried away.

But later, he passed by her room and heard her sobbing softly.

Not a good sign for a bride of less than four hours, he thought. He sighed. Anthony Miller was a good man. And he'd be good to Kiernan. They'd get on well enough, which was what most people did anyway.

But his heart went out to her as he stood outside her bedroom door. She was his only child, and he loved her with all his heart. He prayed for her happiness. When Anthony came for her, when they lived together, when there were little children at her feet, perhaps then she would find the happiness that seemed determined to elude her now.

But Kiernan never had to lie in the bed she had made for herself. Manassas saw to that.

In his hospital tent at Bull Run, Jesse was up to his elbows in blood.

The wounded, the already dead, and the dying were arriving with frightening speed. He was probing a ball from an artillery man's shoulder when suddenly a cry went out that they should evacuate quickly.

The ball wasn't quite out. Jesse gritted his teeth and stood his ground, even as shells exploded nearly overhead.

"Captain Cameron! Did you hear me?" a young sergeant demanded.

"I heard you! And I promise you, son, if there's ever a ball in your shoulder, I'll see that it's out before I hightail it and run, all right?" He looked up, motioning to his orderlies. "Get the rest of these men out of here, and onto the wagons —fast!"

He paused, then set back to his task. Another shell exploded, ripping along his nerves, but he held steady. He could hear the troops racing by him.

They had taken the offensive here at Bull Run. Military leaders had advised Lincoln to use patience, but the northern populace had been clamoring for action. The attack had been sound enough. Under the command of Brigadier General Irvin McDowell, Lincoln had ordered that the troops advance.

But the strategy had not gone smoothly from the start.

Jesse's corps had started out with the campaign on the sixteenth of July. McDowell's army had been thirty-five thousand strong, marching out of Washington with colorful Zouaves in the front.

But two days of confusion and straggling and an incredibly slow pace had followed. They had entered Centreville, Virginia, a town directly east and north of Bull Run, which was a lazy, sluggish stream.

But behind that stream was Confederate General Beauregard and his army, with twenty-two thousand Confederates waiting to defend the vital railroad position at Manassas Junction.

On the day of their arrival, McDowell ordered a reconnaissance probe. That resulted in a skirmish with two Confederate brigades at Blackburn's Ford.

The skirmish resulted in two more days of confusion, days

in which McDowell resupplied his poorly disciplined troops and created his battle plan. Finally, at about 2:00 A.M. on the twenty-first, McDowell had his twelve-thousand-man flanking column marching down the Warrenton Pike from Centreville.

McDowell's plan had been sound enough, Jesse thought. But his troops were still not an army—they were an untrained, inexperienced mob. It seemed painfully clear now that Confederates had been warned of the plan. Beauregard had been reinforced by troops from the west under Confederate General Joseph E. Johnston.

The battle had grown heated by midmorning, when a Confederate colonel led his troops against the Union attack force. Jesse heard from the wounded coming in that reinforcements for the Rebs as well as the Union forces had come piecemeal, as the Confederate and Union generals alike sent men scrambling from the Confederate right to bolster the sagging left flank.

One of Jesse's orderlies, a longtime army man and Virginian from Powhatan County by the name of Gordon Gray, told him dolefully that it had been their own statesmen who bolstered up the day for the Rebs. "Colonel Bartow and General Lee were up there, heading things up. But the Rebs are just as raw and green and scattered as most of these new recruits we got here ourselves. Then that eccentric college professor from the Virginia Military Institute stood up there with his troops—Jackson. Thomas Jackson, Brigadier General Jackson. And he held still up there on the hill. General Lee tried to rally his troops, and his cry went up—'Look! There's Jackson standing like a stone wall. Rally around the Virginians!' " Gordon shook his head sadly. "And by God, they did. Jackson's men on the hill started our troops running, and they've been running every since."

The Federals had regrouped, and savage fighting had continued. Men had streamed into the field hospital. But now, it seemed, they were being beaten back at last.

Shells were exploding one right after another.

Jesse pulled the ball cleanly from the soldier's shoulder

and quickly set to bandaging the wound. The soldier opened pained and opiate-glazed eyes to Jesse. "Am I going to live?" he asked.

"Maybe to the ripe old age of a hundred," Jesse told him.

The soldier grinned. Corporal Gordon Gray appeared to help him scramble over to the wagon where a score of wounded waited. The wagon started off. A shell that exploded overhead missed the wagon by inches.

Gordon forgot his military etiquette. "Jesse, come on!"

Jesse quickly and efficiently closed up his bag and gave orders to save what they could of the field hospital. His cots and bandages and surgical equipment were quickly packed and loaded unto another waiting wagon. Pegasus was tethered to the rear of it. A veteran of many confrontations in the West, the seasoned war horse awaited Jesse's command.

Jesse mounted Pegasus to follow the wagon.

Soon he was part of the Union retreat.

And it was a retreat. Soldiers ran pell-mell from the action. Haphazard shots were fired.

In front of them, Jesse could see the carriages of the darn fool civilians who had ridden out from Washington to watch the rebellious little Confederates get their comeuppance.

Those Confederates had proven themselves not so easy to beat.

Jesse had never expected that it would be easy. He knew too many of the men who fought for the South.

He gritted his teeth, seeing an overturned carriage. "Hold up!" he called to the wagon. He leaped off Pegasus and hurried to the carriage. A civilian man was caught beneath one of the broken wheels. "Gordon! Come quickly. Help me!"

They extricated the man from the debris. Jesse was sure he had a broken leg, but there was nothing that he could do about it now. Thankfully, the man fell unconscious after he was pulled out. He wouldn't feel the pain as the wagon jolted back to Washington.

It was the last time the man would watch a battle for sport, Jesse reckoned.

It had been a grim day all around. He closed his eyes and

thought of all the wounded who had passed through his tent.

He winced when he thought of all those who had died before he'd had a chance to touch them. Hundreds lay on the field today.

Well, they had all wanted war.

Pegasus stopped suddenly without a signal from Jesse. The wagon had stopped, and Pegasus, fine animal that he was, had stopped along with it.

They had come across another hospital wagon, and the driver was calling out to him.

"Captain Cameron! There's another field tent up ahead. It's out of artillery range for the moment. The doc there was killed by a shell. Think you can bandage up a few men who won't make the march back without a little help?"

Jesse nodded. "Corporal, bring my bag," he called to his corporal.

He walked into the tent and looked with dismay at the scared and filthy faces of the men who could sit or stand. He looked with deeper dismay at those unconscious on the ground and on the few cots. The uniforms hadn't been standardized yet, so along with the regular army blue, there were any number of outfits upon the men.

He walked to a cot where a sheet covered a man.

"Oh," said the soldier who had stopped him. "Those are Rebs. Someone brought them here by mistake. Seems they were cavalry and with the dust and powder on them, they looked a lot like the Union boys. Why don't you see to them last?"

Jesse felt his heart beating hard. Reb cavalry—the injured could be any number of men he knew.

Hell, there were hundreds of Reb cavalry men that he didn't know.

He looked across the field tent at the two orderlies who seemed to be doing their best to make order out of the chaos, to make the injured men as calm and comfortable as possible.

"Take me around to whoever needs help first. Don't go by

their uniforms. Just take me to the men with the worst injuries."

"You're going to mess with the Rebs—" the annoyed soldier began.

"Damned right, Private. I'm here to save lives, and I'm not going to ask a pack of questions first. Understand?"

He didn't receive an answer. One of the orderlies stepped forward quickly. Jesse began to look at the men. He was appalled by the number that he found dead already. The tent was a nightmare. The men were gut-shot, they were blinded. Their limbs were so badly battered that Jesse knew amputation was the only way out. But for the moment, he did patch-up jobs. He had no time to do more. He bandaged the men up just enough to enable them to get back to Washington.

He turned in time to see the second orderly pull a sheet over one of the Rebs. He felt his heart quicken. He'd tried hard to be impartial. He couldn't do it anymore.

A cavalry officer could be his brother.

"He's dead, Captain," the orderly said. "Trust me. I've been weeding out the dead ones all day."

Jesse ignored the orderly.

He walked over to the shrouded body. A hot feeling of sickness and apprehension swept through his body. Don't let it be Daniel, God, help me. It can't be Daniel.

He snatched the cover back, and a deep, startled sound escaped him.

The man was dead.

It wasn't Daniel.

It was Anthony Miller.

The Confederates were indisputably able to claim the victory at Bull Run. The Union troops had flown like the green recruits they were, leaving the field uncontested.

But both sides had suffered badly. A *Harper's Weekly* correspondent Jesse saw soon after he finished patching up what men he could told him he estimated the North had probably lost close to five hundred, with maybe twelve hundred wounded. It was hard to make a count and might be hard for some time in all the confusion. Close to twelve hundred men were missing, too, but who knew what "missing" men were lost and shell-shocked and what "missing" men were flat-out deserting now that they knew war wasn't going to be a glorious triumph.

The South had lost, too, the correspondent was convinced. Maybe close to four hundred had been killed, and fifteen hundred wounded—but not nearly so many were "missing." Jesse got what information he could out of the men and learned what he could about the southern troops. He found out nothing about his own brother, but the correspondent knew someone who had said that Jeb Stuart had been leading cavalry damned admirably, and a parlay with him might still be possible.

Jesse didn't seek permission from a superior officer. In the confusion that reigned, he wasn't about to go through military red tape to confer with Stuart, an enemy officer. He sent out Private Gibbs into the recent battle zone with a white flag and a message. It took Gibbs some time, but he managed to reach Stuart and arrange a meeting.

Jesse met his old school chum on a ridge where the left flank had fought.

Bodies littered the ground. Trees and grass had been mowed down from the hail of bullets and artillery. Stuart, an incredible horseman, came galloping upon the field with neither fear nor suspicion. Jesse didn't gallop to meet him, for the body of Anthony Miller was on a litter affixed to his saddle by splints.

The two soldiers—Confederate and Union—met.

Jeb nodded to him gravely. "Jesse. It's a damned sorry thing, but it's good to see you alive."

"You, too," Jesse agreed. "Daniel—"

"Your brother's company was under me. He's fine. He didn't receive so much as a nick."

"Thanks," Jesse told him.

"We can't meet long," Jeb warned him.

"I know," Jesse said. "But I found someone who was once an old friend among our dead and wounded, Jeb. I reckoned you could see him returned to his father for burial."

Jeb arched a brow and looked to the sheeted bundle in the litter. He leaped down from his mount and came around, lifting the sheet.

He looked up at Jesse. "Jesu," he murmured. "I can't take him to his father. Andrew Miller was with Johnston's army. He was killed, too, not far from here, in the early stages of the battle."

Jesse felt his throat tighten. Father and son together in one day? Two bodies would have to be received by the children. All that remained of the Miller family now were Anthony's younger brother and sister, he thought.

"By God," Jeb muttered, "I'll have to deliver both of these bodies to his wife."

"His wife?" Jesse tensed.

Jeb looked up at him. "You didn't know? Anthony married Kiernan Mackay."

"No," Jesse said. "I didn't know." Hot arrows pierced him. She had finally married him. She hadn't loved him, but she had married him.

I'm actually jealous, Jesse thought in amazement. How the hell can I envy a dead man?

Jeb was looking at him again. "It was good of you to come out here like this, Jesse. I'll see to it that Anthony makes it home. I'll see to it that Kiernan knows you got him back to me."

Jesse shook his head. "No, keep my name out of it, please. Give Daniel my best, though."

Jeb smiled with a slow, wry curve to his lip. He knew Jesse's situation. Jeb's own father-in-law was a colonel with the Union Army, and would certainly receive quick advancement now with the war under way.

Jeb knew what it was like to have a family split. "I'll see to it that he gets your regards."

Jesse dismounted from his horse and released the litter contraption. "Take care, Jeb."

"You, too, Jesse."

Jesse mounted and rode along the bloodstrewn trail. His

heart had never felt quite so heavy. He hadn't returned the body of a one-time friend.

He had returned the body of a husband to a wife.

To Kiernan.

Fourteen

A week later, Kiernan stood in the railway station at Harpers Ferry still numb. From head to toe, she was dressed in black. She was now a widow, and she was still in disbelief that Anthony was dead.

Daniel had ridden down the peninsula and brought the news to her.

She had been too shocked at first to truly understand what had happened to her. From the night Anthony had married her and left her, she had dreaded his coming back. She had dreaded lying in bed with him, she had been certain that she could never begin to give him what she had given to Jesse so freely.

And now . . .

Her father left her alone after they received the news. John was busy mourning himself for Anthony's father. Andrew had been one of John best friends, as well as his business partner. Now that fine older gentleman was dead.

"He was too old to go to war!" John said, shaking his head. But he realized that his daughter didn't even hear him. She was silent, numb.

It was summer. Something had to be done with the bodies, even if Daniel had taken it upon himself to see that they were put in fine mahogany coffins. Those coffins had to be interred soon.

Within a day, the Millers' lawyer appeared at the Mackays' door. He explained the circumstances to John.

John Mackay in turn sat Kiernan before him and tried to explain the situation to her.

Andrew and Anthony were dead. Young Jacob Miller and his sister Patricia were the heirs to Montemarte. Anthony, always a gentleman in every manner, had adjusted his will before leaving home to ride to battle—and to try to acquire a wife. Kiernan had been left a sum of gold and a share of the rifle works, which now made her her father's business partner.

With the death of both Andrew and Anthony, she had also been left in charge of the children.

With lost eyes she stared at her father. "Kiernan, do you understand? You must care for them. You must protect their home for them. Kiernan, their lives are in your hands." She didn't answer him, and he sighed. "We can have them brought down here. It will be rough on them to lose everyone and then to be uprooted so cruelly too. But if you can't deal with the situation—"

"No!" she protested, instantly standing. The guilt weighed on her terribly. She hadn't loved Anthony, yet she had married him. She hadn't wanted to sleep with him—and he was dead.

The very least that she could do was to care for his family. That would be no difficulty. She knew the children well, she enjoyed them. She knew the Miller household well enough, and it was a fine one.

It was just so far from her own home. But the next morning, dressed in black and with the coffins in tow, she was ready to travel to Harpers Ferry and Montemarte. John Mackay would have accompanied her, but she insisted that she could manage alone. Thomas and Lacey Donahue were wired to meet her at the station with the children. She would manage well enough.

And so she came back to Harpers Ferry, a little more than a year and a half after John Brown had tried to seize the armory.

As she stood in the railway station in her black, she

looked around and found that the place had changed, pathetically changed. It was very empty. Quiet lay over the streets like a pall. The whisper of the breeze seemed the only sound.

She heard the clip-clop of horses' hooves and the wheels of a carriage. Thomas Donahue stepped down from the carriage and hurried across the platform to reach her.

"Kiernan!"

A big, kind gentleman, he took her into his arms and held her warmly.

She hugged him fiercely in return, then looked at him with wide eyes. "Thomas, what happened here?"

"I'll get you to the house," he told her. "We'll talk there." He lifted her baggage up onto the carriage.

The stationmaster had already been ordered to bring the coffins up to the Episcopal church. There would be a service first thing in the morning.

Thomas clucked to the horses and the carriage was off, bringing them around to the house. Lacey was on the steps to meet her and hugged her warmly. She looked at Kiernan very sadly, then clucked like an old mother hen and brought her inside. "I was going to have the children brought here, but then I thought that we should wait. Have some tea, then Thomas can see you up to the house. The children are fine, of course. They are with dear Janey out at Montemarte, and she's been supervising the dears for so long now—well, everyone is fine, of course, but anxious for you. Oh, Kiernan!" Tears welled up in her eyes. "It is so good that you have come!"

She hugged her again. Kiernan found herself before the fire with Thomas while Lacey went into the kitchen to prepare tea.

"Thomas, what has happened here?" she asked him. "It is so terribly desolate!"

Thomas sucked on his pipe, studying the fire. "It's been bad here, you know." He shrugged and screwed up his face in thought. "Let's see—the vote for secession happened in April. We had a Rebel soldier at the telegraph office and Union boys at the arsenal. It's hard to keep track of things, they change so quickly. On the eighteenth, southern forces marched in. The Yanks had destroyed what they could of the armory before leaving. A local man, an Irishman named Donovan, had shouldered a musket to guard the place, and when the Rebs marched in, poor Donovan was very nearly lynched for his Yankee sympathies.

"It's been a hard road here, Kiernan, what with folks split in their beliefs, some for the old government, some for the new. It was tough with the Rebel soldiers in town—young, green fellows for the most part, brash, and impressed with their own importance. 'Course, they were all Virginians in here then, and I've heard tell that we're the most tolerant of the folk, and that if it had been soldiers from the Gulf states, Donovan would be as dead as a doornail by now. Harpers Ferry is between the hawk and the buzzard, I do tell you!

"Let me see, the Rebs were here a few months. Jeb Stuart came in to form up a cavalry corps—a friend of yours was with him and stopped by, young Daniel Cameron. He was as fine and cavalier a soldier as ever, but I tell you, Kiernan, even though it was our southern boys in here, it was still the downfall of the town. The strutting militia fellows were pulled out and a fine man, a colonel named Jackson—he's a general now, distinguished himself at Bull Run, he did, the one they're calling "Stonewall"—he came in, and things were better. But the town was tainted somehow. Suddenly everyone either was a spy or was thought a spy. There's been black-marketing and the like ever since. With all the soldiers in—well, women of the weaker persuasion have flourished."

"Everyone seems to be gone!" Kiernan murmured.

"Oh, there's still folks about, though not so many. Things got worse. There were cries of 'Yanks!' every other day. One day there was a horrible hailstorm—yes, ma'am, a hailstorm —and the troops all went marching out to meet up with a supposed attack. They came back frozen and wet and soaked through, and their brand-new uniforms a wreck. The machinery in the rifle workshops has all been dismantled and sent south to Fayettesville, in South Carolina. The Miller place was dismantled along with the one-time federal works—but the Rebs did leave payment for that. The Millers' lawyer put it all aside and has taken good care of it. You've still got some control of the place your Pa and Andrew and me set up a year or so ago down in the valley. We can talk on that later."

He fell silent, a sad old man. Kiernan prompted him onward. "What happened then?"

"Let's see. Jackson left, and General Joe Johnston was put in command. Then on June fourteenth, the Rebs started blowing things up. They blew the railroad bridge and the arsenal buildings, and they retreated up the valley. Some Mississippi and Maryland troops came through at the end of the month, and they finished off the bridge. Then on the Fourth of July, there was a lively skirmish. Yanks said they won, Rebs said they won. But at nightfall, the Yanks were firing across the river from Maryland Heights, and they killed a civilian. Then things got worse. A Union general, Patterson, was after the Reb Joe Johnston's troops, but Johnston gave him the slip to make it on over to Bull Run and throw in his lot with Beauregard. Patterson pulled back here to Harpers Ferry. I tell you, Kiernan, whatever prowess the Union soldiers might lack on the battlefield, they do not lack in foraging! They ravaged this town. If it wasn't tied down, they took it. Why, some of the boys have told me that they even stole a tombstone out of the Methodist cemetery!" He paused, and exhaled slowly. "Well, they've gone now. There still seem to be some sharpshooters up on the heights yet, and we get some Confederates running around in town —mostly up on the heights this side—to return their fire. But the town—well, she's been wounded. Sometimes I think it's been a mortal blow."

Kiernan stood up and came to his side, setting an arm around his shoulder and laying her cheek against it. "I'm so sorry, Thomas."

He patted her hand absently. "I'm sorry for you, Kiernan. So quickly a bride, so swiftly a widow. Anthony was a very fine young man."

"I know," Kiernan said.

"Here's tea!" Lacey announced, bustling through from the kitchen. She offered Kiernan a wry grin. "It's not much, but it's all I could muster. There's some fine cold chicken, Kiernan. Those Yanks carried off nearly every feathered creature in town, but Janey sent this one over when Thomas told her you were coming. She wants you to know, too, how happy she is to have you coming."

Janey would have thought of something like that, Kiernan thought. She remembered briefly that Janey had been freed by Anthony's will, but that paper work still had to be taken care of. She would get to it quickly, she promised herself. She felt a chill steal over her. There was so much. . . .

There was the beautiful home in the mountains, Montemarte. Anthony had loved Montemarte very much. It was old, like Cameron Hall. It was beautiful, it was graceful. It had been built nearly a century ago. It belonged to Jacob now—Jacob, a boy of twelve.

She owed it to Anthony to protect that heritage for him.

There was Patricia, too, and there was the business, the Miller Firearms factories.

She suddenly felt weary. She wondered if she was competent to deal with it all.

You will be competent! she commanded herself sternly. You will! After everything that you did to that poor man!

"Kiernan, dear?" Lacey repeated. "Are you all right? Of course, you're not. I keep forgetting that poor Anthony has barely grown cold, that we've not even gotten his body into the ground."

"It's all right, Lacey," Kiernan said. She smiled. She and Thomas sat down to the meal that Lacey had worked so hard and so anxiously to prepare. Kiernan did her best to do justice to the meal. She pushed most of her food around, but her tea was very hot and sweet, and she suspected that Lacey had braced it with a touch of something a bit stronger.

"Was everything all right?" Lacey asked her.

"Everything was wonderful," Kiernan assured her. She smiled, still holding her teacup.

"I'll get more tea!" Lacey told her.

The town had changed drastically since she had last been here, Kiernan thought. When John Brown had conducted his raid, there had been several thousand people in town. It had been a prosperous place. And now?

The silence was oppressive. As darkness approached, it seemed to fall even more heavily. No light seemed to flicker into the house from outside. No street lamps were lit, and inside the house, no light was lit.

Thomas Donahue must have sensed her question, for he explained softly to her, "Can't have too much light. The Yanks over there shoot at anything. We keep it dark."

"Oh," Kiernan murmured.

Thomas leaned close to her. "Kiernan, you've got to take grave care."

"Why is that?" she asked him, her eyes widening.

"Well, Miller firearms have been provided for many a fighting man. Andrew managed to get his stock and himself out of town before the Yanks could come for him. Now Andrew and Anthony are dead, but down in the valley, our employees are still manufacturing arms at a startling rate for the Rebs. The Yanks might still decide to come in for the house."

"Montemarte?" she inquired, startled.

"Montemarte," Thomas said.

"But that would be wanton destruction of property!" Kiernan protested.

Thomas smiled bitterly. "Watch the war unfold, Kiernan. There has already been wanton destruction of property. I'm not saying that anything *will* happen, I'm just warning you that you've got to take care, and be prepared."

She straightened her shoulders, though her heart was sinking.

She didn't want to be here. She wanted to go home to her father. She wanted to endure the war in Tidewater Virginia. She wanted to know what was happening to Daniel.

And no matter how she despised him, she wanted to know of any word from Jesse.

But she had married Anthony, and her place was here now.

"I'll manage," she told Thomas. She realized that her voice was harsh, and she squeezed his hand to take away the

sting of it. But when he looked at her, she knew that he saw
the tears that she held back, and that he understood.

He pushed back his chair. "Seems I ought to be taking
you out to Montemarte now."

She rose. She kissed Lacey and promised that they would
see each other again very soon.

She followed Thomas out to the carriage.

It wasn't a long ride to Montemarte, not more than
twenty minutes.

But that night, the ride was far too short.

Thomas drew the wagon up before the house and helped
her out.

There was a light in the window. They were far away
from the snipers up on Maryland Heights.

Thomas took her arm and led her up the walk. She wondered how the children would react to her. For a moment,
an uneasy fear curled in her chest and constricted her
throat. She was such a sham! Their brother's widow. Oh, if
they only knew! She'd had no right to marry him. They
would look into her eyes, and they would know, and they
would despise her for the hypocrisy they saw.

She slowed her pace and stared up at the beautiful facade
of the house.

"Kiernan?" Thomas said worriedly.

She walked forward, her knees trembling.

For the dear Lord's sake! She was about to meet children!

Children could see so clearly.

They might even see that she was in love with a Yankee
soldier—a man their brother had challenged in a duel, a
man who had shot their brother.

Maybe they would see her as the woman who had caused
that duel.

God, what a coward, she railed silently against herself.
She kept walking.

Suddenly, the door burst open. In a blur of motion, someone was running against her.

A soft body catapulted into hers. Instinctively, she
stooped low, opening her arms.

Patricia Miller, just turned twelve, easily threw herself
into Kiernan's arms. And Kiernan just as easily wrapped
her arms around the little girl, who was so woefully dressed
in gray.

"You've come! You've come to be with us. Jacob said that
you wouldn't, that you wouldn't feel you'd been married
long enough to be obliged. But I knew you'd come." Patricia
pulled away from her, her warm, tear-stained eyes ardently
upon Kiernan's. "I knew that you'd come. I always knew
why Anthony loved you so much. You'll stay, won't you?
You won't leave us too?"

Kiernan returned her stare, and warmth flooded through
her.

Patricia was a child who had lost her father and her older
brother on the same day. She was hurt and lost and alone,
and suddenly, standing there upon the porch, she gave
something back to Kiernan—something that Kiernan had
lost, or perhaps even something that she had never had.

"Yes, of course, I'll stay."

"You're my sister now, aren't you?" Patricia demanded.

"Yes, I'm your sister now. And you and Jacob and I are
going to do very well together." She looked past Patricia.
Jacob, twelve, was his sister's twin, but he was already
sprouting up to be a man and was not so quick to hand over
his love and trust. Kiernan would not force him to do so.

"Hello, Jacob," she said.

His brown eyes, so like Anthony's, were grave. "Hello,
Kiernan."

What was missing in Jacob's greeting was made up for in
Janey's. The black woman had stepped through the doorway
too. "Oh, Miz Kiernan! It is good to have you home!"

Janey hugged her fiercely.

Home.

But it wasn't her home!

She had made her bed . . .

Yes, now it was hers.

Home.

*   *   *

In the morning, Kiernan sat between Jacob and Patricia in the Episcopal church and listened while words were spoken over the bodies of Anthony and Andrew Miller.

The reverend spoke of Anthony's grieving widow, and she realized he meant her.

For the first time she realized that, whether or not she had loved Anthony as she should, she had lost a very dear friend. She would never hear his laughter again, never see the sincerity in his warm dark eyes. Tears welled in her own, and a feeling of pain and loss moved through her with a startling severity. Anthony was dead. The dead did not rise, not here on earth. She would never see him again.

The reverend spoke on about the valor and the courage of these men who had been so swift to give their lives to the great southern cause. The Millers were beloved in this country, and the reverend's words were impassioned and earnest. He spoke of the loss of life, of youth and beauty, and of dreams, and as he did so, Kiernan closed her eyes and saw Anthony as she had seen him that last night. So exuberant, so tender, so excited, and as the reverend had said, so beautiful in his youth and gallantry and courage. Now, that was all gone. All that was left of the fine young man was a mangled body to lie and rot in a graveyard.

Either it was the realization that Anthony was dead and gone, or it was the sudden knowledge, deep, swift and sure, that the bloodshed had just begun. But suddenly the numbness left her, and her tears trailed down her cheeks in silent streams. At last she was able to grieve.

The bodies were placed in a fine black hearse and drawn uphill by an ebony gelding to the cemetery. Behind it, in Thomas Donahue's black-draped carriage, the Donahues, Kiernan, Jacob, and Patricia followed. Up at the crest of the hill, in the old cemetery, Anthony and his father were laid to rest in a gated family plot with their kin.

Dust to dust, ashes to ashes . . .

As they stood by the grave site, even Jacob's fingers curled around hers.

The Confederate flag that had draped Andrew's coffin was handed over to Patricia. The one that draped Anthony's was given to Kiernan. She and Patricia stepped forward to toss summer roses into the ground atop the coffins.

Soon those roses would die, she thought.

Dust to dust . . . like the men beneath them.

The funeral was over.

All that had to be endured now was the meal back at Montemarte. When they returned to the house, there was frightfully little on the tables, but there were very few people there.

The war had already stripped Harpers Ferry and Bolivar and the surrounding countryside of much of their population.

Still, Kiernan thought that she should speak to Janey about the poor spread that had been put on the table for the mourners.

Janey looked at her with dark eyes that were weary and sad. "Miz Kiernan, I put out everything I could manage."

"Janey, if you needed help, you should have gotten it!"

Janey was quiet for a minute.

"Janey?"

"Well, Miz Kiernan, this place never was a plantation, not like your home back in the Tidewater region."

"Well, of course not, but—"

"We have gardens here. Chickens, a cow, and a few pigs. We used to have two more house slaves and ten to tend to the stables and the grounds."

"That's what I mean. If you needed help—"

"That's what I've been trying to tell you, Miz Kiernan. Outside the house, there's Jeremiah and his sons David and Tyne left, and there's me left inside. Mr. Andrew and Mr. Anthony were gone when the Union troops were here. All but Jeremiah's family and me done gone and run off." She lifted her hands expressively. "Mr. Andrew were never a hard man on nobody—he never whipped a man that I know of—but that taste of freedom was too strong. They just run off. Now, if we were on the Maryland side of the river, the law would probably have gone after them all. But this is Virginia, and it's a state in rebellion, and no one were going to try to give slaves back to a southern man, especially not the man who owns the Miller Firearms Factories."

Kiernan looked at Janey, and her heart sank. The huge house had to be taken care of. The gardens and the livestock . . . and they had to eat.

But everyone was gone—everyone but Janey and a man named Jeremiah and his sons. However was she going to manage?

She felt hysteria rise within her. She didn't belong here, she should be home. She hated the empty mountain roads, the shell-shot streets in town, and the darkness and the depression that had settled over the area. She hated the Yankees for killing Anthony and Andrew, and most of all she hated Jesse.

It was all his fault.

No, she couldn't hate him, she couldn't even think about him anymore. She couldn't afford to pray for his life, and she didn't dare let herself realize that she was grateful she hadn't heard about his death.

She inhaled and exhaled quickly. She heard the voices of the mourners speaking softly and gently to Jacob and Patricia. There weren't many of them—the food would suffice. They would do very well there at Montemarte—she would see to it that they did.

There were things to be grateful for.

"Janey, thank you for not running off."

Janey smiled, a proud, handsome woman. "I am a free woman, Miz Kiernan. I love those children like my own, and they love me. Why would I run off?"

"Thank you just the same," Kiernan said. "Because I need you very badly. Tomorrow, I'll go and tell Jeremiah the same." She started to walk away, but turned back. "Janey, I've been in something of a fog lately, I'm afraid. Do you know if Mr. Andrew made any considerations for Jeremiah in his will?"

"I don't think so, Miz Kiernan."

"Then you can tell Jeremiah that I will see to it myself that he is legally made a free man."

Janey smiled broadly. "He'll like that just fine—indeed, he will."

To her complete dismay, Kiernan realized that she was very near hysterical tears. "Oh, Janey!" she murmured. Suddenly, she was in the other woman's arms.

"It's gonna be all right, Miz Kiernan. We're gonna make it."

Yes, Kiernan decided, they were going to make it. And not just make it—she was going to do a damned good job of it.

She pulled away from Janey. "We'll make it just fine, Janey. I know we will. Let's get through the rest of today, shall we?"

By evening, the last of their guests, including Thomas and Lacey, had gone. Jacob insisted on seeing himself to bed. Kiernan tucked in Patricia, staying with her while the little girl clung to her. When Patricia's arms at last went limp around her, Kiernan eased herself away. She left Patricia's room and walked across the hallway to the guest room she had chosen for herself.

She hadn't taken Anthony's room. There was still way too much of Anthony about the room—his combs, his shaving equipment, his clothing, diplomas, papers, and memorabilia. Wandering there, she had felt too much as if he were still alive.

She would never be able to sleep there.

One day, Jacob would grow up and marry. He would be the one to take over his father's room, the big master room with the heavy four-postered bed that looked big enough to sleep six.

She had taken the guest room that looked south over the mountains to the back. It was a peaceful view.

She stood by the window, her hands shaking. Leaning against the window frame, she looked out into the darkness and remembered the day Jesse had left. She had been bitterly miserable. But it had been easy to be miserable then. She had had a home where everything had been taken care of for her.

Now she was here, where everything could only be taken care of by her.

She couldn't fret over it any longer, she decided, and morning would come early. She dressed in a cool nightgown and crawled beneath the covers of her bed. The sheets were crisp and comfortable against her skin. The night breeze carried the scent of jasmine upon it. Tears stung her eyes again, but she blinked them away. She told herself that she had to sleep.

And to her amazement, she did.

Eight weeks later, down on her hands and knees in the garden, Kiernan cried out with soft elation as she studied the tomato vines. Janey, plucking the perfectly ripe red orbs behind her, paused and looked behind her.

"They're beautiful!" she exclaimed, flushing, and then laughed as Janey smiled at her pleasure. Kiernan had turned her attention to lovingly tending the garden, and she was amazed by the perfection of the fruit she was growing.

"I've never seen such fine tomatoes in all my born days," Janey assured her.

Kiernan stood up and took a bow. "My lettuce is equally exquisite," she assured Janey. She noticed that Jacob, who still had not warmed to her, was up on the step watching her. He was smiling.

"Exquisite?" he asked her politely, and a smile that reminded her very much of his brother's smile curved his lip.

"Entirely," she told him. Taking two tomatoes from a vine, she tossed the first one over to him. "Catch!"

His reflexes were good, and he caught the tomato. But his smile suddenly faded, as did Kiernan's, as he heard the sound of hoofbeats.

Kiernan swung around. Riders were coming, three of them, dressed in Union blue.

They must be from the 13th Massachusetts, she thought. Harpers Ferry had been quiet—dead quiet—since she had come. Neither army had occupied the area, and the snipers from both sides kept to their action in the heart of town.

But Union General Nathaniel Banks—whom even the

most stalwart of the Confederate sympathizers regarded as a gentleman—had moved on, leaving only a few troops at Sandy Hook, the Maryland point across the river.

The people hated the 13th Massachusetts. They had harassed and shot at the people and had taken everything that they had ever owned from them. Kiernan had not met up with any of those Yanks, but she had heard about them from Lacey.

She was certain that these three men were from Sandy Hook. They were the only Yanks in the area.

It was too late to get a gun, too late to do anything but stand and wait.

"Kiernan," Jacob said nervously.

"There are only three men. Just stand your ground."

"Kiernan, you've been supplying lots of men out of the factory in the valley!" Jacob reminded her with a wisdom well beyond his years. "What if—"

"If they meant real harm, there would be more of them," she said.

"If they try to touch this house, I'll kill them with my bare hands!" Jacob claimed.

One of the men suddenly let out a loud shot and came tearing down on them. Kiernan's eyes widened with horror and she almost shrieked and turned away.

The rider halted and leaped down. He was young, maybe twenty, and his face was riddled with pimples. "Tomatoes, eh? Well, we'll take them. And anything else that you have, you Rebel-lovin' Confederates." He stepped forward, placing a hand on Kiernan's shoulders. She wrenched free, never having know such deep hatred as she knew that moment.

"You won't touch a thing on this property!" she swore.

"I'll have me those tomatoes, sure as the mornin' comes!" he told her.

She still held the one tomato in her hands. If he wanted it so damned badly, he was going to get it. She backed away and hurled it into his face it with force that surprised even herself.

He swore, and to Kiernan's sudden alarm, he pulled his pistol.

A shot rang out. Her hand instantly flew to her throat, and she wondered, dazed, if she had been hit.

But she had not.

It was the Union soldier sinking down to her feet who had been hit. He clutched a bloody stain at his abdomen that spread to engulf his lower body even as he fell.

Fifteen

Jacob screamed to Kiernan as the fire that had been aimed against the Yankee was returned by his two companions. Instinctively, she fell flat, looking around her.

The barrage of fire was coming from more horsemen, these clad in gray, who were coming up the rise of the lawn. There were two of them, Kiernan dimly realized.

The fight did not last long. Even as she lay flat upon the grass, frozen and numb, the gunfire around her ceased.

The three Yankees lay dead.

There was no question of seeing to their wounds or discovering if they still breathed. The first man lay with his glazed eyes open to the heaven above. The second wore a clean hole through his temple, and the third had been caught in the heart.

She stared at them all, a scream rising in her throat, bile forming in her stomach.

Kiernan looked up. Jacob was by her side, helping her to her feet, even as the two Rebs came riding up. The first instantly leaped off his horse. He was a man of her father's age, white-haired, white-bearded, with fine, weathered features. "Mrs. Miller, are you all right?"

The courteous voice, the trembling in the man's tone, brough the first realization to her that she might easily have been killed by either side. She almost fell to the ground, but she felt Jacob's arm of support and she knew that she couldn't fall apart in front of him. Janey was running to her side too. Patricia would have heard the shots from inside, and she would soon be running out. Jeremiah and the boys were out back feeding the hens and choosing a fryer for the night, but they had heard the shots. It was no time to fall apart.

"I'm fine," she told the man. She glanced back to the bodies on her lawn, then stared straight at the Reb soldier again. "I—thank you. It seems that you came upon us just in time."

The second Rebel, a younger man, had also dismounted from his horse and was inspecting the dead. He spat out a stream of juice from his chewing tobacco, and his voice was laced with disgust when he spoke. "These boys ain't no regular troops. There ain't been none of this regiment around here in months. Looks like a group of deserters to me. Not even guerrillas—just plain old deserters."

He looked from his commander to Kiernan and started to spit again. "Oh, pardon me, ma'am."

Kiernan lifted her arms in a gesture that said he must make himself comfortable.

What was a little tobacco spit after the blood and . . . the blood and innards of a man still warm upon her lawn. The Reb was telling her something very serious. Kiernan looked curiously to him, trying to understand.

"Yanks is still men for the most part, Mrs. Miller," he told her. "My youngest son is bearing arms up there for the 47th Maryland artillery corps, and I can tell you that he may be a ferocious fighter and he may be waving a flag for Abe Lincoln, but if he needed food or to use someone's home—in the South or in the North—he'd be wiping his boots clean before he entered and he'd be saying 'please' and 'thank you' all the while. He was raised right, and so were most of them northern boys. But on both sides you got no-good-no-accounts, too, and that's what you had here, young lady. Them's what you got to watch out for."

"Then I do thank you, indeed, for coming along at the right time," Kiernan told him. "I don't even know your names to thank you properly." She paused. "But you know me."

"Course, we do, ma'am." He lifted his hat to her. "You're old Andrew's daughter-in-law, Anthony's wife. And your rifle works are keeping a lot of boys in good supply. Whatever we can do for you, we'll always be glad to do. My name is Geary, Sergeant Angus Geary. This here is T.J. Castleman, one of the finest sharpshooters you ever will meet."

"Are you stationed near here?" Kiernan asked. "Is a Rebel army moving back in?"

"Well, now, ma'am, we're not exactly moving back in, but we're not exactly moving out either. We've got ourselves an intriguing job, it seems, harassing Union forces in the Shenandoah Valley. We're up and down it seems, sometimes in the mountains, sometimes down low."

"We're with Stonewall—General Thomas Jackson, that is. The finest commander ever drew breath this or any other side of the border."

"Well," Kiernan told Sergeant Geary, flashing a quick glance to his sharpshooting companion, "since you did a great deal to improve my day, I'd very much like to do something for yours. Can we offer you gentlemen a home-cooked meal?" She realized, even as the words left her mouth, that she was inviting them to dinner over three corpses. "Oh," she murmured, certain that she herself could not eat, "perhaps we could—er, get these men onto a wagon, and I could have Jeremiah drive them into town, and they could be sent back—"

"No ma'am, I don't think that that would be a right good idea," T.J. Castleman told her. "Don't you worry none. Sarge and I will see to these Yanks."

She opened her mouth, but no sound left it. Angus spoke to her again. "You see, Mrs. Miller, if we send them back, the Yanks will know we caught up with them, and they'll know just whereabout we caught up with them too. As far as Yanks go, we need them to think that you're just living over here somewhere on the Rebel side just as sweet and quiet as can be. Like as not, sooner or later, someone might decide that this fine house shouldn't stand no more. But till that day comes—" He broke off and shrugged. "You got any weapons in the house?"

Jacob grinned and replied for her. "What do you think, Sarge? Sure, we got a gun in the house. We got a cabinet full of some of my pa's best, and I've got my very own rifle, handmade for me. And I got a fine supply of shells too."

"Well, that's good, boy, that's real good. 'Cause if you ever see a few stragglers like this again, you shoot, and you shoot to kill. But mark my next words just the same—if you see a whole army heading your way, you stand aside. If the army comes, they won't come to hurt you. They'll just rip up the place a bit. 'Course if you shoot at them, they'll have to shoot at you. And even if one Reb is worth ten Yanks"— he winked at Kiernan—"there just isn't any way for one Reb to take on a whole company or a brigade. You understand, Mrs. Miller?"

"Yes," Kiernan said, studying the man's fine gray eyes. She understood completely. She wouldn't let Jacob foolishly kill himself taking on a regular unit.

She understood, too, that there were deserters and some less-than-honorable guerrillas from both sides who might just come by. And if they came by, then they might as well shoot, because if they didn't, there was a good chance that they would die anyway.

"Sarge, I'll take care of the bluebellies," T.J. said. He spat out a wad of tobacco juice, then looked at Kiernan guiltily again. She shook her head, almost smiling.

"Please, sir, you must be comfortable here. We're very grateful."

He grinned to her in turn. She thought that he had the good rugged sense of a mountain man, and that, along with the Virginia gentry who knew so much about horses and guns and riding and the terrain, the fine solid citizens like T.J. were the ones who were going to win the war.

"That meal sounds real fine to me," he told her.

She didn't dare look at the corpses again. She took Janey by the elbow. "Let's go on in and see if Jeremiah has gotten hold of one of those chickens yet. Then we'll get something on the table mighty quick."

* * *

Kiernan never asked what they did with the Yank bodies —she didn't really want to know. She was certain, though, that they had seen to it that the bodies were well away from the house.

Certain that the two men didn't have much time, Kiernan saw to it that they ate within the hour. She was excited at this prospect of company. Not that she'd really been deprived or lonely. Thomas and Lacey had been up to see her several times, and she'd been into town often enough. The foreman of the rifleworks in the valley had been up to see her, and she had sat through her first business meeting with him.

But this was different. She knew almost nothing about the rifleworks, and Thomas was as worthy a partner as her own father, so she had done more listening than anything else, and she had asked them both to assure her that the majority of their sales were to either the Confederate government or to private concerns wishing to equip military companies they were raising on their own.

Bull Run, the first major engagement of the war, had shown everyone that Virginia—so slow to pull away from the old government—was going to pay for her alliance with the new. Their land, it already seemed to be apparent, was going to be the major battlefield.

Having Sergeant Angus and T.J. in the house was the first time she herself was involved in the war effort. She suddenly deeply and desperately wanted to be involved. It seemed to be the only way to survive it all.

She thought about it during the meal. She couldn't eat a thing herself, but she was glad that T.J. and Angus seemed to enjoy every single mouthful as well as the house, and the snowy table linen, and the silverware.

Janey had been against the use of the good family silverware. To convince her that they must put it on the table tonight, Kiernan promised her they would bury it very soon, what with rogue Rebels and rogue Yanks in the area.

She trusted both T.J. and Angus implicitly. She was glad that she did, for T.J.—much more evidently than the world-worn Angus—showed his awe and pleasure at the beauty of the simple things within the house—the fine lace drapes, the beautifully hewn English furniture, the crystal sconces, and the elegant tableware. When the meal was finished, she played old Irish ballads and lively Virginia reels for them on the spinet. Jacob danced with his sister, and then sweet Patricia politely urged T.J. to be her partner. To teach T.J., Kiernan bowed low to Angus and became his partner.

Then it seemed that Angus became serious very quickly, realizing that they had been gone a long time.

He thanked Kiernan and the family, and he promised them that he'd guard them whenever he could.

"We're often near, in the valley," he said, looking directly at her. "In fact, if you've ever a need for us that you might be knowing in advance, you might want to look in that ancient old oak back by the ruins of the old Chagall estate. Do you know where that is?" he asked Kiernan.

She nodded, meeting his eyes. "I rode there once, long ago, with Anthony."

"Well, you keep us in mind," Angus said.

When the two Rebs departed, Kiernan was delighted to see that Angus had left his hat. With a brief word to the twins and Janey, she went flying after him. She found Angus just about to dismount from his horse—evidently, the grinning T.J. had waited to inform him that he was hatless until he was about to ride away.

"Ah, Mrs. Miller, I'll be thanking you again!" he told her.

Kiernan handed him his hat and stepped back, smiling, shielding her eyes from the sun that was slipping into the earth.

"I owe you the thanks, sir," she reminded him. She stepped forward again. It wasn't necessary to whisper—the twins couldn't possibly hear her—but she felt compelled to speak as softly as she could and get as close to the gentleman as she could be. "I'd like to do something that I might be really thanked for myself," she said. Angus stared at her, sternly. "Did I misunderstand something?" she demanded. "Didn't you tell me about the oak because I might be able to bring you information?"

T.J. and Angus exchanged a quick glance. Angus looked down at his hands, then at her. "Yes," he admitted. "Not that I had any right to do so, ma'am. You've already given far and above the call of duty, what with a brave young lad of a husband dead and in the ground. And with the rifleworks."

"I'd like to be a spy," she said frankly.

Angus winced. "Spying is a dangerous trade, Mrs. Miller."

Dangerous, yes. But the mere thought of it made her feel alive.

Male spies, if caught, were hanged, she reminded herself. She gritted her teeth. Not even Yankees hanged women. Not yet.

She had no intention of getting caught. She wasn't even sure what she could do.

She smiled at Angus, for he looked very concerned. "Angus, I'm probably a prime target because of the rifleworks anyway. I won't do anything horrible—I don't think that I'd be able to do anything horrible, I don't know any Yankees that well. What I can do is make sure that anything I hear gets to that old oak as soon as possible."

Angus looked to T.J., and T.J. shrugged. "We need her, Sarge," T.J. drawled. "There's too many folks in these woods who are for the Yanks, and too many folks who just don't really show what they're feeling deep inside. Mrs. Miller, ma'am, don't you risk nothing, but if you hear tell of anything that you think we should know, why, exercise one of those fine horses of yours down by that old oak. I think that would serve us well enough, don't you, Sarge?"

Angus swept his hat up on his head. "Mrs. Miller, we would be forever and deeply indebted."

Kiernan smiled, and she waved as they rode away.

It wasn't long before she made her first trip out to the old oak at the ruins of the Chagall estate.

It wasn't that she had learned anything that was a major secret. It was just that she had some early information on something that everyone would soon know about. And that was because Thomas had been learning things from one of the railroad employees.

The mill on Virginius Island had been partially destroyed by a Union colonel to prevent the Confederates from making use of it. The proprietor of the mill, Mr. Herr, had long been suspected of very heavy Federal leanings. There was quite a quantity of grain within the mill, and Herr had offered it to the Federal officials in Maryland.

Thomas told Kiernan that men from the 3rd Wisconsin regiment would be "supervising" the able-bodied men left in Harpers Ferry as they loaded the grain onto ships, since currently no bridge was left over the Potomac. Supposedly, citizens would receive recompense for their efforts. Thomas said that it was most unlikely that anyone would ever be recompensed for any of these activities.

Thomas had been glum generally. Bullet holes extended over the length and breadth of his house because Union troops shot at anything that moved or seemed to move from their point on Maryland Heights. The once-vibrant town of Harpers Ferry was becoming a ghost town where nothing dared appear by night. As winter approached, the early darkness decreed that some lights must be lit against the early shadows of the evening—which could endanger them all. Kiernan realized that Thomas had loved his town more than either government, and that in his eyes, there could be no winners or losers—his town was dying.

She did her best to cheer him up, then rode home. She wasn't sure why, but she took a roundabout trail. It was a beautiful way to ride. October was new, and the mountains were covered in their most beautiful foliage. The rivers, dangerous for the unwary, were nevertheless beautiful too. The water was high at this time of year, but in places the rushing water still danced over the rocks in a cool white fury, and leaves still fell upon the water, adding a spray of muted, lulling color.

Before she knew it, she had come to a halt before the trail that led down to the fishing shack on the water. She almost allowed her horse to carry her down that trail, for she was feeling very nostalgic. It had been almost two years since John Brown had raided Harpers Ferry.

And almost two years since she had led Jesse here.

She bit hard into her lip. She hadn't thought much about Jesse lately—or maybe she had never really stopped thinking about him, maybe she'd just forced him into the back of her mind. But suddenly everything came rushing back to her. She remembered how upset he had been that day, how the events had seemed to cast his very soul to the devil . . .

And how he had come to her because of it.

He had known, she thought. Somehow, Jesse had known that their world would come to this.

A house divided.

Not even love could change what had come. Angus had spoken proudly of his Yankee son. Harpers Ferry was split in two. Virginia herself was split. What southern mother wouldn't love her northern child? Daniel had not ceased to love his brother.

And I loved you so deeply, she thought of Jesse.

But that was in the past, just as that day of sweet tempest and tender torment they had spent upon the river was past. Their love had never had a chance.

She turned her horse and rode away. But she was too restless to return home to the children, which perhaps was why she headed up to the ruins of the Chagall estate and the oak tree there. Kiernan dismounted from her horse in the high grass and stared over at the estate. It had probably once been very beautiful. The remains of its driveway were overgrown with weeds and long grasses, but four Doric pillars still stood, scorched, but defying time. She stared at the house and felt the whisper of a chill wind that foreboded winter. She shivered and pulled her cape closer about herself, then she turned to the oak.

It was an ancient tree, split once by lightning, big and heavy still. Within its wide gnarly trunk was a deep hole—a perfect place for a message.

Except, she had no paper or anything with which to write her message.

A fine spy she was going to make, she thought.

But even as she stood there, she heard a rustling in the trees. She was about to leap upon her horse in panic and ride like the wind for home, but a voice called out to her quickly.

"Mrs. Miller!"

She paused and watched as T.J. came sauntering out of the bushes, a blade of grass between his teeth, just as cool and calm as a man could be on a lazy autumn's day.

"Hello, ma'am. Reckon you've got something to say to us, is that right?"

"I don't really know," she admitted, but she told him what she knew about the wheat.

He nodded when she was finished. "We've heard something about it already. Thanks for the confirmation. We'll take this one to the militia, I think, and see how those boys feel about the situation. Thank you kindly, ma'am. Thank you kindly. You doing all right, you and those children?"

"Yes, we're doing very well, thank you."

He nodded. "Better ride on home, then. Don't pay to be a woman alone these days, and it's just as well that I don't be seen with you now."

Kiernan mounted her horse and bade him good-bye. He lifted a hand to her, still standing beneath the oak, that blade of grass in his mouth.

She wondered if he'd run out of chewing tobacco.

"Kiernan! Kiernan!"

Late on the afternoon of October 16, Kiernan was out back laughing with Jeremiah. Young David was rushing around the hen coop trying to procure the eggs of a suddenly indignant chicken.

Kiernan's laughter faded as soon as she heard her name called, and she rushed around to the front of the house. To her amazement, Thomas Donahue was there. And he was mounted on his carriage horse, which was unusual since Thomas hated to ride.

"Thomas! What is it? Come on down, come inside. We'll have you some tea or coffee—or something stronger—quick as a wink, I promise."

Thomas shook his head, refusing to dismount. "I've got to

warn a few more folks. Seems the Virginia militia isn't
happy about the Yanks making the folks in town load that
wheat. There've been rumors that Colonel Ashby is on his
way in to put a stop to it all."

"Oh?" Kiernan's heart was hammering.

"Well, the Yanks are coming after the Rebs. Ashby is
supposed to be up on Bolivar Heights. The Yanks are going
to engage him there. Get those young ones inside and under
cover, Kiernan. Who knows where bullets may fly. You
hear?"

"Yes, Thomas, thank you!"

Thomas turned his mount around, and Kiernan shouted
for Patricia and Jacob and the others. "We're going to spend
some time in the basement," she told them. "Patricia, gather
up some blankets. Jacob, why don't you bring your rifle
down? Janey, we can almost make a picnic out of it. Why
don't you see what we have in the larder?"

"Miz Kiernan, does this mean that I don't have to fight
with that chicken no more?" David asked.

She smiled. David was eight, precocious, a whirlwind of
energy. He worked as hard as any adult, and he was smart,
for Patricia frequently read to him. Patricia had never
voiced her opinion on slavery to Kiernan, and Kiernan often
wondered if the younger Millers had an opinion one way or
the other. But Patricia, motherless herself for so long, had
adopted David, and David certainly had prospered for it.

"No, David, you don't have to fight with that chicken
anymore," Kiernan assured him. "You just help Patricia.
And we'll all get down to the basement."

"Miz Kiernan?"

Jeremiah's elder son, Tyne, was no boy. Nearly twenty, he
was at least six feet two inches tall, ebony black, muscled,
sleek, and handsome. Kiernan imagined that he would have
made a fine African prince, for he stood with pride that no
bondage could break.

"Tyne?" she said.

He lowered his voice. "No bluebelly is gonna have any
cause to pay heed to me, nor any Reb for that matter. A
good field hand stays in a field. You take the young 'uns

down to that basement. If you say so, I'll keep my eyes open here."

Kiernan paused. He could run off on her. But he could have run off on her months ago. Besides, she had promised Jeremiah and his sons their freedom.

She nodded. "All right, Tyne."

She herded the rest of her charges into the basement as Tyne had urged.

They had not been down very long before they heard the first shots—and then the sound of the cannon, booming.

As Kiernan wrapped her arm around Patricia, holding her close against the sounds of battle, she realized that it was two years ago exactly that John Brown had come to Harpers Ferry.

In time, the sounds of the shots died away. Kiernan was just rising when the door to the basement opened. She looked up the steps, feeling her heart leap to her throat.

"Miz Kiernan?"

She dared to breathe again. It was Tyne.

"Is it over?"

"Seems to be. It's been mighty quiet for a spell now. I seen some bluebellies heading back toward town and the river, and I seen the boys in gray lookin' as if they was retreating toward Charles Town. They was actin' as if they'd done won the battle, so it's hard to tell what's really goin' on."

"None of them came toward the house?" Kiernan asked him, hurrying up the stairs.

"None that I could see."

She exhaled slowly, then hurried past Tyne to the front of the house. Her fingers curled around one of the pillars. There was a bullet mark in it, and she shivered. She had known that the fighting would be close. She hadn't known how close.

She noticed a body far down in the grass. She walked from the porch and started to run. She came to the body and fell down in her knees beside it.

It was a Yankee. He had fallen on his stomach.

She bit her lip, knowing that if he was injured, she would have to help him.

She turned him over.

She didn't have to help him. His sightless eyes were staring heavenward.

Young eyes—oh, so very young. Once a soft blue, like a cloudy sky, set in a young face. He had barely begun to shave.

It was a handsome face. One that had probably won many a sweetheart, one his sisters would have adored.

"Oh, God!" she breathed.

Tyne was behind her. She swallowed hard. She really couldn't start crying hysterically over a Yankee soldier.

Had she caused his death? No, the Rebels had known about the grain and the mill before she had told T.J. Rebels and Yanks were dying everywhere now—it was a war, for the love of God! She couldn't stop them from dying.

Not even Jesse could stop them from dying.

Jesse. Jesse could be lying like this in blue on some other woman's lawn. He was a doctor, but he never stayed out of the action. He'd ridden with his troops in the West when he should have been in a hospital field tent.

"We've got to—we've got to return him," Kiernan said. This was no deserter—he was a brave young man who had died in battle. "Get rid of his tobacco first," Tyne advised her. Kiernan couldn't move. Tyne stooped down and rifled through the soldier's blood-soaked clothing. He found a pouch of tobacco and a pipe and handed them to Kiernan. "He's just a boy. Too young to be smokin'. His mama probably wouldn't like it real well."

Kiernan nodded.

"I'll get the wagon," Tyne told her.

She nodded again.

She sat with the dead Yank until Tyne returned with Albert, the mule, hitched to the wagon. He lifted the dead man and placed him in the wagon. Kiernan rose from her knees at last and came around to look at the dead soldier who was scarcely more than a boy.

A plaid blanket was balled up in a corner of the wagon. Kiernan laid it gently across the man.

Tyne had been silent. "He's the enemy, Miz Kiernan."

She glanced at him, wondering how serious he was. The Yanks were the ones trying to free the black people.

"My enemy, but not yours, Tyne."

Tyne shrugged, adjusting the blanket. "Well, I'll tell you, Miz Kiernan, I've heard that Abe Lincoln is a mighty good man. Tall and gentle and ugly as sin, but a mighty good man nonetheless. But I hear tell, too, that even though he wants to free the black man, he wants for him an island somewhere, a republic of black men. And I kinda got a hankerin' for Virginia. Some of those folks up north, they don't want the southern folk beatin' us black folk down here, and that's a mighty fine thing for them to be wantin' too. But some of them same folk have a notion that if they rub up next to a black man, why, some of that color is gonna to come off. They're afraid that it might be dirt. Now I may be a lucky man for a slave, Miz Kiernan. But I been around white folk all my life who don't think that taking my hand is gonna make their own dirty. So I'm with you, Miz Kiernan, one way or the other."

"Thank you, Tyne," she told him.

His mouth curled at the corner. "I never did have to pick cotton, Miz Kiernan. I might feel a whole lot different if I'd been a 'field nigger,' " he told her wryly.

She nodded. Tyne was a proud man. She understood that. She had her own pride.

She started to climb into the wagon.

"You don't need to come, Miz Kiernan. I can take care of this for you."

"Tyne, you can't bring him anywhere alone. You're—"

"Miz Kiernan," he told her, grinning. "A black man wouldn't wanta bring a dead Reb back to his regiment, oh, no! But if'n I bring this bluebelly in, I'll be all right. They're the ones fightin' to free us, remember?"

She smiled, lowered her head, and nodded. Tyne crawled up into the wagon and picked up the whip.

"Tyne!" she called.

"Yes, Miz Kiernan?"

"Ride gently with him, please."

"Yes ma'am, I will."

He flicked the whip, and the wagon rolled away. She watched it for a while and then started back for the house.

She sat on the swing for a while and felt the coolness of the autumn breeze. She was amazed by how very calm she felt. She was coming to terms with life, she thought. She would never get over the pain of seeing men die, but she was living in the midst of war, and she was surviving it. Constant gunshots riddled the town far below her home, but she was surviving.

Neither side really had the manpower to hold Harpers Ferry. The heights around the town made it impossible to hold.

She shivered suddenly, remembering that Harpers Ferry was a ghost town. Whether the blue or gray could hold it or not, it was an important railway stop, and they would both be impelled to come back, again and again.

She sighed softly. She would weather it.

And with that thought, she felt surprisingly calm.

She was still calm that night when Tyne returned to tell her there were still Yanks around, and that a number of citizens were being arrested for harboring Rebels.

She wasn't harboring anyone.

That night, when she first slept, her dreams were peopled by dead men. The Yanks who had died on her lawn drifted by, like Irish death-ghosts. The pale blue eyes of the boy today haunted her.

And then she was turning over the blue-clad Yank's body again, and she started to scream.

Because it was Jesse's body.

She awoke with a start and reminded herself that Jesse was out of her life.

But she lay awake for a long, long time.

When she slept again, it was dreamlessly. And she slept late, well into the morning. She went for a ride in the afternoon, and when she returned, she spent time in the stables with Tyne and Jeremiah and David, grooming the horses and mules and deciding which animals did and didn't need new shoes. There were still some Yankees around, near town, she didn't know how many.

But she was very calm. She had her life under the very best control that she could, given the circumstances.

But it was that very evening, in the deceptively peaceful beauty of the autumn night, that the massive blue column of soldiers came riding her into life.

And Jesse Cameron.

The one who wore blue.

Interlude

JESSE

October 17, 1861
Washington, D.C.

"Jesse, can I talk to you?"

From his desk at the hospital in Washington, Jesse looked up. Captain Allan Quinn, 14th Northern Virginia Cavalry, Union Army, stood in front of him. Jesse's first thought was to recall which of Quinn's men were in his wards, and in his mind he quickly went through the names of the ones who were there. He knew the unit—he had ridden with most of them when he had chosen regular cavalry duty. Many from the unit had been with him in the West.

Just as Daniel had been, and Jeb, and some of the others.

Looking at Quinn, Jesse breathed an inward sigh of relief. Two of Quinn's boys were here, fallen in skirmishes, but both of them were doing well. One had been an amputation, and at the time, it had disturbed Jesse greatly because he suspected that the operation would not have been necessary had he been able to tend to the wound earlier. But the cavalryman was doing well now, and he had told Jesse that he'd been grateful to lose an arm rather than a leg. He could ride just fine one-armed, but he'd not have fared so well with only one leg.

The other man had suffered a head wound, but it had been a clean one. A bullet had whizzed by, ripping hair and skin but miraculously leaving bone and brain intact. He, too, was doing well.

But not as well as he might have been doing if medical attention had been more readily available to him.

Jesse didn't like being in Washington. He wanted a hospital closer to the action. By the time the injured were reaching him here, many had received haphazard attention that only complicated the injury. He disagreed with many a man on his own side about the proper way to attend to wounds. A doctor in the West with whom he had worked had proved to his satisfaction that using the same sponges on different men hastened the onset of infection. Most physicians scoffed at the idea, but Jesse had watched his patients carefully. Clean sponges saved lives—just as a good shot of alcohol could sometimes help, inside and out, when nothing else was available.

Something suddenly told Jesse that Quinn hadn't come to talk about his wounded. An uneasy feeling crept over him. He'd known Quinn a long time, and Quinn knew a lot about his life.

"Jess."

"What is it? What's wrong?" Jesse asked tensely. "Have you heard something about my brother?"

Quinn, who was Jesse's own age, was probably destined to rise far in the military. He shrugged. "No, Jesse, I haven't heard anything about Daniel. I'm not even certain that anything is wrong at all. Well, it's going to be wrong, I guess."

By then Jesse was on his feet, his pen clutched tight in his hand. "Then tell me what *might* be wrong, or what it is that's *going to be* wrong."

"Lots of skirmishing going on."

"Yes, I know that. Allan, will you tell me what—"

"Jesse, there was a battle near Harpers Ferry yesterday, up on Bolivar Heights."

Jesse's fingers curled tightly around the pen he still held.

Kiernan. Kiernan would have been very near the battle.

He broke out in a cold sweat. "Any civilians caught up in it?" he asked hoarsely.

"No, Jesse, it's not that. She—er, Mrs. Miller wasn't caught by a ball or anything like that."

Jesse dropped the pen and clenched his hands together tightly behind his back as a sensation of relief flooded over him. She was all right.

Kiernan. Damn her!

Damn, but he'd tried hard not to think of her! It had been over between them, over before it had ever begun.

She had told him that she'd hate him, that she'd be his worst enemy. And she'd married Anthony, who was now dead.

Kiernan was out at Montemarte. Jesse knew it because Christa still wrote him. Christa was as ardent a Confederate as any, but she had never ceased to write him. She didn't write about the war, she didn't condemn him, and she didn't try to sway him. She just wrote about people, places, and events. She had told him that Kiernan went out to take care of her sister- and brother-in-law at Montemarte, near Harpers Ferry.

He had thought of writing Kiernan and telling her that it was a damned fool place to be, but she wouldn't have wanted to hear it from him. She probably wouldn't have even opened a letter from him.

She would be so much better off back home. Harpers Ferry was destined to be in a tug-of-war, and that tug-of-war would affect the nearby countryside.

It already had. And his heart was beating too damned hard.

And Quinn was in the same position that he was. Quinn was a Virginian too. Sometimes it was damned confusing. A number of states had regiments fighting on both sides of the line. Quinn had moved in the same social circles as Jesse, and Quinn knew that Kiernan Mackay was important to him. Hell, Jesse thought wearily, half of the world has probably heard about that insane duel between him and Anthony.

He looked across at his friend. "Quinn, what are you trying to tell me?" he demanded. "There was a battle, but it's over. And Kiernan Miller is all right, no civilians were hurt. Then—?"

"Have you ever met up with Captain Hugh Norris?"

Jesse frowned. Norris—yes, he had met the man at Manassas. He was from Maryland, and he was very bitter about the numerous "traitors" from his own state. He seemed to have a mean streak in him a mile long.

"I've met him."

"His brother was killed at Bull Run, and he's convinced that the Millers were responsible."

Jesse's brows shot up. "The Millers were responsible for the battle at Manassas?" Anthony and Andrew would have enjoyed hearing about their own importance in that one, Jesse reflected wryly.

"No," Allan said. "This Norris thinks that a Miller firearm might have killed his brother because his brother died near the left flank, and the southern troops there were mostly from the western counties of Virginia."

"You can blame it on whoever you want, I guess," Jesse said. Tension began to ripple along his spine. Norris was out there, Kiernan was out there. It was a little more than an hour's journey by train—when the trains were running. Otherwise, it was a very long ride.

Quinn continued. "I heard talk from some fellows who just rode in that Norris has a command there and that he has received some sort of blessing to burn down the Miller estate, Montemarte. I know that you and Anthony had some differences before he died, but—well, I know, too, that you were neighbors with the Mackay plantation. The way I see it, Anthony and his father are dead. There's just his widow and those children out there now, and for the life of me, I can't see how God can be on our side if we burn widows and children out of their homes. I can't interfere—I've got my assignment here, guarding the capital. But Jesse, you've got a lot of freedom, and General Banks is out there, and Banks thinks highly of you. Maybe you can do something."

Jesse's mouth was dry. They'd be burning down lots of houses before the war ended, he thought. Both sides were already well versed in destruction, determined to keep important supplies and resources out of each other's hands.

But Quinn was right. At this stage, there was little reason to burn a widow out of her house.

Even if that widow did have some control over the Miller Firearms Factories.

He had to convince someone of that.

"Thanks, Quinn," he said briefly, then lifted his hat from his desk, and hurried along the corridor. Colonel Sebring was his immediate superior, and Sebring was a reasonable man.

Jesse burst into his office. "Sir, I need to take some operations closer to the field. Now. And I know right where I want to take them."

Sebring looked up from his desk, startled. He leaned back, a bushy brow arching. "Now?"

"Now, sir. I'm requesting permission to leave within the hour. We've discussed this—"

"Oh," Sebring said. "You've heard about the incident at Bolivar Heights. It was a skirmish, Jesse. Nothing major. You're one of the best physicians we've got—no one stands up to battle conditions like you do, and no one works as well in the horrid conditions—"

"That's exactly why I shouldn't be in Washington, sir!"

Sebring leaned back. "I gather, son, that you want to take over the Miller estate—what's it called, Montemarte?"

It was Jesse's turn to be startled. Sebring was definitely a wise old coot. Montemarte was well known, and the Millers were well known. But Jesse had never imagined that Sebring might know about his involvement with either.

"Captain Norris is out there now, determined to burn the place down. I can see no reason for it. The factories are deep in the valley. And it wouldn't be good politics either. A number of the counties in western Virginia are unhappy about being in the Confederacy. They're holding a referendum on it next week. They may eventually secede from the state, form their own state, and move back into the Union. If we go around burning down their homes, it will never happen, sir."

Sebring watched Jesse and twirled the curl on his snow-white mustache.

"I need you here, Jesse. But maybe that's selfish on my part. I've got civilian doctors by the score here."

"Colonel," Jesse reminded him, his teeth on edge, "I could ride regular cavalry, it would be my right—"

"Oh, hold your pants, young man!"

"I can't, sir. Norris is in or near Harpers Ferry. I'm all the way out here."

Colonel Sebring grinned. "You've got a point, you've got a point." He was quiet for a moment, then reached for his pen to write out orders. "I'll be sending you the most shot-up and torn of the men in the vicinity. And I'll also be sending you a few who just need a little convalescence but can fight. And"—he paused, wagging a finger at him—"when it's necessary to pull out, we pull out. You understand?"

"Yes, sir, I understand."

Jesse took the orders Sebring handed to him and started to leave.

"Oh, Jesse," Sebring said.

He turned back.

"Don't let your personal life interfere any more with your military life."

Jesse paused. "If I'd allowed it to interfere, sir, I'd be on the other side."

Sebring shrugged. "You've got me there, son."

Jesse started moving again, but one more time, Sebring stopped him.

"Captain!"

Jesse turned back.

"You watch out for that girl too. There's some who think she might be watching us mighty keenly—and passing on everything that she knows."

"What?" Jesse demanded, startled.

"You heard me right, Jesse. You keep an eye on her. We haven't shot any women yet that I know of, but who knows what this war might come to?"

Jesse nodded and hurried out before Sebring could stop him again.

He wondered how Sebring knew so much about events in Harpers Ferry.

Kiernan might well be watching the Union—it would be just like her. But it seemed that the Union was watching her too.

Damn, she'd be better off, much better off, if she'd just go home, back to Tidewater Virginia.

But she wasn't going to go home—he knew that. There were no guarantees that any part of Virginia was going to be particularly safe now anyway. Virginia, after all, bordered the capital.

With raw anxiety, Jesse was determined to get out there quickly.

He felt as if he owed Anthony something too. He wasn't sure why—or maybe he was.

He'd had Anthony's wife.

But maybe he could save Anthony's house for his family.

And Kiernan, the little fool. He didn't know what the Union would do with women either. He did know that one Washington socialite, the very beautiful widow, Rose Greenhow, was imprisoned. She was suspected of having used her charm and contacts to procure information for General Beauregard that had brought about the rout at Bull Run.

There was talk that she would be brought up on charges of treason. There was only one penalty for treason—death.

"Oh, damn her!" Jesse said the words aloud. With long strides he returned to his desk to issue orders about his current patients to his clerk and, within minutes, he was out of the hospital.

He hitched a train ride for himself and Pegasus for a good part of the way out of Union Station. Once he was seated, he leaned back.

He was going to see Kiernan again. His heart raced, and a wildfire surged through him. It seemed so long ago that he'd seen her last. The chasm between them had never been greater. She had sworn to be his enemy, and she would not let him touch her in any way.

All he could do was watch out for her.

He gritted his teeth tightly together. He might not make it

in time. By the time he arrived, the house might be nothing but ashes. And Kiernan might be on her way into the Shenandoah Valley, far from his reach. She could head for Richmond, she could head for home. Or she could choose to remain.

Was she spying?

I'm going to stop you if you are, he thought. I'm going to stop you for your own good.

Hell, the South didn't need her—not now. The South was doing damned well.

At Manassas Junction, the Union had learned what Jesse had known all along—that the South would not be easy to beat.

Through the long hot nights of the summer, while he had tended to the men and boys wounded here, he had remembered the sight of that battlefield. There was nothing like war. Men who had been healthy and whole had been shot, torn, ripped, ragged and bleeding, lying atop one another in fields of dirt and blood—maimed, crying, dying.

No, there was nothing at all like war.

Manassas had been the true test. Since then, both sides had been learning warfare, learning in life those tactics that they had read about in books at the military academies. When to attack, and when to fall back. How to flank your enemy, how to encircle him. How to fight an army that outnumbered your own. How to win.

The common soldier didn't need to know how to do any of these things. He had only to follow orders and to march without blinking into the thunderous volley of fire from his enemy. And when the volley was over, the soldier had to know when to thrust his bayonet so that his enemy might die, and he might stay alive.

The art of warfare was for the generals and the colonels. The South was filled with brilliant military men. Colonel Lee was a general now—recently put in charge of all of the men in western Virginia, Jesse had heard. And Stuart, his old friend, was General Jeb now. Jackson, that fine gentleman from the Virginia Military Institute, had been called

"General Stonewall" ever since Manassas. The South was indeed in a strong position.

Manassas had been a fine test, and the test was still going on. The war was young, and men were still mastering the arts of it. In August, in the rolling hill country southwest of Springfield, Missouri, the battle of Wilson's Creek had been fought. Like Manassas, it had been a clear victory for the Confederacy. The Union leader had been killed, and his troops had withdrawn. They had not just retreated—they had left most of the state to the Rebs.

In Virginia, men were skirmishing and battling in various pockets. The South had yet to invade the North, but Washington remained ringed by forces. There had been confrontations in a number of places. Union forces had moved against Confederates at Big Bethel, and there had been skirmishing at Piggot's Mill, Wayne Court House, and Blue's House, among others. The action had kept the hospitals filled.

The Rebs were doing all right. They didn't need any help from Kiernan.

Jesse left the train in Maryland and rode until he reached General Banks with his orders from Colonel Sebring.

Banks frowned, wondering what Jesse was talking about at first. Then he remembered that he had given his captain permission to burn the house. "The Millers are hard-core Rebels, Captain Cameron. I've done my best to deal justly and properly with the civilian populations around here, but Captain, the Millers are an exception."

"But the Miller men are dead, sir. The adults, that is. There's a boy living there, a widow, and a little girl. The house would be absolutely perfect for a hospital. Sir, dammit, I can save more of your troops!"

Banks stared at Jesse, startled. Jesse wondered for a minute if he was going to be court martialed, but then Banks smiled. "Go on. Convince me."

Jesse reminded him that western Virginia might come back to the Union fold and that kind treatment of the people —even Rebs like the Millers—might have an influence next week, when it came time for people to vote. Banks's grin kept growing. At the end, Banks nodded, reaching for his pen. "You've sold me, Captain. The place is yours." He frowned for a minute. "Just keep your eye on—"

"I know, sir. Keep my eye on Mrs. Miller. I've been warned." And I know her, he added in silence. I know her very well.

Banks assigned him two orderlies and a small company of guards for his operations. But before the men could be assembled, Jesse was on the road again, very aware of the desperate need to hurry. When he reached the soldiers on the outskirts of Harpers Ferry, he learned that Norris and his men were already on their way to Montemarte.

It was then that Jesse started to race up the cliffs and ragged terrain, anxious to beat Norris.

There was no scent of fire on the air. That was a good sign.

At last he burst upon Montemarte. He saw the ring of soldiers in blue surrounding the place. He saw Norris, mounted, shouting orders.

And he saw the lit torches, ready to be set to the kindling planted about the porch.

Even as he raced onward, he saw Kiernan.

She stood upon the porch, tall, slim, and regal, the very essence of everything beautiful and graceful and charming in the world, her world, their world, the world that they had both known. The sunlight from the dying day caught the tendrils of her hair, and it seemed ablaze itself, a color deeper, richer, more alive than even the true fires that threatened her existence.

She was dressed beautifully, elegantly, as if she had just stepped away from tea. White lace lay over a gown of silver blue, a gown with full, sweeping skirts, its bodice cut to reveal the elegant length of her throat and just a hint of the fullness and roundness of her breasts. Her eyes were magnificent—burning, blazing emerald. With every inch of flesh and bone and beauty, she was defiant. As she stood there, the men began to move toward the house with their burning torches.

"Halt!" Jesse roared. He leaned closer to Pegasus and

raced harder to reach the house. "Norris, halt!" he thundered.

Norris saw him at last. He pulled his horse around and came toward Jesse, but by then, Jesse had nearly reached the house. He reined in hard, meeting up with Norris upon his bay.

"What the hell do you think you're doing?" Norris demanded furiously. "I've got permission to—"

"Not anymore. Read, Norris," Jesse told him, producing his orders.

"A hospital!" Norris bit out heatedly.

"The place is mine. Do you understand?" Jesse demanded.

"You bastard!" Norris hissed suddenly. "I'll get you for this, Cameron!"

Jesse arched a brow to him while Pegasus pranced nervously beneath him. "You'll get me for this? For setting up a hospital? What the hell is the matter with you, Norris?"

Norris rode close to him. "I'll tell you what's the matter. This place should burn! And *she* should burn. They should all burn, right down to the ground!"

"There are children in there."

"They'll grow up to be Rebs! And they'll kill more of us on the battlefield."

"Andrew Miller is dead, Norris. And Anthony Miller is dead. That's enough."

"You watch yourself, Cameron. You just watch yourself!" Norris warned furiously.

"I always do, Norris," Jesse told him. "Douse your torches!" he ordered loudly to the men. He stared at Norris again. "And you watch yourself, Norris. I've chosen a medical command this time, but I was cavalry a long, long time before that. And I know what I'm doing."

"You threatening me?"

"I'm telling you that I know how to watch out for myself."

"Reb-lover! Or are you a Reb?" Norris demanded.

"Get the hell out of my way," Jesse snarled, "before I forget that we're on the same side."

He rode past Norris and reined in right before the porch.

She stood there still, as regal as ever, like a princess, not about to forget her station in life.

"Hello, Kiernan," he said softly.

Her eyes swept over him, cold and filled with disdain. Gone, long gone, was the girl he had once known, the girl he had loved.

She was a stranger now, distant, as cold as the frost of the coming winter.

She didn't respond to him in any way. He gritted his teeth, feeling his temper flare. He wanted to shout at her in fury. He wanted to shake that cold superiority from her eyes and make her understand. "Mrs. Miller, as of this moment I'm taking over this property for use as my headquarters, for hospital and surgical space as is necessary. You will kindly inform your household."

Her gaze swept chillingly over him once again, but at last, she spoke. "Captain Norris has plans to burn the place, Captain Cameron. I'm afraid you'll have to seek your headquarters elsewhere."

That was the final straw. He wanted to do more than shake her. He wanted to draw her over his knee as if she were still a child and paddle some sense into her. He'd half-killed himself to reach her in time, and she was telling him that she'd rather see her house burned than see him in it.

Before he knew what he was doing, he had dismounted and was striding up the steps. His fingers itched to touch her. Somehow, he restrained himself. He spoke through clenched teeth. "I'm trying to save your home and your neck, Mrs. Miller," he told her.

"My neck hasn't been threatened, Captain Cameron."

"Keep talking, Mrs. Miller, and it will be! Now shut up, and the manor can remain standing."

She delicately arched one brow, watching him. "Will you really be taking it over?"

"Yes."

Her lip curled. "Then I'd rather see it burn."

It took every ounce of his self-control to refrain from wrenching her shoulders around to force her to understand the gravity of her position. He fought to speak in a level tone.

"I'm sure you would, Kiernan. Common sense was never your strong suit. But what of young Jacob Miller and his sister?"

"Jacob wouldn't want a Yankee turncoat like you living in the house, either, Captain Cameron."

"You'd rather it burned?"

"Yes."

He stared at her, and he thought of the reckless speed with which he had come here, so desperate to salvage her home for her.

And she'd rather see it burned than see him touch it. He could have killed her.

Instead, he started to laugh. Hard. He turned away from her, starting down the steps.

"Captain Cameron!"

He paused. She was suddenly hurrying down the steps to him. Her breathing was hard. Her breasts were rising and falling with agitation, and for a moment, all he could remember was the feel of the woman in his arms, and the look of those green eyes when they were drenched with passion. She was still so damned regal.

But there was a chink within that armor of hers. She didn't really want the house to burn. She just wanted him to know how very much she hated him.

"Will you—will you burn it now?" she asked him.

He set his foot on a step and leaned an elbow casually upon it. "Well, Mrs. Miller," he told her, "I probably should do just that. But I am sorry to disappoint you. I'm afraid that I can't burn it now. I had to threaten and cajole and just about turn handstands to get the general to turn the place over to me. You see, Millers aren't real popular among the Union men. Lots and lots of them have had friends and kin killed by Miller firearms. They'd like to see the total destruction of Miller property and Miller people."

"That shouldn't be difficult now, considering that the majority of the Millers are dead—thanks to the Union Army."

"I assure you, several hundred Union men died the same
—thanks to the Confederate army."

"They were on Virginia soil!" she said, her eyes narrowing.

"I didn't start the war, Kiernan."

"But we're on opposite sides."

He felt his temper snap.

He loved her so much. . . .

And they were enemies. No words that she had ever spoken had shown him that as clearly as the look in her eyes
today.

"So fight me!" He managed to say the words softly. "But
I'm moving in, with my staff. Take your little charges and
run to your own home. You'll be safe enough there for a
while. I probably won't be able to salvage everything in the
house, but at least I can keep it standing."

"I don't want any favors from you!" she snapped. Again,
the fire was in her eyes. Her breasts rose and fell with her
rapid breathing. "And I'll be damned," she continued, "if
I'll run away from a passel of bad-mannered Yanks!"

His heart seemed to slam against his ribs—and his groin.

"You're staying?"

Her chin shot up, and she might have been the Queen of
England. "Stonewall Jackson will bring his army in here and
wipe out the lot of you," she promised. "I might as well wait
around for him to come. And keep your men from looting
the house blind."

"You haven't been asked to stay, Mrs. Miller."

"Are you planning on having your men throw me and the
children out—bodily?"

"Heavens no, Mrs. Miller. It's war, and I have managed
to send men into battle. But I'm a merciful commander—I
wouldn't dream of sending them in after you."

She ignored his sarcasm completely. She almost smiled in
cool, calculating challenge. "Then I'm staying."

"Maybe not," he told her heatedly. "I didn't say that I
wouldn't come in after you myself."

"What a fine point of valor, Captain Cameron!"

"Go home, Kiernan!"

"This is my home now. And Jackson will come back. Or Lee will come back. Some southern general will come for this land again, and you will be routed."

She was probably right about that, Jesse determined. Stonewall would claim the area again—and again. Or Lee would come back, or someone.

He couldn't hold it long. But when the Union was here, he had to manage to be here too.

He stared at her—at the pride in her stance, at the beauty in her face, at the fire within her eyes and the passion.

And the fury and the hatred.

And still, he wanted nothing more than to strip away the silver finery of her dress and hold her beneath him and take the fury and the tempest into his arms. To lie with her, to bed her again.

His gaze raked up and down her, and then he shrugged and spoke as casually as he could. "That's highly possible, Kiernan. Fine. Stay. But I'm taking over the house. Be forewarned."

"Forewarned, sir?" Her fury was ragged in her voice. "I'll be looking over your shoulder. I'll be making sure that you treat Reb prisoners with the same care that you would give to your own injured."

Oh, how he itched to seize her throat! But she had intended to reach into his soul, and he would never let her know how easily she could do so. He stepped closer to her. "I thought you'd run because of me, Mrs. Miller, like you did before. I won't mind your being around. I'll enjoy it. You're the one who promised never to suffer life with a Yank, remember?"

"I won't be suffering a life with you! I'll be surviving in spite of you!"

He smiled slowly, watching her. Fine, challenge me! You will not win, Kiernan, so help me God, you will not win!

"I'll fight you every step of the way. And the South will win."

"Maybe the battles, but never the war," he said quickly.

He realized that he wasn't talking about the great conflict

between the North and the South. He was talking about the two of them.

Suddenly, the tension was so great that it was nearly unbearable. He felt her heat, felt the raw desperation and fury and determination in her.

And he felt the sizzle of the fire that had always burned between them. Dear Lord, he wanted her! And the memories of the things that had once been between them were suddenly naked in her eyes.

Damn, but I will have you again! he vowed in silence. Perhaps she didn't fully remember. She'd been Anthony's wife.

A black wave of unreasoning anger washed over him. He'd been warned to keep his personal life out of the military.

And here he was, growing heedless of the forces around him, heedless of the autumn day.

Wanting her. Wanting to take her until he could erase the touch of a dead man. Wanting her to remember only him, and hating that dead man for ever having touched her. Hating the emotions that touched him, but still wanting her. Wanting her so badly that he could have swept her into his arms right now and had her, there on the lawn, despite the troops, despite—honor.

"The Confederates will come back!" she cried out suddenly.

"They very well might," he told her. "But until your Rebs come back, Mrs. Miller, it's going to be share and share alike."

He swept off his hat and bowed low to her with a mocking gallantry, with all the fury that still churned within him.

Then he turned very quickly on his heel and walked away from her, shouting orders to the men who still waited. His words came out normally, no matter what thoughts that raced through his mind.

Damn her, damn her, damn her!

It was, indeed, war.

3

War

Sixteen

Montemarte
October 18, 1861

Despite her insistence that she would stay in the house, Kiernan disappeared for much of his moving-in process.

The Miller housekeeper greeted him when he stepped into the hall of Montemarte. He didn't see her at first in the shadows, and for a moment, it was as if the autumn twilight played tricks on his eyes. He could remember the hallway from better times. It stretched from the entry to the rear of the house, much like the breezeway at Cameron Hall. There was a fine spinet set at the end of the hallway, and there were groupings of elegant furnishings. Dead center in the hall was a fireplace. It was warm and inviting. During their balls and entertainments, the Millers had always ordered the furniture pulled back. Dancers in silks and satins and taffetas had waltzed through the evenings. He could almost hear the rustle of skirts now.

"So, Yankee, you're here."

The words made him start. He stared into the shadows and saw the woman. She was tall and handsome, ramrod stiff with graying hair. He remembered her vaguely. She had always held an important place in this household, since Andrew's wife had died soon after the birth of Anthony's younger sister and brother.

She knew him. She'd welcomed him and Daniel and Christa, and she'd accompanied her young charges to Cameron Hall.

She knew him by name. Yet she seemed to prefer calling him "Yankee" at the moment.

He set his hands on his hips and stared across the room at her. Janey—that was her name.

"I see," he said. "You would just as soon the place be burned down too."

She looked at him, then shook her head. "No, not me. I like a roof over my head. I like this roof just fine. But if you think I'm going to welcome you here, Yank, you're wrong."

He shrugged. "Fine. Don't welcome me, but listen to me. If there's anything of real value—"

"We done buried the silver a long time ago, Yank."

"Good. But see that handsome spinet there? It just might be better off up in the attic."

"I hear you loudly, Yank," Janey assured him. "I'll see to some moving right away."

"Good." He started for the stairs. He had to find a place for himself to sleep at night, and he wanted a room with good light so that he could maintain an office in it too.

Halfway up the stairs, he realized that Janey was on his heels. He paused and turned back, and she almost bumped into him. "I'll give you a tour, Yank."

"Oh?"

"That way I can warn you where not to sleep."

They reached the second floor, and Janey hurried on by him. "Not there—that's young Master Jacob's room." She went on down the hallway. "And this one is Patricia's room." She started onward again, but Jesse stopped. A doorway was open to a very large room with windows that faced the east and the rising sun. The massive bed in the room looked comfortable and, after the rush he'd gone through that day, very inviting. There was a desk across from it, and a very large armoire off to the side by the windows. It was perfect.

But it was a master bedroom, he thought. Anthony's room? Or Andrew's room?

Had it ever been Kiernan's room? Had she ever slept with her husband in it?

"Yankee, are you comin'?" Janey demanded.

He ignored her and voiced his own question. "Is this Mrs. Miller's room?"

Janey paused, her jaw twisting, and she hesitated to give him an answer. She spoke at last. "No, this ain't nobody's room right now. Used to be Master Andrew's room, and it would have been Master Anthony's room, except he done got himself killed. So there's no one in there right now. But it'll be Master Jacob's room one day—"

"I'm not moving in for eternity, Janey," Jesse told her, "just for the duration."

"The duration of what?" she demanded.

"The war."

She snickered. "You ain't gonna hold this property even that long, Yank."

"Right. But even if we lose this place, we'll be back for it. The Union will keep fighting for this area. I won't be here long enough for Jacob to grow up, get married, and bring home a bride—I hope," he added under his breath. "This will be just perfect."

Janey turned and started to walk away. Somewhat amused, Jesse called her back.

"What is it, Yank?"

"Where *does* Mrs. Miller sleep?"

Janey's eyes narrowed sharply. "What do you want to know that for, Yank?"

"So that I don't put injured men on her bed," Jesse replied dryly.

Janey inhaled and exhaled with a long sigh. She pointed to the door next to his own. "There's her room. So you'll be all set. The healthy folk will be at this end, far down the hall, and you can put your injured in the rooms closer to the stairs. There's five more on this floor. The one over there will be big enough for a ward. The others can accommodate two or three men."

"Thank you for that information, Janey."

Once again, she started to leave him.

"Oh, Janey?"

"Yes, sir, Master Yank?" Janey slung the field-hand accent at him with fake, wide-eyed innocence. He almost smiled. The woman was as feisty as her mistress.

"Where did Master Anthony sleep?"

Janey paused, and he thought she was hiding a smile. "Why, Yank? He ain't sleepin' there no more, so you don't have to worry about puttin' no injured man in his bed."

"Curiosity," he admitted.

Janey pointed across the hall to the room that she had said was large enough for a ward.

Kiernan wasn't sleeping in the room that had been her husband's.

Had she ever slept in his room? Jesse wanted to know, but he couldn't ask Janey any more questions. Not if he wanted her to keep answering his questions now.

"Thank you," he told her.

"I'm not gonna cook for Yanks," she said flatly.

"I have a company cook," he told her. She left, and started down the stairs. But before Jesse had stepped into the room he intended to make his own, she was back.

"Ain't gonna be no Yanks in my kitchen. I'll cook for the household, same as always. You can eat at the table if Miz Kiernan says—"

"No, Janey," he corrected her. "I've taken over the house. And I dine late. At least eight o'clock because I need all the daylight hours. If Mrs. Miller wants to dine at that time of day, then she—and the children—may join me."

Janey looked as if she wanted to stamp a foot on the floor, but she didn't. Instead, she walked away, and Jesse inspected his new room at last.

Apparently, Kiernan had no interest in fighting him for the dining room. Nor did she fight him on much else during the days in which he took charge of the Montemarte mansion.

After looking over his sleeping quarters, Jesse had found two black men downstairs moving the spinet. One was elderly, and Jesse didn't like to see him huffing and puffing over the heavy furniture. He told them both to wait, rolled up his sleeves, and joined them in moving the spinet up the stairs, followed by several other large pieces.

He wasn't trying to salvage Miller furniture. He needed the space for the cots that would be arriving in the morning.

He didn't speak much with the two men, but he noted that their dark eyes were on him as they worked together. He learned that they were father and son, that the elder was named Jeremiah, and the younger, Tyne. Jeremiah was growing old. Tyne, on the other hand, was young and as strong as an ox.

From Tyne, Jesse learned that they were the only ones who remained on the estate—the two of them, another son, David, and Janey.

He also realized that they were loyal. Whatever came in the future, they would not be leaving Kiernan. That gave him a feeling of some relief. Irritably, he wondered why. After all, if everyone deserted her, then Kiernan might be inclined to travel farther south and keep herself safe.

Neither Kiernan nor the children dined with him at eight thirty that evening.

Janey, however, presented him with a well-seasoned chicken pot pie. It was one of the best-tasting dishes he had eaten since Virginia seceded from the Union.

He was exhausted by the time he climbed upstairs to strip down and stretch out on his bed, so exhausted that he should have slept instantly.

He didn't.

He knew that she was there, just behind the wall. He could leave his room and burst in on hers, and he could force her into his arms, and . . .

No, dammit, he wouldn't do it, ever. The choice had to be hers.

He groaned, turned over, and slept at long last, wondering if he was strong enough to let the choice remain hers. She had told him often enough that she would despise him if he went north.

He had ridden north, and he was wearing blue.

Sometime in the night, he finally slept.

* * *

Downstairs in the dining room, he breakfasted alone. Janey served him a stack of hotcakes while he read the most recent issue of *Harper's Weekly,* brought to him by one of his new company, a man who had taken up residence in a tent on the lawn along with his fellow soldiers.

"Where is Mrs. Miller this morning?" he asked Janey.

"Why, she done gone into town, Yankee."

"I see," he said to her. He complimented her on her coffee, then went out to supervise the setup of his hospital facilities in the large entry hallway. Cots had arrived, bandages, and his surgery equipment contained in his special black bag —the one he refused to ride into battle without, the one with all his field instruments.

By afternoon, Montemarte had been transformed.

By early evening, the first of Jesse's patients had arrived.

A middle-aged soldier who had weathered the war in Mexico and a great deal of action in the West was carried in by his company just as twilight came. Skirmishing was going on in the woods to the west of them. There would be more patients soon.

Jesse hadn't expected help from the household at Montemarte, and he didn't really need it. He had a company of twenty able-bodied soldiers to do his bidding, and two of his men were excellent orderlies.

But Tyne happened to be on the porch when the wounded soldier arrived, and Tyne helped carry him up and into the surgery he had created from the Miller's downstairs office. Absently, Jesse told Tyne that it was necessary to keep the man still while he inspected his leg.

Later, after he had dug out the ball, found that the break was clean, and set the splint, he realized he had given Tyne orders through the whole operation, and that the powerful Negro had silently given him some of the finest help he had ever received in the operating theater.

Nor had he expected anything from Kiernan. She had insisted that she wouldn't leave, but she gave him a very wide berth. When he finished with his patient at last, cleaned up, and came down to the dining room, Janey informed him that Miz Kiernan had retired for the evening, as had the children.

In the morning he was surprised to discover that Kiernan had been in to see his patient. Speaking with the bedridden veteran, Jesse asked him how he had passed his night.

"Right fine, Captain, right fine."

"How's the pain?"

"It's there, but it could be worse."

The man was a grizzled old soldier with salt-and-pepper hair and a fine dark beard. He grinned. "Well, I was feeling the worse for it, but then I woke up, and there, sure as rain, was this angel. She was just standing over me, and when I opened my eyes, she asked me how I was feeling. Why, I told her that I thought that I'd died and gone right on up to heaven, she were that purty. Hair like gold and fire, and eyes greener than me old Pa's tales about Ireland! She brought me a whiskey, and I swallowed it down, and I slept like a babe right after that."

"Whiskey, eh?"

"Whiskey it were."

Jesse wondered if he'd dare drink anything Kiernan offered him if he were bedridden himself—the whiskey might be laced with rat poison. It surprised him that she had been so decent to this Yank in her house.

But maybe she reserved her real hatred for Yanks like him —Yanks who she felt should be wearing the colors of the Confederacy.

He couldn't afford to think about it for long. The men Colonel Sebring was sending him to convalesce were arriving, and he had to go over all their files. By nightfall, the large upstairs room was full.

He had yet to see Kiernan again.

Still, he knew that she was about. She visited his patients. To each and every one of them, she was an angel. She never told them that she was anything but the stoutest of Rebels, but when he slept, she awoke and carried water to his injured crew, whiskey if they needed it. She even wrote a few letters. She might despise Jesse, but just as Tyne was providing him with excellent help in the surgery, Kiernan was proving to be an excellent matron for his ward.

He stayed awake purposely one night to catch her in the act of nursing. He heard her light footsteps hurrying down the hall. He rose and came silently into the hallway in his breeches and bare feet.

He watched her with the men. There were six of them now. She listened to their battle stories, and she retorted to all of them that they should have known that one Rebel was worth ten Yankees. None of the injured seemed to take it ill from her.

She might have called them rats and locusts, and they still wouldn't have taken it ill, Jesse decided wryly. She was simply too beautiful as she tended to them. Her smile was beautiful, her hair was beautiful, floating about her shoulders. She did look like an angel, for she wore a very proper white flannel nightgown and robe, and both drifted about her with her every movement like the white tunic and wings of the sweetest angel.

He felt his pulse beating in his throat, and he longed with all his heart to leap upon her in the darkness of the hallway, and sweep her away the minute she left the sickroom.

But he did not. He moved against the shadows of the doorway, and he clenched his teeth tightly while he allowed her to pass, unaccosted.

Her scent drifted by him.

Swearing, he returned to his bedroom. He didn't sleep. The next day, he was exhausted, and he dragged himself through the day, glad that no soldiers in his care were in need of surgery that day.

The next night, he forced himself to sleep. But he thought that he heard her laughter in his dreams, and he damned her in silence for not having run away, far, far away, after he arrived.

Several days after his arrival, his routine began to change.

It was late at night, not late enough for Kiernan to have begun her nocturnal wanderings, but late enough for him to have eaten dinner, made a last round of the patients, and retired to his room. But he wasn't in bed. Stripped down to a white shirt and his regulation breeches, he was going through the reports he intended to send Colonel Sebring.

His desk faced the windows for the light of the morning and faced away from the door that entered into the room.

He heard the door open and expected it to be Janey. She was careful to keep a certain distance from him, but she was also careful to see to his needs. She cooked him substantial meals daily, and she instructed his men in the use of the laundry for the best output on sheets and bandages. She was remarkable in her management of time and labor, and he realized that it was becoming very easy to depend on her. Despite her avowals that she was only doing her best to keep the house in order for the rightful residents, she often went above and beyond what was necessary for that. At night, when she knew that his candle was burning and that he was still working, she often made him coffee.

He didn't look up when he heard the door close and felt the presence in the room. She didn't like him to thank her—that made it seem too much as if she had actually done something for him.

"Just put it on the desk, will you, please, Janey?"

A moment later he realized that there was silence and that nothing had come to his desk. He frowned, set down the sheet of paper he was writing on, and turned at last.

Janey was not in the doorway at all. It was the boy, Jacob. Tall, lean, with golden-blond curls and wide dark eyes, he was a younger version of Anthony Miller. Right now, he seemed very much like his brother, for he was holding one of his family's special pistols, a six-shooter, and it was aimed at Jesse's heart.

The boy would know how to shoot, Jesse thought. Coming from this family, he would know how to shoot. They were at point-blank range from each other.

Maybe Jacob Miller hadn't seen enough fighting yet to want to pull the trigger. His fingers were shaking, and it was taking him both hands to hold the pistol. His face, in the soft candlelight of the room, was chalk white.

Jesse leaned back in his chair.

"Do you really want to pull that trigger?" he asked Jacob softly.

The boy was silent for so long that Jesse began to wonder if he had heard him or not.

"I want you out of my house," Jacob said at last. "Dead is one way to go."

Jesse lowered his eyes, hiding a smile. Yes, dead was one way to leave. He shouldn't be smiling. A nervous lad might easily shoot him down, where Indians and Jayhawkers and Rebs had not managed to do so.

And Jacob was deadly serious.

"If you shoot me, you must know that one of my men may get a little crazy and shoot you back, even if you are just twelve."

"Nearly thirteen."

"A rotten age to die."

"You brought a whole passel of Yanks here!" Jacob accused him. "You killed my brother!"

Jesse wondered where Jacob had gotten such information. He realized he was talking in a broad sense, that anyone in blue was responsible for killing Anthony Miller.

"I—I don't care if I *am* shot down by a Union company," he told Jesse. "Just as long as I take one bluebelly with me."

"Right," Jesse said. "But what about Patricia? And Kiernan? Once I'm gone, this house is tinderwood."

Jacob blinked once. "They'll go east," he said. "They'll go to Kiernan's father."

It was what he himself wanted, Jesse thought wryly. "Jacob, if you would just—"

"You know Kiernan better than I do," Jacob said suddenly. "You probably know her better than my brother did."

"I lived next to her all of my life, Jacob."

"You wanted my brother dead!" Jacob accused him.

Jesse stood up. The gun in Jacob's hand waved at him, but he was suddenly too angry to let the boy get away with his words. Reason wasn't working. "You're damned wrong, Jacob Miller. I've never wanted any man dead." Hand outstretched, he started across the room. "Now give me that pistol, and go back—"

He broke off, throwing himself down and at Jacob's legs as, to his amazement, the boy actually fired the gun. A bullet grazed Jesse's arm, then hit the desk somewhere. Blood suddenly drenched the sleeve of his white shirt, but he knew he was all right. He had Jacob down on the ground beneath him, and the gun was wrenched from his hands.

"What did you want to go do a damned fool thing like that for?" Jesse demanded furiously.

"I didn't mean to!" Jacob gasped. "Honest to God, I didn't really mean to!"

The door to the room suddenly burst open. Corporal O'Malley, a fresh-faced Irishman hailing from Manhattan, on night duty with the patients, stood there, his rifle loaded and aimed.

"Captain Cameron—"

"I'm fine, Corporal," he called over his shoulder.

"But Captain—"

"I said I'm fine. We had a little accident here."

O'Malley seemed to assess the situation, then grinned and started out of the room. But in his place, another arrival rushed past him in a panic.

Kiernan was dressed in her angel attire, Jesse noted, the chaste white that drifted and wafted around her, that covered her from throat to foot, that made her the most sensual creature he had ever seen.

Angel, indeed. An angel sent from hell to torment his every waking moment and beyond.

But for once, there was nothing in her shimmering green eyes besides fear. Was it fear for his safety? he wondered briefly.

He remembered that he was sitting on top of one of her charges, and that she'd be concerned.

"Jesse, what—oh, my God! Jacob!"

She rushed forward, but Jesse put up a warning hand, his eyes narrowing, and she came to a halt, staring at them both, her lower lip caught between her teeth.

"Jesse, don't hurt him!" she pleaded. "Jesse, please, for the sake of our friendship—"

" 'Jesse'? What the hell happened to 'Captain Cameron'?

he scolded her. "Friendship? What friendship? I'm a Yank, remember? You'd rather see this house burn to the ground than see me in it, remember? Jacob was only trying to help you, Mrs. Miller."

Her face was suddenly whiter than the boy's, if that was possible. Jesse rose to his feet, pulling Jacob up along with him with his good hand. Kiernan issued another gasp. "Your arm! Let him go. Let me see to it—"

"Mrs. Miller, it breaks my heart to turn down an offer of tender ministrations from you, but I believe I'll do just that. Now, excuse us."

He had Jacob by the shirt collar and was starting for the door.

"Jesse—"

He stopped, furious with her. "It's 'Captain Cameron' to you, ma'am, and if you will excuse me, the lad and I have a few things to discuss."

She started almost as if he had slapped her. He ignored her and pulled Jacob along the hallway and to the stairs, then down to the ground floor. He made his way through the cots waiting in the entry hall to the left, to what had been a Miller office but was now his surgery, with big windows that faced the east. He paused to light a lamp. He realized then that Kiernan had followed.

"Jesse—"

"Captain Cameron!"

"Captain Cameron, then!" she snapped, the angel's sweet tone leaving her voice. He smiled. Even now, pretense was so quickly stripped away with her. "He's just a boy, he didn't—"

"He's a big boy, and he did," Jesse told her flatly. "Out." He left Jacob in the center of the room and walked right into Kiernan, forcing her to back up. It was a damned good thing that he had his own anger.

Because it felt good to touch her body, to feel the soft fabric brushing him, to feel the curve of her breasts touching his chest as he forced her back.

"Damn you! I won't leave him here with you!" she cried, and her fists slammed against his chest.

He plucked her swiftly up and off her feet. For one wild moment, her eyes met his, and he remembered all those other times that he had held her so. Fire raged through his loins and tore into his limbs, and still her eyes met his. He felt a shudder rake through her body, and her lashes lowered.

When her gaze met his again, it was all fury. "Let me down, Yank, let me—"

He did let her down. He deposited her flatly outside the door, slammed it in her face, and locked it.

He turned, hearing her pounding on it and calling his name, then any name that seemed to come to her mind.

He looked at Jacob, who now stood wide-eyed in the center of the room, staring at him.

Jesse smiled. "Well, we're alone at last." Feeling a certain sweet satisfaction—even though all the fires of hell were still tormenting him—Jesse strode across the room to the cabinet where he had kept a set of his medical instruments and a supply of bandages. "Here, you can patch this arm up for me. You did it—you might as well fix it."

He paused, glancing toward the door. The house was well built. Kiernan was still swearing away and pounding on the wood.

He ignored her.

Jacob stared at him. His eyes strayed toward the door, then met Jesse's again. Jesse returned the look, as if to assure Jacob that he had no intention of paying heed to Kiernan. "Now, to my wound. You might cause me pain cleaning it out. Think I'll have a drink. Yes, there's a whiskey bottle over there. Want a shot?"

"I—er, I'm not old enough," Jacob told him blankly.

"Sure you are. If you're old enough to run around pointing pistols at men, you're old enough to share a small drink."

Several bottles and glasses stood on a cherrywood table that he had wedged close to the desk to leave as much room as possible in the room. He poured out two shots of whiskey and handed one to Jacob. He swallowed down his own, then studied the boy as he took a sip. Jacob winced, but he didn't cough, and he swallowed down all of the amber liquid.

"You've had whiskey before," Jesse said.

"Once or twice," he admitted. "Pa gave me some the day Virginia voted out of the Union."

"Mm," Jesse murmured. "Well, let's see if it's steadied your hand."

From a basin he poured out fresh water. He ripped off his shirt sleeve and inspected his wound. "Let's see. Do we need to sew it up?"

"Sew?" Jacob said, and swallowed hard.

"Sew," Jesse said. "Maybe just a stitch or two."

He had been hit in the left arm, and for that he was grateful—he needed his right arm. He easily washed away the blood on the wound, and it probably would have been all right without any stitches. But it seemed like a good time for Jacob to learn something, something that might make all the difference for him in the future.

Jesse went through his bag and produced a needle and sutures. He threaded the needle and brought it over to Jacob. "Here, start right here. Just two of them, small and neat. Don't worry about tying them off. I've got one hand left—I'll help you."

"Sew it—just like that?"

"Yep."

"Don't you need something for the pain?"

"It's just two stitches, and I'll take another shot of whiskey. It wouldn't be a good idea for me to go too far under the influence of liquor in this house, do you think?"

Jacob flushed. He had the needle in his hand. His eyes sought Jesse's once again.

"I've had stitches before. Go on, sew."

Jacob was in far more pain than he was, Jesse decided as the needle touched his flesh. He locked his teeth and braced himself hard against the pain. The needle went through his flesh and back out again, then quickly, very quickly, it went in and out again. What Jacob's touch lacked in experience, it made up for with speed.

A cold sweat had broken out on Jacob's brow. Jesse told

him where to hold the suture, and he tied it off. He swallowed down another shot of whiskey and poured a little portion over the wound, wincing at the sting. "Don't know why, but it's good for it," he told Jacob, who was staring at him once again.

Jacob remained silent—and obviously scared. Jesse leaned back against the desk and watched him. "Let's get one thing straight here and now. You're on one side of this war, and I'm on the other. I don't expect you to change sides—I've been given the best arguments in the world, and I'm not changing sides. It's a war. That's what happens in war. But I want you to understand one thing. I didn't want your brother's death, not in any way. I admired him, and in better times, I considered him a friend."

Jacob looked down at his feet, then looked up at Jesse and shrugged. "Yeah, well, I—I guess I know that."

"You do?"

Jacob shrugged, shoving his hands into his pockets. "Anthony told me he challenged you to a duel. He wouldn't tell me what it was about—only that his temper had kind of gone and that it had been real stupid on his part. He said that you wouldn't kill him. He said you were a right good man, that there was only one thing wrong with you."

"What was that?"

"That you were a Yank, of course."

"Oh," Jesse said softly.

"I—I didn't really mean to kill you," Jacob told him.

"I didn't think you did. I never met a Miller who couldn't handle a firearm. If you'd wanted me dead now, I'd be dead," Jesse said.

"Yeah, maybe," Jacob said with a flush.

"I came here because I owe your brother," Jesse said. "We may not be on the same side, Jacob, but I came here fighting for you."

Jacob nodded.

"I'm not asking for surrender. I just want to call a truce in this house," Jesse told him. He offered Jacob his hand.

Jacob stared from his hand to his eyes. "That's it? I shot you, and that's it?"

"Yep. I'd like your word that you won't try to shoot me again."

Jacob shook his hand, still looking into his eyes. "You've got my word. That's enough for you?"

"Yep. I never had reason to doubt a Miller before."

A small smile touched Jacob's face. He nodded. "No, we don't lie. We never lie," he said proudly. He swallowed hard and studied Jesse's face again. "Thank you," he said.

Those two words must have cost him a great deal, Jesse decided. "There's nothing to thank me for. Now, we probably should go up to bed."

"Yes, sir," Jacob said to him. He started for the door, then turned back. "You came here because you felt you owed something to Anthony?"

"Yes," Jesse said.

Jacob gazed at him innocently. "That's funny. I could have sworn that you came here for Kiernan."

His eyes were steady on Jesse's. Jesse kept his eyes steady too.

"Yes, that too," he admitted.

Jacob grinned again, lowered his head, and said good night. He opened the door, and Kiernan nearly came tumbling into the room.

She had given up her pounding sometime before, and she was tired out. But her gaze raced quickly over her young charge, her fear and concern evident. "Jacob, are you all right?"

"I'm fine. I learned how to do sutures, Kiernan." He held her shoulders and kissed her cheek, then walked past her up the stairs.

Kiernan, exhausted, leaned against the wall, her eyes closed.

Then those emerald orbs shot open and gazed upon him with glittering fury and reproach. "You left me out there thinking—you left me terrified and worried sick!"

"You shouldn't have been terrified or worried sick," Jesse said dryly. "You've known me all your life, and you know damned well that I'd never do injury to a child."

"No!" she protested, her eyes still flashing their emerald

fire. "I don't know you at all. Because the man I thought I knew would never have walked away from the graveyard at Cameron Hall that day."

Pain was mingled with the anger of her voice. He wanted to touch her. He took a step toward her. "Kiernan—"

She straightened, pushing away from the wall. She smiled at him, a regal, elegant, very superior smile.

"It's Mrs. Miller to you, Captain Cameron. Mrs. Miller."

She swung around and left the room, her head high, her hair flowing, the angel-white fabric of her gown floating behind her.

He followed her out to the stairway and watched her run up the steps.

He smiled suddenly, then wondered how he could be smiling while everything inside of him ached at the same time.

Sadly, the same conclusive and useless thought that had plagued him since he had come plagued him again.

Damn her.

Damn her sweet, beautiful, elegant, little hide.

Seventeen

During the following week, Jesse had Jacob for a dinner companion.

By the end of the week, Jacob's sister, Patricia, had joined them.

Kiernan kept her distance.

For a woman who so detested Yankees, Kiernan was spending a fair amount of time with them. She no longer waited until the wee hours of the night to move among them. Afternoons, when he looked in on the wards, he usually found her there.

In the midst of the pain and injury and the growing cold of the coming winter, she was the sweetest breath of spring. She smelled delicious. She was dressed elegantly. She moved with a rustle of silk, with that sweet fragrance, with her beauty, her hair always smoothed beneath a net, her fingers thin and delicate upon a pen as she wrote a letter, or upon a cloth as she soothed a man's brow.

They were all in love with her.

"Ain't she just the most glorious thing that ever lived and breathed, Doc?" an old soldier asked him one day as Jesse looked carefully over his chart.

Jesse cocked a brow and grunted. Yes, she was glorious, he thought dryly. But the old coot had never seen her angry.

Of course, the injured men never did see her angry. They

saw her in full skirts, with her demure smile, and they heard her laughter and her teasing tones.

One afternoon, it was almost as if she were holding court. She was seated on a chair in the middle of the beds in the large ward. She wore a beautiful yellow day dress with a lace overlay that covered the bodice to the collar and the sleeves to mid-elbow. A beautiful brooch highlighted her throat at her collar. Her skirt flowed around her. Her eyes were alive and dancing, and her accent was thicker and richer than he'd ever heard flow from her ruby lips before.

The men were enthralled.

"It's not that I don't think highly of you gents," she drawled softly. "It's just that I most earnestly do believe that two of our boys have the speed and the fighting ability of about ten of ya'll."

"Why, that ain't true at all, Miz Miller," a young soldier protested. "We just ain't had all the right opportunities."

"And we haven't got generals like Stonewall or Lee," the grizzled fellow said sagely.

"Men fight very hard to protect their own land."

"We can still outfight the Rebs," another lad offered.

Watching silently from the doorway, Jesse realized that the soldier speaking had just come into Montemarte the day before yesterday with his arm all torn up by shrapnel. Jesse had been sent the soldier to see if he couldn't save the arm. He'd spent hours in the surgery, removing bits of metal and ball.

"You just wait and see, Miz Miller," he was saying now. "When our boys are the ones with the element of surprise, they'll take the Rebs. Why, we've got some boys going down into the valley in just a few days' time. They'll whomp the few troops old Stonewall has sitting there."

"Whomp 'em?" Kiernan asked, laughing sweetly.

"Why, sure. We'll have surprise on our side—and better numbers, too, probably."

"Well, we'll just see then, won't we?" she asked. She stood, and moved among them. "Why, Billy Joe Raily, I declare, your skin looks nice and white and so healthy today. That bit of yellow tinge is all gone." She stroked the man's cheek with the back of her hand.

Billy Joe looked as if he were just about to burst. Kiernan had her bedside manner down pat. A touch, and poor Billy Joe was probably trying hard not to climax.

Jesse imagined that he was saving his men from their battle wounds—so they could die of heart attacks from the excitement Kiernan caused them.

She stooped to place a wet cloth on another brow, then turned and saw him. And stopped dead still.

For a moment, the demure mask of the very sweet belle slipped. She was every bit as beautiful, but her face suddenly appeared sharp and weary, and her eyes bore a trace of wariness. She straightened, still staring at him, and set the cloth upon the table. Then she turned around to sweep the room with her gaze. "Good afternoon, boys," she wished them, serene and innocent. The mask was back in place.

She swept by Jesse.

He breathed in the sweet scent of the woman and her perfume, and he listened to the rustle of silk.

Later that afternoon, near twilight, he looked out of his bedroom window and saw her in front of the house. She had changed into a dark velvet riding habit that had been fashioned more for utility than for elegance. As he watched, she hurried toward the stables.

He dropped the letter he had just received from Washington, grabbed his wool, shoulder-skirted frock coat, and hurried downstairs. By the time he reached the porch, she was just riding out, careful to skirt around the tents of his men and the bivouac on the front lawn.

Jesse hurried toward the stables himself. Old Jeremiah was seated on a chair by the door, leaning back and dozing. But when Jesse strode by him, he opened his eyes wide, then hurried after Jesse.

"Where you goin' there, Master Jess?"

"Riding."

"Don't seem to me like no good time to go ridin'. It's gonna be dark soon enough."

Right before Pegasus's stall, Jesse paused. "Oh, really? You should have thought to stop your mistress then."

"What?"

"Kiernan just left. Mrs. Miller just rode away from here," Jesse said impatiently.

"Did she now?"

"Jeremiah, you're trying to tell me that you didn't see Mrs. Miller riding out, when you were sitting right here?"

"Come to think of it—"

"Right, come to think of it," Jesse muttered. He drew Pegasus's bridle from its hook and moved around to the horse's head.

"Want me to saddle him up for you, Master Jess?"

"No, thanks," Jesse said. "If I let you do it, I have a feeling I'd be sitting here all night waiting for you to finish."

"Why, Master Jess—"

"Step aside, Jeremiah," Jesse said. He pushed on Pegasus's neck, backing him out of the stall. He quickly threw a blanket and his saddle over the horse's back and cinched and tightened the girth. Then leaped upon the horse and looked down at Jeremiah.

"Don't fret too much, Jeremiah. She's way ahead of me."

Jeremiah stepped back; he had no choice. Jesse set his heels to Pegasus, and they started off.

He didn't skirt around his own encampment and made up some time by riding through it. Still, when he reached the place where Kiernan had disappeared into the trees, he reined in. He studied the ground, but it was bone dry, and there were few prints. One trail seemed to have more broken foliage along it, so he urged Pegasus in that direction.

Mentally, he drew a picture of the area. Harpers Ferry was far below, with Maryland Heights, the mounts and hills and crests and valleys, all around. He thought of the manors and the plantations in the region, places where he had attended balls and fêtes and where he had hunted with friends.

He remembered that the trail before him led to the ruins of the Chagall estate.

"All right, Pegasus, let's see what she's up to," Jesse murmured. He tightened his thighs, urging the horse forward.

*   *   *

Some mornings when Kiernan awoke, she still prayed that she would discover that it had all been a horrible nightmare.

Jesse had never come to the house. None of the Yanks had ever come. The war had yet to touch them, and a dozen injured men were not living in her house.

At first, nothing could conceivably have been worse than having Jesse in the next room. Surely not even the fires of hell could bring so much torment as having him so near. She had not slept, just knowing that he was there. Hearing his footsteps across the wooden floor, imagining the movements that he made—she could picture his face because she knew him so well. He would be weary coming in from surgery. He would cast off his coat or his jacket, sit back in the chair at the desk, and prop his booted heels up upon it. He would sink down, close his eyes, and press his temple between his thumb and his forefinger. Then, slowly, his hand would fall, his eyes would open, and he would rise.

She could hear him moving about the room, stripping down. His boots falling to the floor, his shirt over a chair, his breeches, his belt. Then she would hear his weight as he fell upon his bed, and she would picture him again, fingers laced behind his head, his eyes upon the darkened shadows on the ceiling.

In the silence that followed she could imagine no greater anguish than lying awake and seeing him in her mind's eyes, just feet apart from her. He was her enemy now. They had no future together. Jesse had donned blue and gone his own way, and she could never change him. She had sworn to hate him.

And she had sworn to herself that she hated him.

And she did, completely. But love died hard, she realized, no matter what color cloth covered a man.

And now she was Anthony's widow. She had married Anthony, and Anthony was dead, and it had not been that long ago, and she should have been in deepest mourning.

But none of that mattered when Jesse was in a room. No matter how deep her fury, no matter how desperate her situation, when he came near, smoldering sparks came alive, furnaces blazed. Her hatred was intense—and so, too, was her longing.

It was not simply Jesse's arrival that tormented her. It was the men who camped out on the lawn. It was the men who lay in Anthony's room across the hall. Yankees. Sick Yankees, hurt Yankees.

When she had first heard a man screaming in the surgery, she had simply stayed in her bedroom, her hands clamped over her ears. She could have sworn that the victim had died. But there he was that night, alive and well, and with a gentle smile when he saw her looking in on him. He, too, was the enemy.

But how could she wish him dead?

Then the others came. They were men with lean faces and blue eyes and brown eyes, and men with weary and worn faces. Some wore whiskers, and some did not. They, too, were the enemy. They were the same as any man, and as often as not in this region, they had kinfolk on the other side, and they prayed not so much to live as to not encounter their own loved ones at the other end of their rifles. She wanted to ignore their suffering; but she discovered that she could not bear it.

She also discovered that Jesse's patients were a fine way to learn the movements of the Union troops. They had all come in from skirmishes in the countryside nearby, and the information they had was invaluable.

She had already left a message at the oak for foraging Confederates to vacate a place before Yankees with superior numbers could surprise them. Now she had a second opportunity to do so. It pleased her greatly. It seemed, at the very least, some recompense for the anguish of having Jesse in the house and the agony of hearing the screams that came from the surgery.

Night was coming quickly this evening, she realized, riding harder as she neared the Chagall estate. She reined in, seeing the pillars of the burned-out place, white and black and ghostly in the pale moonlight that had replaced the rays of the day's dying sun.

The wind rustled through the trees, and haunting shadows fell over the terrain. Movements seemed to flutter all about her, and for a moment she held still, as a shiver of fear danced up and down the length of her spine.

She had been a fool to come so late at night, she thought. But there was little to fear, she told herself. The Rebs would not hurt her, and the Yanks were already living in her house.

And still . . .

The breeze was very cool, and the night seemed to have eyes.

She leaped off her horse and raced to the old oak. Just as she neared the tree, a shadow stepped out from behind it.

The shadow of a man, and not of a man . . .

Tall, dark, pitch-black, and menacing, the moonlight caught him in a strange silhouette, throwing his shadow far and wide across the tree and all the overgrown lawn before the house.

Kiernan screamed, reeling back, her hand flying to her mouth. Instinctively, she turned to run. She heard a shout, but in her panic, it meant nothing. She tore across the weeds and grass and fallen branches, desperate to reach her horse. The wind rose again, rustling through the trees with sudden vengeance.

She could feel him, the shadow on her back, hounding her. She ran faster, gasping, screaming desperately for every breath, running so hard that her lungs ached and threatened to burst, her legs cramped and burned, and her heart hammered.

Just feet away from her horse, the shadow devoured her. She was swept off her feet, and she screamed again in a wild panic. She felt herself falling and hitting the hard earth, the shadow on top of her.

She fought it, swinging out, kicking, screaming, slamming hard again and again against the blackness and the hard bulk as panic overwhelmed her.

"Kiernan!"

At last, her name penetrated her terrified senses. She went rigidly still.

"Kiernan!"

Jesse! It was Jesse. She should have known. She should have recognized the angle of his hat, even in a distorted silhouette. She should have known the feel of him, the scent of him. . . .

But when she had left the house, he was in his room! He had just finished surgery, he'd probably received messages from Washington, and he should have been involved in all that was going on in his hospital.

How had he reached the oak ahead of her?

"Jesse!" Sanity was returning to her. The wind was high, and it whistled and rustled through the trees like something alive. The moonlight came down upon them fully now, and his face was clear above her own. It was a handsome face with clear, defined features, a rugged face, with fine character lines around his eyes. It was a face she knew so well.

Suddenly, she worried that somebody might be in the area —Angus or T. J. or one of their neighbors. If they saw Jesse straddled over her like this, they might . . .

Kill him.

"Jesse, get off me, you fool!"

"Why, Kiernan?" he demanded. His voice was harsh, his eyes were nearly obsidian in the night. His touch was steel.

"Why?" she repeated, incredulous. "Because you've got me pinned to the ground! Because you just scared me half to death. Because I hate, loathe, and despise you. Because you're the enemy. Because you're goddamned wearing blue!"

His eyes glittered in the darkness. His hands pinned her wrists above her head. He was so close to her. She felt the warmth of his breath, sensed the heat and tension in him, felt the rippling of his muscles. It didn't matter what she said. He ignored her.

"What the hell are you doing out here?"

"What the hell is it to you?" she spat. She stiffened in agony beneath him, praying that he would move, and quickly. He wasn't hurting her; he was just holding her with his thighs, with his weight, with the taut ring of his fingers around her wrists.

"What are you doing out here?" he thundered again.

"I came for a ride!"

"At night?"

"Yes, it's night, isn't it? Bright boy. That must be why you Yanks do so well in battle."

"Stop it!" he commanded her.

"Stop what?"

"Stop acting like that!"

"Acting! I'm not acting, Captain. This is war, remember?" She stared up at him, growing very cold against the damp earth, hating him, and suddenly afraid as she saw a ruthless glimmer in his eyes that was as cold as the night. Had his grasp slackened just a bit? She strived with all her strength to kick him. He swore, and she gasped out, rolling hard to elude his touch.

But he was right with her. Before she had moved six inches, he was on top of her again, splayed over her this time. He held her wrists together with one hand and lifted her chin with his free thumb. "I'll ask you again. What are you doing out here?"

"I came for a ride. What are *you* doing out here?"

"Following you."

"Jesse, I'm not going to tell you anything—"

"Kiernan, they shoot spies!"

"Go to hell, Jesse. I'm not a spy! And if I—"

"Bitch!" he swore suddenly. He rose to his feet, drawing her up before him. His hands were so tight on hers that she almost cried out with the pain. He pulled her so tautly against him that she could scarcely bear it. His fingers wound into her hair, tight and painful. She met his gaze.

"You used my men. You acted like an angel of mercy, but you didn't care in the least that they suffered. You'd just as soon see them dead, right? But you moved among them from that very first night for whatever little tidbit you might pick up from them—men so very grateful for the least little bounty that you offered!"

He was shaking, trembling with his rage. He had her pulled so flush against him that she could feel the beat of his heart. The heat of his words and his anger touched her lips, almost like a kiss.

"Jesse, damn you, I didn't—"

"Damn you! Don't lie to me!"

"Fine, fine!" she cried out. Tears stung her eyes from the pressure of his fingers upon her hair. She could not look away. "I'd use them anytime, Jesse, and I'd use you. You're the enemy. My God, how many times do you have to be told that? I hate you, Jesse, and I hate them! They're invading my land! They've taken over my house! They've killed my friends and my people! What the hell do you want from me?"

He was dead silent as the wind rustled through the trees again and as the night drifted all around him. He swore an oath, still furious, still shaking, his fingers curling around her shoulders. "What do I want out of you?" he repeated savagely. He teeth flashed white in the moonlight. "What do I want out of you? I want to curl my fingers around your throat. I want—"

He became still again. But only a second passed before his lips were suddenly on hers, hard and nearly as savage as her words. His mouth formed, hot and demanding upon hers, igniting an instant blaze within her, a combustion that rocketed the night, that seized hold of all her senses and left her powerless to resist.

It had been so long . . .

So long since he had held her so, so long since she had felt the world tremble beneath her feet, felt joy erupt in her heart and in her limbs and in the deepest, inner core of her body. She could not resist, for she was melded to his form, so tight against him that they might have been one. His arms were so powerful around her. His tongue ringed her lips and forced entry to the sweetest depths of her mouth.

He held her and kissed her. With each passing second the hot, sultry seduction of his mouth and tongue took her deeper and deeper into a no man's land of longing and memory. Bright tears flooded her eyes as the thing that she could never deny to herself sprang into her thoughts.

She loved him.

No war could change that, no color could cover that blindness. She loved him, and she wanted him.

No! She'd never been a wife to Anthony in any sense. At the very least, she could be a decent widow.

She wrenched free from the seduction of his touch. "Jesse. No, damn you!" she cried out, and stepped back a foot, wiping her mouth with the back of her hand as if she could erase what had happened.

"Kiernan—"

"No! Never! Not here, not now! Not near Anthony's house, dear Lord!"

"Kiernan!" His voice was hard and rugged and rasping as he took a step forward.

"I'm a widow, Jesse! Anthony's widow!" she stressed.

He went dead still, his fingers knotted tightly into fists and clenched at his side. "Damn you, Kiernan," he muttered.

"Don't touch me again!" she whispered. "Don't touch me. If he was ever your friend, if you ever had any respect for him. Jesse, this is his home, his land."

"And it was *his* home, *his* land, where we first made love!" Jesse exploded.

It was like a slap in the face—because it was true.

She spun around, anxious to reach her horse. But she didn't get very far before he caught hold of her elbow and spun her back around to face him.

"Where are your widow's weeds, Kiernan? Where is your black, where the hell is your mourning?"

In dismay, she stared at him. She had shed her mourning colors only a few months after she had come. Black had been so hot when she had been working in the garden. They hadn't done laundry frequently enough to clean them.

She had loved Anthony in a way, but she had never managed to feel like his widow, and it had been easy to slip.

Jesse smiled a mocking smile and took a step back. "What a love affair it must have been!" he taunted.

She took a wild swing at him. He caught her arm and wrenched her up against him once more. She felt the awful thundering of her heart when she thought he was going to kiss her again.

"Let me go, Jesse."

He held her still. She couldn't best his strength. His lips would touch hers again, and she would be lost.

"He was your friend, Jesse. He fought you, but he always admired you."

He was stiff, as rigid as steel. He held her in silence, his teeth grating, his jaw clenched. When he spoke, it was through clenched teeth. His eyes were dark upon hers, his features taut. "Damn you, Kiernan! Damn you."

But she was free. She looked at him, quickly backing away from him, hoping that her tears would not fall and that she would not betray her own emotions.

She turned and fled and mounted her horse and galloped all the way home.

He was behind her all the way, but he did not try to catch her again. At the house, she did not dare to look at him again.

She left her horse with Jeremiah, who was worried, and who cried after her. She would not stop. She fled to the house and to her room.

Once again that night, she listened. She listened to his footsteps in the room next to her own. She listened to the creaking of his chair as he sat. She heard his boots fall, heard the very weariness as he shed his clothing and fell into his bed.

She closed her eyes tight, clenching down on her jaw. It would be so easy to rise and walk the few steps down the hall. So easy to open the door and drift in white, like the white of a bride, to his bed.

And lie down beside him.

And feel his arms and the night breeze against her naked flesh.

She buried her face in the pillow.

Trying to hate him . . .

And hating herself.

It was morning before she realized that she had not left her message in the oak. The information she had learned from the Yanks might save a number of lives.

She dressed in a simple gingham and brown day dress in

case Jesse happened to notice her moving about the house. Very carefully, she folded her written message and slipped it low into her bodice and left her room. Knowing that she had to take grave care, she went first to the ward and spoke with the men. Corporal O'Malley was there with an assistant, speaking with the men and looking over bandages and braces and splints. Kiernan swept among them all, offering smiles and assurances, pouring water and providing what little amenities that she could to make them more comfortable.

One moment, she felt as if twin darts of fire were burning into her back, and she turned.

Jesse stood in the doorway watching her. He had accused her of caring nothing for the men, and he had said that spying was her only reason to be among them.

He'd never have believed that she wanted nothing from them that morning, that she had learned that she cared for any man's suffering, no matter what color he wore.

But Jesse would never believe that. The look he gave her now condemned her a thousand times over. It made her shake inside and want to cry out.

She turned quickly from him and changed the cool cloth on the forehead of the soldier who had asked her assistance. When she turned back again, Jesse was gone.

She lingered with the men for another hour. She heard Corporal O'Malley say something about finding Tyne to help Jesse get ready in surgery.

It was time for her to leave.

She hurried downstairs and out of the house. Glancing back, she was certain that no one stood at a window to watch her departure. She ran to the stables.

But when she opened the door, she found two soldiers standing there, staring at her.

"Gentlemen?" she demanded.

The first, Private Yeager, shook his head. "Don't try to sweet-talk us, Mrs. Miller."

"Sweet-talk you, sir?" she said sharply, her brow rising.

"You're carrying information to the Rebs," the second soldier, Sergeant Herrington, said flatly.

"Don't be absurd!" she lied. "Get out of my way."

She started forward, but Yeager stood directly in front of her. "Hand it over, Mrs. Miller. You're carrying a message."

"Get out of my way!" She stepped around him.

To her amazement, he pulled her back. His eyes were bright. "You're carrying a message, and I want it."

"Don't you dare handle me like that!" she cried imperiously.

"I'll handle you—" he began, but then his voice broke. He was staring over her shoulder. His hold went slack, and Kiernan spun around.

Jesse stood dead set in the doorway, his arms folded across his chest, his eyes implacable.

"What's going on here, Sergeant?"

Sergeant Herrington cleared his throat. "Sir, she's carrying notes to the Rebels. We're convinced of it."

Jesse arched a brow and looked at Kiernan. "Are you carrying secret missives to Rebel soldiers, Mrs. Miller?"

"No," she lied flatly.

Jesse looked to the two men. "She denies the charge, men."

"Well, just you let me—let me—" Herrington began.

"Let you what?" Jesse asked.

"Search her!" Herrington spat out with relish.

Kiernan gasped. "Captain! You cannot let this orangutan touch me!"

"Madam, such a comparison is insulting to orangutans."

"Captain—"

"We are soldiers in the Union Army, gentlemen. I cannot let you search a lady. And as gentlemen, men of honor, you are obliged to accept her word. You may return to your posts."

Herrington cast her a furious stare and walked out, the hapless Private Yeager at his heels.

Kiernan's heart sank. She certainly couldn't ride away now. She started after them, but Jesse slammed the door in her face before she could go.

Startled, she looked at him—and her heart began to beat

hard, for there was fire in his eyes, and they were alone, very alone, in the stables.

"Are you carrying a message, Kiernan?" he quizzed her softly.

"You'll never know, will you?" she asked sweetly. "Now, if you'll excuse me—"

He shook his head. "I certainly will not excuse you." He took a step toward her, and she backed away.

"Jesse, what are you doing?"

"I'm going to find out if you're carrying a message."

"What?" she cried. "You can't!" She took another step back, a step that landed her in a freshly broken bale of hay, and she fell back into it.

Jesse stood above her, his long legs straddled over her own as he stared down at her.

"Jesse, you wouldn't dare!"

"I've told you before, I dare anything."

"You just said that a gentleman in the Union Army couldn't do such a thing! You wouldn't allow those men—"

"Ah, but Kiernan, you told me long ago that you considered me no gentleman. And I told those men that *they* couldn't." He smiled wickedly. "I certainly didn't say that *I* couldn't . . . or *wouldn't.*"

To Kiernan's astonishment and rising horror, he was suddenly down upon the hay.

Upon her.

Eighteen

His knee lay at an angle over her thigh. He leaned upon one elbow at her side, while his left arm was braced around her waist. She stared at him furiously. "Jesse, I always knew you were no gentleman, but—"

"Kiernan, let's not go through this again. I want the message."

"There is no message."

"There is. You can give it to me, or I can take it."

He was serious, she decided. But she couldn't just hand over proof that she had been using her association with the hospitalized men to aid the Confederacy. Why in the Lord's name hadn't she waited until she reached the tree before she wrote down her message?

Because he might have followed her, she thought dully, and she never would have had a chance to write it down.

"Jesse," she said very softly, her eyes on his with what she hoped was open honesty, "I'm asking you to stop this. It's totally undignified. It dishonors all—all that we ever were to one another," she added with a note of pathos.

"And what is that, Kiernan?" he asked softly. His knuckles brushed softly over her cheeks, and she was amazed by the warmth that filled her with that touch. The warmth spread the length and breadth of her, the rake of his knuckles was so tender. His lips were close to hers, and the weight of his body was painfully familiar.

She had to seduce him into letting her go free, she reminded herself. She reached up and brushed back a lock of his hair, a dark lock that dangled rakishly upon occasion, no matter how much she knew he tried to subdue it. She smoothed it back and allowed the tips of her fingers to stroke his face in turn.

"Jesse, let me up, please. I have to get away. There are times when I just have to ride away. Don't you understand?"

He caught her fingers and planted a kiss upon them. He held them still, fascinated. Another kiss fell, and another. She felt the hot, sultry movement of his tongue upon them.

"Jesse . . ."

"I understand," he murmured. "There are Yankees in your house. Yankees." He repeated the word, looked into her eyes, smiled, and shivered. "Ugh."

She almost snatched her hand away. She gritted her teeth and pouted. "Jesse, be serious, please."

"I'm very serious," he promised her. He eased back, curling his fingers around hers, allowing both their hands to rest upon her chest, just above the rise of her breasts. "Let's see, you need to ride away because there are Yankees in your house."

"That's right, Jesse."

"You've been good to those poor, sick Yankees."

"Yes, I have. I tend to them daily."

"And now you want to ride away with all the little goodies, tidbits of information, that those poor sick Yankees with their tongues hanging out have given you, right?"

"Right." Her own reply stunned her—she had been so entranced by the cadence of his voice. "No—wrong! Oh, Jesse, you're confusing me so!"

"Like hell I am!" To her great irritation, he grinned. "Ah, Mrs. Miller, it is the dramatic stage's loss that you never tried your hand at acting."

"Jesse, you get off me!" she cried out, twisting frantically to be free from him. But this was one fight that he did not intend to lose. Before she knew it, her hands were slammed down high atop her head. He straddled her and grabbed her wrists together to hold them tightly with one hand. His fingers wound around her wrists hard, pinning them above her head.

And then his free hand was on her, on her breast. His fingers touched her bare flesh, delving with purpose into her clothing. She squirmed in wild desperation that only seemed to entangle them more fully. Buttons gave way, and her breasts seemed to spill forth over the ties of her corset and the soft, now-mangled material of her chemise.

"Jesse, you bastard!"

Her voice broke as the ties of her corset suddenly gave, and her note fell free. Still holding her with one hand, Jesse unfolded the missive with the other, holding it out to read quickly in silence.

His eyes fell upon hers, a bright, hard blue.

"You wouldn't dream of spying, Kiernan?" he asked politely.

"Jesse, you've got what you wanted. Now get off me!"

But he didn't move. His eyes raked over her in the light and shadow of the stables. Her hair, freed now, was tousled and tangled with the hay. Her face was so flushed, her eyes so wide.

And her breasts, naked, spilling forth.

She gritted down hard on her teeth, trying to force his eyes back to hers, for she could feel her nipples hardening beneath his scrutiny. As she lay exposed, she could not hide her emotions.

"I haven't gotten what I wanted at all," he told her.

"You must be insane!" she cried out. He was going to touch her again, she knew it. His hand was touching her clothing. "No!" she breathed, and closed her eyes. God, don't let him touch me, because he'll know how very much I want him. "Please!" she whispered.

But she felt the ties coming together, not apart. The velvet of her bodice was being pulled closed, covering her nakedness, not revealing it.

She opened her eyes. He was watching her still, with a dark and brooding tension. No violence remained, no breath of ruthlessness as he touched her cheek again.

"I could arrest you."

"Then arrest me," she told him.

"I don't want to. I want you to stop doing what you're doing."

"I'm lying on a stable floor in misery. I want to stop doing that myself," she murmured bitterly.

He smiled and sank back on his haunches, lifting her up beneath him. It felt so good, for those few moments, to have his arms around her.

"Kiernan, you can't win this war, you just can't. Do you know that you're suspected as far away as Washington?"

"You—you were warned about me?" she said in dismay.

He nodded. "Don't you see? I can't let you go on doing what you're doing. And I definitely can't let you use my men."

She tossed her head back. "Then arrest me, Jesse."

"Surrender the fight. You've no right being in this war!"

"I have every right to be in this war. This is my home— Virginia is my home. I cannot—I will not—surrender, ever," she assured him passionately.

"Kiernan—"

"No!" She pulled away from him. He didn't try to stop her when she rose and turned away, adjusting her clothing. She swirled back around. "*You* surrender! You've no right being in this war!"

"What?" He, too, was on his feet. "What are you talking about?"

"You've no right being in this war. I'm fighting for my home, but you're making war on yours. What are you fighting for? Some absurd ideal? What ideal? The U.S. Congress says you're fighting to subdue the states in rebellion! Do you think you're fighting to end slavery? But slavery hasn't been abolished in most northern states. What are you trying to do? Why in God's name do you keep this up? You've seen the men come in to you day after day, broken, bleeding, dying! Why the hell are you on their side?"

"Because the Union has to stand!" he shouted back. "It has to stand together. Don't you see that? The halves are nothing without the whole!"

"No, no, I don't see it at all!" she cried back. Why did she always come so damnably near tears every time they got into one of these fights? She had lost this battle with him long before. "Damn you, Jesse!" she cried out. She had to get past him. She couldn't burst into tears, she didn't dare let him come close to her again. "You've got your message, your proof. Arrest me, hang me, do whatever it is you want to do. But let me out of here now! I cannot bear what you've done! I cannot bear to talk with you, to try to reason with you."

He exhaled with exasperation. "You're under house arrest, Kiernan."

"Fine. It doesn't matter. You fool, don't you know that Jackson or someone else will come back here? You'll be beaten, Jesse, because the Rebs are more disciplined. And because they're fighting for their homes."

She gasped when his hands landed hard upon her shoulders again, and he gave her a shake that sent her head falling back and her hair cascading all around, and forced her eyes to meet his.

"Yes! Jackson will come back, or he'll send another commander. And yes, the South can fight. They can ride, and they can shoot. They've been born and bred to horses and guns. And my God, yes, they're good—they run circles around us all the time. But in the end, Kiernan, we'll win. We'll win because there simply are more of us. And we'll win because we have more factories, and more clothing, and more power."

Suddenly, she was more afraid than she had ever been. It had never occurred to her that the South could lose.

She broke free from him, staring at him hard. Her tears were hot behind her eyes now. "I hate you, Jesse!" she reminded him.

To her surprise, he smiled a slow, anguished, crooked smile. "I know," he said, and added very softly, "and I still love you."

"But not enough! Not enough!" she whispered desperately.

He reached for her. "Kiernan—"

"No! For the love of God, let me go!"

He freed her, and she tore away, nearly blinded by her tears as she ran back to the house as quickly as she could.

The next morning she awoke to a tremendous commotion. Rising, she hurried to the window and looked out.

Men were arriving. Two horse soldiers were leading a caravan with a wagon, and beyond the wagon, more men followed. They didn't march like men going off to battle—they came slowly, hanging upon one another, limping men aided by ones with bloodied bandages around their arm.

They were a company of wounded, she realized.

Even as she watched, Jesse came out into the yard. He called out, and she saw that Tyne was hurrying to join him. Janey was out there, too, and then Jeremiah, and then David, and even Jacob.

The cool morning air drifted by her, and a numbness settled around her. They were all Yankees. Bluebellies. They had left behind any number of Rebel dead and wounded.

She heard a cry of agony, and the numbness drifted from her shoulders like a cloak. They were in pain, all of them. They would die, some of them.

She looked away, swallowing hard. She couldn't worry about them, she just couldn't. Every time Jesse patched them up, they just went back to the war, back to killing more men of the Confederacy. More Virginians.

But then Jesse was shouting orders, and everyone was running about to follow them. As she watched, he moved through the men who were able to stand, quickly assessing their wounds. Little David was hurrying about with water for them all, and as Jesse saw each man, he called to Janey to see that the man was sent either to a room or to the hallway to await surgery. He disappeared into the wagon for a moment, then reappeared and addressed Corporal O'Malley. "We've two dead in the wagon, Corporal. See to them, will you?"

"Right, sir!" O'Malley agreed.

A sick sensation stirred in Kiernan's belly, and she hurried across the room to douse her face in her wash water. Then she felt better.

She dressed quickly, then hurried downstairs. The commotion was still going on, men limping here and there, stretchers being borne in by men who were still largely whole. As she came through the great hall, she suddenly stopped dead still. There weren't only Yankees in her hallway.

Three of the men who had been carried in were dressed in gray.

"Mrs. Miller!"

A faint, husky voice called out to her. Her heart leaped to her throat, and she moved quickly through the cots and beds to reach the fallen soldier in gray.

He was in bad shape, she thought. There was blood on the gray wool of his uniform at his stomach, and blood covered most of his left leg. His hair was matted, and his face was covered in mud. She stared at him for a long horrified moment before she recognized him.

"T.J.!" she cried, and curled her fingers over his, looking at him anxiously. She saw that David was moving among the men with a water pitcher, and she called to him.

"David, come quickly!"

He obeyed, and she poured out a cup of water and lifted T.J.'s head so that he could drink. She ripped off the bottom of her skirt to get a cloth to clean away the mud upon his face.

"Oh, T.J.!" she murmured.

His eyes opened to hers. "Don't let them chop me up, Mrs. Miller. Don't let them stick their saws on me."

"T.J.—" she began, but his eyes had closed. His breathing was shallow. She placed her hand upon his heart and found that its beat was slow and weak. "Oh, T.J., don't die on me!" she pleaded.

He needed help, and he needed it badly. Suddenly, his fingers wound around hers. "Let it be, Mrs. Miller. Some of those"—he paused, moistening his cracked lips—"some of those Yank sawbones boast that they can kill more Rebs on their operating tables than the soldiers can in the fields. If they just forget me, I can die in peace."

"You're not going to die, and this Yankee sawbones isn't like the others," Kiernan promised him quickly. "T.J., he'll help you, I swear he will."

But he didn't answer her. His eyes were already closed again.

Kiernan looked across the room desperately. So many men, and they all seemed badly hurt. She saw Janey by one of the wounded men, and she hurried over to him.

"Where's Jesse?"

Janey stared at her, amazed to see her.

"Janey! Where's Jesse?"

Janey indicated the office. "In surgery. He ain't gonna want to talk to you right now, Miz Kiernan."

Kiernan ignored her and hurried to the office, bursting in. For a moment she paused in the doorway, horrified. The man on the operating table was tossing and screaming, thrashing about wildly. Jesse was shouting to Tyne to subdue him and trying to administer a dose of morphine.

The man had nothing left of his foot or lower leg, nothing but pulp that could not be recognized as human flesh.

"Jesse . . ." His name came out a whisper.

He looked up, saw her, and suddenly summoned her. "Kiernan, quick—I need you."

"But Jesse—"

"I need you!"

Suddenly, she was beside him and the maimed man. He gave her an instant medical lesson, showing her the different saws that he needed for an amputation, telling her to staunch the flow of blood instantly and to keep all the sponges and bandages clean.

She looked around. There had to be someone else to help. She was going to pass out.

But there was no one. Corporal O'Malley was stitching up men with minor injuries. Jeremiah was assisting him. Janey was doing her best with the chaos in the hallway.

"Jesse, I can't do this," she breathed, but he didn't seem to hear her. He was telling Tyne to use his mighty shoulders and arms to brace the man, and whether Kiernan wanted to be there or not, she was. The man was quickly prepped, and Jesse was demanding his instruments, scalpel, saw, and bone saw.

She did it. Somehow, she did it. She handed him his instruments as he demanded them, and she caught the bloodied things when he finished. She followed his every order as he packed and bandaged the leg just below the knee, where he had sewn the flesh as carefully as he dared, to give the man a chance to walk with a false limb later.

Tyne carried away the severed calf.

Then she thought she would pass out.

But Jesse shouted for water, insisted upon washing his hands, then demanded to know who was next. She remembered that this was why she had come.

"Jesse, there's a man out there very badly wounded. He needs you quickly."

"O'Malley will see that he's brought in next."

"Jesse"—she paused—"Jesse, he's a Reb."

He stared at her for a moment. "Corporal O'Malley?" Jesse called out. His eyes were still on her. "O'Malley, which man needs me the most?"

O'Malley, tying off a stitch in the hallway, looked up. "I guess the Reb is the next worst off. The worst off of them that's still alive, that is."

"See that he's brought in," Jesse ordered.

Janey saw that the man just out of surgery was taken to a bed. Jesse spread out a clean sheet on the table, and in a minute, O'Malley and a man with a bandaged head were bringing in T.J.

"Hey, Captain!" the stranger complained. "Why the Reb? I've got an awful headache, here."

"Private Henson, I'm sure you do. But it's a superficial wound, and you're going to be just fine. I'll be with you soon enough." He looked down at T.J. "This boy is going to die if I don't get to him soon. He might die anyway."

"He should die—he's a Reb," the man said. "Doc, you shouldn't try to save him."

"Private, when I took an oath to save lives, they didn't

allow me to make any distinctions in the color of the uniform a man happens to be wearing. I'll get to you soon enough, and I'll see that you have some time to get over that headache."

Private Henson's brow shot up, but he no longer argued with Jesse. He turned and left with Corporal O'Malley at his heels.

"Jesse," Kiernan breathed.

He looked across the table at her. "You just stay right where you are. No, wash your hands first, and my instruments. Keep doing what you're doing. You're doing it fine."

He started on T.J. Tyne helped him rip off the uniform that covered the wounds. First Jesse sponged and cleaned the blood from T.J.'s gut, and then he began to demand things from her again—a clamp, and then a probe. She gritted her teeth hard as he searched the battered flesh for bits and pieces of metal. He seemed satisfied, then demanded more things from her—a clamp, a needle, sutures. As she stood silently before him, he began to sew. She lowered her head, then she felt his eyes on her, blue and inquisitive. "Are you going to faint?"

"I would have done so by now," she snapped at him.

He smiled and turned back to his work. He ordered T.J.'s breeches ripped away so that he could get to the leg.

"Jesu," he murmured. "I don't know . . ."

T.J. chose that moment to rouse from his drugged stupor. A hand wound around Jesse's wrist, and Jesse and Kiernan both looked at T.J.'s white face.

"Doc, don't take it."

"Soldier, I don't know—"

T.J. fought desperately to remain conscious. "Doc, I was gut-shot. You don't even know that I can make it now."

"Reb, you weren't that shot up inside. None of your major organs were torn. I did a good job taking out the metal. I can't promise that any man will make it, but soldier, you should."

"Sweet Jesus, Doc, don't take my leg! I'm begging you not to take my leg. Mrs. Miller, don't let him!"

Jesse looked across the table at Kiernan.

"Please," she whispered.

He shrugged. "All right, Reb, I'll try," he said. But T.J., it seemed, had already drifted under again. He had put his faith in Kiernan and surrendered to the morphine.

"Tyne," Jesse ordered, "get hold of him. Kiernan, let's rip up these trousers the rest of the way."

They started on his leg. T.J. screamed when the probe first touched his flesh, then he was silent. So was Jesse, dead silent as he worked. Kiernan responded instantly as he ordered clamps, and sponges, then the probe, then a scalpel, then a sponge.

It seemed to go on endlessly. She sponged up blood and more blood, and she gnawed holes in her lower lip, but she didn't falter.

In time, Jesse sewed and swabbed the blood one last time, then wrapped the limb in clean white bandages. Kiernan watched his hands as he worked, watched the artistry. He moved confidently, competently, with skill and decision — and more. Even his most determined touch was compassionate and gentle.

He finished with T.J., his last orders being to bathe down his shoulders and face. Kiernan covered him in a clean sheet. Jesse leaned over the injured Reb one last time.

"Will he live?" Kiernan whispered.

"He's breathing now," Jesse told her. "Like I told him, I can't promise any man."

Kiernan nodded. Jesse was still staring at her. "Friend of yours?" he asked.

"Yes."

He was still watching her. She felt a flush creep up her cheeks.

"Just a friend," she told him.

A slow curl touched the corner of Jesse's lip, and his eyes caught hold of hers. "I wasn't implying anything, Mrs. Miller."

He turned away before she could respond, calling to Corporal O'Malley to see that the Reb was made comfortable in a ward and that the next patient be brought in.

He looked at Kiernan. "Are you staying?"

She couldn't bear any more of the blood and the screams. She had never meant to come.

But she was staying.

She had already discovered that Yanks were men, too, men who could be broken, torn, hurt, made to bleed in anguish. They were men with families, mothers, fathers, sisters, brothers, and lovers.

They were men who might go back and kill more Rebs. But at the moment, they were men who were hurt. Jesse hadn't hesitated to mend up a Rebel soldier. He had taken an oath to save lives, and that was what he did.

She was here now. She would help him. "I'll stay," she told him quietly.

He looked at her for a moment. "Good," he said briefly. "I can use it." He glanced to Tyne. "She's good, isn't she?"

Tyne, who had kept silent during the time they worked together, grinned. "She's mighty good." He looked at Kiernan. "We had three men fall flat down on their faces last week, Miz Kiernan. Soldier boys. You outdone them all," he told her.

The day wasn't over yet, Kiernan decided. They might yet see her flat on her face.

No, she told herself. She wasn't going to pass out in front of Jesse.

But as the hours wore on, she survived. She discovered she had an instinct for working with Jesse. She sensed just what he would need, and when. Work between them narrowed down to a very few words, and time passed very quickly.

Yankees came and went. The two other Rebel soldiers were treated. Their wounds were very minor. The last of the patients came into the surgery, then went out.

Tyne left with the bloodstained laundry. Jesse scrubbed his hands, and Kiernan sank into Andrew Miller's big swivel desk chair, exhausted.

"How are you?" Jesse asked her.

She felt his eyes on her, but she was too tired to care. Yet she felt more than the exhaustion. She felt a strange exhilaration along with it. She had mattered that day, had mattered very much. She had worked until she was bone tired, but the work had been good.

Even if she had been saving Yankees.

She understood something of what Jesse must feel as a doctor. Life—human life—was sacred.

It didn't matter what color uniform a man wore.

"I'm fine," she said very softly.

"Are you sure?" he queried, his voice equally quiet, and curious. He walked to where she sat and leaned over her, his hands upon the arms of the chair.

She smiled. "I'm tired. I think that I'm more tired than I've been in my whole life."

Jesse nodded, watching her. She'd never seen his eyes look so blue. "It was a darned rough day. You should never have had to see half of what you saw today."

No, she shouldn't have had to see the naked male limbs, and she shouldn't have had to see the dirt and the blood.

Once upon a time, the lady she had been trained to be would have fainted dead away at the thought.

But time had a way of changing things.

"I'm all right, really," she told him. She searched out his eyes. "I even feel . . . good," she admitted. "Is that very strange?"

He shook his head, smiling. "It is good to save lives, very good. And I'm glad that you feel that way." He straightened. "But we were lucky today. We didn't lose anyone."

"Do you lose men often, Jesse?"

"Often enough. Cannons and rifles and bayonets are made to kill. And often enough, they do."

She was silent—he was right. She was happy because she had not had to feel life slip away beneath her fingers.

"I've got to make rounds and see how our patients are faring," he told her. "Get yourself a stiff drink, and go to bed. You'll feel even better."

He left her. She started to drift off to sleep in the chair, but then she heard a soft and soothing voice—Janey's. "Chile, you are done worn out. Come on into the kitchen, I've a hot bath for you. And chicken soup. It's been a long day. Lord, yes, a long day."

Kiernan allowed herself to be led into the kitchen. Once undressed, she sank into the hot bath and found it close to heaven.

Soap had never smelled so sweet. Water had never encompassed her so gently, and heat had never touched her limbs so kindly. She sighed and relaxed. When she emerged, Janey was ready with a towel and chicken soup and a stiff brandy. Kiernan devoured both.

"I really did all right," she murmured out loud to Janey.

"Yes, you did, Miz Kiernan. Yes, you did. Now, get on up to bed, because you'll be feelin' it in the mornin'."

Kiernan knew that she was right. Drowsy, she thanked Janey and gave her a fierce hug. She was hugged just as tightly in return. She wrapped her flannel robe about herself and left the kitchen.

The men on cots in the great hall were quiet now. The house was quiet. The hour had grown very late. Kiernan moved quietly among them, heading for the stairway.

"Goodnight, Mrs. Miller," Corporal O'Malley called to her.

She nodded to him and hurried up the stairs.

At the top she suddenly remembered T.J. She didn't know where they had taken him, but she was closest to the ward that had been Anthony's room, so she hurried in there.

The lights were dim; the men seemed to be sleeping. She heard a soft moan, but when she tiptoed over to the cot from where the sound had come, she found that the occupant was sleeping. She tiptoed away again, ready to leave the room.

"Mrs. Miller!" one of the Yanks called to her softly, a man who had been with them awhile.

"Yes?"

"Are you looking for the Rebs?"

"Yes. Yes, I am."

"They're down the hall, in the boy's room. He's bunking in with his sister. Doc needed the space, and the boy didn't mind none. Neither did the little girl."

"Thank you," Kiernan told him.

She hurried out and down the hallway. She opened the

door to Jacob's room—then backed away from what she saw.

Jesse was bent over one of the Rebs. She started to turn, but he said softly to her, "Come in, Kiernan."

He couldn't have seen her in the dark, but she came in, closing the door behind her. She leaned against it for a moment, then Jesse beckoned her forward. He was seeing to T.J.

T.J. was still. Eyes closed, he was as still as . . .

Death.

"Oh, God!" she breathed.

Jesse looked at her, startled, then shook his head, smiling. "Kiernan, he's doing very well."

"Oh!" She felt weak, but she couldn't faint now, she couldn't possibly, not after the day she had been through.

"He's sleeping soundly."

"His leg—?"

"Only time will tell."

She nodded, and clenched her nails into her palms to fight the dizziness that assailed her. She wanted to tell him that she was grateful, but she was suddenly afraid to talk.

She turned quickly. "Good night, Jesse," she said quickly.

"Good night," he responded.

Next, Kiernan looked in on the children. Curled together on Patricia's bed, they were sleeping sweetly.

She returned to her own room. It seemed like aeons since she had left it, but it had only been that morning.

She stared out at the moonlight for a while then slipped beneath her sheets. She was so exhausted, she should have fallen asleep easily.

But sleep eluded her. All that she could think of was the long day.

And Jesse.

She tried very hard to sleep. She tried to remember Anthony's face, and that she was his widow, and that this was his house.

All that she could see was Jesse.

She rose and quietly left her room, walked quickly down the few feet of hallway to his room, and before she dared to think about what she was doing, she opened the door, entered the room, and closed the door behind her.

Jesse was in bed.

But he wasn't asleep, and he hadn't been asleep. He was sitting up in bed, his shoulders and chest naked. His fingers were laced behind his head and he leaned back against the fine oak frame of the big bed. In the darkness and shadow, his eyes were upon her.

Moonlight danced palely within the room. It touched his shoulders and chest, casting them in a bronzelike light. It did not touch his features and gave away nothing of the emotion in his eyes.

"Well, Mrs. Miller," he said softly. "What are you doing here?"

She left the doorway and walked across the room to stand beside his bed. "I wanted you to know that I'm grateful, very grateful, for what you did for T.J."

He stretched his arm out to her, turning his hand palm out, waiting for her to take it. She hesitated, then took it.

And then she found herself pulled down next to him, and before she knew it, his arms were around her and she was rolled down into the depths of the big master bed, lying on the pillow at his side while he braced himself over her, running his fingers gently through her hair.

"I want you to know," he told her huskily, "that I would have tried to save him whether you asked me to or not." He watched her expectantly.

Warmth, a sweet searing explosion of it, suddenly seemed to streak through her. She knew why she had come, she knew why she wanted to be here. She stared into the blue eyes that were so very intent upon her own. Those eyes held so much care and so much wisdom. They were the eyes of a man who could not be denied for the simple measure of what he was inside.

"There's no need for you to be grateful," he said harshly.

Despite his tone, she smiled. She wound her arms around his neck. "I'm not that grateful," she murmured. "I mean—well, I *am* grateful, but I'm not here only because I'm grateful."

"Then?"

"I'm here because . . ."

"Because?"

"Because I want you to hold me."

He returned her smile, slowly. The moonlight played upon his rugged features, and his smile was crooked and sensual.

"Gladly," he whispered.

His arms encompassed her, he kissed her.

Nineteen

If the taste of his kiss was bittersweet, it was made up for by the simple ecstasy of feeling his arms around her again. So many nights she had lain awake, tortured by memory. So many times she had remembered him when he had been far away from her.

War still raged, and it would go on tomorrow.

But for Kiernan, it would stop this night.

His lips upon hers were ardent, fevered. She felt a trembling deep within him as he fought to leash the passion that ignited swiftly between them. The wanting within him touched her as no aphrodisiac could, sending erotic tongues and laps of fire to dance and sweep over her flesh and through her limbs.

She returned his kiss, eager for it, met the fever of his tongue, gasped and sought him again and again when he broke away to circle her lips erotically, slowly, with the bare rim of his tongue, taking her mouth with the fullness of his own, pulling away again.

His tongue moved over her throat, slowly sliding along the length of it.

She gasped, her eyes closed, as she heard the rending of fabric. He ripped her gown cleanly so that it fell open, baring all her flesh to him.

But she did not open her eyes, for she felt that slow burning touch of his kiss, of his tongue, again. Centering upon her collarbone, it moved again, drawing a hot wet pattern between her breasts, moving sensually over that valley. Her breasts ached to be touched so, to be licked and caressed by the force of his mouth. But he did not touch them.

Rather, he continued the hot slide of his tongue onward over her abdomen. She shivered slightly, for when his mouth did not touch her, she was cold. But she could not move—she could only lie still in the greatest, sweetest fascination.

His kiss moved over her belly, and his tongue entered the cavity of her navel, played there, danced there. Suddenly, she was aware of his whisper against her flesh, a whisper that told her how sweetly she smelled, how wonderfully she tasted. The scent of the lilac from her bath still haunted her flesh, haunted his senses.

Then he was silent, and the searing-hot, wet slide of the tip of his tongue traveled ever more downward. Downward, until she thought she would scream. Her entire body awakened, and both cold and steaming, it was near agony in the tempest, sweet and hungry, that seized her—the wanting, the knowing, the needing.

That searing hot dampness was suddenly within her, deep within her, pervading her. An invasion so sweet, it brought a shattering sensation to burst throughout her. A cry welled within her, touched her lips, but never escaped her.

For he was suddenly atop her, his arms around her, and his lips were hot and hungry and molded over hers, smothering any sounds of ecstasy that might have escaped her. The bare bronze sleekness of his body was pressed taut to hers, seeming to meld with it.

His eyes upon her, he held himself above her and watched her eyes as he began his body's own riveting invasion of hers, coming deeper, deeper, deeper.

A soft whisper of desperation tore from her lips, and she buried her face against his throat, pulling tighter and tighter against him, arching, twisting, feeling him with all her length, inside and out. He was slow, torturously slow, pressing her back and watching her eyes again as he moved against her, seeming to burn inside her until he touched her womb, her heart, her very soul.

Then slowness was wickedly abandoned. Even in the darkness his eyes were startlingly blue upon her, and his smile was as wicked as the storm that he promised. He was suddenly a tempest, a whirlwind. He moved like lightning and swept her into his rhythm. Night breezes moved about, but the heat seemed consuming. Slick and warm, she clung to him, tasting him, kissing his lips, his shoulders, his lips again. She reached for things that, even now, she barely understood. Things intangible, elusive, as raw as the bare earth, as mystical as the clouds in a night sky. Things that made her hunger, and wonder. For it was splendor to be held so, and it was an even greater splendor for which she reached.

And then he was nearly still, rigid and taut. He moved slowly, slowly, then with startling speed, touched all of her inside again. He withdrew and filled her once again, hard.

Again she almost cried out. But his lips were there, and he kissed her, his tongue ravishing her mouth to steal sound away while the pulsing shaft of his body moved as hard and hot as molten steel deep, deep into her, one long, slow, last time, sinking, staying there.

All that she had reached for came cascading down upon her. Great waves of sensation rushed over her, swirled around her, settled into her. Warmth, dampness, and the sweet liquid heat of his fulfillment entered into her and brought with it a new sensation of ecstasy, a shuddering that seized hold of her.

The trembling remained for long, long moments.

She felt his swift movement as he withdrew from her at last, felt the hot slick wetness of their passion trail across her belly and thighs as he fell to her side, enveloping her in his arms.

She felt the breeze in the room, so cold against her naked flesh. She shivered violently, and he pulled her closer against him, bringing the covers over them both.

Little objects in the room suddenly seemed to stand out in the shadows and moonlight. Andrew Miller's desk, his bed frame, the windows that looked out onto his lawn. Andrew Miller's. One day they would have been Anthony's.

And hers.

But she was lying here tonight with Jesse. "Oh, God," she breathed suddenly.

"What is it?" Jesse asked.

"I've got to go."

She tried to leap up, but his arms suddenly wound more tightly around her. "Why?"

She was pinned down. His knee lay over her thighs, and his arm braced her. He didn't intend to let her go.

"Jesse—"

"Why? How can you say that now, after everything that we've just shared?" Fury riddled his question. His features were taut, his jaw nearly locked.

"We have to forget it—" she tried to begin.

They were the wrong words. He pounced on her, and his hand moved over her. "Mrs. Miller, I promise you, I will never forget it. I will never forget the feel of your flesh, the taste of it. Nor the taste or texture of the bud of your breast in my mouth, the feel of your tongue against my own, the scent of your soap, the scent of you as a woman. I promise you that I will not forget the way you move against me." He ran his fingers lightly over the sheen of her shoulder. "I won't forget anything at all, Mrs. Miller. I won't forget your eyes, I won't forget lying between your thighs, I won't forget tasting—"

"Stop it, Jesse!" she nearly shrieked.

"What? It's all right to do it, but not to talk about it?" he demanded. "Or does it go deeper than that?"

"Jesse, I'm a widow!" she reminded him desperately.

His hold upon her eased, then tightened again. "Fine, Mrs. Miller. You are a widow. But he couldn't have given you what I give you. Damn you, Kiernan, you came to me! Don't be a hypocrite. Quit denying me!"

"I'm not denying you!" He had to let go of her because she was shaking in fury. "How could I ever deny you? You had me when I should have been his! You had me first, on his property, when I should have been his fiancée. And now when I'm his widow—Jesse, this is his house!"

He released her. "My Lord. I'm in worse shape with him dead. I'm battling a ghost!"

"It's his house, Jesse!"

"So it's all right if we find a bale of hay in a barn?"

"No, it's his barn, his family—"

"You were never in love with him!" he suddenly thundered.

"Sh!" She pressed her fingers frantically against his lips. He was rigid in his fury. "Please, Jesse?"

He was still, but his jaw remained twisted, his limbs hard, the tension of his body radiating through her like the heat of the sun.

"Jesse, I have to go!" She tried to draw the remnants of her nightgown around her, but his hand was upon her arm again, drawing her back.

"Look at me," he told her.

She met the searing blue of his stare.

"Admit to me that you were never in love with Anthony."

"Jesse—"

"Admit it!"

"You're hurting me!"

"I'm going to hurt you worse!"

"Damn you!" Tears stung her eyes. "All right, all right. You know that I was never in love with him. Why do you have to hear me say it?"

"Why do you have to pretend that there was something between you?" he pressed on furiously. "Did you lie here with him in this bed? Is that what brought on your sudden fit of guilt?"

"It's none of your business, Jesse."

"It is! I'm making it my business!"

"Jesse—"

"You didn't love him. Why the hell did you marry him?"

"Because he wasn't a Yankee!" she spat out, suddenly as furious as he.

His hold on her slackened. She slipped from it, rolled quickly, and leaped to her feet. Holding her gown together, she stared at him and repeated, "Anthony was never a Yankee!"

She turned to flee, but Jesse didn't let her go. In a flash he was up, naked and menacing. He had caught her by both of her arms and dragged her back up against him. "No, he was never a Yankee. But he was never the man for you either. And he's dead now, Kiernan. I didn't want him dead, but he is. Hundreds of men are dead. Maybe thousands by now—I don't really know. But don't pretend that you were in love with him. Not to me!"

"Maybe you can take over his house," Kiernan charged him in a heated whisper, "but you cannot take over his widow! I won't let you—I swear I won't let you!"

She tried to wrench free, but he held her too tight, and his fingers wound harder about her wrists as she struggled. She went still suddenly and met his mocking gaze.

"I already have," he reminded her.

"Let me go, Captain Cameron!" she snapped.

"No!" He was suddenly very earnest. "You listen to me, Kiernan. I have feelings for Anthony, that's one of the reasons why I came here. I know about guilt. I thought that at least I could save his house, his family—something for him. And I've done that, Kiernan, at least so far. It might be a long, long war. You've done what's right too. Jacob and Patricia need you, and they have you. You've loved them and cared for them, and Anthony would have been pleased and proud."

"He'd have been damned pleased and proud to walk in and find me in bed with you, right?" she inquired with a sizzling taunt, her dazzling eyes piercing his, her head cast back imperiously.

"*You* came to *me*," he reminded her curtly.

Hot color covered her cheeks. "Jesse, let me pass."

"No! Not until you admit that you never had with him what you've had with me. Guilt can't change that! And guilt can't keep me away anymore, Kiernan."

"Jesse—"

"Tell me!"

"You bluebellied son of a bitch!" she exploded. "No, I never had anything with Anthony like I have with you. I never had anything at all with him! He married me and rode away the same night."

"What?" he asked incredulously.

"You heard me! Now let me—"

He pulled her close and started to kiss her, a hard, ravishing kiss. She struggled fiercely against him, trying to free her lips, her arms. She didn't win, but he suddenly drew his head away.

"Tell me that you won't want me ever again, Kiernan."

"Will you just let me go!" She tried hard to kick the fine display of naked masculine flesh before her, and she was suddenly very desperate and very determined.

But he dodged all her blows, then spun her around and pulled her hard and flat against his body. "Tell me, Kiernan." The sound of his voice, the hot whisper of it, bathed her ear and her throat. Even as she hated him, she felt the sweet fire of wanting ignite within her all over again. His fingers just edged over her breasts, and his hand moved downward as he held her taut against him.

"Jesse—" She jerked within his arms, trying to stamp on his feet but managing only to dislodge most of what remained of her torn nightgown.

"Oh, shut up, Kiernan!" he commanded her with throaty laughter. He lifted her by her upper arms, and even as she stared down at him, her eyes wide with alarm, he tossed her into the air and she fell flat upon the bed once again, her nightgown lost completely.

Her eyes narrowed in fury. "Jesse, you—"

He dived down upon her, and his lips were upon hers.

She struggled, but the warmth of his kiss was undeniable. Something languid and sweet swept slowly through her. She touched his hair, feeling the texture of it, only then realizing that her hands were free.

She was free.

But by then, she did not want to go. She did want what he had to give her.

He made love to her a second time that night, and she made love to him in return.

Later, she awoke and felt the probe of his sex at her but-

tocks as they lay curled with his arms around her. He made
love to her so, and when it was over, she drifted to sleep
again, content to feel his arms around her.

She was still at war—at war with Jesse.

But she was too tired to fight at the moment.

She awoke as dawn was coming through the windows,
and then she was upset. As his arm curled around her, she
pleaded, "Jesse, I have to go now. The children."

Some emotion passed through his eyes. He understood,
she knew. He released her.

"Your gown," he began, his tone almost apologetic.

"I've got it. I'll wear a sheet," she said quickly, wrapping
herself up in one even as she spoke. She prayed that she
wouldn't meet anyone in the hallway as she hurried toward
the door.

"Kiernan!"

She turned back. His hair was tousled, his shoulders very
bronze against the white of the sheets, his eyes very blue.

She wondered if she would ever stop loving him.

"Jesse, I have to go."

"Kiernan, I want you to marry me."

"I can't marry you, Jesse!"

"Why the hell not?" he demanded irritably.

"You're a Yankee! I didn't marry you before because
you're a Yankee. And I won't marry you now for the same
reason. Don't you understand?" Why was he always able to
bring her so dangerously close to tears? "I'll never marry
you, Jesse! Never!"

She spun around and tore out of his room, almost care-
lessly, desperate not to meet anyone.

There was no one in the hallway. She could hear sounds
in the ward—the "hospital" day was beginning.

Shaking, she sat on her own bed, the sheet pulled about
her tightly. She looked out at the dawn breaking through
her windows. It would be a beautiful day.

No one, no one but herself or Jesse, would be any the
wiser about the night that they had passed together.

But how would she survive the days to come? Wanting

him, loving him, having him so very near, knowing he was just beyond a doorway.

And that she had to stop seeing him.

She sat in torment for a long, long time. But in the end, her dilemma did not matter. It was taken care of for her.

By nightfall, new orders had come for Jesse. He had been commanded to move out.

Kiernan washed and dressed and began to move about the house with its many rooms of injured soldiers. Corporal O'Malley was very pleased that they hadn't lost anyone during the night. " 'Course, that don't put any of the men in the clear, but living is a darned good sign, if you'll pardon my language. Don't you think so, Mrs. Miller?"

"Oh, I've come to pardon quite a bit," Kiernan assured him.

"Even the Reb who was hurt bad is doing fine. But then again, if they send him to a prison camp—oh, I'm sorry, again. I keep forgetting where your sympathies lie, Mrs. Miller. You're so good to all of us. A couple of the boys say you spy on us, but I know real compassion when I see it, and that's what you've got, ma'am, that's what you've got."

Real compassion? But I *was* spying, she wanted to cry out.

It didn't matter. Maybe O'Malley needed his few illusions, and maybe she was one of them.

"Thank you, Corporal. But I am a Confederate," she told him, "and this morning, I think I will see to the Rebs."

She smiled at him and hurried down the hallway. T.J. was awake, sitting up in his bed. Patricia was already up and about and perched on a stool by T.J.'s side, writing a letter for him. She gave Kiernan a brilliant smile. "Kiernan, they told me yesterday that T.J. might die, but look at him! He's doing very well!"

T.J.'s gaze met Kiernan's. They both knew that it was too soon for the little girl's hopes to be so raised.

"It's good to see you doing so well," she said, and coming to the bed, she soaked a cool cloth in water and set it upon his forehead. He was scarcely warm. That, too, was a good sign, she knew.

T.J. grasped her hand warmly. "You saved my leg."

"T.J., you can't be certain. You mustn't—"

"Look at it!" He was too excited to realize that he shouldn't be exposing his masculine limbs to a lady and a little girl, even though that lady had been present for far worse. He lifted away the sheet so that she could see his leg, and she was amazed. The stitches were very neat. There was no sign of swelling, and barely any discoloration. She remembered Jesse working on it the day before, and she felt a strange shaking take hold of her. He was very, very good.

"Still," she warned, "you know that infection may set in during the days to come."

He nodded. His fingers were shaking, and he wound them together in his lap to still them. "I wanted to die," he told her. "When I realized that I'd been picked up by the Yanks, I was so damned afraid of what a Yankee sawbones might do to me that I wanted to die. But he's good. Hell, he's brilliant."

"Yes, he's very good."

"Too bad he's a Yank."

"That's what my brother says about Jesse," Patricia said airily, studying the pen. " 'Course, he really shouldn't be one at all."

T.J. looked surprised, and he glanced from Kiernan to Patricia. "Sounds like you've known him awhile."

"We have. We've been out to his place a number of times, and before the war, Jesse was welcome here. He didn't have to take the place over then. I love Jesse," she said enthusiastically, then reddened. "Oh. I love him as much as you're allowed to love a Yank."

T.J. grinned. "Don't worry, Patricia. You can't love a word—you can love a person, a man. It's all right."

She looked worriedly from T.J. to Kiernan, hoping that it really was all right. "They would have burned my father's house down if it hadn't been for him. Jacob didn't care at first, but even my brother likes him now. We don't know him half as well as Kiernan does."

T.J.'s eyes shot to Kiernan's. In seconds, she was certain
T.J. understood everything there was to understand about
her relationship with Jesse.

He wasn't going to say anything, though.

Patricia leaped off her seat when one of the other men
turned over and let out a soft croak for water.

Kiernan leaned close to T.J. "War is funny, isn't it?" she
said softly. "I'd been trying to reach you with information
about Union troops making a foray into the valley."

T.J. closed his eyes and spoke wearily. "There's always
someone near the oak," he said. "The war is over for me
now. I imagine I'll be spending it in a camp."

"Maybe not."

The masculine words spoken behind Kiernan sent shivers
racing along her spine.

She had absolutely no idea just how long Jesse had been
standing there. Was it long enough for him to hear what she
had told T.J.?

She spun around. His eyes were fire when they touched
hers, but he had come to see T.J. He pulled back the sheets
and looked at the leg, then inspected the wound in T.J.'s gut.
He seemed pleased. He pulled the sheet back up over his
patient.

"I'd have liked more time," he murmured, "a lot more
time. But I've been called back to Washington."

Stunned, Kiernan stared at him. Just that morning she
had been praying for a way . . .

But this wasn't it. The Yankee patients would be all right.
They'd receive careful passage back to Washington. But
what would happen to T.J., and these other two?

A prison camp would kill T.J.

And where would Jesse be?

"Jesu, Doc," T.J. said. "I won't stand a snowball's chance
in hell!"

Jesse was silent, contemplative. "We'll see, soldier," he
said at last.

He nodded to Kiernan, then left the room.

During the day she tried to see Jesse alone. She was more
than willing to plead for a miracle to save T.J.

But she couldn't even get close to Jesse. He was a whirl-wind of activity. Wagons had come for his patients, and he had to make sure that every one of them was as comfortably prepared for travel as possible, bandaged and bedded down for a journey across the river.

Corporal O'Malley advised her about the sudden hurry.

The area didn't really belong to anyone at the moment, either the Rebs or the Yanks. Sharpshooters and skirmishes were the rule of the day here. But a rumor had reached Washington through spies working for a man named Pinker-ton—who was organizing something called the Secret Ser-vice—that Stonewall Jackson was coming in somewhere nearby with a major troop movement.

Jesse was very important to the Union because he had a way of making men live. He was going to be promoted with his new orders to full colonel.

There was no stopping him. Whenever she came near Jesse, he immediately put her to work preparing patients for the trip. She didn't mind the labor. She had helped him stitch up most of the patients the day before, and she couldn't help but care about them.

After working late into the night, she still had not man-aged to speak to Jesse. Not until midnight had the last of the injured Yanks been bedded down in wagons to move back to Washington.

And now, the house seemed empty.

Patricia and Jacob had fallen asleep on the steps of the front porch, and Tyne and Jeremiah had long since carried them up to bed. With the last soldier bedded down, Jer-emiah had gone to his quarters to find his own rest. Tyne and Corporal O'Malley were still with the Rebs, and Janey was in the kitchen.

Alone in the great hall, Kiernan stared about at the emp-tiness and felt the sound of silence.

She heard a slight noise and turned. Jesse, in his full blue uniform, leaned against the doorway to what had been his surgery, watching her.

"You must be very happy."

She shrugged. She wasn't happy at all.

"I don't suppose I can get you to leave the area?"

She shook her head. "The Rebs won't hurt me," she murmured.

"Personally, I don't think the Rebs are coming right now. They've got other things to do," he said flatly. "It's deserters and stragglers I'm thinking about."

She smiled. "We've had them before, and we handled them. Well"—she paused—"T.J. handled them for me, actually. But I'm prepared now. I'm a good shot, and Jacob is a great shot."

"I've left word with General Banks that I might need the house again. He'll see that none of his troops threaten it again."

"Thank you," she murmured awkwardly.

"I've only one thing left to attend to," he murmured. He started across the empty hallway, his booted heels clicking harshly on the floor.

He headed upstairs to the Rebels. There was a wagon waiting outside to take them away.

Kiernan tore after him and caught him halfway up the stairs, her skirts sweeping wildly around as she tried to stop him.

"Jesse, you can't let T.J. be taken to a camp! You just can't! He'll die there, and you know it."

He paused, a curious smile curving his lip. "Kiernan, you are so damned beautiful, and you plead so elegantly with me. But it's always over some other man!"

"Jesse, please!"

"Kiernan, get out of my way. Please."

"Jesse, I won't—"

"Kiernan, you fool! You're the one who gave that boy information he could use against the Union troops!"

"But I didn't!"

"You might have jeopardized everything."

"Jesse—"

"Kiernan, move!" He picked her up by the waist, and for a moment he held her above him. The air crackled between them, and when she met his eyes, the sweetest memories of the night came flooding back to her.

She felt the tension and the passion in his touch.

He set her down, very gently.

"Excuse me."

He walked past her, reached the room where T.J. was lying, and entered it. He leaned over T.J., checking the texture and temperature of his skin, looking into his eyes.

"How're you feeling, Reb?"

"Good as can be expected, Yank."

"Jesse!" Kiernan started into the room.

"Corporal O'Malley, stop her! That's an order!" Jesse said.

O'Malley caught her just before she could fling herself at Jesse.

"If she can't shut up, remove her from the room!"

"Yes, sir!" O'Malley said unhappily.

Held back by O'Malley, Kiernan bit hard on her lower lip and held still.

"Soldier, you know that this war is over for you now, right?" Jesse demanded.

"Yes, sir, I reckon it is."

"You're a Virginian, right?"

"Yes, sir."

"A man of your word?"

"Always, Doc."

Jesse nodded. "That's what I thought. I've drawn up papers for you and these boys."

"I can't be a Yank, sir."

"You don't have to be a Yank, soldier. The document just promises that you won't take up arms against the Union again. Can you live with that?"

T.J. smiled slowly and exhaled a long breath. "Yes, sir, I can live with that. So can the boys."

"One more thing. Anything Mrs. Miller told you dies in this room. Is that understood?"

He turned and looked at Kiernan, then spoke to T.J. again. "Have I your word?"

"Yes, sir, you have my word."

"Kiernan?"

His blue eyes blazed into her like blades of fire, demanding, always demanding.

She was trembling. Jesse meant to leave T.J. and the two other Rebs here with her, free to go home as soon as they could.

"You—you have my word," she breathed.

"Good. Damn, it was nice not to have to argue with you for once! O'Malley, I guess it's safe to let this Reb go. Get signatures from these other soldiers, and I guess we'll be out of here. Gentlemen, good luck to you," he said, doffing his hat to T.J. and the two other men. Then he strode out of the room.

Kiernan was still for a minute, then she turned and went after him. He was gone from the stairway, and for a moment, she thought that he had left without even saying good-bye to her.

She heard sounds coming from the office that had been his surgery, and she realized that he was gathering the last of his personal instruments. She crossed the great hall quickly and opened the door to the office.

His greatcoat was already over his shoulders. His back was to her, but she knew that he realized she had entered the room. He had cleaned his instruments, and he was repacking them in a large black leather bag. It was a fine surgeon's bag, with his initials embossed into it with large bold script.

He picked up the instruments she had come to know yesterday: Bullet forceps, bone forceps, dissection forceps. Gnawing forceps. Bone scraper. Capital saw, chain saw, metacarpal saw, bone file. Different scissors and scalpels and tourniquets.

All went back into the bag.

Kiernan walked to the rear and collected his suture materials, the black silk thread, his curved and straight needles. She brought them to him and watched him pack them into his bag. His hands brushed hers, and he glanced at her.

She stayed before him, silent. He turned away and reached for the last of his anesthetics, the chloroform and ether, then his pain killers, the opium and morphine.

He hesitated, then turned back to his bag and produced the small syringe he had used for injecting morphine. "I'm leaving you this for T.J. I'll write a prescription for you. Be very careful with the dosage. I'll leave you this too: powdered sassafras, to lower his body temperature if it starts to rise. Keep his bandages clean, and treat the wounds with simple cerates. Can you manage?"

She nodded. "I'll manage."

He closed his case. "Well, then. That's the last of it." His hands moved over the leather. "It's handsome, isn't it? Daniel bought it for me as a Christmas gift a few years ago. I never imagined that I'd be using the amputation instruments so frequently. And I never imagined that I'd be looking at it and wondering where Daniel might be."

"Jesse—"

He turned and faced her. "I have to go. I swore when I received permission to come that I would pull out promptly when I was ordered to do so."

"Jesse, thank you," she said quickly. How was it that they had been so very close last night, yet now she could barely muster words and sounds? He was leaving again, riding away. And once again, there seemed to be nothing at all that she could do about it. "Thank you for T.J.," she said quickly, "and for Jacob. For the house."

"But not for you?" he said softly.

She wanted so very much to run to him. He stood so tall and straight, striking and dark, with his sharp blue eyes, his slouch hat low over his forehead, his greatcoat emphasizing the breadth of his shoulders. He was leaving.

She didn't know when she would see him again, if ever.

"Come here, Kiernan. Please. I'm leaving—what danger can I be to you?"

She walked across the room to him, and he raised her chin with his thumb and forefinger. His lips touched hers gently, tenderly, poignantly. Then his mouth rose, and he whispered softly above hers, "Take care, Kiernan. Take care."

She stared at him, willing the tears in her eyes not to fall. He smiled with a bittersweet curve to his lip. "Still can't wish a Yankee well, eh, Kiernan? Well, that's all right. I understand."

He released her, lifted his bag, and started for the door. He did not turn back.

She closed her eyes. She heard the door shut softly, heard his booted footsteps ringing as they crossed the empty hallway.

She came to life. She ran across the room, threw open the door, and raced out to the porch.

Jesse was just mounting Pegasus. The few men who waited to ride escort with him were down by the end of the sloping lawn, standing sentinel in the moonlight.

"Jesse!"

Mounted on Pegasus, he waited. Kiernan ran breathlessly across the lawn.

"Jesse—" She paused before Pegasus. Jesse waited patiently, his eyes still filled with tenderness, with weariness, with sorrow.

"Jesse, take care," she whispered. "Please, take care of yourself."

He smiled, his lip curling into the slow grin that she loved so very much.

He touched the brim of his hat. "Thank you, Kiernan. I'll do that." He started to urge Pegasus forward. She suddenly rushed forward, touching Jesse's calf, pressing her face against his knee. "Don't die, Jesse, please don't die."

He reached down and touched her hair, then stroked her cheek. "I won't die," he promised her. She looked up at him. "I love you, Kiernan," he said.

She was silent, afraid to speak. He smiled again, aware that she could not reply. Then he nudged Pegasus forward and cantered across the field to join his men.

"I love you, Jesse!" she cried softly.

But it was too late—he was gone.

She had no right to love a Yankee, she told herself fiercely.

But then she remembered what T.J. had told Patricia earlier, and she realized that it wasn't a Yankee that she loved.

She loved Jesse.

She loved a man.

And once again, that man was riding away.

4

A Separate Peace

Twenty

December 1861

Kiernan didn't think she'd ever seen a drearier time than the winter that followed.

Much of Harpers Ferry and the surrounding countryside had been devastated by both armies. The Union soldiers had destroyed munitions and food supplies, and the Rebs had come back and destroyed everything that could be used by the Union troops.

The exchange seemed never ending.

Things seemed to be the very bleakest in the heart of the town. The continual Union sharpshooter fire from Maryland Heights—returned by Rebs up on Loudoun Heights—had nearly stripped the streets of human habitation. Harpers Ferry had once been a thriving town with a population of six thousand. But so many people had fled the devastation that it was now a ghost town, with only a few hundred dazed but dogged souls remaining.

Thomas and Lacey Donahue came out to Montemarte on Christmas Day. Kiernan had done her very best to make it, if not a joyous occasion for the twins, at the very least a pleasant one. It was a difficult day, for it was the first Christmas they would spend without their father or brother.

She couldn't help feeling a pull of nostalgia herself, for just last Christmas she had met Jesse at the summer cottage

at Cameron Hall, and just last Christmas she had been filled
with dreams. Everybody had thought back then that the
South would whop the North, and that it would all be over
very soon.

No one had realized just how tenacious Abe Lincoln
could be, and no one had imagined that John Brown's
prophecy about the land being soaked in blood would prove
so true.

Christmas was a quiet day. After church, Jeremiah killed
one of their last big chickens, and Janey cooked it up with
cranberries and turnip greens and sweet potatoes. Lacey had
brought along an apple pie, and the meal was delicious. T.J.
was still with them, healing nicely, spending more and more
time outdoors. Kiernan often found him looking off into the
distance, as if seeking out the war with his eyes. But he
wasn't going back, he had told her. He'd given his word, and
if his word didn't mean anything, what were they fighting
for?

When dinner was over, they exchanged gifts—little things
that year, all made by hand, socks for T.J. and Thomas,
handkerchiefs for Kiernan and Lacey, a chemise cut down
from one of Kiernan's own for Patricia, and a sheath for
Jacob for his hunting knife. Then Kiernan and the twins
accompanied Thomas and Lacey to their home in town.
Kiernan planned to stay over in Harpers Ferry to witness
certain documents for them.

But she didn't go to their house with them right away.
She asked Thomas to let her off on High Street for a minute,
and he obliged her. She stood in the center of the once-busy
thoroughfare and felt the cold and the emptiness. Dead
leaves rustled on the ground as she looked down the steep
incline and at the windows of the homes and shops along the
street. Everything was silent.

Depression weighed down upon her, and she realized that
she was probably standing on Union soil. Harpers Ferry was
one of the counties that was determined to form its own
state. A lot of Union soldiers had been around when the vote
had been taken, but there were still plenty loyal to the old

government hereabouts. There'd be a new constitution soon, and a new state soon enough, she reckoned.

She hugged her arms close to her chest and shivered.

A new order to things had arrived, she admitted to herself at last.

And there was another admission she had to make. She was going to have Jesse's baby.

Just last year, she hadn't thought it would be so horrible. Last year, she simply would have married Jesse.

But this year she was Anthony's widow, and she should still have been wearing black. And Jesse was gone, fighting the war. She might never see him again. Even if he had been standing in front of her right then, she didn't think that she could tell him she was with child. Even to tell him might be to surrender.

People around here would ostracize her cruelly. People everywhere, for that matter, might feel obliged to do so.

She didn't really care about people in general, but she did care about Patricia and Jacob.

There was nothing to be done, she thought. She couldn't leave the twins, although they might prefer to come home with her.

But she would have to tell her father. He would offer her no cruel words. He would never think of throwing her out into the world. And he would, she was certain, love the baby too. But he would be very disappointed in her. His fine old shoulders would sag with the weariness and weight of what she had done.

The cold of the day touched her cheeks, making them numb. She clenched her teeth and welcomed the cold inside her. She needed that numbness. She didn't have to say anything to the twins yet. When the time came, she would.

Resolute, she walked down the street to the Donahue house.

By February, the newly formed state of West Virginia had written itself a constitution. Kiernan listened while Thomas and T.J. discussed the meaning of it all, but for Kiernan it had no meaning at all. When the Union was in residence, they held the town and the area. When the Confederates were around, it was as southern as pecan pie.

The Union was still destroying the town. A few soldiers had rowed over from Maryland Heights early in the month, and one had been killed by Rebs trying to return. The Union had retaliated, and troops under Major Tynsdale destroyed the section of town where he suspected the Rebs hid. Earlier, Tynsdale had accompanied John Brown's wife down from Pennsylvania acting as a protector, and he had been with her to see that her husband's remains were brought home for burial.

Tynsdale now had those who remained in the town whisper. For John Brown had prophesied the destruction of the town, and now, a little more than two years after his death, the destruction had come—implemented by Tynsdale.

At the end of February, General Banks was in possession of the town. Kiernan didn't breathe very easily with so many soldiers so close, but no one disturbed them, which she was certain was Jesse's doing.

One day while she was out in the laundry, she found T.J. behind her, ready to take the heavy basket she was carrying. He set it down for her, then leaned in the doorway, watching her. She stared at him and finally demanded, "All right, T.J. What is it?"

It pulled out his corncob pipe and lit it, taking his time. "Mrs. Miller, this ain't none of my business, and it ain't my place to say anything, but you're working too hard."

"We all have to work, T.J., if we want to keep eating and wearing clothes."

"But you're working *too* hard"—he hesitated a second—"if you want that young 'un you're carrying to make it healthy and well into this world."

She felt the color fade from her face. Instinctively, protectively, she clutched her stomach. "Is it so very obvious?" she asked worriedly.

T.J. shook his head. "No, not when you're wearing your big, er"—T.J. flushed himself—"your petticoats and all. It's just that I know you, and I see you sick, and I see you very tired. I see you just stare out the window, with eyes as sad and weary and bleak as the winter itself. You helped me, just like that Yankee doc helped me, and I'd like to help you in return."

"No one can help me, T.J. I'm not sick at all anymore. I feel very well. But thank you." She was silent, biting her lower lip. "Do you think I have some time left before I have to tell the children?"

T.J. nodded. "Just don't come out with those big baskets no more, Mrs. Miller. You call me."

"I will, T.J. Thank you."

"You know," he began. "I'm sure the Yank would be more than willing—"

"I don't want to hear it, T.J.," Kiernan said stubbornly.

"He'd marry you."

"I still have the children, T.J. They'd never live among the people who killed their father and brother!"

"I think you're mistaken, Mrs. Miller. I think they have a better perspective on this war than you think."

"That may very well be," Kiernan told him. "Let's just see how things go, shall we? I need some time."

But she wasn't to have much time. The next week she went into town with the children to see what supplies they could purchase. It wasn't easy, for she received her income from the rifle works in Confederate currency, and when the Yankees were in residence, no one wanted to accept it. Still, she was able to do some shopping. One good thing about the Yanks being around was that the strict blockade that went on all winter had been lifted, and northern goods were in abundance.

But as she was leaving a shop, she was stunned when a flying missile struck her in the chest. Patricia, at her side, screamed, and for a wild moment of panic, Kiernan thought she had been hit by a bullet, for a red stain was spreading out on her breast.

She realized that it was a tomato.

"Yankee lover! Whore!" came a call from a window.

She spun around, but it was too late. The tomato hurler hated Yankees, but he didn't feel like getting caught by one.

"Kiernan!" Patricia cried in dismay. "Why—"

"Let's get out of here," Jacob said very angrily. "Kiernan, get between us. If they throw anything else, they'll have to hit me first!"

"If he hits me again, I'll throw it back at him!" Kiernan declared. She was furious, but she was shaking, too, and very close to tears.

"Let's go!" Jacob insisted.

She allowed him to lead her along. At the Donahues' house, Lacey tried to clean up Kiernan's dress and assure herself that Kiernan wasn't hurt. Thomas watched in silence from the fireplace. A while later, he walked to the doorway to pick up his rifle, and Kiernan realized with alarm that he was about to go after the man who had offended her.

She flew up and over to him. "Thomas, no!"

"Kiernan, that man had no right to dishonor a lady!"

"Thomas, please don't go after him." If he were to die because of her—for her honor, or lack of it—she didn't think that she could bear it. "Thomas, you can't go after anyone. I—I *have* been seeing a Yankee, or I *was* seeing one. Please, Thomas, put down the gun."

Lacey gasped. "Do you mean Captain Cameron? Kiernan!" she began.

"That's enough, Lacey!" Thomas said quickly—the children were in the house. His eyes were on Kiernan. "The man still had no right!"

"Please, please, Thomas. Put the gun down. I have to take the children home before the sharpshooters get started. Please promise me that you'll put the gun down."

He sighed at long last and set his rifle down. "All right, Kiernan."

She smiled at him and called to Patricia and Jacob.

They were both silent as she drove the carriage back to Montemarte. When they arrived, Jeremiah was there to take the carriage from her, and she hurried into the house.

Dusk was just falling. She sat in a rocker in Andrew's office—or Jesse's surgery, all scrubbed down now, the cots and bandages gone, no trace of blood remaining. She sat and stared out at the coming darkness.

She felt someone enter the room. Somehow, she knew it was Jacob.

"You're going to have a baby, right?" he demanded.

She nodded, still rocking, still staring.

"It isn't my brother's baby, is it?"

She turned to look at him at last. "Oh, Jacob. I'm so very sorry."

Jacob stood stiffly by the door. His brown eyes seemed to be touched by so much pain, and so much wisdom. He was too young to have that kind of wisdom.

"What are you going to do?" he asked her.

"I don't know yet."

"Are you going to—to leave Patricia and me?"

"No, Jacob, I'd never leave you, I promise you that. Unless, of course . . ."

"Unless what?"

"Unless you wanted me to."

He was silent again. "No. No, I don't want you to leave us. I reckon I don't want to go into town too often, but I don't want you to leave us." He sighed, and his shoulders fell as if he carried the weight of the world upon them. "We'll get by, Kiernan. I know we will."

"Thank you."

He hesitated a minute. "You know, you could marry that Yank." No matter how well Jacob had come to know Jesse, he still seemed to find it necessary to keep his distance.

Kiernan shrugged. "I don't even know where he is, Jacob. I swore to him once that I'd never marry him."

"But you're in love with him, aren't you?"

"Jacob, I—"

"You are. I saw the way he looked at you when he was here. And I saw the way that you looked at him." Jacob frowned suddenly. "He never—I mean, he didn't—he didn't *make* you do anything, did he?"

She shook her head, trying not to smile. Jacob could be so very fierce. What a fine man he was going to be one day!

"No," she said softly, "Jesse never forced me to do anything."

"Well, whatever, we will get by," he promised her. To her

surprise, he walked across the room and set his arms around her shoulders. He hugged her briefly, then left her, and she sat alone in the darkness.

Jesse, she thought. Where was he tonight? She prayed that he was warm and safe from danger, and then she wondered what she would do if he were here right now, sitting with her.

He was a Yankee, and he was never going to change. She certainly could not change him—at least, not his sense of right and wrong and his loyalty.

For his part, he had never asked her to change. He had understood that she had her convictions. But she wasn't certain anymore herself, either about right or wrong, or about their fine southern cause. All she knew was that war killed and maimed, and that it was bitter and painful, no matter what the color of the soldiers' uniforms.

But could she marry him now?

Yes, she decided she could. But only if he wanted her, really wanted her. Not because of the baby, and not because of honor. Love, finally, must be enough.

And she would marry him only if he came to her, of course. She still couldn't quite swallow her pride enough to court a Yankee.

She was so calm, she thought, as a slow smile curved her lip. Not so very long ago, the mere thought of her present position would have been scandalous, a horror within the society that had been hers since birth. Her situation would have made matrons whisper and pull their children aside on the sidewalk when she came by.

Hers was the type of situation that would make those who considered themselves very righteous throw things at her, like tomatoes. It was every father's nightmare.

It was not simply that she was expecting a child. Surely any number of hasty marriages took place, and of course, whispering went along with them.

But Kiernan's scandal went beyond that. She was the widow of a fine southern soldier who had laid down his life at Manassas. She was expecting the child of a Yank, and her husband had not even been dead a year.

But Jacob loved her, despite everything. He meant to stand by her. That was what mattered now. If she only had sure knowledge that Jesse was alive and well.

Suddenly, she felt a fluttering deep within her abdomen. She thought that she had imagined it, but then it came again.

Despite everything, a thrill burst through her as sweet as any she had ever known. Her baby was alive and well and moving. Her baby was real. Her baby, Jesse's baby, their flesh and blood.

Conceived in war . . .

But conceived in love.

"And I will love you, little one!" she vowed vehemently. "I will love you enough to make up for everything!"

She smiled. She was suddenly glad that Jacob knew. Patricia would be all right if Jacob was all right. Both twins could help her now, and she might even begin to live with enthusiasm, with hope.

The fluttering movement came inside her again, the quickening. She wrapped her arms tenderly over her abdomen, and she started to cry softly, tears of a curious joy.

Daniel Cameron had been in the Shenandoah Valley, running spying and harassment raids with a crack company of horse soldiers. Now, in March 1862, his most recent orders had been to move east—Lincoln had put a General named McClellan in charge of his eastern army, and McClellan was planning a huge assault on Richmond by moving up through the peninsula—the Tidewater region.

Daniel had been living in a state of tension ever since the orders had come. For one thing, he was certain that Jesse was with McClellan's army. For another, this campaign was also going to bring the battle frighteningly close to home. He was anxious, damned anxious to be a part of it. If Union soldiers came anywhere close to Cameron Hall, he'd be on the doorstep waiting for them.

It wasn't just his home that concerned him so. Christa was there alone. And John Mackay was near, too, alone what with Kiernan caring for the Miller children in Harpers

Ferry. Kiernan was doing well enough. Daniel hadn't heard from Jesse, and he hadn't heard from Kiernan, which was strange—they had once been such avid correspondents. But time was scarce these days; he'd barely had time to get notes off to Christa. Christa kept him advised, because Jesse wrote to her too.

Seated at his desk in his field tent, Daniel felt his fingers tighten around his pen. War was so damned strange. All his life, he'd followed his brother, followed him to West Point, followed him to Kansas. He hadn't attended medical school like Jesse—he'd never had Jesse's calling for it. But otherwise, they'd been as close as brothers could be.

But now he hadn't seen him, hadn't heard a word from him in over a year. If he did see Jesse, he was supposed to shoot him.

Jesse wouldn't be riding into battle, Daniel knew. He would be taking his skill into field hospitals. Daniel knew that Jesse was trying his best to save lives in this war, but he had been a cavalry soldier for years. There was no telling that he might not mount up in the heat of things and come riding into battle himself—maybe even against orders.

That was Daniel's biggest fear. Not death, not capture, not loss—just meeting his brother in battle.

He sighed, crumpling up the orders he had been writing and starting over again. Suddenly, there was a fracas outside his tent. For a moment, he thought the canvas structure was going to fall over. As he stared at the support pole in amazement, he heard his name called.

"Captain Cameron! Captain Cameron!"

"What the hell is going on here?" he demanded with a roar, leaping up at last.

His aide, Corporal Beal, came through the opening, following an indignant young lad with handsome blond curls and dark eyes. Corporal Beal nearly had his hands upon the boy's nape, but the lad seemed tough. He eluded Beal and strode to Daniel's desk, saluting him quickly.

"Captain Cameron," the boy began.

"Captain Cameron," Beal interrupted, "this wild young pup wouldn't listen when I said that you were busy, that we had to pull out. He ran right past me, and when I caught up to him, why, he took a swing at me and I had to take one back, but he's a scamp, he is, wild and—"

"It's all right, Corporal Beal," Daniel said. He took his seat behind his field desk, frowning as he recognized Jacob Miller. "Jacob's an old friend of mine."

"I done told him we were moving out in a hurry—"

"The Union hasn't done anything in a hurry yet, Corporal. I think I can spare a few minutes for an old friend." He smiled, his gaze on Jacob. "You can leave us now."

"He could be a spy," Beal warned dourly.

"Not this one. The boy is as loyal as they come. Right, Jacob?"

To his surprise, Jacob reddened, but he replied, "Yes, sir, Captain Cameron."

"You can't trust no one these days," Beal muttered, "not no one, not no how!" Daniel grinned at Jacob, and Beal sniffed again, but he left them at last.

"You haven't turned Yank, have you, boy?" Daniel asked. He indicated the folding field chair opposite his desk, and Jacob took a seat.

"No, I haven't turned Yank."

"You're not trying to join the army?"

"No, not yet."

"That's a relief," Daniel told him. "Does Kiernan know that you're out here?" He stiffened suddenly. He'd heard rumors that Kiernan had been giving good information to the troops in the valley. But she wouldn't allow a child this age to engage in espionage, would she?

Still, the war had made people do all kinds of things.

"Did she give you a message for me?"

"No, no!" Jacob protested. His hat was in his hands, and he twisted it between his fingers, looking down at it. "No, in fact"—he paused, looking up at Daniel—"she'd probably have my hide if she knew that I was here."

"Oh." Puzzled, Daniel leaned forward. "Then . . . ?"

"This is a matter of the strictest confidence," Jacob said, sitting very straight.

"The strictest," Daniel agreed somberly.

"I'd like you to get through to your brother, sir. I know he's a Yank and you're a Reb, and that you probably don't talk to each other much anymore. But I want you to let him know that . . ."

"That?"

"That he's going to be a father."

For a moment, Daniel was stunned. Then he said, "Oh!" very softly, and leaned back in his chair. It shouldn't be such a surprise. Anybody who knew Jesse and Kiernan could feel the electricity in the air when they were near each other. If anyone had seen what Jesse meant to Kiernan, it was Daniel himself. And if anybody knew Jesse's heart, well, that was Daniel, too. That the two of them had consummated those feelings, even in war, wasn't that much of a surprise.

He leaned forward. "Is Kiernan well?" he asked Jacob.

"Just fine. But—but she'll never let him know. Don't you see?"

"Proud, huh?"

"Very. And, well, he's—"

"A Yankee."

"Right," Jacob agreed miserably. He looked at Daniel anxiously once again. "Can you get a message through to him?"

Daniel nodded. "Yes, I can."

"You have to be very, er . . ."

"Discreet?"

"Yes."

"I'll write to my sister," Daniel said, "and she'll get through to him. No others will be involved—unless I can think of something else, equally discreet. Do you trust me?"

"Yes, sir, I do."

"Good. Then you'd better be on your way. You don't want Kiernan to start worrying about you."

Jacob Miller saluted him, slammed his slouch hat back down over his head, and started out. Then he looked back. "Maybe you could not mention my name? No, wait—never mind. That wouldn't be very honorable, would it? Go ahead and use my name in this if you want. Make sure you let him know that Patricia and I are all right with this thing. Your brother is a darned good man, sir, except that he's a Yank."

"I've felt that myself, Jacob," Daniel assured him.

Jacob grinned at that, and then he was really gone. Daniel sat back and drummed his fingers on his desk.

It occurred to him that he was going to be an uncle, and he grinned.

"Why, you little hellions!" he thought fondly of his brother and Kiernan.

But his smile faded. This was war. He wasn't at all sure that anybody could do the right thing by anybody else.

He'd try, though. He'd sure as hell try.

Twenty-One

It was late afternoon when Thomas Donahue came riding up to Montemarte at a gallop. It was a fast pace for Thomas —he didn't like his old bones to rattle, he had told Kiernan often enough. Seeing him come so quickly, a sweep of dread instantly wove through her.

She raced out onto the porch. The Yankees were heading out to the house again, it was about to be burned, something horrible had happened, the war had been lost.

"Kiernan!" Thomas wheezed as he dismounted. She ran to him, offering him support. "You've got to go home."

"Home! What's happened?"

"It's your father, Kiernan."

"Oh, God! Oh, no!" She felt faint. Black waves washed before her eyes. "He's not . . . he's not—"

"He's sick, Kiernan, very sick. Christa Cameron managed to get a letter through with an employee of the railroad. She thinks you should come right home. But she's also aware that it's a long and dangerous journey right now. She wanted you to know that she'd be with him, that she'd take care of him. That she'd do everything in the world for him that she could."

"But she wouldn't be me!" Kiernan whispered. "And if Papa is very sick . . ."

No, she thought suddenly. War was awful, and it already

had taken so very much from her and from everyone. She wouldn't let it keep her away from her father too.

She stood very straight. "I'm going home, Thomas."

"But there's troops aplenty on all these roads!" Thomas warned her. "Troops in blue and troops in gray, and I don't know which are more dangerous."

"I'll be all right. Who would disturb a woman in my—er, delicate condition?"

Thomas hesitated. He didn't want to tell her that she was still very beautiful, and that war does strange things to good men and worse things to bad men.

"I'll come with you," Thomas offered.

"You'll do no such thing. You hate to travel, and I'll be moving very quickly. I'll bring Janey and Tyne with me." She couldn't bring T.J.—she'd have to leave him and Jeremiah and David at Montemarte. But the twins would come with her too. She couldn't leave them. She had promised she wouldn't.

"I can't talk you out of this, can I?" Thomas said.

"No." On her tiptoes, Kiernan gave him a kiss. Then she shooed him on his way home and hurried for the stairs, calling for Janey to help her pack. Patricia ran into her room, and Kiernan told her to hurry and pack for the trip. She was in a whirlwind of motion, getting her things together. Janey helped her, then ran to the kitchen to find Tyne and Jeremiah and see that the wagon was readied.

When she had finished with her clothing, Kiernan hurried back down the stairs to the office and went through the medicines that Jesse had left. Her father was sick—but with what? She stared at the bottles with their neatly printed labels and decided to take them all.

Her fingers were trembling, but she was determined to leave then and there, just as soon as the children were ready.

She was going home.

She touched her stomach and felt a strange excitement sweep through her. The baby could be born at home, in Tidewater Virginia.

Suddenly she was very glad, if breathless. She pulled out

the swivel chair and sat. The baby began to move vigorously inside her, as if caught up in the frenzy of her emotion.

Home, she was going home.

The door to the office suddenly swung open, and Jacob appeared. Kiernan looked up at him and realized that she hadn't seen him all day.

"Where have you been?" she asked.

"We're going on a trip?" he asked incredulously.

She nodded. "We have to. My father is ill, Jacob. I have to go home. I want you to come with me."

"But I just—"

"You just what?"

"Nothing. Of course, I'll come with you. I'd never let you go alone," Jacob said. He turned around. "I just hope he can find us now," he murmured.

"Pardon?" Kiernan called after him, trying to rise. It was becoming very hard to do. "Jacob?"

But Jacob was gone, and an hour later, when they were ready to ride out, she didn't remember that she had been questioning him.

All that was on her mind was that her father was very sick.

She was going home.

It was nearly dawn, and the day was going to bring more fighting, Jesse knew.

He was with George B. McClellan's troops on the peninsula, moving toward Richmond.

So far, the Peninsula Campaign had been a lesson in confusion.

McClellan had taken his troops to the tip of the peninsula. There, during the first week of April, a Confederate line had stretched from the York across the peninsula to the Warwick River.

The Union had laid siege there for a month, a slow and overly cautious siege, giving Confederate General Joseph Johnston time to join Confederate General Magruder and shore up his troops. On May 4, McClellan began a grand assault, but Johnston had already moved up the peninsula.

On May 5, the Union vanguard overtook the Confederate rear guard, and action followed at Williamsburg. There had been more and more fighting. The Union took Norfolk, and the Confederate ironclad *Virginia* was destroyed. The James River was opened to the Union, but on May 15, at Drewry's Bluff, seven miles outside Richmond, the Confederates were able to employ river obstructions.

Rains washed over the Chickahominy River, and two Union corps were isolated near the villages of Seven Pines and Fair Oaks Station. On the Confederate side, General Johnston suffered a severe wound.

General Robert E. Lee was put in command.

McClellan remained cautious.

Jesse had it on good word from scouts whom he trusted that they should never have been in their present position. There'd been only seventeen thousand Confederates on that defense line at Yorktown when they'd started their Peninsula Campaign. Now they were facing far greater numbers.

It was ceasing to matter to Jesse. They came in, and he did the best he could to patch them up. He watched them die after he had done his best to make them live. He realized that every day more would come to him. His promotion to full colonel hadn't changed anything. Now he was responsible for other doctors as well as for his own patients.

Very early one morning, Jesse was bandaging the arm of the scout, a man with dark, soulful eyes, a drooping moustache, and a weary knowledge about him—Sergeant Flicker.

"There will be action aplenty this morning, Colonel," Flicker said.

"Oh? I heard we were away from the main body of Confederates."

"Hell, no—there's cavalry out there! Our best intelligence says there's no Rebs out there, but our boys've been trading all night with fellows dressed in gray who look a whole lot like Rebs to me."

Jesse arched a brow at him. It was common knowledge that Union "intelligence" tended to be either exaggerated or dead-out wrong.

But cavalry!

His heart thudded. His brother could be out there.

The thought had just crossed his mind when an enlisted man came running into his tent. "Colonel Cameron. Sir!"

"Yes, what is it?" Jesse demanded.

"Reb to see you, sir!"

"What?" Jesse demanded.

The soldier hesitated at his tone of voice. "Sir—"

"For the love of God, spit it out, will you?"

The soldier grimaced. "We were passing some fine Virginia tobacco over for a pound or two of decent coffee, sir."

Jesse grinned. The man shouldn't have been admitting this to him, but trading went on all the time. Men in blue and gray often talked all night, then fired at and killed one another at daybreak.

"It's all right—keep going. There's a Reb to see me?"

"Claims to be your brother, sir!"

"And there's cavalry near us? Then, soldier, he most certainly is my brother. Where are the Rebs?"

"Right across the stream. We got the message from a little boat a Reb whittled out of a tree branch. We'll probably start fighting real soon, but since it's not quite daylight yet, the major can make sure there's no firing till you both get back to your right sides. The Reb says that if you'll see him, he'll be waiting just downstream."

"Hell, yes—I'll see him!" Jesse announced. He donned his overcoat against the coolness of the morning air and followed the man out of his tent. The Union troops were already dug into their positions for the morning, ready for trench warfare. Jesse hurried down the line toward the stream.

"Make way!" The soldier leading him along called out. "The colonel here has got some kinfolk to see!"

Men made way for him. He passed by Colonel Grayson, in charge of the infantry unit on the front of the line. He saluted, and Grayson returned the motion. "Don't take long out there. I've orders to start shells flying by the first real light."

"Thanks," Jesse told him. He kept walking, leaping out from the trenches to hurry along the stream. Surrounded by the mist rising from the water, he could already see the figure of his brother. He wore an overcoat and a plumed hat, both of a gray color that seemed one with the mist of the morning.

"Daniel?" Jesse called. His footsteps moved faster. He was running.

"Jess!"

Suddenly he stood dead still in front of his brother. They looked very much alike, he knew. He was older, but Daniel might have been a mirror image of himself in the mist— except that one wore blue and one wore gray.

Daniel might have been thinking the same thing. For a long moment they stared at one another gravely. It had been a long, long year, and they had both changed in that time.

And yet they hadn't changed that much at all. Jesse took a step forward, and they embraced, and he saw that they were both trembling.

"Daniel," he said, stepping back. "Damn, it's good just to see you well and alive."

Daniel grinned. "You too, Jess."

"It's been a long time."

"Too long for brothers, Jess."

"Been home recently?"

Daniel nodded. "Christa's fine. I've been worried, though, what with the Union troops on the peninsula. I'm not real popular with some of the Union troops. My boys and I have done a fair amount of harassing of Union troops. I'm worried about Cameron Hall."

"Cameron Hall?" Jesse exclaimed. "Why would Union troops want to burn the hall? Legally, it's mine, not yours."

"Well, Jess, it's in Virginia, and it's in the Confederacy, and I'm part of that Confederacy. I reckon that's the way they see it, I don't know. I've told Christa to go stay with John Mackay until it's over. Mackay's been ill, and he can use her over there. I don't know if word's gotten through to Kiernan yet about her father."

"Mackay is ill?"

"I'm afraid so."

"What is it?"

"Something in his lungs. But Jesse—"

"I wonder if I can get a leave, get to him. You all are giving us such a pounding here—"

"Jesse, stop. You've got to listen to me."

"There's more?"

"Kiernan is—"

"Oh, Lord!" Jesse breathed, gripping his brother's arm. "What's happened? What's wrong with her? Where is she?"

"Jesse—"

"Daniel, if there's anything—"

"Jesse, I'm trying to tell you!" Daniel exploded. "She isn't ill! She's going to have your child!"

He might have been hit by bricks, he was so stunned. Of all the things he had expected that morning, the last was the information that he was going to be a father.

"But how—"

"Jesse, you know damned well how!" Daniel said, grinning with a mild rebuke.

"How do you know?" Jesse demanded.

"Jacob Miller came to see me right before we headed out this way. He thought you should know. He also thought you should know that he and his sister think you're all right— for a Yank. I told him that I felt the same way myself. Jesse, you've got to marry her."

"Daniel, I've been *trying* to marry her!"

"Hey!" came a loud shout from Jesse's lines. "Tell the Reb to get his head down, and you get back here, Colonel Cameron. The fightin's about to commence!"

"Get back, Daniel," Jesse said. He embraced his brother fiercely one last time.

"Hey! Hey, sir! The firing is going to start!"

"Keep your head down!" Jesse ordered Daniel.

"Yeah—and I'll expect to hear about a wedding!" Daniel retorted.

"Is she still at Montemarte?"

"I don't know, she might be on her way home. Jesse, damn you, now you get back, and keep your head down!" Daniel said. Jesse nodded, and they both turned away, hurrying back to their lines.

The first firing started the minute Jesse stepped back down into the trenches. It went on for hours.

Jesse worked mechanically through the day. There were long spells when it seemed that his mind was completely empty, numb. Shells exploded overhead, and screams and screeches could be heard constantly. At one point his field hospital seemed overrun by the Rebs, but then they were repulsed, and the Union managed to move forward bit by bit.

The wounded poured in.

Five doctors worked under Jesse, and all five worked feverishly. He searched for bullets with his bare fingers and bit down hard on his jaw every time he saw that there was no way to save a man's life but to remove a mangled limb.

At least he had chloroform and ether. He had heard that the surgeons on the other side had run out. It was difficult to believe in the field tent that they were lucky in any way, but Jesse believed that they were. He had sufficient help to make the operations successful, a man to deliver the anesthetic and make sure that the patients were receiving enough air along with it, a man to secure the patient, a man to hold the limb, and a surgeon to carefully sever flesh, then muscle, then bone.

By the end of the day, he was weary of it, and weary of war. He wanted to go back to treating influenza and stomach disorders. He wanted to deliver a baby.

He wanted to deliver his own. Jesu, Kiernan! There were other things out there in the world. It had been a day just like this when she had stood by his side, the perfect assistant. She had never blanched, she had never failed him.

She had promised that she would never marry him.

You *will* marry me! he thought furiously.

Calling to an orderly, he had the last of his patients taken on a stretcher from the field surgery and proximity to the field to a wagon. Then he was listening intently.

The firing had stopped. The battle was over.

He stepped out of the tent. It was nearly dusk, and it was quiet on this side of the stream, and quiet on the other.

A soldier was hurrying past. Jesse caught hold of his arm. "What's happened?"

"We got beat back in most places, Colonel. We're pulling out of here now. Setting up camp due east. There's still some wounded right across the stream. But be careful, sir. There's still Rebs around."

"Order my men out except for Corporal O'Malley. Tell them to break down into the wagons, but leave the canvas standing and leave behind my instrument bags. If I find anyone, O'Malley can assist me."

"Yes, sir, Colonel Cameron. Don't forget there's still Rebs out there."

"Thanks. Don't forget I rode regular cavalry for years."

"Yes, sir!" The soldier grinned. "Is that all, sir?"

Jesse nodded, then hurried to the stream. He crossed through the water, and it was so cold that he could feel it even through his high black boots.

Then he stood still. The scene before him was one of contrast. The stream itself was peaceful, with its cool water dancing over rocks and fallen branches.

But by that stream lay the bodies of the fallen. Jesse looked from the bloodred skies of the coming dusk to the devastation in human life spread before him.

He went from man to man. Bodies covered in blue were intertwined with bodies clothed in gray. He bent down and sought pulses on both.

"Jesse!"

He was startled to hear his name called. Standing, he looked around the field. He felt a shudder rip through him.

An officer was calling to him, a cavalry officer in gray.

Daniel.

He ran across the field and fell to his knees at his brother's side. Daniel's hand was clutched low over his gut. His fingers were sticky with blood.

"Damn you, Daniel!" Jesse swore. "I told you to keep your head down."

"I did keep my head down!" Daniel insisted. "He shot me

in the gut!" He tried to smile but winced and went white, and his eyelids fell as he lost consciousness.

Jesse ripped open his brother's frock coat and shirt. A quick probe with his fingers told him that the bullet was still in Daniel's body. He had to remove it as soon as possible. And he had to suture some of the blood vessels. But Daniel was weak. He'd lost a lot of blood and was losing more and more of it as minutes passed by.

"I've got to get you to the field tent."

"Yank, you touch the captain again," a voice suddenly warned him, "and you'll need a field tent yourself!"

Jesse turned around, inwardly damning himself. He should have been listening, he should have been paying attention. But his brother was wounded, and he hadn't heard the approach of the two Rebel soldiers who were now aiming their rifles at him.

"He needs help," Jesse said.

"Well, he don't need it from no Yank! We've come for him —he's our captain."

"You can't take him. If he's not helped right away, he'll die."

"Hell, you'd kill him if we gave you a chance! But we ain't gonna give no Yankee surgeon that chance. Get your hands off him, and we'll let you live. We've got some fine southern prisons."

"You fools!" Jesse swore suddenly. Ignoring them, he hefted his brother into his arms and faced the two. "He's my brother! And I'm a damned good surgeon, and I won't let my own flesh and blood die! I'm taking him. So shoot me!"

The two men looked at each other, then stared at Jesse.

"Tom," one said, "the captain does have a Yank brother who's a surgeon."

The other man asked suspiciously, "How do we know that you're his brother?"

"Hell, just look at me!" Jesse swore with exasperation, and started walking forward. "I haven't time for this."

He heard the click of a gun. He scarcely hesitated. Daniel was rousing.

"Daniel, will you tell these blind soldiers of yours that I'm your brother?"

Daniel grimaced. "Boys, he's my brother! Oh, hell, Jess! Are you taking me back to the Union lines?"

"Yep." He didn't add that he had no choice if he was going to live.

"Captain!" the soldier called Tom called.

"Get on back, boys. Jesse'll patch me up right as rain, and I'll be back myself then."

The Rebels still wouldn't let Jesse pass. Tom stubbornly stood his ground.

"Supposin' you save the captain, Doc. They'll take him to one of your Yankee camps. Maybe they'll try him and shoot him as a spy. Maybe one of those other Yank sawbones will get his hands on him—"

"You think I'm going to let them take my brother to a prison camp!" Jesse exploded.

The men stared at him for a minute. "How you gonna stop 'em?" Tom asked.

Jesse could feel his brother's blood, warm and wet against him. "I give you my word, I won't let them take my brother. Now, either shoot me, and shoot to kill, or let me pass. He's bleeding, and he needs help fast."

This time, the men let him pass.

Jesse bore Daniel's weight across the stream. Daniel's eyes were half open.

"Am I going to make it, Jess?"

"You sure are. I won't let you die."

"If you think I'm going to die, will you try to get me home? I sure would like to go home, Jess."

"So would I," Jesse told him. "So would I."

He had never felt the yearning to be at Cameron Hall so strongly. He wanted to be home, and he wanted Kiernan to be there. He wanted to hold her in his arms, to touch the beauty of new life, to sit before a fire with her, to stare out upon the river. He could almost see it.

Daniel groaned, and the image was dispelled. His throat tightened until he almost choked on it.

God, if you ever let me save a life, please, let it be this life, he prayed.

The last daylight faded as he carried his brother into his hospital field tent and tenderly laid him down.

Twenty-Two

Kiernan didn't think she'd ever been on a longer or more grueling journey than the one she took that April.

Rains had washed away much of the roads. The war had kept them from being repaired.

She often climbed down from the wagon to walk as Tyne and Jacob set their shoulders to help the horses pull it over a deep pock or scar. They had to stop for fallen trees and move them, and they had to stop from sheer exhaustion. With no accommodations nearby, they slept in the wagon, the four of them together, huddled tight for warmth.

There were continual stops for the soldiers.

Just as they had come down the drive from Montemarte, Thomas had returned and given Kiernan a pass that he had procured from a Yankee colonel. It would get her through the Yankee lines, he had assured her.

She thanked Thomas heartily. It had not even occurred to her that she might need such a document. But during the journey, it had stood to her advantage a number of times.

Northern Virginia was a very curious place these days, she realized quickly. Yanks were here, Rebs were there, and towns of total devastation lay in between.

It was not possible for them to take a direct route. They were on the road for a week before they reached Richmond, where they learned that the armies were engaged in a number of serious battles right on the outskirts of the city. Yanks had come from the peninsula in huge numbers. All along the frontiers of the southern capital, the magnificent boys in gray were repelling the invaders.

"On to Richmond!" the Yankees cried.

But the southern boys, commanded by the genteel and remarkable Robert E. Lee, were holding them back. Jeb Stuart's cavalry had actually ridden right around the enemy.

The tension in the city was crackling. She had never imagined that Richmond could be anything like it was now—so vastly overcrowded. The roads were filled with soldiers— and politicians. Prices had skyrocketed with the influx of so many people. Janey went off to buy food and came back grumbling that she hadn't even enough money for a potato.

Kiernan, exhausted and overwhelmed by all they had learned in Richmond, stood by the wagon and told Janey not to worry. "Spend whatever you have to spend. We'll rest tonight here and try to make home by tomorrow night."

"Miz Kiernan," Tyne told her, "you ain't been listening. The soldier boys been fightin' right outside the city. There's a defense ring around it. They ain't gonna let us through."

"They're letting us through," Kiernan said stubbornly. "All I want is to go home!" she exclaimed. "And they're not going to stop me—the Rebels or the Yankees!"

She took Patricia and Jacob to a restaurant near the beautiful capitol building while Tyne and Janey went to see about accommodations for the evening.

She remembered the restaurant well. She and her father had come here often enough in earlier years. Now there was a crowd in the front, waiters in line to get in. She managed to get close enough to see inside.

At least it hadn't changed. The tables were covered in snowy-white cloths, the silver and crystal were elegant, and a violinist played while the diners ate and chatted. Entering the restaurant, Kiernan realized they were hardly dressed for the elegance of the place, which had persevered despite the war. Her voluminous cape hid her condition amazingly well, and the children somehow managed to present themselves at their best despite their days upon the road.

She was dismayed by the line of people waiting for tables.

The sight of them all nearly made her burst into tears, she was so exhausted. Worrying about John Mackay had taken its toll on her, and sleeping in the wagon had not been easy. She was always uncomfortable these days with so much weight to carry about. But she was also determined, and usually, no matter what, she was able to remain calm.

But this long line to eat a decent meal was nearly her undoing.

"Why, Mrs. Miller!"

A man was coming across the room toward them. He was tall and lean and dressed in an impeccable dove-gray frock coat and white ruffled shirt. Kiernan could have sworn she had never seen him before, but he seemed to know her.

She glanced at Jacob anxiously. "Who is that?"

"I'm not sure!" Jacob whispered back. "Maybe he's one of your business partners."

"Business!" she exclaimed suddenly. Patricia, exhausted too, opened her innocent brown eyes wide to Kiernan. Kiernan just smiled. "Miller Firearms," she murmured. "They'll get us home."

"Mrs. Miller!"

The man was upon them. A spark of life invaded Kiernan's system, and she extended her hand for the man to kiss. "I saw you last in Charles Town," the man said, "at the trial of the detestable John Brown. You were still Miss Mackay back then. I heard about your husband, and I'm so very sorry. Still, everything is still moving smoothly here in Richmond. Andrew Miller, Thomas Donahue, and your father picked the perfect site for their operation in the Shenandoah Valley!"

"Yes, they were very clever, Mr. . . . ?"

"Norman. Niles Norman, Mrs. Miller, at your service. If there's anything at all that I could do for you—"

"Why, actually, sir, there is. My throat is parched, and the poor children have been standing for ages. You see, I'm trying to reach my father right now. He's quite ill, I'm afraid. We've taken a loathsome journey in a wagon, what with the railroads being so dangerous, to be with him. And now—well, we're famished, and exhausted, and . . ."

She allowed her hand to flutter in the air and a tear to moisten her eye.

Jacob looked at her with a cocked brow.

Niles Norman was immediately at her service.

They didn't have to wait a moment longer. Niles knew someone in the right place, and soon they were sitting. A few minutes later, a beautiful rack of lamb sat before them with mint jelly and sweet potatoes and green pole beans dripping with sweet-cream butter.

Kiernan didn't think that food had ever tasted quite so good.

Niles Norman remained with them, chatting about the war. The Yankees were breathing right down their necks in Richmond, but they weren't afraid, not a bit. General Lee would keep them out.

Kiernan smiled sweetly. "Then we shouldn't have any problem getting through down on the peninsula, should we?"

Niles Norman frowned. "Now, Mrs. Miller, it just doesn't seem to be the right time—"

"But it has to be, Mr. Norman. I must get through!"

She brought her handkerchief to her eyes. In seconds Norman was assuring her that he would get her a pass; after all, she was part owner of Miller Firearms, and where might confederate boys be without those arms?

Jacob continued to stare at her with questioning eyes. She kicked him beneath the table, and Niles Norman fluttered nervously about her.

She gave him a sweet and dazzling smile.

Although accommodations in the city were extremely scarce, Niles Norman found them two rooms, with space for Tyne and Janey too. When Niles said good night to Kiernan, he cleared his throat several times, then told her that he would love to see her again. Surely, the time wasn't right, but . . .

"Mister," Jacob snorted, "you just don't know how wrong the time is!" he proclaimed.

"Jacob!" Kiernan protested warningly.

It was Jacob's turn for a sweet and innocent smile.

"Sorry, Mr. Norman, sir. But trust me. Kiernan is not ready for anything at the moment."

"What in God's name did you think you were doing?" Kiernan demanded furiously of Jacob after Niles Norman left them at last.

Jacob planted his hands on his waist, staring her down. "You were flirting!"

"I had to flirt!" she responded, astonished. "How else were we going to get anything done?"

"Seven months gone with another man's child—"

"Jacob!" Kiernan gasped. She was suddenly so furious that she could hardly stand it. She almost slapped him. Tears threatened at the back of her eyes, and she clenched her fingers tightly and stepped back rather than take a chance of striking Jacob.

"Even *you* are defending Jesse!" she whispered. "Dammit!" She was so weary, and the baby was so heavy, and as much as she loved the life building within her, her pregnancy was a strain. She couldn't help resenting Jesse at that moment. "You're defending him, and he's a Yankee! The Yankee who took over your house!"

"He's the father of your child," Jacob reminded her. "And I know that it would matter very much to him that you flirted. I—I know it, because I know him!" After his first faltering, Jacob was now firm in his conviction. "I know him, and so—well, you just haven't got any right to flirt like that!"

She hadn't any right to flirt—because of Jesse? Oh, if it weren't for Jesse—if it weren't for the foolish fact that she loved him despite all odds—she wouldn't be in this predicament now.

No, no—she wanted her baby.

"You've no right—no right at all, young Mr. Miller—to tell me what I can and cannot do," she snapped to Jacob. She was wrong to fight with him, but she was too tense and weary to try to explain. And she was frightfully close to tears. She couldn't fall apart now. She was too close to home.

"Oh, please! Stop it, both of you!" Patricia implored.

Kiernan swung around to look at Patricia, startled by her words.

"Jacob is—" Patricia hesitated, not quite as bold as her brother. "Jacob is only standing up for Captain Cameron. And Kiernan, you do love the captain, don't you?"

Kiernan swallowed hard, then nodded. "I have loved him a very long time," she admitted in a soft whisper. "Long before the war. If the war hadn't come along when it did, I probably would have married him. But you must understand about Anthony."

"We do understand," Jacob interrupted her with quiet dignity, and offered her a crooked smile. "You have been a very good widow to him. You would have been a good wife."

He kissed her cheek and went on into the bedroom where he would sleep. Kiernan looked after him, and then Patricia slipped an arm around her. And then the tears did slip down her cheek.

"Kiernan!" Patricia whispered with alarm. "What—?"

"I love you. I love you both," she said, and quickly wiped away her tears, bringing Patricia into the bedroom they would share.

They set off in the morning.

Tyne snapped the reins over the horses' backs, and the wagon moved down the pike. They had barely left behind the city with its fine red-brick row houses when they were stopped by a sentry. Kiernan produced the Confederate pass that Niles Norman had procured for her, and the soldier scratched his head.

"Mrs. Miller, with all due respect, ma'am, there's fighting out there."

"The fighting is out past Williamsburg, isn't it?" she asked.

"Yes, ma'am."

"Then that's the way I'm going," she said sweetly.

Reluctantly, the soldier agreed to let them pass. A quarter-mile down the road, though, Kiernan asked Tyne to pull in on the reins. The wagon rolled to a stop, and she turned back to talk to the twins.

"I've no right to bring you both through this. I'll take you back to Richmond, then I'll come through myself."

"We can't take the time," Jacob said stubbornly. "What if your father . . ." He let the words trail away meaningfully.

"My father may already be dead, Jacob. And it won't help him to endanger you." If John were dead, she thought, she wouldn't be able to bear it.

But she would have to bear it. No matter what happened, she must survive it, and she must make herself be strong—for Jacob, for Patricia, and for the baby.

"We're going with you," Patricia said. "We're not afraid of Yankees. We've already lived with them, remember?"

"Yes, I remember."

"You should," Jacob said softly. He was grinning. He seemed to have become Jesse's champion—and to enjoy taunting her about her transgressions.

"How nice of you to remind me," she said sweetly, gritting her teeth. "Tyne, let's go forward."

Down the road, they met another Confederate sentry. They were given another warning.

An hour later, they moved past a scene of utter devastation. Fighting had just preceded them. Patricia cried out at the sight of a body on the road before them, and Kiernan quickly forced the little girl to lay her head against her shoulder and close her eyes. She had to grit her teeth herself as they moved onward.

"Come on, good Lord Jesus!" Tyne prayed. Kiernan looked from Patricia's blond head to the road. There were more sentries up ahead, dressed in blue. Troops, scores of them, marched along the road. Tyne pulled in on the reins, and Kiernan felt her heart beat furiously.

"We're going to be all right!" she assured Tyne and the children. But she was shaking. She'd seen Yankees before. As Jacob had been kind enough to remind her, she'd seen them rather close.

But she'd never seen so many.

"Halt!" A voice commanded.

Tyne pulled in on the reins, and a footsoldier strode over

to the wagon. A young man looked up to Kiernan. "Lady, where do you think you're going?"

"Home," she told him. "I'm trying to go home. And you're in my way."

"There's been fighting all around here, ma'am, and all down the peninsula."

Her heart slammed hard against her chest. She prayed that she still had a home to go to.

"You have to let me by."

"I'm sorry, ma'am. I can't do that."

"But why?"

"Darkie," the soldier said, addressing Tyne, "draw that wagon over there. Lady, I'm afraid that you and the children will have to come with me to see the general. Come right along."

There was no choice. She stepped down from the wagon, helping Patricia. She reached for Jacob, but he eluded her touch.

"You must behave here," she warned him.

He arched a brow at her.

"Jacob—"

"Lady, you must follow me now," the soldier told her.

"Lead onward, sir. I'm following."

She pulled her hood farther down over her forehead, more as a cover against the stares directed their way than against the coolness of the rain-dampened morning. The soldier led them past rows and rows of marching men—tired men, wounded men, men who marched covered in mud and bandages. Some limped along, using their rifles as crutches.

"Burial detail, halt!" an officer commanded.

They moved past the soldiers performing the weary task of laying their own to rest on foreign soil. They passed by men who seemed to be at leisure. Some were in the grass with their mess kits, gnawing on hardtack, lying back and chewing blades of grass. A number of men had bandaged heads, and feet, and arms—and some had bandages where there should have been limbs.

Kiernan's heart hammered hard, her muscles contracted. Deep within her womb, the baby suddenly moved, violently, swiftly—as if it, too, had seen the ravages of battle and turned against them.

The men watched her walk along with Jacob and Patricia. Some smiled and tipped their hats. Some were appreciative, some were curious, and some were just weary.

And some looked at her as if she were the enemy as much as any gray-clad man they faced in battle.

Kiernan hurried along, putting an arm around Patricia's shoulder. Suddenly, the soldier leading her came to a stop outside a large tent.

"You wait here, ma'am," he told her, and left her standing with Patricia and Jacob. Jacob stared across the road to where a number of injured Yanks sat on their coats in the field.

"Jacob, please be careful here. I know you hate them, but we've got to get by them."

Jacob arched a brow at her, indicating a fellow on the ground who was missing his left calf and foot and his right hand.

"It's hard to hate a man who looks like that, Kiernan," he said softly.

"Kiernan, how long will we have to be here?" Patricia asked urgently.

"I don't know," she answered honestly.

The Yanks were being rather rude, she decided, leaving her standing out here. Her back was killing her. The cape she was wearing grew warm as the sun rose high in the sky, but if she removed it, her condition would become very apparent. She wondered if it mattered, if any of these men cared one way or another that she was carrying a child, in or out of proper wedlock.

Minutes passed by. The sun grew hotter, and her back began to hurt badly.

"Excuse me," she told the children.

"Kiernan," Jacob began, but before he could stop her, she had turned around and burst into the officers' field tent.

A group of officers were huddled around a table covered with maps. She stared straight at the Yankee faces, framed by their fine plumed hats.

"Excuse me. But you gentlemen are not simply the enemy —invading my home, my state, my land—you are excruciatingly rude!"

Dead silence followed her arrival, then one of the men attempted to hide the maps. A gray-haired gentleman stepped forward. "Your pardon, madam. We *have* been excruciatingly rude. Why wasn't I informed of this lady's presence?" he demanded.

The soldier she had first met stepped forward, saluting sharply. "General, sir, the colonel said I was not to interrupt."

"Madam, just what is it that I can do for you? I'm General Jensen, and I wish to be at your disposal."

"I want to go home, General, and your troops are preventing me from doing so."

"Is it urgent that you get home?"

"My father is ill, sir."

A snort suddenly rang out, and a man stepped forward. Kiernan's eyes widened as she recognized Captain Hugh Norris, the cavalryman who had been so eager to burn down Montemarte.

"Norris, I demand a reason for your behavior!" General Jensen said sharply.

"She's a Miller, General."

"Meaning, sir?"

"That should be answer enough, General. Miller Firearms. She's part owner of the company."

"I see," the general murmured, stroking his chin as he surveyed Kiernan.

"And beyond that," Hugh Norris went on, "a number of men are convinced she was spying in Harpers Ferry. The Rebs over there eluded us any number of times."

"Those Rebs eluded you, sir, because they are far smarter than you," Kiernan told him sweetly.

For the moment she thought Norris was going to assault her. General Jensen, however, stood between them. Norris clearly hated her, and it was obvious the man wanted her blood.

She stared at the older officer. "General Jensen, I swear to you that I am not spying. My father is ill. I am desperate to reach him."

"Mrs. Miller," Jensen said with a weary sigh, "I will have to ask you to wait outside for a few minutes while I straighten a few things out. Private Riker, bring the lady a chair, and see if she'd like some coffee."

Kiernan's heart sank. Hugh Norris would have plenty to say to the major.

Riker, who was the soldier who had escorted her to the tent in the first place, took her arm to escort her back out. She knew she had to appear as sweet and innocent and harmless as she could for the moment.

"Please, sir," she told the general, looking back over her shoulder as Riker led her away, "I just want to get home."

"And where is home?"

"An hour's ride from Williamsburg," she told him.

"Give me a minute, madam," he said.

Having little choice, she lowered her head and allowed Riker to lead her out. Jacob seemed oddly exuberant—she had expected him to be at some Yank's throat by now.

She cast him a frown while Riker dragged out a folding field chair. Jacob looked like a cat who had swallowed a canary.

She wanted to demand what was going on with him, but Private Riker wouldn't leave them. She asked for coffee, but the coffee was right there, just beyond them at a fire. He stayed with them.

A soldier suddenly came running by them. "Message for the general, Private! Make way!"

The private stepped aside, and the soldier went in. Still, they waited.

An officer came out of the tent, and Kiernan leaped to her feet. "Sir—"

"I am sorry, ma'am," the man said. "The colonel's insisting that you stay."

"The colonel?" she said, wondering what colonel he meant.

"Have a seat. He'll be right with you."

She had just taken her seat again when she heard the clip

of horses' hooves coming at them quickly. She leaped up, certain that animal was about to run her down.

Her eyes widened in amazement as she recognized the horseman.

Jesse.

He was the colonel who had demanded she be held!

He reined Pegasus in abruptly and leaped down. Before she knew it, he was before her, looking wilder than she'd seen him since Harpers Ferry.

But this was a different kind of wildness. He seemed to be absolutely furious.

His hair was totally disheveled, his black locks falling over his stormy eyes. He was hatless, and his high black boots were covered with the mud that had splashed him on his way here. His fingers, closing harshly around her arms, were hard and taut, almost brutal.

But his whisper, brief, desperate, was intended for her ears only. "Help me, Kiernan. Play along with me."

Instantly his manner changed. His words and his tone of voice matched the fever and fury of his touch. "Kiernan!" He spoke so harshly and so loudly that his voice carried into the tent. The general suddenly threw open a flap, came out, and stood before them. Jesse, incensed, seemed not to see him. "Yes, I heard of your condition, Mrs. Miller. But it never occurred to me that you would hunt me down across a warring countryside! Yes, I'll ask for leave to take you home, madam, but don't expect any more from me! I'll not marry you to save your honor! Who knows what you were up to with those Rebel friends of yours, coming in and out at all hours!"

Play along with me! Had she imagined the words, or had they been real? What was he doing to her? Everyone could hear his voice as he made a horrible mockery of her and everything that had passed between them. Her cheeks were surely bloodred, and despite his whisper, she was hurt and furious.

"What are you talking about!" she demanded.

"I won't marry you, Kiernan. I won't do it!"

She gasped, stunned. What could be bringing about this

kind of behavior in Jesse? "I don't need to be taken home, and you're the last man I'd ever marry!" she cried out, shaken and enraged. Dear God, this couldn't be Jesse, with his eyes on fire, his hold so brutal, doing this to her in front of all these people—making a fool of her, and a bastard of himself!

Play along with me! he had said. Well, she hoped she was playing along as he wanted. She was confused and furious and miserable, and she wanted desperately to be away from him and every Yankee there.

"Let go of me!" she demanded. Wildly, she tried to kick him. He wrenched her hard against him, and she struggled more desperately. "Jesse, you bluebelly fool! I'm not in any condition—"

"Liar!" he charged.

In a minute he would hold her too close, and he would feel her abdomen, and he would know her condition for certain.

She was close enough now. Now he knew he was going to be a father soon.

But he was still playing some game.

"Damn you, lady! I won't marry you!"

This wasn't Jesse. Because of his upbringing and his sense of right and wrong, he would have demanded that the mother of his child marry him, no matter what his feelings for her.

At least, the Jesse she had always known would have done so.

She lifted her chin. *Play along with me!* What was this ruse? It was humiliating!

"Jesse, damn you! Let go of me!"

But before she knew it, he had ripped off her cape, and her condition was very apparent to everyone there.

Then General Jensen snapped out Jesse's name.

"Colonel Cameron!"

"Sir!"

Jesse swirled around, saluting sharply, as if he had only just noticed that the general was present. Hugh Norris was beside him, sniggering at Kiernan and Jesse.

"What in God's name is going on here?" the general insisted.

"It's personal, sir!" Jesse said.

"Colonel Cameron, with the lady in front of us all, it ceases to be personal. Is this child yours?"

Jesse stood very stiffly, taller than anyone, his feet firm on the ground, his stance entirely military. Static seemed to leap from him. "Maybe," he replied.

Kiernan gasped with fury and amazement.

"Maybe!" Hugh Norris repeated, laughing. "He took over the house! I told you, she's a spy! She has her way about her, but I was able to see through that, sir. Cameron here was duped."

"I was never duped, sir. She was a seductress and intended to do me in, but I was never duped. She was under house arrest."

"I have had enough!" Kiernan exclaimed in fury. "I am going home. I will walk if you confiscate my wagon, General, and I will keep going unless you choose to shoot me. And if you do, God will see to it that it is spread across every newspaper in the known world!"

But before she could turn around, Jesse stopped her. "You're not going anywhere!"

"Colonel!" General Jensen snapped. "Young woman, my men do not shoot women in the back."

Kiernan was at a complete loss to understand Jesse. Why was he making a scene? She loved him, she wanted him, no matter what—she knew that. But again the colors seemed to come between them—blue and gray—so vividly, so painfully. She just wanted to go home and see her father.

She wanted to have her baby.

Jesse's baby.

She straightened her shoulders and spoke with dignity to the general. "You bastard Yanks!" she said softly. "You invaded my house and used it as you would. You've threatened my life. You've killed my husband, and now you—"

"I'm about to rectify the situation, Mrs. Miller," the general insisted. "Union soldiers in my command are gentlemen. Is the child that you're carrying Colonel Cameron's?"

With everyone looking on, Kiernan wanted to deny it, to strike out at them all—and so she hesitated too long.

"Yes!" Jesse snapped out. "All right, yes! *I'm* sure that it is my child."

"Get Father Darby. They'll be wed right now," Jensen ordered. "Do you hear me, Colonel Cameron? Marry this woman immediately. That's an order! I will not have this army accused of peopling the South with bastards!"

Jesse was silent. His jaw twisted as if he were in a rage, and he seemed to be looking for some way to avoid marrying her. But finally he looked straight ahead and waited.

"Do you hear me, Colonel?"

"Yes—sir!" Jesse snapped at last, doing his duty like a man of honor.

"Wait!" Kiernan protested. She wasn't going to be married here and now—not when she couldn't talk to Jesse first! Not when she didn't understand what was going on! "Wait! I will not—"

Suddenly Jesse pulled her into his arms again and held her so tight against him that she thought she was going to pass out. His blue eyes bore into hers, bluer than the summer's sky, a piercing, vibrant, blade-sharp blue. His whisper, as his lips touched hers, was hurried and desperate: "Agree now, Kiernan!"

"Let me g—!" she began.

But his arms tightened, and his whisper came urgently. "I desperately need a reason to leave. I have to take you home. Daniel is here. He's injured. I have to get him out and hide him. Daniel's life is at stake!"

Daniel!

She went dead still, understanding at last. Jesse had been forced to make a big scene, to do this to them both, so that no one would question his leaving his company while battles were raging all around them.

The twins were standing together at a distance, deadly quiet. Jacob hadn't said a word in Kiernan's defense through all of this—feisty, proud Jacob—because he knew. Somehow, he had found out about Daniel.

Where was Daniel now? How badly was he hurt?

"Mrs. Miller," General Jensen said consolingly, a hand upon her arm and a hand upon Jesse's shoulder, "we will right this problem. The colonel is a fine man, and usually, he's even a gentleman. But let's get on with this, eh? Here's Father Darby. Father, Colonel Cameron stands there. Mrs. Miller, come—we'll have you right here."

Father Darby was a tall, lean man with a sorrowful face that indicated he'd brought far more solace to the dying lately than anything else. Being ordered to conduct a wedding under fire seemed to be quite a surprise for him.

"They must agree to be married," he said, seemingly puzzled as he studied Jesse.

"They agree!" General Jensen said.

"Jesse?"

"Yes," Jesse said with a long, exaggerated sigh. "I agree."

"And you, Miss . . ."

"Mrs. Kiernan Miller," Kiernan supplied, "and I—"

Jesse's foot slammed down on hers so hard that it brought tears to her eyes. Daniel was somehow at stake.

"I agree!" she exclaimed.

Before she knew it, Jesse was holding her hand.

Patricia and Jacob stood silently in the background, and Private Riker and Hugh Norris looked on, Norris sniggering all the while.

General Jensen gave her away.

In less than five minutes, she and Jesse exchanged their vows. Jesse's signet ring sat around her finger, heavy, too large, and Anthony's gold band was tucked away in her pocket.

Darby cleared his throat. "Well, Colonel, now is when I should tell you to kiss the bride. But you seem to have taken matters into your own hands. I needn't advise you to kiss her."

Jesse's eyes were on Kiernan's. "Ah, but Father Darby, I intend to have a kiss."

It wasn't a customary kiss. She was not pulled reverently into his arms, and she did not feel the gentle press of his lips.

Instead, she was swept into his arms and carried to the

rear of the tent, away from the others, held tightly in his arms. Only then did his lips touch hers.

All the fire was there, a taste of heaven, a hint of the blaze of hell. She wanted to fight his touch, and she struggled against him for the disgrace he was bringing down upon them now that they were married. She fought hard . . .

But nothing could ever sweep away the magic of his kiss. Nothing could quell the burning deep inside. Nothing could take away the sweetness and the warmth, when he had been away again so very long.

Nothing—except Jesse himself.

His lips broke from hers just slightly and hovered above her own. "We have to leave!" he whispered fervently. "I have to bring Daniel through the lines secretly. Do you understand?"

She must have been slow to respond, for he shook her as he held her.

"Do you understand?"

"Yes!" she hissed back.

"Colonel!" Father Darby called, choking on the word.

Kiernan was suddenly on her feet, and Jesse was pulling her back before the general.

"Sir! Request leave to bring my wife home!"

General Jensen shook his head. "Colonel, we're in the midst of a major campaign. I can't let you go."

Kiernan wanted to slap Jesse's face as hard as she could. But she realized that he was in difficulty, and she knew that he would not be lying about Daniel, no matter what. She instantly realized how she could help.

He had once accused her of being a wonderful actress. Now it was time for her abilities to be tested.

"Oh!" she cried out. She fell flat upon the ground, doing her best not to jeopardize the baby. Jesse was instantly at her side, setting his arm around her shoulders, pulling her against him. "Oh, Jesse! The baby! Ohhhhhh!" she wailed.

"Colonel Cameron! Take your wife where she'll be comfortable!" General Jensen ordered.

"No!" she screamed. She struggled against Jesse's hold as hysterically as she could. "No, you despicable Yankees! You invade my home, you take everything! You ravaged my life, and now you expect me to have a child in a battlefield!"

Patricia stepped forward. "You cad!" she told the general indignantly.

Kiernan wailed again, moaning with true dramatic purpose. She would never have fooled Jesse with her performance. She had never fooled Jesse in all of her life.

But something more was at stake at the moment. She screamed as if she had been cut with a knife, then she grated out, "I want to go home!"

"What you want, Mrs. Cameron," Hugh Norris said flatly, "certainly can't matter! This is war!"

"I want to go home!" she wailed again. Norris! That bastard. He sensed that something was going on, and he seemed to hate Jesse almost as much as he hated her. "Please! I want to have my child at home!"

"Dear Lord!" General Jensen was a good man, and he was obviously very upset. "But your husband is here, Mrs. Mil—Mrs. Cameron!" the general tried to soothe her. "He may be a knave, but he's one of the finest physicians in the Union Army! You'll be in his hands—"

"I hate him! I want to go home! My father is ill, and I want to go home! I want my baby born at home! If you force me to have this child in a battlefield, I swear—"

"Yes, yes! Every newspaper in the known world will know about it," Jensen finished wearily. "You win, Mrs. —er, Cameron. Colonel, take your wife home. Madam, you've twenty-four hours to deliver that baby. Then I want you, Colonel, back in the field!"

Jesse saluted sharply. "Yes, sir!"

Hugh Norris narrowed his eyes and gritted his teeth, but there was nothing he could do. General Jensen had given his orders.

Jesse swept Kiernan up into his arms and carried her from the tent. Jacob and Patricia followed quickly behind.

There was no romance to his hold. As soon as they arrived outside, he slid her to her feet and barked instructions to the others.

"Get Tyne and the wagon, quickly, Jacob! Follow me and

Pegasus around to the med tent. Kiernan, get in the wagon and look as if you're in agony."

She nodded briefly. A jagged pain swept through her, and she clenched her teeth very hard.

With amazement, she realized that she wouldn't be acting anymore.

Twenty-Three

They traveled a good distance from the main camp to reach Jesse's field tent. Kiernan realized that the bulk of the army must have pulled in on a tactical retreat, leaving Jesse to take in the last of the wounded.

She didn't feel any more pain, low and deep in the small of her back, as they traveled to Jesse's tent. She began to think that she had imagined the sensation, but then it came again. She was tempted to scream and beg some assistance as panic nearly overwhelmed her. The baby was early, not due for another four weeks. She was suddenly terrified that in her desperation to reach her father, she had jeopardized the safety of her child.

She bit down hard on her knuckles and remained quiet. She still didn't understand quite what was going on, but Daniel's life was at stake too. Lacey had told her that first babies take forever to come—sometimes all day and all night and part of the next day too. She had to keep her silence. The pain finally subsided.

When they reached the tent, Jesse dismounted from Pegasus and called sharply, "Tyne, give me a hand! The rest of you, stay there."

Ignoring the order, Kiernan braced herself carefully on the wagon and stepped down from it. She hurried after Tyne, who had followed Jesse.

Jesse, realizing that she was there, spun around furiously. "I told you to wait in the wagon!"

Hot tears stung her eyes, tears she wasn't about to shed. "You've been telling me what to do and what you will and will not do ever since I've seen you!"

His hands fell hard upon her shoulders. "Daniel—"

"Yes, Daniel! His life is at stake, and if you had just told me from the very beginning, I wouldn't have felt so humiliated when you forced me to marry you!"

"I would have said more if I could. I asked you to play along with me! And don't you think it's convenient that I've married you?"

"I didn't have to be married for convenience!" Kiernan protested in a rush. "I can take care of myself very well."

"But maybe my child wouldn't have appreciated growing up a bastard!"

"This conversation isn't necessary now," Kiernan informed him coolly. "If you had just told me—"

"I couldn't have walked up and told you! I'd requested a leave earlier and been denied it. It was the only way."

She twisted from his hold, still wanting to scream. "I married you for Daniel's sake," she said stubbornly. "The least you can do is let me see him. He's in here, is he not?"

"Miz Kiernan," Tyne said, stepping around her diplomatically, "let's get Captain Cameron into the wagon, and then you'll see him fine enough."

"Yes, and we've got to hurry," Jesse said sharply. "Troops of every color are all over the place. I want to get him home." He started to turn away but came back and faced her, pulling her against him.

"I need you, Kiernan, I need you now! Say what you want to me. Leave me, if you want. I'm still everything that you hate and loathe in the world. But for the love of God, help me now."

She choked at the intensity of emotion that welled within her. So very much was at stake. "I want to help you—that's obvious, you fool!"

"I should be offended that my wife of a bare few minutes is calling me names," he told her. The words were soft and tender, his lip curling into a rueful grin as he spoke. "What we need, madam, is a truce. A separate peace. A cease-fire. Have we got it?"

She nodded. "Jesse, how bad is he?"

"I pulled the bullet out last night. It didn't injure any major organs. He's strong as an ox. He just needs to heal somewhere where the air is cool, where the breeze is clean. I can't let them take him to a prison camp. Do you understand?"

She nodded. In the filth of a prison, he would surely die. "Yes."

"You're with me? A truce?"

"A truce. A separate peace," Kiernan agreed.

"Kiernan," Jesse warned her tensely, "this could be the most dangerous thing any of us have ever done. The Yanks will be after Daniel, and the Rebs will be ready to shoot me down. Are you still willing?" His eyes were bright upon hers. Their differences would have to come between them later, not now.

"I was going through the lines one way or the other, Jesse. I'm going home. My father needs me, and I need him. Now Daniel needs me too. I'm not afraid, Jesse."

"You never were afraid," he said softly. "And that, my love, could be your downfall. Trust me. I'm afraid right now —damned afraid."

Startled, she looked at him.

"I don't intend to die before a firing squad," he said briefly.

Kiernan watched him, silent and still as Jesse walked by her. A second later, he appeared with Tyne and Corporal O'Malley, carrying a stretcher to her wagon. The figure upon it was swathed in a white sheet. "Make way!" Jesse called to Patricia, Jacob, and Janey, and the trio moved to allow the stretcher to be laid out on the wagon's floor. Kiernan stared at O'Malley, who surely knew that he'd had a Reb in his charge.

O'Malley, with innocence that would have stood him well in a poker game, tipped his hat to her. "Mornin', ma'am."

"Good morning, Corporal," she said.

"Nice day for a ride."

"I imagine so, Corporal. Are you coming with us?"

"No, ma'am, the colonel won't allow me to do that. I've got to see that the colonel's orders are carried on to the other surgeons."

"I see," she murmured.

"You look after the colonel, ma'am."

"I will."

O'Malley took a step closer. "Look after him well!" he said in a rush. "He's so all-fired determined to save his brother that he's risking his own life. For hiding a man in gray, his own side could shoot him for treason. And if the Rebs get hold of him, they may well shoot him for a spy. Lady, you're taking a treacherous journey!"

"Kiernan!" Jesse called to her sharply.

Oh, Jesse, she thought briefly, you are indeed a fool! Yet what else could he do? As he had chosen to fight for the Union, now he had chosen to fight for Daniel. She couldn't change him. His mind was set. But she loved him. Even if the circumstances of their marriage had enhanced their differences, she still couldn't change that fact.

"Kiernan!" Jesse called again.

"Yes, I'm coming." She stiffened, O'Malley saluted, and she hurried to the rear of the wagon. She looked up at Jesse for a moment and saw exhaustion in his features, tenacity, determination. She knew why she loved him, even if he was the enemy.

She lowered her lashes. She still knew little about Daniel's condition and wanted to see him for herself.

Jesse lifted her into the back of the wagon. A blanket had been arranged over Daniel, and the twins and Janey sat near him. "Kiernan, lean back so," Jesse instructed her. She nodded. His blue eyes met hers. His features were more tense and weary than she had ever seen them. "Don't let anyone see my brother," he said softly.

"I won't."

He was quickly gone, crawling up front alongside Tyne. O'Malley saluted sharply to Jesse.

"Thanks, Corporal," Jesse called to him.

"See you soon, Colonel!" O'Malley returned. Jesse flicked the reins, and the horses started off. O'Malley trotted alongside the wagon. "Congratulations, ma'am. The best to you and the colonel."

Kiernan waved to O'Malley, and the wagon, with Pegasus tied to the rear, moved away very quickly. They had begun the journey. Patricia looked at her with wide, frightened eyes. Jacob was still and stoic and silent, every inch the young man.

Kiernan tried to smile. She dared not think of the danger.

She thought of her circumstances instead. She and Jesse were married. It was what she had always wanted, it was right. They were about to become parents.

But nothing had changed. If anything, their world was a nightmare. Daniel was lying by her, seriously injured. He might be dead, or he might be dying, and she couldn't even touch him.

The countryside was combed with troops.

And Jesse was still a Yankee, a bitter enemy.

She closed her eyes as fear swamped over her. They still had hours to go. On the way, Yanks might well threaten Daniel.

And Rebs might well shoot Jesse down before asking any questions.

"Halt!"

Kiernan's heart began to hammer at the command. Jacob sat across from her. She couldn't see the road, but Jacob could.

"Reb or Yank?" she mouthed the words. How would she ever bear this? She clenched her fingers together so that they would not tremble. Lucky, lucky Daniel! He was either unconscious or sleeping, unaware of their situation.

"Yank," Jacob mouthed back.

Jesse was producing his pass, and she heard his easy drone as he talked to the man who had stopped him.

"Sorry, Colonel, we've orders to stop everyone," the man was telling him.

"Good to see you obeying orders, soldier!" Jesse responded. Kiernan heard him pick up the reins again.

Daniel moaned loudly from beneath his cocoon of blankets and covers.

"What's that?" the soldier demanded.

Kiernan tensed with every inch of her body. What if the soldier insisted on searching the wagon? Jesse might have no choice but to shoot the man. Would he be able to live with himself if he shot down an innocent man?

"What's what?" Jesse said casually. "My wife is back there with the children and the darkies. My leave is to take her home."

"It sounded like a man," the soldier said. "I could have sworn." He started around the wagon.

"Ohhhhh!" Kiernan cried out, drowning out Daniel's moan. The young soldier moved around the back and stared into the wagon. She covered her rounded abdomen with her splaying fingers. "Please, sir! We must hurry. Please!"

"Of course! Of course!" The soldier backed away. Jesse flicked the reins, and they were moving again, fast.

Thirty minutes later, she heard Jesse call a soft "Woah" to the horses. The wagon halted beneath huge shade trees, and she heard him leap to the ground. He appeared around the side of the wagon. "Janey, Jacob, Patricia—there's a stream down the embankment. Get yourselves some water." He looked at Kiernan, then pulled her to her feet, setting his hands upon her to lift her down beside him. He took her right hand within his own and kissed it softly.

"Whatever you think of me, Kiernan, or ever feel for me, I want you to know this. I will be eternally grateful for this."

"I love Daniel. He is one of my best friends," she said softly.

"Yes, I know. And that is why you agreed to the marriage. Not for our child—you would have allowed him or her to have been born a bastard. And not because you love me. Ah, no, you can't love me, can you? I'm the enemy." His voice had a bitter sound to it.

"Jesse, what do you want from me?" she cried out softly. "You are the enemy. I don't know what I think or feel anymore."

"You're my wife now. You've vowed to love me, Kiernan. Love, honor, and obey, until death do us part."

"And this war, Jesse. And death could come too quickly."

"And if it did?" he queried her softly.

She didn't know what to answer him. They were married, they were having a child together. And they were traveling a countryside that was laden with danger. She wanted to tell him that she loved him. Pride and fear kept her silent.

"I'm just wondering, will you ever be my wife in truth? Will you ever get past the fact that I chose to serve the Union? Or have I now condemned us both?" Cobalt blue and probing, his eyes searched out hers. She still had no answer.

"Never mind, you've been brilliant, and I am more grateful than you'll ever know," he said with a weary sigh.

Suddenly a pain, deep and cutting and sweeping away her breath, seared into her lower back as they spoke. She almost gasped out loud, but she would not let him know her condition, not at this moment. With sheer will power she kept from crying out.

"We've Daniel to worry about," she said.

"Indeed, we do."

He turned from her and leapt into the wagon, hunkering down by his brother's side. He pulled away the covers, touched Daniel's cheek, and then found the pulse at his throat. Daniel's eyes flickered open. "How're you doing?" Jesse asked him huskily.

Daniel nodded, and asked for water. Jesse was prepared, finding a canteen beneath the covering. He let his brother sip the water, then he set the canteen aside. "Let me just see to the bandage," Jesse said.

Kiernan clamped her teeth shut as she saw the bandage that wound around Daniel's gut. Red was slowly staining it.

Daniel was pale, but remained conscious. He looked at his brother and grinned. "It's a dangerous region for a man in blue."

"He's right!" Kiernan murmured. "Jesse, you should put on something of Tyne's—"

"As soon as I take off this uniform, I'm a spy," Jesse said.

"I'll wear my colors, thank you. Kiernan, get some water so that we can get going. Refill the canteen, please."

She took it from him as he handed it over, and turned awkwardly and hurried to meet the children by the stream.

When she came back, Jesse lifted her up beside Daniel once again.

"You'll be all right with him?" Jesse asked her.

"Fine," she replied briefly. He took his seat in front with Tyne. The reins cracked, and they were moving again.

She thought Daniel was sleeping, his lids were so low. Then he grinned. "I'm going to be an uncle?" he said softly.

"Yes."

"Did he do the right thing by you?"

"Yes," Kiernan replied, then lowered her head to speak to him with mock anger. "Thanks to you, Captain! It was the only way to get you out of the Yankee camp. You'd best get well after all this!"

Daniel grinned complacently. "Well, hell. I managed to make Jesse do the right thing after all. You two could have been a little easier on me, though. I had to get gut-shot for you two to tie the knot!"

Kiernan's quick retort was ready, but they moved over a pothole in the road and Daniel winced. She curled her fingers around his tightly. His eyes closed. Moments later, they opened again.

"Kiernan, your father . . ."

Her pulse quickened as his voice trailed away. "Daniel?" Her fingers tightened. "Daniel, my father! Have you heard something else?"

His eyes opened, just barely. "No, no, I haven't heard. But make sure Jesse stops by your place first. I'll make it. He's already pulled the bullet out of me, and I'm on the mend."

"Daniel, you're bleeding."

"And I'll bleed again before it's over, no doubt. Your place before ours, anyway. We'll see how John is doing, and we'll be just fine."

Torn between her father and Daniel, Kiernan looked across the wagon at Jacob. He shook his head miserably, having no help to give her. To complicate matters, she felt another searing pain. She stiffened, bracing her hand against her back, and resolved not to alarm the others.

Janey, looking at her, was about to speak. She knew what Kiernan was going through. Kiernan shook her head fiercely, and Janey closed her lips with disapproval.

Kiernan leaned back and felt the breeze bathe her face. The wagon jerked to a halt, and she heard Jesse swearing softly. Jacob, across from her, called out, "Rebs!"

"Jesu!" Kiernan whispered in panic. Their worst nightmare was now upon them.

"Hey, it's a Yank!" drawled a thick southern voice. "A go'darned Yank! You, Yank! Get out of that wagon. What you got in it?"

Kiernan struggled to look. With alarm, she saw they were surrounded by a party of five Rebs. The one speaking had ridden forward and close and was sneering at Jesse. There were too many of them! Without daring to think, she launched into a reckless speech. "He's got nothing in it! Nothing but an expecting wife and an injured man! Please, sir, let us pass—"

"Kiernan, shut up!" Jesse demanded furiously. He stood on the seat, one hand lightly on the Colt in the holster by his side, as he looked at the five rough-looking men in gray surrounding the wagon.

She stared at him blankly. "But, Jesse, if they only knew—"

"If they knew," Jesse informed her flatly, "they'd still be deserters, Kiernan! Now shut up and sit down!"

"Deserters!" the leader of the Rebs said in an irritated cry. "Yank, what are you—out here all alone?" Kiernan shuddered, studying the man. He was unshaven, and his uniform was muddied and dirtied. She suddenly sensed that Jesse was right. The man smiled at her. "Well now, there's a comely lass for you, even if she is in the family way!" He looked back to Jesse. "She'll be some lively sport once you're dead, Yank."

"Son of a bitch!" Daniel hissed softly at her side.

The Reb grinned and aimed his Enfield rifle at Jesse. But

he never had a chance. Jesse moved like lightning with the Colt. Then he spun around and caught the second man in the hand. The third managed to get off a shot that sent the Colt spinning from Jesse's hand.

Kiernan screamed, but Jesse ignored her, leaping from the wagon with his saber drawn. The third Reb deserter didn't have a prayer of getting in a second shot with his muzzle-loading Enfield. He turned the weapon to use the bayonet, charging at Jesse. Jesse instantly parried the first blow—and the second, and the third. The two were quickly embroiled in a lethal and deadly dance.

The fourth man, shaking, took aim at Jesse's back. Kiernan cried out, but a shot rang out from behind her. She spun around. Daniel was up, and he'd fired at the man.

And hit his target clean through the heart.

Then Kiernan saw another man emerge from the trees. She jumped from the wagon, hurrying to find the Colt in the dirt. Her fingers had just closed around it when a booted foot landed hard upon her hand. She looked up to see a man looming over her, laughing. "Come on, boys, get the hell out of here before they shoot us all down!" the man called out. To Kiernan's horror, three more unshaven and muddied soldiers came crashing out of the trees. Jesse was engaged with two of them, while Daniel fought to keep shooting from the wagon.

"Get up!" the deserter raged at Kiernan. He reached down for her with his hand. She twisted and managed to kick him with all her strength in his groin. He screeched like a banshee, doubling over, then pulled a pistol from his belt and aimed it straight at her.

But he never fired.

His eyes widened, and he swirled about. Kiernan realized that Jesse was behind him, the point of his sword in the man's back. "Throw it down!" Jesse ordered, indicating the pistol.

The deserter refused. He lifted his arm to shoot Jesse, a cocky grin on his face. But Jesse's sword waved in the air like silver lightning. The man spun around again. He stared at Kiernan, stunned. A red stain was spreading across his chest. He fell down dead on top of her. She screamed wildly, and Jesse quickly shoved the man's body aside, reaching for her.

"Jesse!"

She crushed herself against him, her head next to his heart. She felt the pounding of his pulse, the heat of his body, and the tenderness of his hands as he stroked her hair.

"Jesse, get down!" Daniel shouted.

A shot rang out. Kiernan and Jesse spun to see another deserter Reb fall dead to the ground behind them. Jacob had taken the man with Daniel's service revolver.

Jacob leaped from the wagon and rushed to Kiernan's side. He led her away from Jesse, who strode off to search out the nearby trees.

"Is it the last of them?" he demanded of his brother.

Pale, Daniel nodded. "I wasn't a hell of a lot of help," he said.

"Damned good for an unconscious man," Jesse told him. Daniel grinned weakly.

Kiernan started toward the wagon, leaning on Jacob, then staggered at the worst pain yet took hold of her. She couldn't help but cry out.

Jesse swung back, startled by her cry. With his sword still in his hand, he ran to take her from Jacob's hold and support her weight.

"Kiernan!"

"I'm fine," she insisted, and started for the wagon. But as she did, a shot rang out from the trees.

Jesse let out an oath, spun around on the dirt road, and fell flat.

Daniel instantly returned the fire, and a man fell out of a tree, stone dead before he hit the ground.

But Kiernan barely noticed him, for her eyes were upon Jesse lying in the dirt, his eyes closed. She threw herself down upon her knees beside him. Blood stained his arm and his chest, where his arm lay flung over it. "Jesse!" Tears running down her cheeks, she lifted his head into her lap, cradling it. "Jesse! Oh, my love! Where are you hit? Jesse, open your eyes! Damn you, Jesse! Just live! I'll be your wife

in truth, I'll love you, I swear, I'll love, honor, and obey
until death do us part. Oh, Jesse, I do love you. You can't
leave me. Jesse, please, I love you. I love you so very much. I
want to be your wife, to love you forever—"

Her words choked off as he opened his eyes and smiled at
her. "Really?"

"Really. Jesse, just live!"

"You'll love me forever?"

"Forever!"

"Swear it?" he whispered huskily.

"I swear it!"

To her astonishment, he sat up. He pulled her into his
arms and kissed her, and it was hardly the kiss of a dying
man at all. He kissed her in the dusty roadway with fever
and passion and tenderness, so much that she nearly returned the urgency of it, nearly forgot where they were.

She jerked away from him, staring at him hard.

He grinned ruefully. "I was only nicked by the bullet.
See? It caught my arm here. Just a little bit of blood on my
chest—"

"Oh, you blasted Yankee scoundrel!" Kiernan accused
him.

His smile broadened. "That's fine, just as long as I know
you'll love me forever."

"Jesse!"

"Horses!" Tyne called out.

Jesse leaped to his feet, pulling Kiernan up and pressing
her body behind his. Tyne jumped down from the wagon,
making a dive for the Colt.

"Tyne! Give it to me! If it's Rebs, they'll shoot you for
having that weapon."

"Master Jess, I'm willing to fight for you."

"No, dammit man, you won't hang for me!" Jesse
snatched the weapon from Tyne. With his sword in one
hand and his pistol in the other, he shouted to his brother,
"Daniel, get down!"

"No, damn you, Jess, I'll fight with you too!"

"It's Rebs!" Jacob cried out. "Look!"

Kiernan looked. Horsemen were coming, Rebel horsemen. They broke upon the road, a bearded cavalry captain with a company of twenty or so.

The bearded man reined in and raised a hand to stop the troops behind him. He saw the gray-clad men on the ground, then looked hard at Jesse.

"Well, Yank, what have we here?" the Rebel captain asked. His gaze took in Jesse's medical insignias—and the weapons he held with such menace.

He dismounted from his horse. Kiernan felt Jesse stiffen, felt his hand tighten around his sword.

"It seems that I have a prisoner, one who might well meet with a firing squad. Who in the hell are you, sir? What in God's name is a Yank doing in this neck of the woods? Colonel, you are mine!"

"I'm afraid I can't let you take me, Captain."

The captain's brows raised. "Sir? I seem to have the greater number, since you are dealing with a boy, a girl, two darkies, and a lady very far gone with child, it seems. Ma'am, I'll ask you to move away now."

Kiernan shook her head fiercely. She tried to step around in front of Jesse to protect him.

"Kiernan!" he thundered, stepping back around her, his sword flashing. "Sir, I repeat, I cannot allow myself to be taken." He actually grinned a reckless grin. "And I beg to differ with you, sir. I am an extraordinary swordsman, and the boy in the wagon is one of the best shots in the world, I dare say. As to the lady, here, why, she may well be the most dangerous of us all."

He was teasing her still, Kiernan thought. Tenderly, gallantly teasing, when they could no longer wage battle and win, when the odds against them were overwhelming. He intended to fight these men, until he could fight no longer.

"Wait!" she pleaded.

"Why, it's Greenbriar!" Daniel's voice called suddenly, interrupting her. Holding his gut, he had managed to stand up almost straight in the wagon.

The captain spun around. "Cameron!"

"In the flesh," Daniel grinned. "I'd stand with more ceremony to greet you, Greenbriar, if I could. But I'm in a rather sad position here. And this Yank—who *is* an extraordinary swordsman, by the way—is my brother, Jesse. He's also the best surgeon in or out of Virginia. Colonel Jesse Cameron, Captain Nathaniel Greenbriar, Virginia militia."

Greenbriar stared from Daniel to Jesse, and back to Daniel again. "Captain Cameron—just what is going on here?"

"I was shot up keeping the Yanks out of Richmond. Our troops were gone, and I looked up, and there was Jesse. So he spirited me across the river, and then my sister-in-law here made a timely arrival, and Jesse's been trying to get me home ever since. Greenbriar, it isn't a spying mission, I swear it. He's trying to take me home. You can't take a man in for that!"

Once again, Greenbriar looked from Daniel to Jesse, and back to Daniel again.

"Sir!" one of the men said from behind him.

"Yes, Potter, what is it?"

"That's Shelley on the ground there, sir. He deserted last month, raided the Halpren estate last week, and was accused of a lot more. We've been trying to chase him down for ages. He shot down three men in cold blood when they were trying to arrest him. Seems like this Yank did us a bit of a favor."

"Is that a fact?" Greenbriar said. He scratched his chin.

There didn't seem to be a breath of movement on the roadway. The leaves didn't rustle in the trees, and the stillness seemed to last forever.

Greenbriar moved at last. He mounted his horse. "Let's ride," he told his men.

"What about the Yank?" Potter asked.

"What Yank?" Greenbriar said. He set his heels to his horse's flanks and rode by.

All the Rebels rode by, looking straight ahead and seeing nothing in their path. Potter held back and spoke quickly to Daniel.

"That Yank who isn't here had best be gone within the next few minutes. We'll have to come back to bury that riff-raff, and I'm afraid of what will happen to him if we get a glimpse of him on the road again."

"He'll be gone," Daniel said. Potter smiled and rode off.

When he was gone, silence reigned once again. Kiernan was aware of the tension all about Jesse and in the air—and then the sweet explosion of it as they all realized they were safe.

"Jesu!" Daniel exclaimed. "We've made it!"

"Thank the good Lord!" Janey breathed.

Kiernan wanted to laugh and to hug Jesse. She wanted to hug Daniel, and she wanted to thank the good Lord too.

But it was all suddenly too much for her.

The light paled all around her, and she felt herself falling.

"Oh, Jesse!" she whispered as she toppled to the ground.

He swept her up and walked fast. She fought the darkness descending upon her and opened her eyes to his.

"Why the hell didn't you say something?" he demanded.

"About what?" she said weakly.

"You're having the baby now."

"I can't have the baby now. You have enough medical emergencies at the moment."

"Whether I do or don't, Kiernan, you're having the baby. And you'll have it right here on the road if we don't get moving!"

"No," she told him, her eyes were wide, dazzling and emerald on his. "I'm having the baby at Cameron Hall!" she insisted.

But then darkness did descend upon her, and for the moment, she could argue no more.

Twenty-Four

Kiernan awoke as an excruciating pain tore across her lower back and curled around to the front of her abdomen, as tight as an iron band about her. She awoke to the sound of her own scream, for the pain had taken hold of her so severely, she hadn't had the awareness to fight it.

"It's all right, Kiernan. It's all right. Hold my hand, and it will pass."

Fingers curled around hers. She heard the soft, husky sound of Jesse's voice, and she looked up quickly into his eyes. He was with her, a rueful, tender smile curved into his lips. He placed a cool damp cloth upon her brow.

They were home, she realized.

They had made it to Cameron Hall.

It was her home now. She was his wife, and they had made it. The child would be born here. She was lying on the huge four-poster bed in Jesse's bedroom. Beyond the windows she could see the gardens and the slope of the lawn. If she moved just a bit, she would probably be able to see all the way to the river.

The pain was easing. Even as he spoke, the pain was easing.

"Jesse, how long have I been out?" she whispered. Her lips and her mouth were so terribly dry. She was no longer clad in her cumbersome travel clothing and cape. She had been changed into a cool cotton nightgown with fine embroidered sleeves and a smocked bodice. She recognized the gown vaguely, then realized it was her own.

It wasn't one she had brought with her in the wagon. It had been brought from her own home on the peninsula.

She jerked up, grabbing Jesse by the shirt collar. "My father! Jesse, my father! Have you seen him? Is he well?"

He caught hold of her hands, pushing her back down. "Kiernan—"

"Jesse!" she cried, pushing against his hold. Then, exhausted, she allowed him to push her back down.

"Kiernan, you're very close to giving birth to our child. You must relax and save your strength."

"Jesse—"

"Wait!" he told her firmly.

He walked across the hall to the door and threw it open. "John!"

Once again, Kiernan jerked up. "He's here? Can he walk?"

"What do you mean, 'Can he walk'?" John Mackay's voice boomed out to her. A second later, he was brushing past Jesse and coming to her bedside. "Ah, Kiernan, it's glad I am to see you lying there awake and aware now. I was worried half out of my mind when you were lying there so still." He perched at her bedside. Scanning her father's face anxiously, Kiernan decided that he was slimmer and his face was pale, but his eyes were bright and filled with mischief, and his grip upon her hand was strong.

"Oh, Papa, Christa sent word that you were sick."

"Yes, I was sick. Miss Christa Cameron was a saint, she was, keeping up with me. They've something of the healing touch in this family. I had a fever for days and days, it seemed, but she was patient as could be. And I was beginning to feel just as right as rain—until Jacob rode up on that horse of Jesse's to find out how I was faring. Then I heard about you, young woman!"

Kiernan swiftly lowered her lashes. After all she had done on her own, she felt like a chastised child. She realized that it was because she loved her father so, that she did not wish to disappoint him.

"Why, I was ready to run for my old shotgun, daughter, until I found out that the man had done right by you."

"John!" Jesse protested calmly, standing behind her father, "I'd gladly have done right by her long ago, had she ever given me half the chance."

"Right," John Mackay agreed. His cloud-blue eyes were on his daughter's. "Daughter, you might have written me!"

"I didn't want to hurt you!" she said. "But I was coming home—I've been trying to come home."

John Mackay grinned. "Kiernan, you have come home. Still! You should have had more faith in your old father. I'd not have been angry with you, ever, Kiernan."

"I love you so much, Papa."

"And I love you, daughter. But you shouldn't have come across country like that. Jesse says the baby is early. We'll pray that the little one is well. You shouldn't have caused that on my account."

"But I had to."

"And if I heard things right, it's well enough that you did. Daniel is here safe too. And you're a married woman again." He leaned close to her and winked. "Married to a Yank—but legally wed, and my grandchild will have a name. Mackay's a fine enough name for any man or woman, but a child wants his own father's name, and that's a fact."

"Oh, Papa—" she began, but she broke off, breathless, tensing and bracing against the pain. It was coming, and it was getting worse and worse.

She fought the urge to scream, grinding down on her teeth. Her fingers wound like steel around her father's. She was able to best the urge to scream out with the agony that assailed her, wrapping all the way around her again, but a whimper did escape her lips, and her father was quickly upon his feet.

"Jesse! Do something for her!"

"Sir, she's in labor. There's very little I can do."

"She's your wife, son!"

"And she's in labor."

He smiled when he sat beside her again. His fingers, so strong, gripped hers. "Kiernan, don't tense so—go easy, it will be all right. Breathe, my love, you're turning blue. You'll manage. I'm here with you."

The pain was blindingly intense. Tears sprang into her eyes, and she felt as if she were being cut in two. It went on and on.

"It's all right, Kiernan," Jesse soothed her.

"Go to hell, Jesse!" she whispered.

"Jesse," John Mackay began in distress.

"John, you'd better leave me with her now," Jesse said, grinning. "The baby will come very soon. Send Janey and Christa in, will you?"

Kiernan closed her eyes tightly. The pain was just beginning to fade.

"Right!" John said.

Jesse eased his fingers from Kiernan's and ripped back the covers. She started shivering fiercely. The pain had ebbed, but she was miserably cold.

"Jesse, give those back!" she pleaded.

"Kiernan, I need you to sit up more."

"Oh!" she screamed, startled when the pain seized her again so quickly. The last pain had barely ebbed away, but already the new one was upon her. It was strong, sweeping from her back to her front with near-blinding agony.

She seized hold of Jesse, gasping as an overwhelming desire to push suddenly mingled with the pain. "Jesse, the baby is here!"

"Wait, Kiernan, let me see. If you push too soon, you'll injure yourself!"

She fell back, feeling her cheeks flood with color. She felt so wretched. She was in such terrible agony, and Jesse was seeing her so huge and ungainly, and so intimately, at such a wretched time.

He moved to examine her, and she wrenched her knees together tightly.

"Kiernan, I'm your husband!" he told her.

"It hurts!"

"Well, of course it hurts—you're having a baby."

"Jesse—"

"I'm a doctor, Kiernan."

"You've never had a baby, so don't tell me how it feels!"

"Kiernan, please!" he whispered with exasperation.

To her distress another cry escaped, and she was certain that in a few minutes she would be a fountain of tears, it hurt so much. But he was beside her again, holding her in his arms, cradling her. "Kiernan, I love you. I don't know how it feels, but I've delivered other babies. I'm nervous about delivering my own, but I'm also ecstatic, Kiernan, because in just a few more minutes we can both cradle our child. Our child, Kiernan. A beautiful, precious new life, something wonderful that came from love, despite all the horror of war. Something that is love and defies the fact that life would call us enemies. Kiernan, trust me. I love you, with all of my heart. And I am doing my best for you and for our babe."

Tears glittered in her eyes, but she went easy in his arms. He started to push her back again. Then he whispered mischievously in her ear. "Besides, I've been between your thighs often enough before."

"Jesse!" she cried out.

But he laughed, and despite her refreshed anger, she was filled with new-found strength. She gritted her teeth against his touch when he examined her, and when she cried out that the pain was coming again and that she had to push, he cried out in turn, "The head is here! Just the tip, but it's here, Kiernan. Dark as a raven's wing. It's fine, Kiernan, push!"

Christa was up by her shoulders supporting her, while Janey waited to take the babe. Kiernan pushed and pushed and pushed, and the three of them encouraged her. Exhausted, she fell back. She cried out that she was too tired, that she couldn't go any further.

She told them all to go right to hell.

Jesse called out, "Kiernan, the head is free, our child is nearly born. Push again—hard!"

She pushed. She felt the child expulse from her body, and she was relieved and exhausted and ecstatic all at the same time. "Jesse!"

Everyone was silent. There was no cry. She pleaded, "Jesse, is the babe—"

She broke off as she heard a little cry at last, and Jesse was at her side, showing her the child. It was dark, as he had told her, slick from birth. But its little arms and legs were moving madly, and suddenly the babe wasn't giving out little cries—it was screaming.

"Oh!" she gasped in gratitude. "Jesse—"

"A little boy," he told her. "Mrs. Cameron, you have given me a son. I thank you with all my heart." He cut the cord swiftly, coming around to her.

He kissed her, his lips warm on hers. He placed the screaming bundle into her arms, and her arms closed around her child. She looked into the squalling little face that she and Jesse had created, and love surged through her that was deeper than any she had ever imagined.

"We've a son!" she said softly. She protested when Janey reached to take him away.

"He's got to be bathed, Miz Kiernan."

"And we've got to finish with you!" Jesse informed her. "You've torn, Kiernan. You need a few stitches."

"But I feel so good, Jesse!"

He laughed, and she leaned back, and she listened to Christa describe the baby. She didn't feel a bit of pain or unease while Jesse delivered the afterbirth and stitched her up. Christa held her bundled son, while Janey brought her water to bathe her face and a new nightgown. There seemed to be so very much activity, but when she tried to hold tight to Jesse again, he forced her back down. "Sleep, Kiernan."

"Jesse, he's so beautiful."

He kissed her brow. "Indeed, he is."

"I want to see him. I can't possibly sleep."

But even as she said it, an overwhelming exhaustion laid hold of her. Jesse pressed her back into the pillows. "How nice. For once, my love, you don't have the energy to fight me!"

She smiled, her eyes closed, and she slept.

* * *

She was awakened soon after she fell asleep, it seemed. Janey had brought her son, and he was squalling furiously. "He's very hungry," Janey told her.

Kiernan fumbled with her gown, then marveled that instinct showed her how to bring him to her breast. The first little tug he made upon her nipple brought a gasp to her lips. Then a sensation of wonder filled her.

She had married her enemy, and they'd had a child together, she mused.

And she'd never known such a sweet sensation of peace.

After a while, Janey took the baby from her and tiptoed away as she drifted off again.

When she awoke again, it was morning. Birds were chirping wildly, and the sun was streaming through the windows.

Patricia was at the foot of her bed in a rocking chair with the baby.

"Oh, Kiernan, he's just beautiful!"

"Is he? I think he is, but is he really, to everyone?"

"Exquisite!" Patricia told her. Kiernan smiled, and reached for him. She set him on the bed and unwrapped his blankets and cotton breeches and looked at him.

"He has all his fingers and toes," Patricia assured her. "He's just a little bit small, but that's because he's a little bit early. Jesse says he's well developed, though."

That was what mattered, Kiernan thought. She smiled. Her new son was staring at her. His eyes, for the moment, were bright blue. His cheeks were perfectly rounded and flushed. His lips had a sweet pucker, and his hair, cleaned and dried, was raven black. "He's a Cameron, all right," Kiernan murmured. She looked at Patricia, feeling a twinge of guilt. But Patricia's warm brown eyes were filled with nothing but tenderness as she studied the baby. "He looks just like Jesse."

The baby's face screwed up into a scowl, and he let out a fierce scream. Kiernan laughed. "Sounds like him, too, doesn't he?"

"Are you casting aspersions on my brother?" a masculine voice asked.

Kiernan looked up. Daniel was standing in the doorway. He was pale, but he seemed stronger.

She let out a little cry and slipped from bed herself. She winced as she realized that it wasn't easy to walk, and he scolded her for getting up just as she scolded him.

"Daniel, you should be in bed!"

"Kiernan, you get back in there!"

They laughed, and then she hugged him carefully. He placed a kiss on her forehead.

"Daniel, are you going to be all right?" she asked anxiously.

He nodded. "I'm going back to bed. I just wanted to tell you that my nephew is beautiful."

She nodded, meeting his eyes, and bit her lower lip. "He's part Yankee," she said, "but I love him anyway."

"Yes," Daniel said with a soft sigh and a slow smile. "His dad is a Yank, and I love him anyway."

"So do I," Kiernan admitted.

Daniel grinned. "Good. Now get back to bed, and I'll do the same."

Kiernan did so. She and Patricia played with the baby, and Kiernan nursed her son again. Then Janey brought her breakfast. She was ravenous. Her father came to see his new grandson, and Jacob came, and even Jacob admitted that for a little thing, he was a fine-looking boy.

Everyone had come—except Jesse.

"Where is he?" Kiernan asked Christa.

"Oh! He was down in the office. I imagine he fell asleep down there. I'll go see."

"No," Kiernan said, "I'll go."

"Wait!" Christa protested. "He'll be furious that you're up."

"I feel very well, and I'll be good like Daniel and come right back to bed. But I want to see him now."

Christa worried that Kiernan might not be able to walk down the stairs, but Kiernan insisted on brushing her hair and donning a clean gown. She studied her reflection in the mirror, watching Christa's secret smile as their eyes met in the glass.

She left the room and went to the portrait gallery. She smiled up at the handsome faces of the Cameron men and the beautiful faces of their women. "I really have come home!" she whispered. She smiled, and wondered if any of the Camerons past smiled in return.

Kiernan carefully descended the stairs. She was weak, she realized, and she would have to be very careful. But she was filled with a certain energy too. She had to see Jesse.

She passed the parlor and came to the door of the office and looked in. Jesse was indeed there, his feet up on the desk.

His head was back against the edge of the captain's chair, and his eyes were closed. His white shirt was open at the collar. He had bathed during the night, and he was dressed in civilian trousers and a simple cotton shirt.

He was sound asleep.

She bit into her lip, thinking that she should leave him undisturbed.

He had to go back to the war, and he needed his sleep. He'd certainly had enough family crises to deal with.

But he was going to go away again.

And because of that she had to have this time with him.

She stepped into the room, closing the door behind her. As she did, his eyes opened. He frowned when he saw her. "Kiernan! What are you doing up?"

She walked over to the desk and discovered that she was suddenly shy.

After all of this, she thought.

All the years, and all their times together.

And now, the birth of their child.

She stopped in front of the desk. "Jesse, I had to see you." Suddenly, she could say no more.

He stood, his boots falling hard on the floor. He walked quickly around the desk, sweeping her up into his arms. And he carried her back around with him, holding her tightly against himself as he took a seat in the captain's chair once again.

"Did I thank you sufficiently for my son?" he asked her softly.

She nodded. "Oh, Jesse, did I thank you?"

He laughed. "The pleasure was all mine."

She flushed, but laughed along with him. "Oh, Jesse!" She wanted to say more—there was so much to say. She set her fingers against the tight black curls where his shirt lay open against his chest. She whispered, "It all came out right! Daniel is home, and he looks wonderful. I know he's going to be fine."

This time, she thought. The war was still going on. But she was careful not to say it.

Like Jesse, Daniel would go back to it.

She refused to worry about it now. "My father is well, Jesse. And we've a son. He is small, but he seems so wonderful too." She was suddenly speaking very quickly. "I'm even glad he's a boy. Girls are wonderful children, too, of course, I've learned that with Patricia. Would you have minded a girl?"

"I'd have loved a little girl," Jesse told her solemnly. "Except that I suppose I am pleased we had a son." He smoothed her hair back from her forehead. "We're still at war. I on my side, and Daniel on his. I'm pleased, for I know that my father would be glad, and his father. Since . . ."

His voice trailed away. "Since the Cameron name will go if you and Daniel are both killed?" Kiernan said, her voice breaking.

Jesse tightened his arms around her. "I love you so much, Kiernan. I've loved you for years. I've been thinking all night. I've always believed that I had to fight for what my conscience dictates to be right. But I love you so much, Kiernan, I'll resign my commission. I can't fight for the South, but we'll go to England if you want, or maybe we could head west, or—"

She pressed her fingers against his lips. Tears came to her eyes and fell. "Jesse, you would do that? For me?"

He smiled, slowly, crookedly. "I would lay down my life, my heart, my soul—everything."

She shook her head vehemently. "Oh, Jesse!"

"Can you love me, Kiernan? I am a Yank at heart, dressed in blue."

"I do love you, Jesse, so much. And once it worried me, that I could love a Yankee so thoroughly, so desperately, so completely. But a friend told me something once. He said that I don't love a Yankee, I love a man. And I do, Jesse, I love you. And the color that you wear can't change the man that you are. I love that man."

His lips found hers, and he kissed her. It was a long kiss, warm, flamed by passion, held in check by the depths of tenderness that overrode all else.

When he broke away from her, her eyes were dazzling upon his. She smiled. "I don't want to go west, Jesse. And I don't want to go to England."

He frowned, his blue eyes very sharp, his raven dark hair disheveled upon his brow. She smiled, loving him so.

"Jesse, you're a doctor, and a good one—no, you're the very best. You save lives, you don't take them. I know that you'd feel as if you'd betrayed your calling if you didn't go back."

"Kiernan—"

"I'm not changing sides, Jesse. No one can change their heart. The war will go on until someone wins it. And if you're posted in Washington again, I'll come there. I won't spy ever again—I'll promise you that. The other day, you asked me for a truce. A separate peace. And that's what I want now, Jesse. A separate peace."

He smiled, and once again he kissed her. He kissed her warmly and deeply. He kissed her with remarkable tenderness, and he kissed her so long that she grew dizzy, feeling a sweet delirium sweep over her. And at last his lips lifted from hers.

He stood up, holding her securely in the strength of his arms. Brilliant blue eyes blazed down into hers, and he smiled. "A separate peace, Mrs. Cameron, is so declared. Now, let's go to see to young Master John Daniel Cameron."

"John Daniel Cameron?" she queried.

"Do you like it?" he asked.

She leaned back in his arms, delighted, secure. "I love it," she assured him, and she curled her arms around his neck. "Just as I love his father!"

Jesse smiled again, tenderly, then turned.

They left the office behind, and Jesse climbed the stairs with her in his arms. They passed by the watchful eyes of the Camerons in the portrait galley until they came to the master bedroom once again.

And there they doted upon the newest Cameron.

The cannons of war raged on, but Jesse and Kiernan had indeed found their separate peace.